An Uncollected Death

A Charlotte Anthony Mystery

Meg Wolfe

ISBN-13: 978-1496163370

This is a work of fiction. Names, characters, businesses, places, events and incidents are either the products of the author's imagination or used in a fictitious manner. Any resemblance to actual persons, living or dead, or actual events is purely coincidental.

For Steve:

Thank you for making it possible.

Acknowledgments

Writing a novel requires a nearly sociopathic degree of focus, yet it can't happen without the help of the world outside the writer's head. I feel so fortunate to have an enthusiastic Reader Team whose feedback, input, editing and proofreading kept me going from the first third of the book all the way to the end and beyond. The first one out the gate has always been Karin Kirulis, backed up by her husband John, with fine-tooth comb proofreading and copy editing—and bonus fellowship, meals, and wine. Tamara Brown and Linda Minard caught typos and loose ends, and along with Marilyn Phillippi took Charlotte and her friends into their imaginations, which was invaluable for developing the characters and inspiring future story lines. Additional thanks to Linda Price, Ian Johnson, LaDonna Pride, and Alice Sasak, and to the many others since for final-draft and advance reader copy feedback and encouragement.

A special thanks to my son, Nick Maxwell, who showed me how I could write seriously again at a time I thought I didn't have any more options, and for bringing Amy and Ellie into our lives. Thanks also to my mother for showing me how to make up stories and poems when I was very small, taking me to the library in town every week during the summers, and teaching me to type really fast—I think it did some good.

Most of all, thanks to my husband, Steve Johnson, who actually had to live with Meg-as-novelist, then provide encouragement, feedback, editing, technical help, layout, cover design, and tea—all on demand. Yet there's so much more to this story than meets the eye; my gratitude runs very deep.

An
Uncollected Death

One

Friday, September 13th

Charlotte Kleid Anthony took a big red mug of black coffee out to the deck, and the first cold barefoot steps in the morning dampness shocked her head clear. The hot mug felt so good in her hands. She took some deep breaths of fresh air, just making out the first ripe tang of autumn, and heard the crows calling to one another in the pines behind the house. Back in the kitchen the letter from the lawyer sported several purple rings from the Merlot she drank the night before. Her mouth was dry, she'd burned her breakfast bagel, but, all in all, it had been worth it.

She squinted from the bright reflections of the sun off the lake, and off the bank of windows at Helene's old house across the way, where it nestled amid the tiers of other hillside houses and trees. It was almost time to go to Olivia's, but she took a few more moments to ground herself, her fingers stroking the bleached cedar deck rail. Her instinct was to commit the texture to memory, because at some point that is all it would be. The crucial clause the lawyer quoted from the settlement played over and over in her mind: "*...or at such time as the child should begin college or professional training, at which time the support money will cease and the expense will be borne by the father.*"

He was right. It was always there, had been for the past ten years, of course, only not in the front of her mind in her rush to prepare Ellis, who had just turned sixteen, to attend the Paris Conservatoire to continue her piano studies. And not in front of her mind after the news last Friday (had it only been a week?) that both *Fine Design* and *Emerson Home Monthly* suddenly ceased publication, leaving Charlotte without a quarterly check for the first time in years.

Diane, her accountant, boiled it down: "You can't afford to live in your house anymore. You can't afford anything much, actually." Then came a flurry of phone calls to the bank and the publishers, all to no avail.

Charlotte realized that she was going to have to throw over her entire life for the second time in ten years. But a few hours of wine and brooding in front of the fireplace was enough to get past the initial panic and see, if she was perfectly honest with herself, that she welcomed the distraction from suddenly having an empty nest. And now, as she surveyed the sparkling blue water surrounded by hills, architectural homes, and dozens of For Sale signs, she no longer saw Lake Parkerton as a magical valley but as a money pit.

Snap out of it, she told herself, and strode back into the house. Time to get ready. Charlotte added a cardigan to her white tee and straight jeans, and slipped on a pair of loafers. At the last minute she dabbed on a bit of lip color, and bent down from the waist to fluff up her shoulder-length hair. Helene warned her not to wear anything that required dry cleaning, describing her sister Olivia's house as "cluttered" and "a bit heavy on the potpourri," but it was the little things, thought Charlotte, that gave one confidence. Strictly speaking, she was qualified for the job, but her academic chops were rusty.

The news was on the kitchen TV, and her attention was caught by the young female reporter standing in front of Warren Brothers' Pawn and Payday. One of the pawnbrokers hit the jackpot when he found a rare first edition of the novel *Least Objects* and sold it at auction for some ungodly amount of money. The story was getting a lot of play, and now everyone thought they might have a valuable book, too.

Charlotte watched as the camera panned the parking lot full of cars, pickup trucks, and potholes, to a line of people with books extending out the shop door across the length of the strip mall. She was working up the nerve to go there herself and pawn her jewelry and silverware. The Jeep needed work, and Diane warned her not to use credit cards anymore, no matter what.

The reporter wrapped up. "There you have it, Floyd, rare book fever among the truck stops. This is Judy Sargent, reporting from Elm Grove, Indiana."

Floyd the news anchor followed it up with a two-sentence bio of the book's author, Seamus O'Dair, whose photo was up on the screen next to him. Charlotte wondered if someone at the studio chose it deliberately, playing up the dullness of the blow-dried talking head on the left side of the screen with the auburn shock and hollow cheeks of the genius on the right. Couldn't blame them if they did.

She switched off the TV, packed up a notepad, pen, bottle of water, sunglasses and reading glasses (that badge of one's middle age), and loaded everything into her sand-colored Jeep. She let out a breath of relief when it started up. Day by day. It was Friday the 13th, but she felt that enough bad things had happened lately that, even if she was superstitious, the odds were against her luck going any further south.

The thirty-minute drive on the four-lane highway from Lake Parkerton to Elm Grove was a lovely stretch of rolling farmland and trees, save for the billboards every half mile or so. Most of them featured giant grinning proprietors of real estate agencies, car dealerships, jewelry stores, insurance companies, and law firms. There was a new one, featuring a linebacker type wearing a backwards baseball cap and a hammy surprised expression. He was holding a book, and next to him was "ASK BOSLEY," under which was, *"It might be worth more than you think!"* It was the pawnbroker whose shop was on TV that morning, and it looked like he didn't lose any time taking advantage of his good luck.

Luck, thought Charlotte, had an amazing amount to do with whether or not one was successful in a bad economy. She thought it was pure luck, for instance, that Helene thought of her for Olivia's project just as the magazine work dried up. Gratitude surpassed whatever pretense to dignity she harbored about needing the work. But when Charlotte expressed that she hoped to be able to return the favor one day, Helene shook her head and said, "Just finding a way to work with my sister will be favor enough. Trust me."

Olivia Targman, *née* Bernadin, turned out to be a crabby, impatient nonagenarian with a hard-done-by attitude who had been keeping a series of notebooks, part memoir, part novel, for the past forty or fifty years. When Helene performed the introductions, Olivia just grunted and asked, "So what do you *do?*" It took a while to assure her of Charlotte's credentials, but she seemed to relent and handed over a spiral-bound notebook.

"You must find *all* of the notebooks," she asserted. Her bony finger pointed at Charlotte for emphasis, and her dark eyes framed by an aquiline nose warned against argument. "The one you're holding is the *last* one. They are in order. I don't remember exactly where the first ones are anymore, some upstairs, some in the basement; it'll come back to me as we find them. I'll show you when you come over. I can't lift things much or go up and down those stairs. But I know they are in order and that there are nine or ten of them."

Once Charlotte found all the notebooks, she was then to work with Olivia to transcribe, edit and prepare them for publication.

Charlotte's Internet search for Olivia Bernadin yielded a single paragraph in an article about "Women of the Beat Generation," in which she was described as having written a well-received book of poetry and a few short stories in *The New Yorker,* and was briefly an editor of the literary journal *Sibylline.* From there Charlotte searched *Sibylline* and learned much the same, along with the fact that Olivia was commissioned to co-write a screenplay for a French New Wave film, but then "disappeared."

The prospect of editing and publishing the novel/memoir of a writer presumed missing for half a century was irresistible, and an incredible bit of luck. Charlotte's enthusiasm for the project grew as she realized this was no mere indulging the bucket list of an elderly eccentric, but a potentially important contribution to the literary world, depending on the quality of the notebooks. It would be good to work on a project different than the articles on trends in the design industry that had been her bread-and-butter for years, a fresh start that might even lead to a completely different path as she rebuilt her career.

Her enthusiasm for the project, in fact, made up for her reluctance to spend so much time back in Elm Grove, a picturesque college town with well-preserved brick storefronts, an ornate 19th-century courthouse, and several streets of stately old houses. It was also graced with many large, shady trees, although, as in most communities these days, few of them were elms. At one time she loved its quaint, almost story-book appearance, before it came to represent everything she hated once her marriage was no longer happily-ever-after. Her cell phone beeped as she turned off the highway onto winding Sheffield Street, which led to the downtown area, and a quick glance showed it was Diane. When the traffic slowed to stop-go, she called back.

Diane's near-tenor voice was both mellow and chipper, as usual. "Good morning, glory."

"Hi Diane. What's up?"

"I ran through your numbers again and created a budget for you, if you'd like to come by and pick it up. It'll give you a better idea of how much you should downsize."

"Downsize. Is that what they call hitting the skids now?"

Diane chuckled. "You knew the risk, Charlotte, when you moved there."

"I know, I know. It's okay. I don't have any regrets; it's just that it's all happening so suddenly. I'm on my way to a client's, so can't stop by for a while yet. Give it to me now. How much can I afford a month?"

Diane paused. "Twenty percent of what you have been living on."

"A fifth?" The sun glared off the back window of the car in front, flattening the world around her. Her ears rang with the noise of cars, the chatter of young mothers pushing strollers to the park, the music playing from speakers attached to the streetlights, the breeze through the maples and oaks around the courthouse square. She remembered pushing Ellis in a stroller down these sidewalks, too, and buying hot dogs and sweet, quickly-melting vanilla cones from the vendors setting up on the corners.

Her hands were cold and clammy on the steering wheel. To live on a fifth of what she was accustomed to meant not only no house, but no new car, no manicures, no hair salon or massages, no good wine or gym membership, no food deliveries, no eating out, and no shopping whatsoever. No new shoes, new coats, not even a bandana. No cleaning lady. No laundry service or dry cleaning. No lawn service, gutter cleaning, guy to plow the driveway in the winter. Most of all, no trip to Paris to see Ellis. "So I'm supposed to, what, live in a tent?"

"Hopefully, no. But you need to eliminate as many expenses as possible right away. Cancel memberships and subscriptions, cable, all that kind of stuff. Watch the eating out and clothes shopping. Minimize, minimize, minimize. Get everything you can down to zero, and of course get that house on the market a.s.a.p. Cut up your credit cards like, *now,* and pay off anything you owe on them, though thank god that doesn't look too bad. You'll want to avoid accumulating debt. That way, after selling your house, you'll have enough to live on while you get your career back on track."

Charlotte could think of nothing to say. The words did not come, just a sensation that life as she knew it had stopped, right there in the middle of a street in a busy village, while she inhaled exhaust from an idled truck. A fifth. The delivery truck started moving again and she drove on through the downtown to the residential area, as if on automatic pilot.

Diane cleared her throat, reminding her that she was still on the phone. "Charlotte, I've got another call I should take. If you can, come in this afternoon to pick up the packet I've prepared for you, and we can take it from there. I'm really sorry all this is happening. It's like a perfect storm."

"Yeah. Thanks, Diane. I'll see you later."

She sighed. The news was even worse than expected, but on the whole she felt better knowing. Good news or bad, having the facts gave things *shape.* With facts, she thought, one can take action. Wondering and worrying about what you didn't know just led to all kinds of problems. It was actually easier now to give Olivia's project her full attention. Or so Charlotte told herself as she turned off Sheffield and onto Pierce Street, passing by Helene's condominium and a row of 1920's bungalows until she reached Olivia's house, the last one on the block.

She pulled the Jeep left into the driveway that led to the detached garage, then backed out and turned to park on the street in front of the walk to the front door. It felt strange to be going to someone's house for a job. She saw that it could use new paint around the door and window trim, the bridal wreath shrubs around the raised foundation were overgrown and covering the windows, and the chain link fence enclosing the yard had dents here and there. A few large branches in the patchy grass looked like they'd been there for a while. The gate squeaked as she went through it, but it worked and latched just fine. Charlotte recalled passing this very house many times when she lived in Elm Grove ten years before, following as Ellis learned to ride her first bike. She might have even seen someone on the old-fashioned swing on the front porch. The breeze carried the cheerful sound of children playing in the schoolyard across the street and up one block.

Olivia did not answer when Charlotte knocked, but the door was unlocked, so she tentatively opened it a crack and called out, "Hello, Mrs. Targman? It's Charlotte." Still no answer. "Hello? Olivia?" she inquired again, as her eyes adjusted to the gloom of the front room after the glare of sun outside. She was sure she'd gotten the appointment time right.

Helene's description of the house as "heavy on the potpourri" was an understatement, and Charlotte couldn't help but think of the morbid rose-heavy scent of funeral homes. It was going to take some doing not to feel queasy, and she wished she hadn't burned that bagel earlier. She rapped on the door again, in case Olivia was asleep, or in the bathroom or simply didn't hear, but there was still no answer. By this time Charlotte's eyes had adjusted to the light and she beheld a small living room with a mix of vintage furniture. There was a blue Queen Anne style sofa at the back, facing the front door, a heavily carved mahogany coffee table in front of it, a worn brown leatherette recliner by the sofa, and end tables with mismatched lamps next to the chairs. Near the door there was a tapestry-covered wingback chair and ottoman. A narrow space behind the sofa was filled with glass-fronted oak curio cabinets displaying porcelain and crystal figurines. There was a doorway opposite the front door that led through a dining room and into what was probably the kitchen. On the wall to her right there was a small writing desk with cubbyholes, a lyre-back chair, and a three-shelf bookcase. The entire wall to her left was covered with utilitarian board-and-bracket shelving crammed with a mix of new and old books, all surrounding a single window draped with sheer Priscilla curtains. Olivia was certainly a reader, if not much of a decorator.

There were some books scattered across the oriental rug, as if they'd fallen from the shelves or had been thrown, and a few loose pages had separated from the covers. Another step into the room revealed a floor lamp and small round chess table that had fallen over next to the wingback chair, along with a tea-stained cup and a book of crossword puzzles. Then as Charlotte turned, she saw the reason why there was no answer to her knock:

Olivia Targman was lying on the floor between the bookshelves and the coffee table, her limp hand holding a baseball bat.

Charlotte's heart fluttered as panic set in. Was Olivia dead? There was a nasty bruise on her forehead. Charlotte had never seen a dead person before, at least not outside of a funeral home, so she wasn't *sure* if she was looking at an actual dead person. She swallowed hard and stepped over the books to reach Olivia, and was relieved to feel that the "body" was still warm, if barely breathing. Her hands trembled as she struggled to call 911 for an ambulance, and then to call Helene. She hardly heard her friend's distress through the ringing in her ears, and took shallow breaths to calm down. It was as she waited for help and started to cover Olivia with a crocheted afghan from the sofa that she noticed the sticky stuff at the business end of the bat: blood. And then she saw another big streak of blood across the rug, which she hadn't spotted at first against the dark red pattern. She called 911 again, this time for the police. Something very bad had happened here.

Two

Also Friday, September 13th

"Hello? Ma'am, are you there? Hello?"

Charlotte started at the dispatcher's voice, and realized she had spaced out for a moment, staring at Olivia's unconscious body, her permed steel gray hair, baggy brown polyester pants, a man's oversized bright green sweatshirt, and skinny ankles sticking out of scruffy gray walking shoes, quite possibly the same outfit she wore when Charlotte met her the other day.

"Yes! I'm here." Charlotte's voice was hoarse, and she cleared her throat.

"Ma'am, are you alone in the house? Is there any chance the person who did this is still in the house?"

"Um, I'm alone, yes, and um—oh dear, I see what you mean—"

"Ma'am, please leave the house and stay on the line. Wait outside for the officers to arrive."

Charlotte's heart started fluttering again, and she staggered back onto her feet, feeling dizzy and short of breath. Of course! Whoever did this to Olivia could still be here, armed and dangerous, even! She picked up her bag and started to make her way out, but stopped cold when the front door opened and a tall man walked in, his features blacked out by the brightness of the light behind him.

She felt herself make a weird squeak as she gasped and clutched her bag even tighter, prepared to use it as a weapon. *Oh my god, oh my god—*

The tall man stopped upon seeing her, and then stepped further into the room, which made his face visible. He looked down at her with eyebrows raised in either surprise or anger, she couldn't tell which in her fraught state of mind.

"Charlotte?" he asked.

How'd he know my name? Did he force it out of Olivia? She nodded, ever so slightly.

The dark eyebrows relaxed. "I'm Simon, Helene's neighbor. She's on her way over and sent me ahead to help. Where's Olivia?"

Charlotte began to breathe again, if just a little bit, and cautiously moved to the side so that he could see Olivia. She heard the dispatcher still on the cell phone again. "Ma'am, are you alright? Do you hear me?" She stepped back more as this Simon fellow moved past her to check on Olivia for himself.

Her wits returned with her breath. "Yes! A friend of Olivia's sister is here now, and I'm—I'm going outside now." She clicked the phone off. But instead of leaving she watched Simon, who was moving around carefully, taking pictures of Olivia, the bat, the books, and the bloodstain on the bat with his cell phone.

"What on earth are you doing?"

"Getting the scene of the crime before the cops get here. If they're good cops, it won't matter. If they're bad cops, these might help prove we didn't do the deed ourselves, or at least didn't mess with the scene."

"That's awfully cold."

Charlotte looked more closely at him and realized they were roughly the same age, making him much older than the impression she first got from his thick hair, black leather jacket, long-legged jeans and energetic movements.

He didn't even turn to look at her. "Not really. You'll see." He continued with pictures of the table and lamp, and even the chair, from several different angles.

This man has an impossible level of self-possession, she thought.

She also realized he had an English accent. Interesting. Didn't the villains in movies and crime shows always have English accents? *Snap out of it,* she thought, this isn't the time to be silly.

"Careful around the bloodstain."

He nodded. "Spotted that. I wonder who it was she whacked. Was the door open when you got here?"

"It was closed, but unlocked. I was just about to clear out when you came in. The dispatcher said whoever did this might still be in here."

Simon nodded as he looked around carefully, taking more pictures here and there. "Let's check the other rooms," he said, moving toward the doorways to the hall and the dining room. He stopped abruptly and Charlotte almost walked into him.

"Bloody hell! This is like an antique shop," he said, trying to look around without knocking over anything.

Here the scent was decidedly floral, and emanated from two crystal bowls with potpourri on the lace-covered Duncan Phyfe table. It was a small dining room, yet still packed with the table and six chairs, a large sideboard, and two more glass-front curio cabinets. The top of the sideboard was covered with three tarnished silver tea sets, around a dozen large silver candlesticks and several tiered petit-fours stands. In addition to the bowls of potpourri, the table was laden with crystal candlesticks, candy bowls, footed bowls, and colorful McCoy and Roseville pottery vases. The curio cabinets were crammed with porcelain boxes, delicate Capodimonte floral baskets, and salt and pepper shakers.

They continued carefully to the kitchen, where there were stacks of mismatched dishes and crockery on the counters, cook books stacked four feet high on the chrome dinette table in the corner, and on the floor stacks of old margarine and whipped topping tubs, cardboard boxes full of empty glass pickle and jelly jars, and cardboard boxes of more glass jars, each filled with a single kind of item, such as buttons, screws, tiny toys, and marbles. Another box held several large rubber band balls. Shelves ran across an entire wall from floor to ceiling, filled with cookie jars, banks, collector liquor bottles, and what had to be a hundred souvenir models of the Eiffel Tower in various sizes and material from wrought iron to embroidered fabric stuffed like doorstops. There were also brightly-colored Fiesta Ware teapots, pitchers, and cup and saucer sets. Yellow vinyl dinette chairs sat against the wall on either side of the table and supported stacks of folded rag rugs and tablecloths in every imaginable color. Under the table were stacks of picture puzzle boxes, some of which looked quite old. The only semblance of the room being used as a kitchen was immediately around the sink, which had a plate and mug on the drain rack, and around the stove, which held a tea kettle. A chrome and vinyl high step stool was situated in front of the drain rack. A bottle of home fragrance stood open on the windowsill above the sink, and smelled of apples and cinnamon.

The kitchen door to the basement was locked, as was the door to the back porch; Charlotte peered out the curtained window and saw stacks of newspapers and more plastic containers, and plastic bags full of more plastic bags. A clothesline stretched across the length of the porch, and hung low with the weight of drying towels and nightgowns. She turned to Simon, who was still taking pictures.

"Just more of the same out here."

He turned to look at her, his mouth hanging slightly open, his eyes wide, and shook his head in amazement. "Good lord!"

Charlotte felt better for knowing that someone else found this house as overwhelming as she did, and just nodded.

They moved back out of the kitchen into the dining room, where they turned into a dark hall with several doors.

The first door was for the bathroom, an old-fashioned one with its original claw-foot tub, mosaic tiled floor, and heavy white pedestal sink, all of which had seen better days. Shelves over the old toilet were crammed with perfume bottles and containers of products that Charlotte hadn't seen since childhood. The next room had bedroom furniture in it, but every inch of floor space was filled with garment racks, each of which was crammed with clothes on hangers. More floral potpourri was in a bowl on the nightstand.

The second bedroom was much the same, except the bed and dresser drawers were more accessible, and there was a small television set atop a chest of drawers opposite the bed. As in the rest of the house, the scent was as pervasive as the clutter.

I wonder if I would have been able to work in this house? She then realized that there would now be some doubt as to when, or even if, the transcription and editing project would happen. She could just make out the whine of approaching sirens as they moved back into the living room, where Olivia remained unconscious.

"I'll go meet Helene," she said, turning to leave, but gasped as she felt the floor soften under her feet. Simon moved quickly to grab her around the waist and nearly lifted her out the room and out to the swing on the porch.

"Hey there, now. You okay?"

"Oh, yes, I'm fine. The fresh air helps." It wasn't just the fresh air, she thought. It was the ease with which he was able to steady her five-foot ten frame, and how it reassured her. Strange how certain things were noticed even when under stress.

Helene was approaching from her condo at the other end of the block, her white swept-back hair glowing like a halo in the sun. She was elegant and dignified, wearing a slim gray skirt, cream knit tunic, and gray and blue wool challis shawl; Charlotte thought that Helene could not look less like Olivia's sister. Simon helped Helene up the steps and went with her inside the house for a few moments until the ambulance and EMTs arrived. When she came out, she sat on the swing next to Charlotte and sighed. "Poor Olivia! Who could have done this?"

Charlotte's heart went out to her dear friend. She couldn't recall ever seeing Helene so distraught, even when her husband died. But the circumstances were of course so different. He had been ill for a long time, whereas Olivia was still going strong and had been assaulted.

The police arrived, to ask their questions and make their reports. It was going to be a long morning.

Tea was the only thing that would help, strong and black. Making tea was as soothing as drinking it, Charlotte thought as she sliced lemons and placed cups and spoons and a plate of cinnamon palmier cookies on a tray. The morning had indeed been long and stretched into mid-afternoon, full of questions from the police, and getting Olivia situated in the hospital, where she remained unconscious and under observation. Charlotte leaned against the countertop as she waited for the electric kettle to boil, enjoying the serenity and simplicity of Helene's kitchen. It could not have been more different than Olivia's: the surfaces were nearly bare, there were no boxes on the floor, the cooking things were contained within cabinets and drawers, and the space was suffused with natural light. Charlotte recalled that the kitchen in Helene's former house at Lake Parkerton, while much grander in scale and rich with granite, mahogany, and high-end appliances, had been equally serene.

Here in the white and birch galley kitchen, Helene still had her striking Belle Époque poster of Loie Fuller in swirls of reds, oranges, and yellows against a black background. And on the bistro-style table there was the same clear green-tinted longneck bud vase with a white orchid that had always graced her breakfast bar at Lake Parkerton. The simple white plates and tea pot were the same. And the zen-like simplicity and airiness —they were the same. Completely different house and location, completely different scale, and yet nothing, really, was lost.

Charlotte brought the tea tray into the sitting area, which, like the kitchen, overlooked the courtyard garden through a series of French doors. The doors led out to a small veranda, making the room seem part of the garden.

Helene was propped up sideways on a white slipcovered sofa, her legs stretched out and covered with a soft throw. She was exhausted, but still too shook up to nap, and Charlotte wanted to be sure she was going to be okay. Simon had taken off his jacket and was slouched in the dark brown leather club chair. He, too, looked exhausted.

From what she could gather of their conversation, Simon had just returned from a week in Japan, and the jet lag was catching up with him. He eyed the tea tray but didn't look happy. Charlotte wondered what was wrong.

"A problem?" she asked.

He hesitated, but Helene looked over and smiled, which only emphasized the dark circles under her eyes. "Would you be a dear and bring a little milk? Simon always takes his tea with milk and sugar instead of lemon."

Charlotte resisted the temptation to tell him to get it himself, since Helene actually made the request. "No problem." Simon has jet lag, Helene is old and worried, and my nerves are shot, she thought. The sooner we all have our tea, the better.

As she returned with the milk and sugar, she heard Helene talking about Ellis.

"Charlotte is Ellis Anthony's mother."

Simon's face lit up, making him look friendly for the first time that day. "Ellie's mom? That girl is talented!"

"You know Ellis?" Charlotte felt the pang of the joint-custody parent at the reminder of just how much of her child's life was a mystery to her. And it was only going to get more so. Ellis had never mentioned this tall man with the abrupt manner. And she *let* him call her "Ellie?" As she listened to Helene's account of how Simon had met Ellis when he stopped by on an errand for Helene, Charlotte took in his black boots, the broken-in jeans stretching up long legs, the black long-sleeved tee with the sleeves shoved up to the elbows, the broad shoulders, the slightly craggy face, blue-green eyes and shaggy, grey-streaked dark blond hair that had only receded a small amount.

"So you're from England, I assume?"

"London." He poured milk into his cup, topped it with tea, then stirred in a spoonful of sugar. "But I go all over. Got a stint with the university here for a bit, thought I'd get to know this part of the States."

"Simon's a photographer, Charlotte," said Helene. She took her own cup of tea, and squeezed in a bit of fresh lemon. "He's been in all kinds of publications and galleries and he's written quite a few books. He was a guest lecturer at Corton last year and they asked him to continue for another. I'm lucky to have him as a neighbor. He lives in the upstairs unit next door." Helene beamed at Simon. Charlotte kept a neutral expression; if she didn't know better, she would have thought Helene had a crush on him.

"Well, I'd like to see your work some time," she said. A photographer. Perhaps that would explain his almost compulsive picture-taking at Olivia's house?

Helene pointed to the shelf under the large coffee table. "You have, actually. There's his big book, right there." Charlotte drew it out, and was stunned. He was Simon *Norwich?* She'd admired this book during many of Ellis' lessons and visits with Helene, and said so. She opened the cover and read Simon's inscription: "For Helene—your example of the beauty of the essential is with me wherever I go. Warmest regards, Simon."

"So you're that guy," Charlotte smiled. "Given all the places you've gone to and photographed, I'm surprised you'd want another year here in the boring Midwest."

"Oh, it's not bad, you know. It's comfortable, and makes a nice base of operations. Cheaper than home, too, and know the language and all. Or enough of it," he laughed, and Charlotte thought his baritone was in scale with his physique. "Sometimes—sometimes it's good to just do some art for art's sake and not have to worry about basic survival and money, weather, shelter, military coups, epidemics," he made a wide gesture with his hands that encompassed all the world's many ills. "The older I get, the more I appreciate home comforts."

Helene sighed. "Is anyplace really safe? Poor Olivia."

They returned to the present problem. Charlotte replaced the book under the table and poured more tea for everyone.

Simon helped himself to another palmier, holding the dessert plate close to his chin to catch any crumbs of pastry.

"Poor dead guy is the other possibility," he mumbled, then swallowed and licked his lips.

Helene shook her head in exasperation. "I *told* her that baseball bat was ridiculous! Who did she think she was going to scare? She's had it by the front door for years."

Charlotte tried to imagine the scenario, and came to a realization.

"It had to have been someone she knew and let in, even invited. That was no break-in. Why would she take a bat to someone she let in herself?"

"Or maybe he found the key under the mat and thought she wasn't there?" said Simon. He turned to Helene. "Maybe she was getting an appraisal and was insulted by the offer?"

"Not impossible," said Helene. "I think she's had appraisals before, and she was interested in talking to the fellow who has been in the news for the past week, the one who found the Seamus O'Dair book. It's not unlikely that she had something along those lines and thought she could get a good price."

"That still blows my mind," said Charlotte, shaking her head. "*Least Objects* isn't on your typical high school or even college sophomore reading list, and, well, I'm sure I'm being a real snob here, but if Bosley Warren is anything like how he looks on TV or that billboard he has up, he would have Cliff-noted his way through every English lit class. Would he have even known it was a rare book? But of course it might just be an act."

Simon was shaking his head. "He wouldn't have had to know anything about literature if he kept up with the trade news. Not long ago someone donated a Samuel Beckett novel to a charity fundraiser in England, and it brought something like 12,000 pounds—made headlines. If you follow auction reports, which I'm sure Warren Brothers would do, it's a matter of keeping an eye out for what's hot." He seemed to smile to himself as he looked straight at Charlotte. "It's a university town, so it's not impossible someone had a first edition of it."

Charlotte found herself drawn in to share in his speculation. "Maybe they knew Olivia from appraising her pottery vases, then remembered seeing a lot of old books in the house, too?"

The three of them sat in silence for a moment, contemplating the possibilities.

"Whatever it was," said Simon, "it went pear-shaped."

Well, Charlotte thought, there's a phrase you don't hear every day on this side of "the pond." She spoke to Helene.

"I think you said Olivia has a son?"

"Yes," said Helene, nodding. "Donovan. I haven't seen him in years. He would be a few years older than you, about fifty-five, fifty-six, I think. Olivia didn't talk much about Donnie. There was a rift many years ago and they just kept their distance. She could get hold of him, I think, and every so often he'd check in with her, especially after Ronson died. As you saw yourself, she isn't easy to get along with. But she seemed to be mellowing these past two years. She really seemed to want to connect again, at least with me." Helene let out a deep, regretful sigh.

Charlotte looked around the room, the uncluttered elegance of a few loved things brought together with good comfortable furniture.

"One thing that struck me," Charlotte said, picking her words carefully, "was the remarkable contrast between your home and your sister's."

"Yes. Well. Olivia's a collector gone haywire. Hoarder." Helene shrugged, as if to say, *there it is.*

"And the fragrance was over the top," added Charlotte. "It was like being in an incense shop."

"Oh, I know. She always did go too heavy with the potpourri and air fresheners. I couldn't stand being in her house for long, I'd get asthma. So when we did meet up, it would usually be here or at a restaurant. It was a sore point with her, but if I couldn't breathe, I couldn't breathe. I haven't been in that house for longer than five minutes since before Ronson died. In fact I sometimes have to air this place out after she's been here, it just gets into everything!"

Simon smiled at Helene wrinkling her nose. "I think I still have it up my nose, can't stop smelling it." He made a small shiver of horror. "I've come across hoarders before, but Olivia is a different sort. The front room is over-furnished and has all these curio cabinets and bookcases and whatnot, but you can still sit down in there. So she is somewhat aware of what she's doing, and puts on a good front. But the rest of the place was packed to the ceiling! And we didn't go in the basement or look in the closets, either."

"So it is even worse than I thought," said Helene. "And now there is an injured missing person and Olivia is in the hospital. I hope the police have reached Donovan. He's going to have a huge job on his hands if she doesn't recover."

The sun was setting and the last of the afternoon light turned the white walls to gold. Simon set down his cup and stretched his arms and slowly tilted his head from side to side to stretch his neck.

"I'm going to have to take leave of you ladies before I fall asleep in this chair. Been a long day."

"Oh Simon, of course, and I'm so sorry everything turned out like this, especially the moment you came back," said Helene, as she tried to get up from the sofa.

"I should be going, too," said Charlotte, helping her up, "I need to stop by my accountant's. But are you going to be alright? Would you want me to come back and stay over?"

Helene shook her head. "No, no, I'm quite alright, really, just very tired. If you could help me tidy up that would be perfect, then I will spend the rest of the evening reading in bed. Jeanette, my cleaning lady, comes in the morning, and she's bringing homemade *pain au chocolat.*" Helene's eyes twinkled in anticipation.

Thus reassured, Simon took the tea things into the kitchen and did the washing up while Charlotte put away the remaining milk, sugar, and lemons. Then she suddenly realized he wasn't there. Helene came into the kitchen.

"Where's Simon?" Charlotte asked.

"He's gone home."

"Oh. He can be a bit abrupt."

"He's not one to wax sentimental, certainly, but he's a lovely soul.

You'll get used to him."

"Is that an English thing?"

"It's a Simon thing."

Three

Friday, September 13th (a very long day)

Pellegato Accounting was nestled between a florist and a bike shop on one of the streets across from the courthouse. Charlotte had called Diane while waiting for Helene to get Olivia settled in at the hospital, explained what was going on, and was grateful that she was able to drop by after regular office hours. One bonus of the late hour was being able to get a parking space right in front of the office's window, which was outfitted with Venetian blinds with red cords, and slats alternately tinted cream and pale green, giving it the appearance of a giant ledger book. Diane actually did everything on computers, but the local Chamber of Commerce encouraged downtown businesses to use traditional visual signifiers, such as the red-and-white striped pole at Phil's Barber Shop, and the giant nutcracker-style wooden soldiers that stood guard at the Toy Emporium.

The staff had already gone home and Diane herself unlocked the door, looking every inch *not* like a traditional accountant. She took Casual Fridays seriously, wearing pale purple jeans and a long deep purple sweater that set off her peaches and cream complexion and black short-cropped hair. Her high-top sneakers were purple, too. Only the horn-rim glasses suggested her profession, and they were the kind of assertive glasses that made Charlotte reach up to touch the reading glasses shoved into her hair like a head band just to make sure they were still there, and not, perhaps, left behind in the Jeep or at Helene's. Diane gave Charlotte a hug, then held her at arm's length and looked her over with genuine concern.

"How are you doing? How's Helene's sister? How's Helene?"

"Helene is calming down, mostly. Olivia's still unconscious. There's bleeding in the brain, so the prognosis isn't good, especially given her age."

"Coffee? Tea?" Charlotte said thanks but shook her head no, and Diane continued. "That's such a shock, somebody hurting an old woman like that, and just a few blocks away, and connected to someone you know."

They moved from the waiting room to Diane's office, where they sat down in the pair of armchairs in front of the desk. Charlotte rubbed her eyes, then forehead and the back of her neck. The strain of the day was catching up with her.

"You look exhausted. Is there anything I can get you? An aspirin? A smoke? Bourbon?" asked Diane.

Charlotte smiled. "That's a great selection, Diane, but I'd better not. I don't know that it's exhaustion so much as a combination of shock and weirdness. Maybe even a little bit of fear, especially for Helene. I mean, we have no idea what actually happened there, who did this or why. It's mystifying."

"I would imagine the first question would be, who benefits?" said Diane. "I mean, that is, if Olivia dies. Do you think?"

"Her son, I would imagine. But he evidently hasn't been around much, and I don't think his own mother would use a bat on him."

"Not unless he came in in the middle of the night and she thought he was a burglar."

"She was still dressed in street clothes, and there were books scattered on the floor."

"Sounds like a murder mystery. Complete with bloody baseball bat. That is, if she dies. Close enough. Or sounds likely." Diane had picked up on Charlotte's fear of the unknown, and her eyes were wide and bright behind her glasses. "So the police haven't a clue?"

"They might, but if they do, they're not telling us. I hate not knowing, you know? Makes me want to *do* something, anything!"

"Maybe something will come to light tomorrow, or you'll remember a detail that will help the police."

Charlotte smiled ruefully. "Yeah, right, like I'd make a good Miss Marple. I'm so observant I didn't even see my own disaster coming." She looked down at the office carpet, tracing the pattern with her toe. "Between coming to terms with what's happened in my own life and now this, my head is in a whirl. Maybe it's crass of me to be thinking about this when someone's life is hanging by a thread, but I'm also afraid that now there probably won't be an editing job. I was really looking forward to it, too."

"Yeah, it's crass, but we can do crass just between the two of us," said Diane. "Your situation is serious enough to make it understandable."

She handed Charlotte a folder that was lying on the desk, and went into accountant mode.

"The first thing I wanted to say, is that you've been a long-time client and I consider you a friend, so I'm waiving my fee until you make enough to pay taxes again."

Charlotte started to protest, but Diane was having none of it. "Shut it. Don't argue with me. It's just between us. Here's the budget, the numbers you need to work with. But those are just the numbers. Obviously there are different ways of going about reaching these numbers, and some will be more challenging than others. As we discussed before, the first thing is to sell your house as soon as possible, which will get rid of that mortgage payment, and the insurance and utilities, and of course those ridiculous property taxes. As you can see," she pointed at a couple of different columns, "if you eliminate your housing-related expenses, you'll have a much better chance of making ends meet with a reduced income. That will put *you* back in charge of your life."

Charlotte felt her glasses slide down her nose and her heart sink when she compared the numbers. "You're not kidding. Seeing it laid out like this really brings it home. I guess it is time to get hold of a real estate agent and have a moving sale."

"Do you have an agent in mind?"

"No, actually. I used Bernie Baysell last time. He was so annoying. But I think he's retired now."

Diane laughed. "Why, didn't you like being called 'sweetheart,' and 'little darling?'"

"No!" Charlotte laughed.

"Actually," said Diane, "Baysell Realty is still going strong, and there's a Women's Business Forum member working there, Lola McKennie, who everyone says is a very hard worker, very dedicated to getting houses sold quickly. She's done the whole single mom thing, too, and I suspect she would be appreciative of your situation right now."

"Thanks for the recommendation. I'll give her a call tomorrow."

Diane hesitated and looked at the clock. "Would it be okay,

Charlotte, if I give her a call right now? The Women's Forum really encourages us to make at least three personal-contact referrals every month, and this one would count. The advantage in it for you is that you'll get more priority than otherwise."

"Sure, fine, that would be great. Glad to be of help."

Diane made the call in her usual cheerful phone voice and Charlotte heard herself being referred to as a "friend," and her situation as "a perfect storm," and could make out a woman's voice saying, "YES!" when Diane mentioned Lake Parkerton.

Diane looked over. "Nine o'clock tomorrow morning okay?"

Charlotte nodded, and was impressed by the speed of doing things this way. Diane confirmed the appointment, along with Charlotte's address and phone number.

"You're all set, then. Go home, Charlotte, take a long bath, have some wine. Time enough to deal with all of this tomorrow."

Anticipation for a long bath and a glass of wine kept Charlotte going during her sunset drive back to Lake Parkerton, but after turning into the entrance gates and following the road that wound around the lake and up the hills, the many signs saying Foreclosure and For Sale brought her firmly back into the present. The national economy was supposedly on the upswing, but many local economies were just as bad as ever. One of the area's biggest steel mills had been purchased by a foreign conglomerate right before the recession, but instead of expanding it as promised, the new owners shut it down altogether. Lake Parkerton was where many of the original company's executives and upper management lived, and it was now showing the effects of the economic downturn. Several lawns were looking unkempt, and a few houses had gutters coming loose. The Velez' house was still boarded up, officially the result of a kitchen fire, but Ernie next door swore it was an insurance scam. The parents of Ellis' first boyfriend from junior high still lived two doors down from there, but Charlotte had heard that they were splitting up. He was a funny boy, who once said that her hair was the same color as the cottontail rabbit that lived under the far end of the deck. He had been sent to a military academy, and she wondered what would happen to him now. She drove around a tow truck that was loading up a repossessed Hummer. It just wasn't the same place it used to be. Her own For Sale sign would be going up soon. She was going to have to tell Ellis, plan a moving sale, find more work—

Charlotte parked the Jeep in her garage and walked into the kitchen, thinking about something quick she could make for supper. Anything to put the events of the day—of the past few days, actually—out of her head and pretend life was normal again.

Normal, however, wasn't particularly welcoming. First, there was the clutter: countertops crammed with jars of pasta and dry beans, spices, bottles of various flavored oils and vinegars, a dozen bags or boxes of snack foods, most half-full or almost empty, a large knife block, an unpacked box containing a darling new hand-painted pasta set (bought four months ago, right before they learned Ellis was going to Paris), overhead racks with dozens of pots and pans, some of them rather nice and some simply decorative, figurines of animal cooks, including a three-foot high one of a squirrel holding a spoon and a walnut, a stack of clean dishtowels and a pile of dirty ones, a laundry basket of clean unfolded towels and napkins, and several crockery jars holding spoons, whisks, spatulas, and such. What bit of counter space that was available was occupied by a dirty cutting board with the uneaten burnt bagel from breakfast. The sink had several plates and cups and last night's wine glass because the dishwasher hadn't yet been emptied. Then there was the pile of mail, mostly junk advertisements, several magazines and catalogs, five days' worth of the newspaper as yet unread, two broken plates from months ago set aside to be repaired, and by the door three large garbage bags of old school papers and girlish things that Ellis threw out and Charlotte had yet to bring herself to throw in the trash.

No actual crime happened here, but the difference between her kitchen and Helene's was not unlike the difference between Helene's kitchen and Olivia's, and this realization stopped her in her tracks. *I'm turning into an Olivia,* she thought. *If I drop dead right now, other people would come in here and say, "Bloody hell!"* She imagined Simon looking over her kitchen, and, if she was honest, her bathroom, bedroom, basement, and garage in slack-jawed amazement. And she wouldn't have faulted him. And she thought, too, that if she died, poor Ellis would have to set aside time in her own life to deal with all this *crap.*

Her stomach growled. She grabbed a clean wine glass, a fresh bottle of pinot noir, and heated up a frozen diet lasagna dinner in the microwave while she looked for the corkscrew, which after ten minutes' search was discovered under the pile of dirty towels. She took her dinner and the folder from Diane into the living room—like Olivia's, the one room that wasn't too bad—to get away from the mess. She settled into her usual corner of a tan Italian leather sectional and clicked on the gas fireplace with the remote. A sip of wine, then a bite of food—for prefab frozen lasagna, it wasn't too bad, she thought. As she looked over the budget plan, however, she knew that convenience food wasn't likely to be on future grocery lists, along with a lot of other things.

With only the light from the fire in the living room, Charlotte could look over the darkening lake through the clerestory windows and see the lights from houses on the other side. It looked like the Olewskis were having a party, or maybe it was their kids, it was a little too far away to tell for sure. She had seen a lot of them when she first moved here, as their daughter and Ellis were the same age, but as the girls drifted apart in high school, so, too did the adults. Next door to them was the Pannetti's house, dark, foreclosed and deadly silent without the happy racket from their five kids. She had liked them a lot, too. At one time there was such vitality in Lake Parkerton, and all of a sudden it seemed there was nothing. Perhaps her only connection to these people was as Ellis' mother.

Charlotte never admitted to anyone, not even Diane, her real reason for moving here: she wanted Ellis, who showed great promise even at the age of six, to have piano lessons with Helene Dalmier, one of the most well-regarded and well-connected teachers in the region. She'd heard that Helene had cut back on her teaching schedule, but still seemed willing to take students from Lake Parkerton. Charlotte had quietly gone with her instincts on this, because talking about one's child's "gift" was to invite all sorts of eye-rolling and talk about stage-mothering and such. It was a gamble, but it paid off. Ellis flourished under Helene's calm but firm assurance, so different than Charlotte's own style, which was more akin to putting out fires. Charlotte never wanted Ellis to know about the gamble, to feel guilty if it didn't work out.

But now Helene was no longer in her grand house, which was one of the original fifty houses designed and built by Paul Dalmier and his associates when they founded Lake Parkerton, in a variation on Frank Lloyd Wright's Usonian style that featured pitched rather than flat roofs. The house-slash-studio he built for himself and Helene was the most striking, with two levels of glass windows facing the water. It was a pleasure to take Ellis to her piano lessons where Helene's matching pair of grand pianos—which she referred to as "The Twins"—seemed to float in the sky.

The house, however, was not well-suited for an aging widow: 6,000 square feet of open staircases, multilevel floors, terraces, a steep driveway, and a long drive from doctors, hospital, drugstores, grocery stores, and other services. So Helene, with a graceful acceptance of reality, sold up and moved to the 1,200 square foot Elm Grove condominium two years ago, just down the block from her older sister. The Twins were now nestled together like a yin-yang symbol in what most people would have used as the living room.

Charlotte's house was one third the size of Helene's old house, but it was one of the original fifty; buying it gave her an instant introduction to Paul Dalmier, and in turn to Helene. She looked around at her own living room, from the wood-and-steel open staircase, to the baby grand piano, to the collection of art and sculpture and books, a room which was now full of contrasting areas of gold and darkness from the fireplace. She loved fireplaces, had never had one until she moved here—would she ever have one again? The wine in the glass glowed blood red. It was tempting to just lie here like she did the night before, for hours and hours until she fell asleep in a stupor under the soft silk-and-merino throw.

Charlotte's thoughts this evening, however, hurtled through her brain in a random whirl: split-second images of Ellis hugging her goodbye at the airport, Olivia's senseless body on the oriental rug, Jack handing her divorce papers, house-hunting in Lake Parkerton, the blood on the bat, Simon's long legs in snug black jeans, Ellis at the state competition, Jack on their wedding day, Helene beaming at Simon, Olivia pointing at her with a bony finger and saying, "So what do you *do*?"

The notebook Olivia had given her the other day was on the coffee table. Charlotte picked it up and shifted her position to get more light from the fireplace. The first thing that caught her eye was the words written on the inside cover: *Put the pieces together and bloom*. Then she began reading the first page, which was dated several years ago. Some words were immediately clear, some became clear in context, and a few remained garbled, as if Olivia had given up trying to correct them. But Charlotte was able to understand that these opening paragraphs were written during her husband Ronson Targman's dying days.

You call for him, and he will not come, you call for me and only part of me arrives. I go through the motions, wash your body as if I were washing the floor: wet, swab, polish dry, just another one of your soldier boys.... The pain seizes you and you blame me. They tell me that you don't mean it, this is the dementia, but it is not, it is the same thing you have always said have always done....Now they can care for you and I walk away, they will wipe my spittle from your face, thinking it is yours....

The dark sentiment took Charlotte by surprise, yet she knew it shouldn't have done so, after meeting its author. Was the entire notebook like this? She moved to the last paragraphs on the last page in the notebook, dated roughly six months ago, the writing marginally clearer:

Golden girl, I always knew you would end up in the same place as me, small and insignificant, alone alone alone.... What good do your glory days do you now? We're just a collage of ticket stubs from journeys to other times. The fat conductor never cared how much you paid, he would only look you over and decide if he would collect your ticket or not, if he would let you ride. But there were no free rides, only uncollected deaths.

This was not the sort of reading she needed at the moment, and she tossed the notebook back on the coffee table.

Housework. Housework was her catharsis. She suddenly

remembered that the real estate agent was coming tomorrow morning, as well, and at the very least she ought to get the kitchen sanitary. She switched off the fireplace, took her dinner things back into the kitchen, put on a pot of coffee, turned on the TV for company, and set to work, starting with taking the clean dishes out of the dishwasher and putting the dirty ones in, folding the clean linens and gathering the dirty, dumping the burnt bagel and scrubbing the cutting board, putting the trash bags in the large wheeled bins in the garage, and getting out a roll of new trash bags to tackle the junk mail and other papers.

Charlotte looked at the covers of the magazines and catalogs, their enticing headlines and pictures of perfect rooms and perfect outfits. The new reality that these things were no longer within her reach—or even her professional business to know about—suddenly made them abstract. The brown cashmere sweater with the fake fur collar on the cover model was as out of her price range as a ticket on the space shuttle. She found a notepad and wrote "TO DO" at the top. The first item: cancel subscriptions and mailing lists. It was one of the items on Diane's budget plan. Canned laughter from the sitcom on the TV reminded her to add canceling the cable service, as well.

The refrigerator and freezer came next, tossing out expired food and putting the empty containers for the next dishwasher load in the sink. She made a decision not to buy any more food until she ate up everything she already had in the freezer, fridge, and pantry. That should save a few dollars on groceries and get the kitchen emptied out at the same time. The junk food, however, she sent straight to the trash. It was time to stop the pity-party food. Her jeans were getting tight, and it wasn't like she would be able to run out and buy a new pair. It also made her feel guilty to have it around, because she didn't let Ellis eat much junk food, no matter how much she begged for it.

There was still too much stuff on the counters: all the containers of utensils and dry goods, along with the toaster, the food processor, the large stand mixer, the blender, the coffeemaker, the microwave, and the many decorative things. Apart from the coffeemaker, most of it ought to go in the cabinets, she thought—or just go. But there wasn't room, because the cabinets were full of old things she hadn't used in years, and a large assortment of plastic containers. She recalled Olivia's back porch, unusable because of the huge stacks of those containers and newspapers. *That is not going to be me, I swear it*, she thought. She moved all the containers into the recycling bin, collected the vacuum sweeper from the hall closet and used it to get the now-empty cabinet spotless, then moved all the appliances save the coffeemaker and the microwave into it. She did the same with another section of cabinet, and moved in the jars of dry goods and bottles of oil and vinegar.

That left the jars of utensils, the knife block, and the collection of animal cook figurines. She pulled out the only two knives she ever really seemed to use, and moved the block in with the appliances. The utensils could go in a drawer. That's how Helene's lovely kitchen was set up: everything stored in the cabinets and drawers. Her own four drawers, however, were full: one had the everyday flatware and another the good silver and serving pieces, but the other two were crammed with the miscellany every household seemed to collect: the junk drawers. Charlotte looked over the tape, scissors, envelopes, stamps, rubber bands, twist-ties, corks, matches, marbles, tiny pieces from doll clothes and puzzles, fast-food toys, miscellaneous spare parts for appliances she no longer had, recipe cards from friends and family, manufacturers' coupons, and a mass of nearly unidentifiable objects that once had a designated purpose, now long forgotten. They reminded her of the jars full of such trivia in Olivia's kitchen, only here they were unsorted. She took the drawers off their tracks and then over to the breakfast nook to sit and have coffee while she cleaned them out.

The TV was replaying the morning show from earlier in the day, with world news, bad news, economic news, mortgage crisis, political promises, and new diseases, interspersed with celebrity and sappy stories. Mixed in were commercials for cars, insurance, cell phones, and, for all she knew, magic wands. There was a story about some guy living with fifty things in a loft with beautiful windows. The simplicity of the space with its beautiful light caught her attention. Ten of his fifty things were in his closet. A small closet. A laptop. His well-fitting jeans and the laptop were expensive. No furniture, just some kind of roll-up bedding right on the floor. He called himself a minimalist, and he wrote a blog and some books about it. He said he was happy and free, and he looked it. Then came more commercials for cars, insurance, cell phones, and magic wands.

The morning show hosts were still talking about the guy with fifty things. The woman said it was weird. Elegant but weird, and couldn't imagine any sane woman doing the same. The man said he couldn't see his wife doing it, either, but thought a lot of men could, especially young men without kids or a house to worry about. The sports guy said he thought it was cool. The weather guy said, well, that might be okay in Southern California, but folks we have a big cold front blowing down from Canada next week and sure hope that one of those fifty things is a nice warm coat. Then a sports update, but Charlotte ignored it while trying to imagine herself living with only fifty things.

If, right at the moment, she only had fifty personal items to worry about, she would not be cleaning and sorting into the wee hours of the morning, particularly these five hundred pieces of trivia in two drawers on the breakfast table. She could "walk" from this house if she dared, like the Panettis did last year—just packed some bags, went to Argentina, and left everything else behind, from furniture to lawn mowers, for the bank to sort out. With only fifty things, she could live in a single room, like she did in her college dorm days, back when all she needed was a room of her own, simple and quiet, in which to do her work. Charlotte imagined what those things would be: her laptop, certainly, and her cell phone. A few clothes, grooming items, then cooking things, a decent bed—sleeping on a futon mattress on the floor like the guy on TV would not be doable for long—her favorite pieces of art, the photo albums, her favorite dishes, rugs, and —!

The so-called minimalist probably had a storage unit somewhere that he raided on a regular basis, Charlotte thought. It would be hard to know how to live with so few things, since she was attached to an awful lot of her stuff as well as her creature comforts. She'd just spent the last ten years, after all, writing about stuff, caring about it, having opinions about it, and making recommendations about it. But when she looked down at the jumble in the drawers, her brain hit the wall and she was overwhelmed by an almost life-or-death urge: *No more.*

She worked quickly, picking out a few things from the drawers that she knew were needed or used fairly recently, then dumped out everything else into a cardboard box. A quick wipe and sweep of the drawers, then in went the things she used the most. It was now easy to find and grab every single item, every spoon, spatula, scissors, knife, ball of twine, roll of tape. Everything *current.* She now had two entire drawers that looked like she wished life would be: comprehensible.

Charlotte gathered some more boxes from the garage and filled one of them with the cooking utensils she didn't often use and the jars that held them. She filled another two boxes with the animal cook figurines, and recalled how she and Jack would pick them up at restaurant gift shops, resorts, antique shops, and flea markets. She had actually been tired of them for a long time, and they were a pain to keep clean, especially in a kitchen. She wiped down each one before it went into a box.

By the time her mind felt clearer and more settled, it was two in the morning and she'd consumed an entire pot of coffee. But she felt happier than she had in a long time. She grabbed the list and added to it: take all magazines and newspapers to the big public recycling bins at the grocery store, sort through the baking things and dishes in the upper cabinets, weed out the cookbooks. Then she added: Moving sale.

Charlotte looked at the clock again and realized that Ellis, in Paris, would likely be awake, and hopefully not in class or at practice. The conversation had to happen sometime. She decided not to say anything about Olivia, at least not until more was known. She smoothed out her hair; she was nervous about breaking the news to Ellis that she had to sell their home. Then she set up the computer for video chat.

It was a lovely morning over there, the sun through the dorm window illuminating Ellis' cheerful face. Mother and daughter shared the same blue eyes, high forehead, long nose, and long neck, but Ellis had her father's light freckled coloring and curly dark brown hair, which Charlotte thought so much more attractive than her own straight drab hair and sallow complexion. They caught up on the small things of life and school, with Ellis doing most of the talking, happy and excited. Charlotte swallowed hard, feeling a lump in her throat.

"Mom, what's wrong? You look like you're going to cry."

"Oh, I just miss you, that's all. It's so quiet around here and I wish I could be there, too."

"Why don't you fly over, then? I have a long weekend in a couple of weeks and we can go all over Paris and shop and—" Ellis stopped as Charlotte shook her head in regret.

"I can't, Ellis. Something's come up, and it's one of the reasons for the unplanned chat." Charlotte went on to explain about the magazines shutting down, the finances, and the need to sell up and downsize.

Ellis' reaction was better than Charlotte had hoped for—serious, but not crushed. "Mom, I think you're doing the right thing. It's a great chance for you to do something else with your life, too, when you think about it. I mean," she wisecracked, "I'm Dad's problem now, right?"

"Oh, you were never a problem for me, you know that!" Charlotte laughed. "I was worried that you'd be upset that I was selling our home, that you wouldn't be able to come back to it anymore."

"You know, just as long as you're there, it's home." Her smile was as sweet as it was when she was small.

"You're great, kid, you really are."

"It's no problem, honestly, Mom. I had a home with Dad, too, in Elm Grove, and now I'm at home here, and I think I'll probably always be able to be at home wherever I need to go. So it's all good. It's a great house, but there's lots of great houses in the world, and I'm sure you'll find another great place to live, too."

"I just wish I knew where. But I need to do all this very soon. I want to know what to do about your piano, the sheet music, and the other things you have here. I can sell them and put the money in your savings account, or I can put them in storage if your Dad would be willing to pay the fee."

"Oh, that's right, my piano," said Ellis. "I love it, but I've outgrown it, you know? If I stay with piano I'm going to want a proper grand, and if I stay in Paris or in Europe a long time, I might not ever need it again."

"*If* you stay with piano? What do you mean? What else would you play?"

"I'm really getting into electronic music and composition. There's some amazing stuff happening and it's *right now*, not just resurrecting the past."

Charlotte just smiled through the edges of her dismay, reminding herself that teenagers liked to try this, try that. "I'm sure you'll find your path, wherever it leads. What does your dad say about it?"

"Oh, he's pretty cool about it." Ellis smiled wryly, as if she knew what Charlotte was thinking. "Don't worry, Mom, I'm not throwing away all those years of piano, I'm still playing and in fact I'm starting on the middle-period Beethoven Sonatas now." She went on to describe her piano teacher and his style. Then Ellis turned to look elsewhere in her room; Charlotte heard a girl speaking French and Ellis answered her in French, as well. The girl, whose short, side-parted black hair nearly obscured her pretty face, appeared behind Ellis, and waved at Charlotte.

Ellis explained. "Mom, this is my roommate Camille. She says hello, and nice to meet you."

Charlotte waved back with her own *bonjour,* and Camille went on her way.

"So what about your piano? Do you want to talk to your Dad first, since it was Grandma and Grandpa Anthony who gave it to you?"

"Good idea. I'll send you an email later today after I talk to him. I packed up everything I definitely wanted to keep before I left, and those are the big boxes in my bedroom closet. If you could hang on to those or put them in storage, that would be great. And save my music books.

Everything else you can sell. I can sort out the boxes and music when I'm home next time."

"Any idea when that would be?"

Ellis shrugged. "I really don't know, Mom. It's kind of expensive and it costs *so* much more to live in Paris than it does back home. I always thought Parisians would be chic and glamorous, but it's only the wealthy ones who are. The rest of the people really have a hard time making ends meet, and now I know why."

"Well, I sympathize with them, although I shouldn't complain, really. Still trying to get used to the idea of what I have to do. I started cleaning up this kitchen because the real estate agent is coming tomorrow morning, and it suddenly hit me that I'm becoming a hoarder, and I hate that, and I've just been clearing it all out." She turned the laptop so Ellis could see the cleared-off counters and the stuff she'd boxed up.

"Wow!" Ellis exclaimed.

Charlotte turned the laptop back around. "Looks different, doesn't it?"

"It looks amazing! Reminds me of Helene's kitchen."

Charlotte felt a glow of satisfaction. "Helene's kitchen was the inspiration. I've got a lot to learn from her, I think. That reminds me, I met Helene's neighbor Simon Norwich today. He spoke highly of you."

Ellis nodded and grinned. "Say hi to him for me, will you? He's so cool and funny." She leaned forward, as if speaking in confidence. "You should ask him out, Mom."

Charlotte was taken aback and shook her head. "Not going to happen! But I will tell him you said hello, and Helene as well."

"Thanks. Look, Mom, I've got to get to practice, I've got a piano room reserved for ten minutes from now, and it's an eleven minute walk

—"

They did their usual affectionate goodbyes with promises and reassurances, and ended the chat. Charlotte thought she would be in tears at the end of the "call," but instead found herself calm and even a bit content. This was going to be the new normal. As she went through the archway to go upstairs to bed, she passed Ellis' baby grand piano, which sat forlorn in the corner of the living room. Its only purpose now was as a shiny black compositional element whose open lid pointed to the apex of the cathedral ceiling. Charlotte closed it, and knew for certain this was the beginning of the end.

Four

Saturday, September 14th

At eight-o-five in the morning, Charlotte stood in the middle of her walk-in closet, swaddled in a bathrobe after her shower, and glared at the mass of clothing piled on the floor. She should have felt much worse, given the events of the day before, drinking a pot of coffee late at night and getting less than five hours of sleep, but she was energized by the prospect of talking to the real estate agent, Lola McKennie, and getting this whole life change thing going. She had Ellis' support, too, and that counted for a lot. At the moment, however, she was convinced that her stuff "knew" she was getting rid of it, and was conspiring to give her a hard time. The clothes had been so crammed together, that the rod had popped out of its bracket when she tugged at a hanger. It had then swung down to the floor, creating a waist-high mountain of shirts, jackets, dresses, skirts, pants, sweaters and coats in many colors and fabrics, some pieces going back to her college days.

She began to get dressed, automatically, in jeans, tee, and chambray overshirt, pulling each thing from the pile. Then she paused. *I've got all these nice things and no place to wear them. I'm not living the life I bought the clothes for.*

So what life was that? The lunching-lady life? The endless cocktail party life? The life of constant vacation? The executive woman life? The perfect wife and mother life?

None of the above.

Reality: she was a middle-aged writer, a single empty-nester, and broke broke broke.

She looked at herself in a full-view mirror for all of five seconds, then went back to the closet and quickly undressed. This was not business as usual. This was the beginning of a new life. As a member of the style and design media, she had written and promoted many an article with the theme: New Life = Wardrobe Makeover! She found and pulled on skinny black jeans (barely acknowledging to herself that Simon was the inspiration) and a black tank top, and slipped on a supple pearl gray silk safari-style shirt with the sleeves rolled up and tabbed and the front left unbuttoned and draped. Another look in the mirror. It was still warm enough for flat black thong sandals. A bit of lip color. Silver hoop earrings. A head shake to fluff up almost-dry hair. A silver bracelet Ellis gave her last Christmas. It was a good look for her, not too dumpy, but still comfortable and practical. An upgrade. A keeper.

Inspired, Charlotte pulled out two suitcases and opened them up on the bed, and began to fill them with a few clothes, a few shoes and boots, a few accessories and jewelry she couldn't part with. It went quickly: one little black dress and black pumps, a pair of wool trousers, a pair of chinos, cropped pants, shorts, a good wool skirt and a gauzy summer one, two favorite summer dresses, the jeans and chambray shirt (one doesn't clean house in good clothes), some tees and a couple white shirts, a cashmere sweater, a cotton one, and two wool ones, exercise clothing, robe, two sets of pajamas, slippers, the best of her lingerie and socks. Scarf, hats, gloves, a wool coat and a trench coat, a denim cropped jacket. A pashmina from Helene. Enough clothes for two weeks without worrying about laundry, enough clothes for all seasons and occasions, and it all easily fit in the two suitcases, with enough room for various things from the bathroom. This was doable. The knowledge that she was looking at what was very likely to be her future wardrobe excited her, as if she was packing for an extended journey. The only thing missing was knowing where she was going, but all in good time.

It was quite a bit more than fifty things, thought Charlotte, remembering the young minimalist guy, but less than a twentieth of what remained in the closet. If she was honest, a lot of it was hopelessly outdated or little better than rags, a lot of it just never fit right or looked right, a lot of it had associations with past relationships, past life roles.

Time to live—and dress—for the present.

Time, also, for breakfast before Lola McKennie was due, and this time she promised herself she wouldn't burn the bagel.

At eight forty-five, Charlotte entered the kitchen for the first time since her chat with Ellis, and it took her a moment to recognize what she'd done the night before. The blur of long-familiar clutter was gone, and in its place was—*space.* Sunlight on an empty smooth countertop. A subtle flow of air. Serenity. The kitchen also looked twice as big. There were still the boxes of stuff over in the corner, but it was as if the doors of possibility were suddenly flung open—and she was ready. Had the security of familiar things been a trap, a prison, all along? Was she entering a dream, or leaving one?

The surrealness of the scene hit Charlotte all at once, and she grabbed the back of a bar stool at the island counter to steady herself. Part of her thought it was a blood sugar deficit—breakfast was late, after all—but another part of her knew it was mild shock. She looked at the boxes of things in the corner, things that were now removed from their long-time familiar places, and their dislocation set loose a dislocation of the emotions attached to them. This was saying goodbye, goodbye to all of that, goodbye yellow brick road, goodbye, Mr. Chips, goodbye, so long, farewell, ta ta. She felt a pang just short of tears, and then just as quickly, she smiled.

One of the animal cook figurines, the pig in the white toque and apron, stared at her with insane blank eyes and she recalled the very moment when her friend Hannah first gave it to her, and the *real* feelings she had repressed in a microsecond upon feeling them, the truth. She remembered Hannah's words, "For the cook in the family," knowing that Hannah knew that Jack did nearly all of the cooking at the time, in a burst of gourmet enthusiasm. He was a pig, Hannah was telling her, he was a ridiculous pig. And yet she and Jack kept collecting them, and she kept on collecting them after the divorce, and her friends kept giving them to her, and even Ellis contributed one or two.

This, she thought, was the real meaning behind the collection: her fierce determination to put a good face on things, to bury the truth of Jack's personal character in an anthropomorphic collection.

What have I done, what have I been doing?

That pig was next to the squirrel holding a spoon and a walnut. It cost three hundred dollars. In the next box there were decorative jars filled with colorful layers of beans and rice, a dozen different jars, maybe. Some of those were pricey, and some weren't, but she dearly wished she had the cash instead of the beans and the jars. And she dearly wished she had back the time she'd spent on the shopping and browsing spent on each one, and on the work she'd done to earn the money she'd spent on a bunch of jars filled with dyed beans that were not likely safe enough to turn into a pot of soup.

All those hours and years of working for the magazines, and now the work wasn't there; she'd been discarded right along with the magazines themselves.

There are no free rides, just uncollected deaths.

Lola McKennie strode through the house in her short-skirted pastel pink suit and matching stiletto slingbacks, taking dimensions, pictures, and notes, and exclaiming with a soft Georgia accent over each room's attractive features, which seemed to be legion.

Charlotte struggled not to roll her eyes at the real estate agent's strangely perfect hair and manicure, and the illusion of youth in a body so toned that when she arrived, Ernie next door said, "You could bounce a quarter off that butt." Charlotte punched him in the arm and shooed him away.

After the tour, they sat in the breakfast nook and Lola got down to business, setting up a laptop, several folders and papers, and a calculator. She presented similar properties for sale in Lake Parkerton, and Charlotte was dismayed at the relatively low list prices, as well as how many there were.

"I'm going to be honest, Charlotte, you've got a lot of competition and unless we get the perfect buyer, you'll be lucky to get what you paid for it ten years ago. But I'm a selling machine. If you're willing to get this place staged, we can make it more competitive."

Charlotte felt a bit defeated before they'd barely started. Ten years' mortgage payments hadn't built much equity, and if the house didn't sell for more than the mortgage, it wouldn't leave her much to live on while rebuilding her career. She'd also forgotten about staging, which, as she now remembered, was creating an environment to help potential buyers imagine their own stuff in a space, or at least imagine living there. This usually meant neutralizing a homeowner's personal touches, like toning down a color scheme or swapping a ratty old throw for a new silk one, and bringing in better-suited pieces of furniture. She thought to herself, *I work in the design industry, I'm supposed to have good taste and a sense of the trends, and this woman wants to "stage" my home?* Then she caught sight again of the pig cook in the box and decided that Lola might have a point.

"I'm not even sure where I'm going from here," said Charlotte, "let alone what I would do with all my stuff."

"That's alright, it's part of the conversation we'll be having this morning. No matter what you decide, to leave your stuff here or take it with you, you'll want to get all the windows professionally cleaned, and keep the big one overlooking the deck and the lake extra-clean, even if it means cleaning it every day and after every showing. That window is gonna sell this house, what with the view and the light and airiness it brings to the living room. And then—"

Charlotte tried to contain her frustration, but had to stop this line of thinking before it got out of control. "Look, Lola, I don't have enough money to hire professional window washers, or to pay for storage and staging."

Lola just looked straight at Charlotte, expression neutral. She spoke quietly. "We'll get it figured out, even if I gotta come over here with a bucket and a squeegee myself. I've got a whole set of squeegees in different sizes and a couple of extension poles. It takes practice to get it right, but I've had more practice lately than you would *ever* believe."

"You certainly seem, um, fit." Charlotte couldn't resist.

Lola laughed, her whitened teeth glowing against her bright pink lipstick. "Oh, yes, Charlotte! I've done the window-washing, *and* the hedge-trimming, *and* the furniture-moving, carpet cleaning, replacing light bulbs, fixing broken doorbells and leaky faucets. But there's only so much I can do, and the more the homeowner does, the more I can put my energy and good attitude into creative selling." She stretched out her perfectly manicured hand and snapped off a polished pink nail: it was fake, and covered a fingertip that showed signs of gardening, scrubbing, and even exposure to bleach.

Charlotte's first impression of Lola began to change. The Barbie-doll facade was exactly that, a facade that was chosen because it gave Lola another edge in a competitive field. It wasn't only homeowners taking a hit in this economy, it was also the real estate agents, who were getting less commission, what with lower prices and sluggish sales.

Lola saw that Charlotte understood, and continued, pressing the fake nail back on. "Charlotte, I don't want to pressure you, but I'd like to get this house listed and ready to show within a couple of weeks. Sales are always so much slower in the winter. This area is also really beautiful in the fall, and the leaves are going to start turning pretty soon."

"Two weeks?" Well, Charlotte thought, in for a penny, in for a pound—the sooner this is all over with, the happier I'll be, too. "If I could get some help with all the boxes and furniture moving, maybe, but I'd have to have a moving sale, and after the last garage sale we had a few years ago, Ellis and I swore never again—too much work."

"There's no time, really, for a garage or moving sale, especially not if you're doing it on your own. What I have in mind is using an estate liquidator. They literally do *everything*, from set up to clean up. You won't have to do much work other than just picking out what you want to keep and setting it aside. Diane tells me you need to downsize, and estate liquidation is a very efficient way to do it. I could get Warren Brothers Estate and Auction out here to start setting up as soon as next week and have the sale the week after. The house will be emptied out, and you'll have some cash to tide you over until it sells."

"Wow!" Charlotte thought about all the foreclosure signs she'd seen. The competition was indeed stiff. The faster she could sell this house, the more likely she would be able to sell it at all. "How much do they charge?"

"They would only take ten percent of the sales. You pay nothing up front. They take care of the advertising, all the paperwork and taxes, and it's also a good way to get a lot of people going through this house, too. You've got some nice stuff here, like the sectional, the rugs and the piano, unless of course you were planning to keep them."

Charlotte's thoughts bounced between excitement at raising cash within a couple of weeks and not having to set up a moving sale herself, and dismay at the idea of no longer owning any of her stuff. Lola went through a folder and pulled out a spreadsheet with a list of names in the first column and services offered across the top, along with commission percentage and contact information.

"Here's the list we use at Baysell Realty, all the estate liquidation services in the area. As you can see, most of them charge a higher commission, or they specialize in business or farm auctions. Any of them can handle your sale, but Warren Brothers charges the least commission."

Charlotte noted that Warren Brothers didn't offer cleanup after the sale or delivery of unsold items to charities, as did Stanton Estate Services, the next one on the list. But Stanton charged thirty percent commission. That was a lot higher.

"Warren Brothers, that's the same people with the pawn shop, as in Bosley Warren?"

"Yes it is. He's got a high profile right now, and that alone will help draw in people for a sale. Let me give them a call right now and see if they can come out and give you more information and a time frame."

"Hey, sure, thanks, if that's no problem." Charlotte was curious, both about Bosley Warren and about how the estate sale would work out. But mostly she was fascinated by the process of business networking, first with Diane calling Lola, and then now with Lola calling Bosley Warren. Was it a small-town thing, a Chamber of Commerce or other small-business thing? As a writer who worked mostly online from her home office, Charlotte's range of influence had been her name in the column under the magazine mast head, but nothing more. The last time she'd needed to network locally, it was to access the Lake Parkerton babysitter referral list. Ernie next door had reliable referrals for everything else, like plumbers.

Lola walked around while making the call, and went out onto the deck. Her arms moved while she talked, as if she was describing the house and the lake view. Charlotte heard her laugh briefly before ending the call and coming back into the kitchen.

"Bosley Warren himself will be here in about forty-five minutes. As soon as I said Lake Parkerton and estate sale, he rearranged his day. The real estate market might be struggling, but estate sales are where it's at."

Charlotte laughed, remembering the way Lola shouted "Yes!" when Diane mentioned Lake Parkerton. "Yeah, it's a good time for turkey buzzards." Lola seemed not to hear as she brought up a listing form on her computer. Was Lola offended by the remark? "Thanks again for making the call and getting him over here so quickly."

"No problem. It looks like you've taken action already," said Lola, pointing at the boxes with the figurines and other clutter. "I'm impressed."

"I started tackling everything quite suddenly. Had an epiphany of sorts. I think I know what kind of lifestyle I really want for myself and I'm ready to make the changes. Now I just need to find a place to move *to*."

While they dealt with the listing paperwork, Lola told her about the more remarkable houses she'd sold and the difference in prices that a couple of years made, as well as the differences in the impact the economy had from town to town.

"Do you want to stay here in Lake Parkerton, or move away, do you know?"

Charlotte thought a moment. "Mostly I just want to get away from Lake Parkerton, to go someplace where there's not so much upheaval, and of course much less expensive, but still a pleasant quality of life, if you know what I mean."

"I think I do. What you'll want is an established neighborhood, but an affordable one. Some place like Elm Grove, actually, with that nice historic downtown."

"I used to live there before my divorce, and thought I'd never go back, to be honest."

"I understand. But it's evolved a bit in the last ten years. It's a good walking and biking town, there's lots of entertainment and restaurants and theater, and of course events at the university if you wanted. There's some quirkier neighborhoods, too. And the property taxes aren't anywhere near what they are here!"

Lola's phone rang and she excused herself, needing to take the call, and once again walked around and orchestrated her statements with her arms. When she finished, she said she had another showing back in Elm Grove, so they wrapped things up for the day, with Charlotte agreeing to let her know how things went with Bosley Warren. Charlotte liked Lola more than she expected to, but nonetheless was relieved when the real estate agent's effervescent presence was gone and things were nice and quiet again. She rubbed the back of her neck and checked the time. Fifteen minutes until Bosley Warren arrived. She went to her office to space out and play solitaire on the computer, let her mind relax and wander.

Could she move back to Elm Grove? Could she see herself living well in a place that had so many old memories, many of which weren't very good? It would be a practical location. Her doctors were there, her hair salon, and she knew where to find goods and services. There were good grocery stores, her car mechanic—just about everything she needed was there, as was Helene, and Diane. Being able to walk along tree-lined neighborhoods would help make up for losing this wonderful view of the lake. Ellis would love it on visits home, as she still had a lot of friends there from weekends with Jack.

She got online and did a search for apartments in Elm Grove, which revealed that the average rent in the big complexes was higher than what Diane recommended in the budget. Then she searched for the kind that weren't part of complexes or run by management companies. There weren't many, or they were temporary sublets, or they were duplexes that were both too much space and too much money. Several were renters looking for roommates to share the cost. Charlotte preferred to have as much control over her space as she could, so a roomie was out.

Then she spotted a terse listing dated the week before, "Studio, downtown, second floor, utilities included." And a high rent. There was something about it, though. She didn't know if she was projecting her hopes, or if her intuition was giving her a nudge, but she picked up her phone and called the number, which rang for a bit, and then suddenly a man's voice answered, "The Good Stuff. Larry speaking."

The Good Stuff? The gift shop in Elm Grove? "Hi. I saw an ad for an apartment with this number, and wondered if it was still available."

Larry let out a snort. "Oh, it's still available. Why? You wanna take a look?"

"Well, can you tell me more about it?"

"It's a studio above the store, Harvey Street entrance, long flight of stairs, lotta windows, bathroom, efficiency kitchen, one closet, utilities included."

"When can I see it?"

"Anytime you like, just come to the store and ask for me. Larry."

"I'm surprised it is still available."

"You won't be when you see it. It's a dump."

Charlotte laughed in surprise. "You don't sound like you are trying too hard to get it rented out."

"Eh, well, I am and I'm not. The previous tenants made a mess of things and I haven't had time to get it cleaned up. And I'm warning you I'm gonna be picky about the next renter."

"What did they do to it?"

"They lived like pigs! A couple of law students, looked real clean-cut and serious when I rented it to them, but then they'd have these screaming rows when I got customers here, and had all sorts of strange-looking people coming and going and making the customers nervous.

Then a few weeks ago they got busted for dealing coke, cops all over the place, making me and the shop look bad, you know? I don't need the grief. You another law student?"

"Oh, wow. No, Larry, I'm old enough to be a law student's mom, and I don't deal drugs. Just looking for a little apartment with an Internet connection and reasonably comfortable."

There was a pause. "You'll wanna come see it, then. It needs some fixing up, but I'll work with ya."

"I'll stop by tomorrow, if that's okay?"

"Yeah, I'll be here all day. Hope you won't be discouraged, but it's a cute place when it's fixed up."

It felt so strange to look around at her house and her things and to be thinking about them as if they were already history, especially since she had only an abstract idea what kind of home or lifestyle was going to replace them. Charlotte felt she needed something to plan *towards*. Downsizing, facing life on a pittance, felt negative unless one could replace it with attractive possibilities. She imagined feeling unfettered by stuff, bills, and upkeep, free to focus on work and maybe even resurrect a hobby. A minimum of expenses meant a small income would go a long way.

What she needed was to make it feel real to her in a positive way: the space, the furniture, the neighborhood. The windows here needed to be replaced in her mind's eye by the windows of a new space, the quality of the light, the view, the kinds of trees, the kinds of activities and people and cars and noises and smells. Would the windows of the studio above Good Stuff do the job? One of the crows that nested in the pine trees flew by the window. She would miss him, but there would be other crows in other places, wouldn't there? And other rabbits and squirrels and deer? Well, maybe not the deer in downtown Elm Grove. She'd heard a coyote was spotted there last summer.

And what furniture would she have, what layout of the rooms? Would she be able to make it *her* space if she was only renting? Of course she would. She loved nesting. Big or small, her space was always her space.

Charlotte heard the doorbell ring, and took a couple deep breaths to calm her nerves.

Five

Saturday, September 14th (Another long day)

When Charlotte opened the front door, she almost gasped.

Bosley Warren wasn't much smaller in person than he was on the billboard. She wasn't sure if she'd ever been up close to someone this large in her life: just short of seven feet tall and nearly four feet wide, with eyes that looked twinkling and smiling on the billboard but in person just looked like small round black beetles buried in fat.

But those beetle eyes were moving around fast as Charlotte walked him through the house, taking in every square inch of the entry, the kitchen, the living room, taking in every object large and small. She could almost see the calculations occurring behind them. He reeked of strong aftershave or cologne, which made her nose itch.

"Well, now, Ms. Anthony," he drawled—and it was a good imitation of an authentic drawl, designed to make others think he was just an ordinary good ol' boy there to do some honest business with them —"you've got some mighty fine things here, all in a real beautiful house. It'll put people in a buying mood, and I'm sure there will be no problem making a tidy sum from it."

"That's good to hear, Mr. Warren. How would you proceed? How much of the set-up do you take care of, and how much would I have to do, that sort of thing?"

"Call me Bosley, Ms. Anthony, and if I may call you Charlotte?" he asked, with an inflection that automatically made Charlotte feel she was in a used car lot, and not in her lovely house. But she nodded her assent, and he continued,

"Okay, Charlotte, here is how it works. I see you've already started cleaning things out and boxing up stuff, but I want you to stop, as you might be throwing out something that somebody might want to buy. You'd be amazed at what people will pay money for at these sales, and even something that goes for a couple of dollars adds to the total. As we like to say, 'it might be worth more than you think!' Even any clothes you don't want, you can leave those for us to sell, too."

Charlotte knew he was thinking of the pile in the walk-in closet and felt herself blush. "The rod fell down this morning...."

Bosley grinned and lifted his hand to stop her. "I unnerstand."

She then felt less embarrassed and more irritated, as if he now had something on her, which was of course ridiculous, wasn't it? *Snap out of it and pay attention,* she told herself.

"Anyhow, my team and I would then come in with big banquet tables and set out some things by themselves and group some less expensive items together in boxes. This tends to speed things up, as many people will spend five dollars on a box of stuff that has only one thing they really want in it. We like to call 'em treasure boxes. That's part of the enjoyment folks get from going to sales like this, as sometimes you never know what else might be in a box you pick up for the one thing you thought you wanted." He nodded in a knowing manner, almost winking at her, as if to imply another side of things that were known, but not directly spoken of.

"That's good to know." Charlotte paused, and watched Bosley's eyes do their darting around thing again, as if he didn't even realize she'd stopped speaking. Maybe it wasn't so unlikely that he found a first edition of *Least Objects.* "Is that how you found that book?"

Her question took a full two seconds to register in his brain. He didn't look at her this time, but smiled more to himself and said, "Somethin' like that."

Then he continued with how things would be set up. Charlotte found it a lot to take in, but heard nothing that differed from the details in the spreadsheet Lola had given her to look over. "What should I do with the things I want to keep?"

"That's up to you. Generally, we mark items not for sale as such. Some clients move everything to a lockable bedroom or study, particularly small things. You might want to use your office. There will be a representative in every room of the house to keep an eye on things, don't you worry about that." He opened his notebook to a calendar page. "My crew and I can come in and start setting up two weeks from today. We work fast and can have your sale a week after that. That'll give you some time to sort through anything personal you want to hold back."

"It sounds good, but it's a lot to take in. How soon would you need to have my answer?"

"The sooner the better, and—."

Bosley's cell phone interrupted him, and he surprised her with the speed with which he pulled it out of his jacket pocket and answered it, as if he had been waiting for the call. "Yeah," he said into the phone, turning his back to her and moving away to stand in front of the fireplace.

"*What?*" He paused, then drawled, "Oh, for cryin' out loud." He turned back toward Charlotte as he ended the call with, "I'll be there in about half an hour."

Charlotte had to give the man credit for quickly getting past whatever news was disturbing enough to take the color out of his face, and resume his smile, even if he couldn't control the way the flesh around the outside of his eyes sagged with worry.

"Charlotte, here's a copy of our standard agreement, if you'll just look it over, plain English, all straightforward," he handed her the paper from the folder, and then offered her a pen.

"I want to sleep on it, Bosley. Like I said, it's a lot to take in. I can drop this off at your shop, though, right?"

"Yes, ma'am, that would be perfectly all right. Lola said you are in a little bit of a hurry, and I've set this date aside for you, so don't wait too long if you wanna keep it. Best you let me know one way or the other no later than 6 p.m. on Monday, okay?"

Charlotte had the sense that if he didn't have someplace else he had to get to he would have pressed a lot harder for a decision right then and there. As it was, however, he made his way back through the kitchen and out to his Esplanade, drawling remarks about the weather and the "cute knick-knacks," as if he really wasn't in a hurry, even shaking her hand with the tips of his fingers. He took his time backing out of the driveway, but she could see him driving faster and faster down the lakeshore road, and blow the stop sign on the way to the highway.

Back in the house, she looked over her "cute knick-knacks," and felt her mood turning dark. She knew that she ought to go with Bosley to get as much cash as she could from everything—who knew how long it would take before the house sold, if it would sell enough to cover the mortgage, or how long it would take to rebuild her career and income? But it was hard enough to effect a complete life change like this without feeling like one's dignity was also being liquidated. The smell of whatever fragrance Bosley Warren was wearing still lingered in the living room, and she felt smothered by it.

A cup of tea in her familiar, cozy office put Charlotte in a better frame of mind. She called Helene, and asked how Olivia was faring.

Helene sighed. "I went to see her this morning, and thought maybe she was coming to, she started talking. I was holding her hand, and then she looked right up at me and said, in French, "It's *my* book! *My* book!" I asked her what book that was, but she drifted off again, and went back to sleep."

"Maybe she meant the notebooks?"

"Possibly. It seems likely. But there were those books on the floor. I wonder if whoever else was there took something that belonged to her. I did call the police detective and told him, but it is hard to tell if we should take it seriously or if she was just talking in a delirium."

There was a lull in the conversation, and Charlotte looked down at the various papers Lola left behind. The chart with the estate liquidation services was on top, and it dawned on her why one name in particular seemed familiar.

"Helene, when you were preparing to move to Elm Grove, you had an estate sale, right?"

"Yes, that is right. Paul and I had so many things in that big house and of course I could not take much of it with. Why do you ask?"

Charlotte told her about Diane's budget plan and about listing the house with Lola McKennie. "She recommended that I use an estate liquidation service, and I seem to recall your sale was handled by Stanton's, right?"

"Yes, Martin Stanton handled it. He was great. He's done a lot of high-end sales in the region and draws a lot of antique and art dealers as well as collectors. He keeps very accurate records, which helps appraisers with knowing the provenance of a work of art or fine crafts like rugs and pottery, and when it was over with, the place was spotless. I can't recommend Stanton's enough."

"That is high praise. He is worth the thirty percent commission, then?"

"Oh yes. If I had tried to sell everything on my own it would have taken forever, and I would have left myself vulnerable to fraud, maybe even theft. And I might not have been able to sell all of it, because I don't have his range of contacts, the potential market."

"Did you consider anyone else before you hired Stanton?"

"No, actually. Paul knew him well, and I admit that was enough for me. I know there are other companies out there, and other ways of doing it. Olivia was toying with the idea of using Warren Brothers if she would ever have a sale."

"They are on the list of liquidators that Lola gave me. They only charge ten percent, but they don't do clean up afterward."

"They might be just fine for some sales, I wouldn't know. But if you have high-end things, you want to draw the right potential buyers, and Stanton can do that. I'm not so sure a pawn shop would."

"I must admit I don't like Bosley Warren very much." She went on to explain about his visit.

"Oh, dear, that sounds like the stereotype of such businesses, like used car dealers, although I admit I've known a couple from years ago that were rather low-key and well-mannered."

"Something bothers me about his whole set-up. I mean, he's got the pawn shop, the payday loans, he's evidently an expert on model trains and old books, if what I read in the news is accurate, and he's got estate liquidation and even auction services. Somewhere along the line there's going to be a conflict of interest, wouldn't you think?"

"That's what I said to Olivia!" exclaimed Helene. "She has so much small stuff it would be hard to keep track if they held back something for themselves, to sell in the shop. But she was impressed by the publicity they got for that book."

"Helene, do you think Stanton's would be suitable for me, even though I don't have as much as you did, although there are some nice things here, and given that I need to keep as much cash as possible?"

"Well, I'm biased, obviously, in favor of Stanton. But let's do the math." Charlotte could hear Helene scribbling on a piece of notepaper. "Let's use Ellis' piano as an example. Say Stanton, who draws big spenders, sells it for five thousand dollars. He keeps thirty percent, which is fifteen hundred, netting you thirty-five hundred. Now let's say Warren sells the piano for only four thousand. But he only takes ten percent, which is four hundred, which nets you thirty-six hundred. Warren comes out on top, by a hundred dollars. But, and this is where things like reputation come in, Stanton's client list brings people who are more likely to find your house appealing and affordable, and to recognize and buy other things like your art collection, and that beautiful leather sectional. It's impossible to predict the actual outcome, but you can get a sense of the odds."

Charlotte laughed. "Helene, I don't know what I'd do without you. I'm sold. I'll call them first thing Monday."

"Well, thank you, dear heart. But there's a bonus if you want to go with Stanton."

"What's that?"

"I've got Martin's home phone number, and I am confident I can get this going *very* quickly, if you'd like."

Et tu, Helene? Somehow, Charlotte thought, she'd never before noticed the extent to which people seemed to like to take care of their own.

A scant two hours later, Martin the liquidator was at the door, a compact man in his fifties with smile crinkles around his eyes and the muscles of someone who moved furniture on a regular basis. He wore tan chinos and a royal blue polo shirt with an embroidered Stanton Estate Service logo. He was using a tablet computer and stylus, but was clearly struggling. "Sorry about this. Hold on." He went back to his truck and returned with a clipboard and pen. "My company is trying to go paperless, but obviously I need more practice before actually using that thing on the job. This way I know I won't make any mistakes." His voice was deep and pleasant, and Charlotte imagined he was a good singer.

"Thanks so much for coming over so quickly!" she said, when he came into the house.

He smiled at her effusiveness. "Not a problem. Helene Dalmier is a good friend. Her husband played a big role in my getting my company started." He took a long, sweeping look over the kitchen and the deck, then entered the living room, making notes along the way.

He immediately zeroed in on the baby grand. "This would be a good draw."

"I've asked my daughter and her father about selling it."

"Great. I hope they okay it. I see you have a Hannah Verhagen!" He pointed at the big painting above the fireplace, and they all admired the abstracted floral still life, done in the artist's signature layers of translucent colors. It was called "Blossoming," and Hannah had painted it for Charlotte in honor of beginning a new life after her divorce.

"Oh, you know her work, too?"

"Yeah," Martin nodded, not taking his eyes off the painting. "She's pretty popular around here, and quite a few locals have her work from back when she lived in the area."

"We went to Corton together, and she gave that to me as a housewarming present when I moved here. I wasn't planning on selling it, though, as I love it and she is a good friend."

"Well, if you change your mind, I know it would make another draw. Her work has shot up in value over the last few years."

"It's highly unlikely. I'm getting rid of the vast majority of my things, but plan to keep the best of the best if I can, and that painting is one of them. I've got a few other pieces of art that can be sold, though some of the artists are probably better known in Chicago."

"Not a problem, and in fact what I can see of your collection in here will appeal to our client list. We draw buyers from Chicago and the suburbs, as well as Milwaukee, Indianapolis, and even Detroit."

They continued through the house, and Charlotte again felt embarrassed at the mess of clothes in her closet, but Martin was nonplussed, saying "that's an easy repair," and she even lost her self-consciousness about the clutter in the other rooms and the basement. After Martin saw everything and made a call to the main office, they settled in the kitchen.

The basics, as he explained it, were not that different than what Bosley Warren described: tables set up in every room, items not for sale were marked or moved into a locked room, and a representative in every room.

"Do you make up boxes of a lot of small stuff to sell as a lot?"

Martin shook his head. "Not as a general rule. With common household items we are often offered a price for several things, where the customer creates their own lot and we use our discretion whether or not to accept the offer. You have a lot of things, but not a lot of junk, so there's no need to go that route, and it wouldn't appeal to our client base, either."

Charlotte's self-esteem got a much-needed boost from his words. She did, after all, have quite a collection of art and fine crafts and had acquired good furniture through her designer connections; it was a relief to talk to someone who recognized them for what they were.

Martin continued his explanation of company policy. "Anything that doesn't sell, we can donate to charity, and you can choose from our list of charities where you'd like it to go, if you have a preference. We take 30% of the total sales. All we need is proof of ownership of the house and homeowner's insurance, and your signature on our contract. We have a large crew, so we are able to handle several sales in different locations at the same time, and we have a crew available to set up and conduct your sale two weeks from today. We ask that you not be present during the sale, but you are more than welcome to be here during setup and immediately after, in case you change your mind about anything that is up for sale or if it doesn't sell, whether you want it back or it should continue to charity. Our service includes hauling away whatever doesn't sell, plus general cleanup, such as vacuuming and bagging up trash."

"I have so many boxes of things in the basement that I haven't looked through in years and really ought to go through them before anyone else does!"

He laughed, and once again she was struck by his pleasant voice. "It's generally a good idea, yes, but we've seen it all, Charlotte. We are often hired by the children of elderly people who are going into nursing homes or hospice, and the children live hundreds of miles away and can't get out here to do the sorting. We uncover thousands of personal items like photo albums and mementos and letters. We'll usually set them aside. We're efficient, but I'd like to think we aren't ruthless."

"That's reassuring. On one hand, I know the faster all this happens, the better, but on the other hand, I don't want to get rid of anything I'll later regret." She paused for a moment, to take a deep mental breath. Here it goes, she thought.

"Let's do it."

Six

Sunday, September 15th

Charlotte had allowed herself too much time, arriving at the strip mall twenty minutes before the pawn shop opened. It was a ratty place on the far north side of Elm Grove, along a trucker's route with access roads to the steel mills, and the trucks rumbled and whined as they accelerated and decelerated through the intersection. The pawn shop took up three store fronts out of the six, as if the business grew and swallowed up the spaces to each side. There were no lines of people waiting to get their old books appraised. A large sign in the window said NO BOOK APPRAISALS TODAY.

The fast-food coffee she was sipping left a lot to be desired, but it was hot, caffeinated, and free, thanks to the coupon in the paper that morning. It was her last issue of the paper, too, now that the subscription was canceled. Reading the paper over breakfast was something she'd done nearly every day since graduating from college, especially enjoying her favorite comic strips and working the crossword puzzle. Would reading the news online ever feel as familiar?

Her purse was on the floor behind her legs, and crammed with a plastic bag of mostly gold jewelry, with some silver and diamonds mixed in. Her set of sterling flatware was in a large shoebox on the passenger seat, the individual pieces rolled up in the pockets of silver cloth. She was parked near a pay phone, off to the side of the cracked and potholed asphalt lot. Places like this made her nervous.

The very idea of handing over her jewelry and silver, even temporarily, felt all wrong, but she needed enough cash to get through the next two weeks. The Jeep was acting weird more and more often, not always starting, having trouble accelerating quickly, vibrating a lot, and she just knew she was in for an expensive repair job at any moment. This was the sort of place she imagined bad stuff happened. There was a motel across the street, and several semi-trucks parked in the large lot next to it. A woman with dark eyes and bright magenta hair came out of one of the rooms, smoking a cigarette and hoisting an oversized designer knockoff tote bag over her shoulder. She waited at the busy four-lane highway and saw her chance to get across, strutting furiously with tiny steps in her spike-heeled shoes and pink spandex skirt. Once across, she continued straight to the shop and unlocked the front door.

By now the coffee had gone cold and lost whatever charm it had, as did the pawn shop. Charlotte was just about to give up, then decided that maybe it would be easier to talk to the woman instead of Bosley. She had to let him know that she was going with Stanton. And he was also the only pawn shop in town, the only place she knew about within safe driving distance in the Jeep. It wouldn't hurt to ask. She hoped. She wouldn't get much money, she knew this, but she needed every dime she could get. It was only for a little while. She started to pull up to a parking space in front of the shop when a large black sedan blew into the lot, raising dust and coming to a halt in the space she was planning to take. Two men got out and strode into the shop; the older one walked in like he owned the place. Maybe he did.

Charlotte thought about it for a few more minutes. When she started to pull up to the shop, she couldn't do it. When she tried to leave, she couldn't do that, either. But this was the only shop of its kind. *Snap out of it! People have to do this kind of thing sometimes.* There was a quarter in the cup holder in the console, and she picked it up and flipped it, heads go in, tails go home. Heads.

The shop was not quite what she expected, given the moped and racing bikes in the front window, the neon signs saying "OPEN" AND "PAYDAY LOANS." There were, for instance, things that looked like antiques, and even some old books. Pawn shops bought valuable things cheaply in order to sell them for a little more, but still cheap, and those items usually meant jewelry, up-to-date electronics, silver, sports equipment, power tools, and the like. There was still evidence of the former Hobby Shop. Maybe it wasn't such a coincidence that Bosley Warren found a valuable first edition.

The redhead was on the phone and looked up briefly as Charlotte came in, but kept on with the call that included an account of who was dating who on the night somebody went to jail and where the kids were going to end up. Even as Charlotte reached the counter and placed her purse and box of silverware on it, the redhead kept talking on the phone, while moving to a door leading to the back, and yelling, "Mr. Banks! Customer!" Then she kept on talking on the phone.

Charlotte waited, taking in everything in her line of sight, particularly the model train that was running on a track around the perimeter of the shop, up near the ceiling. There was a large locked glass case with various model train engines and cars, some with original boxes, plus scaled models of trees, buildings, people, and animals. She remembered reading in the newspaper that Bosley Warren was known for his expertise in model trains.

The older man who had gone into the shop before her came out from the room behind the counter. He was wearing a sports jacket over a polo shirt and dress pants, and appeared average in every way, save for the almost total lack of expression on his face or in his eyes. Charlotte couldn't decide if he was beyond bored or if the neutrality was part of being a professional pawnbroker. Even his voice, as he placed his hands flat on the glass case that served as a counter, asking how he could help her, left Charlotte feeling uncertain, with nothing, not even trite pleasantries, giving her any firm ground to stand on.

"Um, I have some jewelry, and silver?" In her nervousness, it came out like a question. Her palms were sweating.

"Yes. Pawn or sell?"

"Um, pawn, I think." She set the box on the counter, then drew the gallon-size plastic food storage bag out of her purse and handed it over.

"Doc," said the man. Charlotte looked at him, confused.

The driver then emerged from the back room. He looked larger in person than he did in the parking lot, perhaps because dark brown turtleneck sweater was slightly tight, revealing muscles in his arms and the start of a paunch above his belt. His face was red and pocked with burn scars on one side. This was evidently "Doc." The older man, presumably "Mr. Banks," nodded for Doc to deal with the bag of jewelry, while he unrolled and examined the silver.

Doc calmly emptied the bag of gold chains, earrings, bracelets, and watches on the counter, and his big hands were surprisingly deft as he untangled the lot. He turned on a bright desk lamp and used a jeweler's loupe to examine each piece, making notes as he went, all without comment.

The redhead, in the meantime, didn't stop talking, and was gushing about not knowing where Wesley's been, and how worried everybody was and how "Bos" was really getting out of line. Without any warning, the older man turned to her and hissed, "You will stop!"

She stopped mid-sentence and they stared at one another for a few seconds that felt like half an hour to Charlotte. The woman looked seriously worried and hung up the phone without another word, and went into the back room. Doc resumed his study of Charlotte's jewelry, taking particular care with a diamond tennis bracelet. When he finished, he wrote down some numbers on a note pad, handed it to the older man, then answered his cell phone, which had been on vibrate. His voice was so quiet, Charlotte couldn't hear what he was saying.

Banks added the value of the silver and the jewelry and showed it to her, without saying a word. His expression had changed to slightly lifted eyebrows, as if he was bored—and she could take it or leave it. The terms were better than she hoped, but still not much. She nodded her acceptance, also without saying a word. He gave her a check and a receipt on which was printed she had one month to return for the items, after which he would have the right to sell them.

No thank you, have a nice day, or if there was anything else he could help with. Just a noncommittal look that said they were done. And that was it. She felt compelled to get him to say something, just to humanize the situation for herself.

"You've a lot of books and model trains. That's unusual for a pawn shop, isn't it?"

"It's a sideline." He turned and went into the back room.

So much for that.

The redhead came back out, looking more worried than ever. Charlotte was about to give her a message for Bosley, when the shop phone rang and the woman answered it, saying "Warren Brothers Pawn and Payday, Ilona speaking," then gasped in relief.

"There you are! Banks is *not* in good mood, you need to talk to him *now*!" She stretched her hand into the doorway of the back room, and Charlotte saw Doc's hand taking the phone.

Ilona finally gave Charlotte her attention. "You need something?"

Charlotte tamped down her irritation at the woman's why-are-you-still-here expression.

"Yes, I have a message for Bosley. I'm Charlotte Anthony. I've decided to go with another service for my estate liquidation, so he doesn't need to hold the date for me."

"Ilona!" shouted one of the men, unseen, from the back room.

Ilona started to leave the counter, turning to nod at Charlotte. "Yeah, no problem, I'll tell him."

And that was that, leaving Charlotte with a great sense unease about the whole thing.

The next stop was back in downtown Elm Grove, to check out the apartment. The stretch of storefront windows on either side of the entrance to The Good Stuff displayed a variety of home decor items with an autumn theme, including Halloween and Thanksgiving. As Charlotte walked up, one of the items moved, and she stopped to look more carefully. It was a large black cat—a real one, and when it turned to face her she saw it had white tuxedo markings on its chest and paws. It yawned and stretched, then sat on his haunches and tilted his head as he sized her up. Two small girls ran up the sidewalk ahead of their mothers and tapped on the window to get the cat's attention. He touched the glass with his nose, then abruptly turned and jumped off the display ledge, disappearing into the store.

Charlotte once loved The Good Stuff as a young newlywed, completely smitten with the cheerful, colorful selection of lamps, posters, crockery, and other accessories assembled by the original owner. But now, the sheer mass of items was overwhelming—not unlike the pawn shop, she thought, as she went inside and became reacquainted with the place. There seemed to be a zillion small things on various display units, handmade jewelry, tiny bottles of essential oils and packets of incense, wind chimes and sun-catchers hanging in clusters along the windows, stacks of tablecloths and napkins, shelves of stuffed animals, party-favor toys, dozens of greeting card displays, and several aisles of kitchen and bathroom gadgets, garden ornaments, and pottery. It was three times the size of the original store, as well. Charlotte assumed the content changed because this was the stuff that sells.

There were quite a few customers and clerks milling about. Charlotte recognized Larry's voice from the phone call, and followed it to the far end of the long checkout counter, where he was talking to a woman holding a pan for baking madelines. He was slightly shorter than herself, very tubby, and bald on the top of his head. He was wearing a bright blue t-shirt with large white letters that proclaimed: The Good Stuff.

She got his attention after the customer left, and introduced herself. He beamed at her with a toothy grin framed by his bushy mustache, every inch a man happy to sell things to customers. They shook hands, and he told the staff he'd be back in a few minutes. Charlotte followed him outside and then through the door to the apartment, which opened to a long, narrow foyer with stairs immediately to the right. He reached up and pulled on a lamp chain, which lit up a space that reminded her of the foyer in the first apartment she had in college. The old-fashioned floral carpet runner on the stairs looked much the same, as well. As she followed Larry up to the apartment, her nose twitched at the mustiness and faint herbal notes that might have been from weed, but it didn't distract her from the glow of sunlight at the top of the stairs; she felt excited by the implication of many windows. Would they turn out to be as pleasant as all the windows at her house?

Well, she thought as they reached the top and she got her first view of the place, they are and they aren't. The three large windows across the wall that faced the street reached from three feet off the floor to nearly the twelve foot high ceiling. But Larry hadn't been exaggerating about the condition of the place: the walls were dirty and loaded with the remains of papers and posters that had been taped to the walls, the carpet was old, ratty, and stained, there were a couple of broken chairs and an ugly card table, and there were large plastic bags of trash cluttering the kitchen area. The upper part of the windows didn't look too bad, but there were fingerprints and other grime on the lower panes. One wall was painted black, another purple, the rest were a dingy white. Papers and old t-shirts littered the floor. A tall stepladder was propped up against the wall near the stairwell, along with a bucket and cleaning supplies.

But there were a couple of surprises. One was a huge, old-fashioned library table with legs like balustrades. Another was a well-worn Chesterfield-style sofa in oxblood red leather. Both were as grimy as the rest of the place, but seemed to be in one piece.

"Does the furniture stay?" she asked Larry, pointing at the sofa and table.

"I sure as hell hope so," he moaned. "Do you have any idea how *heavy* that sofa is? That stuff belonged to the grandfather of one of the law students. He was a lawyer, too. I don't know how they got this stuff up here, but it's mine now. Along with the crap."

Larry threw up his hands in defeat. "I've been up here a couple of times to clean, but I don't really have much time, and frankly, I wonder what's the use—the next people will probably trash the place, too." He went over and opened up a window, and Charlotte was glad to see that it wasn't painted shut. The sounds of traffic flooded the room, along with the mixed scent of exhaust and pizza.

They made the usual landlord/prospective tenant conversation; she told him she was a writer, an empty-nester, and in the process of selling her house. He confirmed there was cable Internet available, but that it wasn't included in the rent, which she had expected. The area behind the apartment was storage for the shop, and he and his wife lived in the large apartment on the floor above. She wandered around to get a closer look at the kitchen area—it needed a good scrub and sanitizing. There was an under-counter refrigerator and a small stove. They both needed cleaning, too, but seemed to be in working order. The bathroom had a large claw-foot tub and pedestal sink, similar to the ones at Olivia's house. Both begged for a hit of disinfectant. The place was a mess and needed a good cleaning, but it wasn't absolutely squalid. Back in the main area, she lifted up a corner of the carpet and saw there was a reasonably intact wood floor underneath. It gave her an idea.

"Larry, I'll be upfront with you. The rent is actually too high for me, even with the utilities."

He nodded and put up his hands to stop her. "I know it's high for a studio. I was trying to discourage students and lowlifes, to be honest."

"I see. Would you consider giving me a break if I get this place cleaned up and redecorated for you?"

He looked surprised, but intrigued. "What do you have in mind?"

"If you provide the supplies, I'll paint it and get it squeaky clean again. It would also help if you could get this nasty carpet out of here, too."

Larry thought about it for a minute, walking around with his hands in his pockets, sucking his lower lip, then turned to her. "I tell you what. You get rid of the carpet and the rest of this garbage, you can use the dumpsters out back, and I'll provide the paint and brushes and stuff, in exchange for three months' rent."

So far so good, thought Charlotte. "But then what will the rent be?"

"Take a third off. I like you. It'll be worth it to have a nice, quiet lady writer living up here, someone who won't scare away the customers."

It was an offer she couldn't refuse.

Helene's condominium building still looked like a church on the outside, complete with steeple and stained glass. Charlotte wondered if people who visited the town after many years away were ever confused by the changes. Did the residents have many strangers at the door on Sundays, for instance? Strangers pulling at the locked doors, banging on them, even, wondering what was going on? She rang the bell, and as she waited for it to be answered she looked down the end of the block at Olivia's house. The yellow crime scene tape was gone, thankfully. What was going to happen to the place now? And the project? Helene answered the door with a smile, and Charlotte could smell a light touch of perfume. Such a light touch compared to Olivia's, certainly.

She admired her friend's never-failing elegance and ageless appearance, the beautiful cheekbones, the white swept-back hair. Helene wore one of her signature outfits, a dark gray cashmere tunic-length sweater over a slim camel-colored wool skirt, with the long sleeves of the sweater pushed up to three-quarter length. A silk scarf in off-white, gray, and tan with a tiny bit of black softened the neckline; a silver and polished stone bracelet and low-heeled camel tan pumps completed the look. The shoes were custom made. Charlotte realized that even on days like today, when she made an effort on her appearance, she looked scruffy by comparison to Helene, but that didn't seem to matter. One felt lifted up around her.

They sat down at the little table in the kitchen, with cups of lemon tea. Helene placed a hand on Charlotte's arm, said, "So, how did you like Martin? Isn't he the most reassuring person you've ever met?"

"Oh, yes, undoubtedly. I felt so much more relaxed with him, and felt so much better about myself and my stuff. It's hard enough to go through this without feeling like your whole life amounts to little more than a tag sale."

"Even if something doesn't bring as much as you hoped, you can be sure it brought as much as could reasonably be expected, especially these days."

"Now I need to decide what I'm going to sell and keep. But I've got more news."

"There's *more?* You've been a busy bee."

"I've found an apartment!" She described it, Larry, and the terms of renting it.

Helene marveled at Charlotte's good fortune. "I'm thrilled! You'll just be four or five blocks away. But won't it be an awful lot of work?"

Charlotte nodded. "It will be, I won't kid you or myself about that. But I think it will be cathartic. Other than making sure I've selected everything I want to keep, the estate liquidators don't want me involved—they will do it all. It will help me a lot to have a place to move things to, to help me decide what to keep, and what I can't realistically keep. It will help to make it more tangible, if you know what I mean."

"Oh, I do know, I do know. I went through that when I sold my own house. Obviously, I couldn't take most of my things with me, and I had to allow room for two pianos on top of it. Not too many people can visualize space accurately."

"It's going to be hard to make the choices, though. I really like a lot of the things I have." She took another sip of tea, and asked, "What would you do if you were in my shoes?"

Helene nodded slowly and thoughtfully. "I think," and here she paused, as if still gathering the thoughts or finding the words, "I think I would travel light. In my experience, the people who survive are the ones who are willing to travel light. It's the people who cannot part with their possessions that end up being trapped by them, and sometimes the cost can be very high."

"Sounds like being a refugee."

"More like a traveler to unknown parts. It's good to have the right stuff, but not too much, so that you can move quickly when conditions change. Being independent is important. It's also important to know that you don't need to keep stuff in order to keep memories."

Helene's phone rang, surprising her, and after answering it, spoke little but quietly, and then hung up.

She turned to Charlotte. "Olivia's dead."

Seven

Monday, September 16th

It was seven a.m. on a Monday morning, and Charlotte showed up for work with an everything bagel and the big red mug of coffee despite the fact there was no work to show up for. The email inbox held more junk than missives from colleagues and friends, so she browsed through her various social media accounts to find out what everybody was up to.

The furor over the sudden loss of jobs when the magazines folded had died down only slightly, with many of her former colleagues still in shock or feeling outrage, some of it aimed at Charlotte herself under the assumption that she knew what was going to happen and didn't warn anyone. A key few, however, seemed absent from the discussion entirely. Where were they? Some said that the absentees had found work elsewhere, or had life-raft work lined up before their own ship sank. Could it be so? For that matter, were there *any* jobs out there in such a shrinking field?

She thought of rival magazines and trade publications which would make a good fit for her, and checked their online editions and made various inquiries. With Olivia's death, Charlotte felt it was likely the transcription and editing job would be canceled or delayed indefinitely, and if she needed to stay in the design field, she had best do so while she still had fresh credentials and contacts.

The jobs boards showed little that was current, unless she wanted to jump fields and edit publications for gun aficionados, which was highly unlikely. Out of curiosity, she went back through the listings for the past several weeks to see which design-related publications had posted jobs, then to the publications themselves. And there they were, the colleagues missing from the forum discussions, already holding masthead or department positions. Charlotte contacted three of them, and learned that they had, indeed, known the end of the publications was coming, and were surprised that she hadn't also known and acted on it. Charlotte looked through the backlog of messages and emails from the weeks before Ellis went to Paris, spotting cryptic messages from these very people, carefully worded invitations to lunch or drinks or online chat rooms. She had been too busy and too emotionally distracted by the prospect of Ellis leaving home to read between the lines, to make the time to join in.

The realization that she had left herself professionally vulnerable and out of the loop manifested itself as heartburn before she could even put it into words in her mind, and as the words finally did form, *it really was your own damned fault,* her chest tightened and her heartbeat fluttered, the old signs of an incipient panic attack.

Breathe, she told herself. Shallow at first, then deeper and slower as the seconds and minutes ticked by. It's too late now, the damage is done, and maybe—just maybe—it was something her subconscious mind actually wanted, a change in her own life as large as Ellis'? As the hands of her inner control freak loosened their strangulating grip on her windpipe and stopped pouring acid into her stomach, she even managed a little smile as she saw the three "For Sale" signs up and down the street from the window in front of her desk. In a way, she'd been as vulnerable to suggestion as her intended magazine audience.

It wasn't as obvious as the words "For Sale" working on her mind in subliminal ways. Rather, it was the shift in what they meant. When this all started, she knew deep down that life wasn't going to be the same without Ellis, nor were her relationships with her neighbors, and these things in turn changed the value of her house, the value of her lifestyle, and, by extension, the value of her job. Her line of work, the world of predicting, reporting on, and marketing design trends, meant constantly changing and updating the notion of what was desirable, and doing so in ways both obvious (the "new succulent plums" over last year's "tired old teal") and subliminal (an evocative photo of a chair draped with a soft, luxurious shawl in a deep purple cashmere).

Changing and updating the notion of what was desirable was also an essential part of marketing in a capitalist economy, inspiring consumers to purchase new fashions or new cars, tying in an ability to display what was desirable to own with one's sense of self-worth. It wasn't something Charlotte took seriously in the days before writing about it regularly and moving to Lake Parkerton, and in fact at first it was fun, like getting paid to shop and compare purchases with other shoppers. But then it changed, becoming more serious the more she was drawn into the world of design and marketing, the more responsibilities she had as she moved from staff writer to the editorial teams, where the financial clout of the advertisers determined policy. The better she got at her job, the more she bought into the values it promoted, without ever fully realizing it.

When the economy crumbled and people no longer spent money decorating their increasingly devalued homes, the advertisers in turn could no longer contribute their revenue to the magazines. The signs of the troubles to come, however, were in the neighborhoods and shops long before they were in the editorial offices. And she hadn't been paying attention to those signs, either.

The meaning of things could be changed deliberately by marketing, but they could also be changed inadvertently by time, place, or circumstance. Either way, she thought, humans can perceive these changes and change their actions and their own value systems accordingly. As Charlotte considered the changes that occurred over the past few weeks, the desire to step outside of the deliberate, marketed side of things became stronger and clearer. Independence was now the most beautiful and desirable thing in the world, principally financial independence, but of a kind that turned commonly held values on their head.

It did not matter, she thought, if one was wealthy or not: the less you felt compelled to spend, the more less income sufficed. Diane suggested that downsizing and selling everything was a temporary move until Charlotte rebuilt her career and income, but the more she thought about it, the less she wanted to work in a field that depended on convincing people like herself to buy what they really didn't need, to make them think that there was something better than what they already had. She logged out of the chat rooms and closed the tabs for the magazine websites.

Every Monday for the past several years, Charlotte sat down in her office and wrote her editorials and blog posts for the magazines. It was a simple and gentle way to begin the work week, a routine that helped her to stay on track, often a problem for telecommuters. Once a post was written, the other routines seemed to fall into place. The sudden reality of not having a post to write, let alone two or three, made her restless. A writer, after all, has to write, just like a cat needs to stretch and sharpen its claws. She needed to write, just to be writing, to organize stray thoughts into coherent ones, to express herself, to feel a little more real now that there was no longer a readership to provide feedback.

Should I start a personal blog? She wondered if she should, to keep her byline, C. K. Anthony, out there and alive—and findable on the Internet. What would she blog about? What was fit for public consumption? Clearly, she couldn't write publicly about what happened to Olivia. She also couldn't write about the transcription project, assuming it would even continue with Olivia's death. And she didn't really know what to say about her own circumstances that wouldn't make her look pathetic to her former co-workers and employers, or to prospective ones. As she thought about this, a pickup truck with the Baysell Realty logo pulled up in the front of her house. The muscular young driver pulled out a sturdy timber For Sale sign from the back and began to set it in into the ground.

She could write for herself for the time being, keep a journal of sorts. She kept one while going through the divorce and getting settled here, and on and off through the years, but nothing regular. There was a journal template in her writing software, so she opened it and set up something simple, a plain screen with a blank white rectangle page on which there was only a blinking cursor at the top left. A fresh start. She began to type.

Every Monday for the past several years, I've sat down at this computer to write editorials and blog posts, and I signed them "C. K. Anthony." But today, there is no C. K. Anthony. There's only me, Charlotte, a woman in limbo, and on this particular Monday I'm watching a young man install a For Sale sign in my front yard. I feel both loss and anticipation, of being neither here nor there....

Charlotte and Helene sat in the quietest corner of The Coffee Grove. The proprietor, a lanky man in a gray ponytail and round wire-rimmed glasses named Jimmy Frobisher, brought over a tray with lattes in big white cups and plates with croissants. "Ladies," he said in a soft easy tenor. "Fresh from *la boulangerie*, and a square of chocolate to round it out." Jimmy was very fond of Helene. Charlotte noted that just about all men (and here she thought of Simon) were fond of Helene. She also remembered Jimmy before his hair went gray.

"And welcome back, Charlotte," said Jimmy. "It's been a long time." He gave Helene a hug and his condolences before returning to the counter.

Charlotte smiled with anticipation as she opened her napkin. "You know, I always used to think that the French had croissants for breakfast every day, and a lot of other rich things, too."

"Oh my goodness, no! Not unless you want to get very fat. They're really a treat, or for company, or for eating out when they're 'fresh from the boulangerie,'" She pulled a tiny bite off the end of her croissant and ate it slowly. "Of course," she smiled after a sip of latte, "there are frequent reasons to celebrate and have a treat or eat out, too."

"The French paradox." Charlotte dipped the end of her own croissant in the latte, and relished the blend of coffee and pastry, a treat that was now no longer in her budget, but she was here at Helene's invitation. "Jack and I used to eat these like mad for years, and filled with all kinds of things, and also with extra butter and jams and such. Wow." She shook her head at the memory of youthful metabolism. "We bought the mass-produced ones, of course, some already filled with ham and cheese, and we'd just pop them in the toaster oven. They don't compare with these."

"I should hope not, but I've had that kind, too. Evidently more and more in France are mass-produced, as well. Very sad."

Helene looked out the window at the people and cars going by, her expression neutral, but Charlotte knew her sadness about Olivia was very close to the surface.

"Do you miss France? Or Monte Carlo?"

Helene turned back, and managed a smile. "I don't know if I would call it *missing*, because that was then and this is now. Even if I could go back to Monte Carlo, what made it what it was for me is no longer there. We left, after all, in 1941. I was just barely nine years old."

"Olivia would have remembered Paris, though, right?"

Helene nodded. "Olivia was born in 1921, and I came along in '32, the year we moved to Monte Carlo."

"That must have been a beautiful place to live, very glamorous, and seeing all the famous people and the race cars."

"Oh, it was! And we lived in one of the grandest villas, too."

"So your family was wealthy?"

Helene burst out laughing, shaking her head. "Oh, heavens, Charlotte, no! We were just plain *lucky*. Our father was a sous-chef in Paris in the twenties, at one of the more exclusive restaurants. Eventually he was noticed by Beaufort Lamont, a wealthy American with a place in Monte Carlo. Mr. Lamont was a widower with two children. He entertained lavishly, as the wealthy did in Monte Carlo, and he asked Papa to come and be his chef. It was a no-brainer for our father: good money, regular money, and a chance to shine professionally. Best of all, in my mother's opinion, we would have our own apartment in the villa, as Mr. Lamont had more room than he knew what to do with. We moved there shortly after I was born, so I only know Paris from occasional visits and when Paul and I lived there for a year.

"Olivia, however, loved Paris, and adored Papa's sister Anastasia, who had a bookshop on the Left Bank and knew all sorts of writers and artists. When she was a teenager, Olivia drove our mother crazy until she promised to let her stay in Paris for a few weeks with Aunt Sasha. Then she would make regular visits, sometimes staying for a month or two at a time. Olivia wanted to be a writer, and thrived by being around writers. To me she seemed so glamorous and independent, and I was sure she was going to be a famous writer, just like Collette.

"The last time she stayed with Aunt Sasha, it had to be 1939, because France had just declared war on Germany, and my parents were out of their minds with worry that Olivia would be stuck in Paris, which the Germans would be more likely to either bomb or occupy, while we were relatively safe in Monte Carlo. Mr. Lamont sent Papa in a car with a chauffeur to go and get her. We were getting nervous, too, because Mother was Jewish, and we were hearing of all sorts of atrocities. Olivia was so upset that Aunt Sasha chose to stay in Paris, but then Paris was declared an Open City in the spring or summer of 1940, so we kept our fingers crossed that our aunt would be okay."

"Your mother was Jewish, but your father wasn't?"

Helene nodded. "My mother was from Scotland. There was a sizable community of Jewish scholars there. My grandparents took her on a European Tour, and happened to stay at my French grandmother's lodgings in Paris, and that's how she met my father and a long-distance courtship ensued. My grandfather was evidently not too happy that mother was marrying "a cook," but when he saw how well-educated Aunt Sasha was, he realized it was a family after his own heart, and gave his consent."

"That's a great story!" said Charlotte. "So if your mother was from Scotland, you must have learned English from her?"

"That's right. Mother was a whiz at languages, and made certain we were as fluent in English as in French, with passable German and Italian, as well. Mr. Lamont asked her to translate on quite a few occasions."

"Your mother sounds like an amazing person. I take it that your family didn't stay during the war, though?"

"No, thank heavens, but it wasn't easy to get away. Mr. Lamont realized it was time to go back to the States, to his flat in Manhattan, and he wanted to bring the entire household along, chauffeur, chef, butler, housekeeper, the whole kit and kaboodle, even the piano teacher, but to his great surprise he couldn't get visas. It was simple enough in the past, but all of a sudden the United States got very fussy about issuing visas. Later we realized it was because they didn't want an influx of German spies posing as Jewish refugees." Helene paused, as if she still thought it was preposterous that her family could ever be suspected of being German spies.

"I can't imagine how worried your family must have been, not knowing if they could get away," said Charlotte.

Helene nodded. "Money eventually talked, or at least Mr. Lamont did a lot of talking to one of the American ambassadors in Marseilles. Months of talking, actually. The ambassador was secretly trying to get as many Jews out of France as he could, but could only do it by issuing forged visas. I think we got out at nearly the last possible minute!

"I fell in love with our new home, the incredible view of the city and Central Park, the sense of being safe because my parents and Mr. Lamont weren't so worried anymore. I got full run of the music room, because by this time Mr. Lamont's children had all grown up, and I continued my studies at Juilliard. There were so many wonderful teachers there, a lot of Russians who came here because of the Revolution or the First World War, and then like us, the Nazis and another war. For a few months I even studied with Siloti, who was one of Franz Liszt's most renowned students; his cousin was Rachmaninoff, who we got to hear perform several times. So many wonderful artists and teachers." Helene's expression was wistful.

"Did Olivia take to life in America?"

Helene shrugged. "Not so much. Olivia went to Columbia University soon after our arrival. She had always had a single-minded intensity about her writing, but she changed a lot during her time in university, developed a wild streak. She seemed more brittle, and always angry, impatient with America for not getting involved in the war soon enough. She went back to Paris as soon as she could after it was over."

By this time they'd long finished their lattes, and Jimmy brought them regular coffees to nurse while Helene continued her reminisces.

"Olivia went to live and work at Aunt Sasha's bookstore, it was called "Sibylline," and like some others they had their own little literary magazine or journal, too, but by this time Aunt Sasha was dead—something to do with the war—and her partner Henriette was running it. Olivia published her poetry and stories in *Sibylline* and in a couple of the other literary magazines over there, and also back here in the States. In time she took over Henriette's editing duties. But Henriette was ill, and the bookstore was struggling—she eventually had to sell it to pay her bills. After she died, Olivia came back and lived in Greenwich Village for a while. I saw her every now and again, because the music students at Juilliard would go down to the Village or up to Harlem, and Olivia and her crowd loved jazz. I'd sometimes meet up with her when she was on her way to some club or other. But we traveled in different circles. She loved to dance, jazz dancing in particular. That reminds me, I found a picture of her from those days, and brought it to show you—."

Helene rummaged through her purse and pulled out a black-and-white photograph of a classic Beatnik girl in tight black capris, striped French boatneck sailor top, and black ballet flats. Her dark hair was pulled back into a pony tail. It was the eyes that Charlotte recognized, dark and daring, looking right into the camera. Olivia Bernadin had once been a strikingly beautiful woman, but the eyes said that her beauty was irrelevant to her.

"I'm so glad you showed me this. I can just tell she was unconventional, as well as beautiful."

"Oh, that she was, much more than I was, certainly. It wasn't long after that photo was taken that I got a postcard from France—Olivia was in love with a writer, living in Paris, and writing some plays. After that, I heard almost nothing from her, nor did our parents, for two or three years. One day out of the blue she shows up with an American army officer for a husband—and a baby boy. I don't know for certain where she met Ronson, but I think at the time he was stationed at the American base in Orleans. Maybe they met at a nightclub. He was a rigid, traditional sort of man, the perfect soldier. We all wondered what in the world he saw in *her.* Maybe opposites attract? They moved here when he was given a new duty station, because it is halfway between Camp Atterbury and Fort Custer. Not quite sure what he did, but he was gone a lot, mostly to one base or the other, and especially during the Vietnam War.

"Then, as you know, Olivia evidently stopped writing. She never did do anything more with her education and talent, just stayed home, a wife and mother and homemaker. In fact, she went from completely wild and independent to quite stodgy and even critical of my life as a pianist and the wife of an architect. I just assumed it was because we traveled so much and never had children. Paul always said that she was jealous and disappointed, but I didn't want to believe it of her.

"Ronson seemed to not care if she was happy or not. He did provide for her and Donovan, but he wasn't *engaged*, if you know what I mean. I know she went on various antidepressants through the years. You could tell when she wasn't—she'd fly off the handle at stupid stuff, slap Donovan if he didn't hand out Christmas presents fast enough, snap at us all. Even through those fits Ronson seemed unconcerned, just ignored it and went through all the motions of doing what was needed—everything except a hug, it seems.

"But after he died, about five years ago, I would hear from her a little more often. After a time, I could say that we had something of a restored relationship, if not close, but there we were, both widows, and her own child so absent that she might as well be as childless as I am. Perhaps old age is a bit of an equalizer. Or maybe she just felt freer to say and do what she wanted once Ronson was gone. At any rate, it seemed reasonable to move here, and closer to her, when the house at Lake Parkerton was just too much and too far from things I needed.

"Sometimes she'd open up a bit and tell me more about her time in Paris, both before and after the war. She'd met Hemingway, Jean-Paul Sartre, James Baldwin, and so many others. And she'd talk about Kerouac and Ginsberg and Burroughs, she knew them when they were still in New York, and there were several others in that circle. She never did say which one she was in love with. Once she married Ronson, though, I don't think she ever went to either New York or Paris again."

Eight

Tuesday, September 17th

Donovan Targman unfolded himself from the armchair and rose to shake hands with Charlotte as Helene introduced them. He was thin and looked much taller than he actually was, in part because his sports jacket was slightly too big in the body and slightly too short in the sleeves, in part because of the shock of auburn hair that rose up nearly two inches before it draped over to the sides. He had the bony, long-fingered hands of a pianist, but they bore the scars and calluses of manual labor. He looked sadder than Charlotte had expected him to be, given Helene's description of his relationship with his mother. Or perhaps he was simply tired or unwell; his glasses emphasized his eyes with black rectangular frames over slightly sunken cheeks. His manner was pleasant, if somewhat quiet; there were awkward silences during which he looked preoccupied and nervous, rubbing his hands, and he glanced frequently at a simple bronze urn on the coffee table. Charlotte did, too, as she had never seen it before, and then it dawned on her that it held Olivia's ashes.

During one such awkward moment, Helene brought Charlotte up

to speed.

"I was saying to Donovan that I was so sorry we couldn't find him before Olivia passed away, but...."

"That's okay, Aunt Helene, really," said Donovan, as if he felt bad that she felt bad. "You know how hard it could be to do the normal family thing with my mother. And I did speak to her not too long ago."

Charlotte found herself wanting to know more about this unusual-looking man. "Did you have far to travel, Donovan?"

He shook his head. "No, actually. Just down from South Bend."

"Ah, that's not so bad, then. Have you lived there long?"

"Just a few years, worked in Elkhart before that, Detroit before that, and, just, you know, where the work was."

"What kind of work do you do? Oh, I'm so sorry," Charlotte stopped herself. "I don't mean to interrogate!"

He smiled a little and laughed. "It's okay. At the moment, not much. Automotive type work, factory, repair shops. Economy's shot, my health isn't the best—not a lot of options out there. You could say I'm between gigs at the moment."

Donovan was leaning forward in the chair, arms on knees and hands loosely clasped, making him look as if he was all limbs, and a bit lean and hungry.

Helene leaned forward and patted his hands. "Well, maybe that's a good thing, because dealing with your mother's house is going to be a job and a half."

He rolled his eyes and nodded in agreement. "I was thinking of having an auction or something, just getting it dealt with, but maybe I should take my time and just put a few things on eBay. Don't know, though, if I want to stay in the area. Was thinking of going down to

Mexico or Costa Rica. The winters here are getting to me and the dollar goes a little further there." He was rubbing his hands again as if they hurt, but Charlotte wondered if it was simply a nervous tic, he did it so often.

"Have you been to Mexico or Costa Rica before?" asked Helene.

"Mexico once, long time ago. But I've been to Arizona in the winters a few times and I think maybe it would be good to relocate altogether."

"I sympathize about the economy," said Charlotte. "I've taken a hit with my work, too, and have to rethink a few things."

"Yeah? What's your line?"

"I was a writer and editor for design publications. The two main magazines I wrote for have folded, and others are reorganizing, going online instead of in print."

He nodded his understanding. "It's not like it was for our parents' generation, is it? No working at one place until you retire, and a little nest egg to live on until you die."

"No—no, it's not. So many of my neighbors have either lost their jobs, or they're underwater on their mortgages, or have health problems with unimaginable medical bills, or even a combination of those things. A lot of credit card debt, too. Saw a Hummer being repossessed the other day."

He grinned, one side of his mouth turning up more than the other. "Yeah, I've seen that, too, some nice cars, big trucks and fancy SUVs, there they go, bye-bye."

Charlotte thought he was funny at first, and laughed, but then sensed there could be a tinge of his mother's hard-done-by spiteful glee in others' misfortunes. She glanced at Helene, who was smiling more politely than genuinely.

Helene hesitated for a moment, then gestured toward Charlotte. "Charlotte is here because she is not only a close friend of mine, she is a professional writer. Your mother had just hired her to find and transcribe her notebooks, and then to edit them into something that could be published."

Donovan looked puzzled. "What notebooks?" There was complete silence while Helene and Charlotte took in the significance of his statement.

"Did you even know your mother was once a writer?" asked Charlotte.

"I knew that, yeah, but it wasn't talked about like it was anything special. I thought maybe it was just a newspaper article or something like that."

"Oh, my," Helene sighed. "She had published several stories, books of poetry, and a couple of plays. She was commissioned to write a screenplay before she married your father. Then she stopped. Just stopped."

Donovan looked as surprised as if someone had told him his mother was a secret agent. "I had no idea Mom had so much going for her. What happened? What made her marry somebody like my dad and leave all that behind?"

Helene shrugged. "I don't know. You have to realize that times were very different back then, women still had a difficult time professionally, even as writers, and many women were pressured to give up their careers if they married. Your father was a military man, very conservative and strict, so I wouldn't have been surprised if he had something to do with it."

Donovan's eyes went dark and sharp and his jaw tensed. "I hated him. He would never let my mother do anything kind for me, saying I had to learn to be a man, be tough. Even before I got into high school. When he would stay on the base for a while, things would be a little better, but I would still be angry at Mom for letting him be so abusive to us both. She would be angry, too. Sometimes I didn't know if she was angry at him for the abuse, or angry at me for existing. It drove me crazy. I'd sneak out at night to have fun with my friends or even just to do something I wasn't supposed to do, and the older I got, the more I just did what I wanted to do, even when she'd whale on me. After getting knocked around by the old man, she was nothing. But then she'd be all sorry and wonderful and really interested in me, and I'd fall for it again and again. I loved her. I hated her. But him, I just plain hated."

Charlotte listened in silence. This was not the time to reveal Olivia's harsh account of Donovan's dying father.

Helene seemed to age visibly as she took in this account of her sister's and nephew's life; the circles under her eyes darkened and her voice became less clear. "Oh, Donny, I had no idea it was that bad. I wish your mother would have said something. I should have realized her moodiness was from a terrible marriage. Your mother and I had not been in touch very often between the time you were born and a couple of years ago, even though we didn't live far apart for the last twenty years. She didn't really start opening up until after your father died, so I'm sure he was the biggest obstacle in all of this. When Paul and I would have dinner with you all during Christmas or Thanksgiving, it always seemed strange and tense."

Donovan shrugged, resigned about the past. "It was rough. None of my friends lived like that. If their dads were abusive, it was usually from drinking. These days it's harder to get away with that kind of thing, but back then *nobody* got between parents and kids unless it happened right out in public, which I don't remember ever happened. It was always in the house, in private." Donovan gazed out the doors to the veranda. "He wanted me to go into the army, my mother wanted me to go to college, and I didn't want part of either one. I left home the day I graduated from high school, and went to work in the mill."

Helene's phone rang and she went into the kitchen to take the call. Donovan looked down at his hands and began rubbing them. Charlotte remained silent; she was at a loss for something to say, and couldn't stop thinking about Olivia's hatred for Ronson as he lay dying. No wonder she wrote what she did.

Helene came back in, looking distressed. She held the cordless phone out to Donovan. "It's your mother's lawyer. He wants to talk to you."

Charlotte rose and offered to make tea, uncertain what to say or not to say in front of Donovan. Helene nodded, but didn't take her eyes off Donovan as he spoke on the phone.

Something was clearly up, and Charlotte assembled the tea as quietly as she could in order to listen to whatever snippets of conversation came from the sitting room. The electric kettle began rattling as it heated the water, however, and drowned out everything until a sudden shouted "*What?*"

She went to the archway between the rooms to see Donovan, who was now standing and staring at Helene in a mixture of disbelief and outrage, his hand holding the phone dangling at his side.

"You have got to be kidding! What have you two old bats *done?*"

Charlotte could hear the lawyer's voice coming through the phone and Helene went over to take it from Donovan, but he pulled it away and spoke into it himself.

"You have no idea what pile of troubles this has caused, and it will be challenged!" He then pointed the phone at Helene as if it was a gun. "And you will be, too!"

He was so furious that he threw the phone at the urn, knocking it over, and stormed out of the condo.

Helene was shaking, and Charlotte put her arms around her and led her back to the sofa.

"What happened, Helene?"

Helene took a deep breath and shook her head in disbelief. "It's Olivia's will. She's evidently left me the contents of the house, and named me as executor. There's some other things, too, but that's the main thing. Donovan can't sell the house or even take possession until after I deal with the contents."

This was clearly unexpected, Charlotte thought. It was also a little unfair, given how much there was to deal with.

Helene's own outrage grew the more she thought about it. "That dratted sister of mine! What was she thinking? What on earth am I going to do with a house crammed with all that *junk*? This is her way of getting back at the both of us, Donnie and me both! Paul was right about her—this is sheer spite!"

"Let me bring you some tea, and then call the attorney back and maybe make an appointment?"

Helene just nodded and stared out the French doors and at the garden beyond. Charlotte worried that all the stress would hurt her friend's health. She picked up the urn from the floor and set it back on the coffee table, grateful that the lid hadn't popped off and spilled the ashes.

While Helene talked to the attorney—and she made no secret of her dismay—Charlotte considered this new side of things. As Diane said, the first thing to consider is who benefits by someone's death, and the most obvious one was Donovan, or at least would have been Donovan in most circumstances. His outburst, while disturbing, was understandable, especially if he was counting on it to make a move to a warmer climate. Charlotte, however, couldn't help but wonder if there was a connection between Donovan's reaction to the terms of the will and the violence surrounding his mother's death. What if he was the one Olivia had hit with the bat? And if he was the one who pushed her? If Olivia hit him first, one could understand his reacting instinctively, and pushing her away in self-defense, even if the intent was not to hurt her or kill her. But he did not appear to have any injuries, or to move as if he'd been beaten with a baseball bat. And if her head injury wasn't intended, wouldn't he have called for an ambulance? Or would he?

Donovan had appeared tired, and somewhat ill at ease. He almost constantly rubbed his hands as if they hurt, and indeed the knuckles were knobby from arthritis. But hand-wringing could also mean nervousness, distress—and guilt. Charlotte wondered if he was always like that, no matter the situation, or if it would get worse, say, in Olivia's house, the scene of the crime. Or maybe, she sighed to herself, he's just upset and that's the way he shows it. She didn't have enough information to form an opinion, and certainly not to pass judgment.

Helene ended her call, having set an appointment for the following morning, but had nothing more to add to what they already knew. Since she had a student coming in the afternoon, she wanted to rest and reclaim her equilibrium with a nap, and Charlotte left when she was assured that Helene would be okay.

It was another marvelous early autumn day, which was fortunate since Charlotte had dropped the Jeep off at Elm Grove Auto and Body on the way to Helene's and had to get around on foot. She walked down to Olivia's house, to see if Donovan had gone there, worried that he would do some damage to his mother's house in his fit of anger. All seemed quiet, however, as she passed the front of the house, and turned the corner to check the back door and garage. She continued on. The sounds of children playing in the schoolyard in the next block brought back memories of Ellis' kindergarten days at the same school, of walking her there, of volunteering in the classroom. It was a good school. Charlotte sometimes wondered how things would have been different if Ellis had remained there, if she would have done as well in her piano studies living in this small town with its traditional public school and neighborhoods. But of course, Helene didn't live here at the time, and Charlotte herself found life here untenable in the days during and immediately after the divorce, and then of course Jack lost no time in marrying Mrs. Jack—.

She walked up past the school, then turned toward Bellamy Street, which was pure Historical District, lined with turreted Queen Anne houses, columned Greek and Colonial Revival homes, Second Empire houses with high mansard roofs, and frothy Eastlake homes decked out with spindle work. It was rich with oaks, maples, ash, linden, and tulip trees that had been planted to replace the elms which gave the town its name a hundred and fifty years before.

None of the houses were larger or grander than the old brick Blumenthal mansion, built shortly before the crash of '29, which sported a "For Sale" sign. Charlotte wondered if the Blumenthal family was finally, ironically, falling on hard times, but she doubted it. They probably didn't want the bother of keeping up a house designed for a much more formal lifestyle. What would become of it?

Charlotte continued to Cortland Street, to walk by her old Greek

Revival-style house, and received another surprise. The original six over six windows that she had once spent excruciating weeks fixing and painting were in the process of being replaced by modern ones with vinyl snap-in grids to simulate the panes. Cortland Street was not limited by the strict Historical District regulations that governed Bellamy Street, but the homeowners were encouraged to preserve the original style as much as possible. Charlotte sighed, but walked on, making her way back downtown to Harvey Street. It wasn't her problem anymore. She had enough of her own.

Jack had sold the house quickly six months ago, in anticipation of moving to Paris, where both he and Mrs. Jack were either teaching or doing research at an institute at the Sorbonne. Charlotte never did get it straight. She also wasn't clear as to what role, if any, their relocation played in Ellis' acceptance to the Conservatoire. But they were there, and now Ellis was there—and she herself wasn't.

There are days like this, she thought, when it seems the entire world has gone contrary to expectations. It put her in an impatient mood, wanting to get as many things out of gray areas as possible. She wanted things to be *settled*—to be living in one place, to have one town, one life, and not this in-between shuttling back and forth between one place and another, with neither feeling like home base, if not home. She wanted friends to stay friends, families to stay families, homes to stay homes, neighbors to stay neighborly, employers to remain employers. But they didn't. It was the worst feeling in the world for a nester like Charlotte, and it seemed like the upheaval would never come to an end.

She called Elm Grove Auto Repair to see if the Jeep was ready, but they said not for another couple of hours yet, they ran into "a little problem." She sighed as she disconnected, after asking them to let her know if it was going to cost much more before proceeding with the work. By this time she had reached Harvey Street, where many people were taking advantage of the summery day, sitting at umbrellaed tables on the sidewalks in front of various restaurants and looking as if they didn't have a care in the world. Inspired, she called Diane.

"Can you come out to play?"

Diane chuckled. "Actually, I can. Where are you at?"

"In front of Ramona's Resale, but I was thinking more along the lines of a drink."

"Have you had lunch yet?"

"Um, no—"

"I haven't either, and I've got a craving for a ribeye sandwich. Cole's Pub, five minutes?"

Diane ordered martinis for them both. "I insist—my treat. You look like you could use a treat right about now."

"That is so nice of you. I'm very grateful, and enjoying this immensely," said Charlotte, as she slid further back into the booth. Cole's Pub was a restaurant/watering hole favored by lawyers and deal-makers. It was old and dark but comfortable; faint music played over the speakers, the kitchen sounds were faint, the murmurs of conversations were faint, the baseball game on the television above the bar was faint, and together they made a pleasant white noise that fit Charlotte's mood better than the pretty, ladies-luncheon al fresco option they could have had at another restaurant. The martinis arrived and she knew that they would soon make the ambiance even more pleasant.

"It's really hitting home just how little I've relaxed lately. I'm getting too irritated at things which are beyond my control." She took her first sip. The gin made her nose twitch, but it was not unpleasant. She pulled an olive off its plastic spear and savored it. Wonderful.

"It's understandable, but don't worry about it," said Diane, patting Charlotte's hand. "This is only temporary. In fact, everything you're doing now almost guarantees that you will bounce back and have financial security within a year or two."

"Actually, there's some question in my mind what form that will take." She brought Diane up to date about Lola, the estate liquidation, the apartment, and her realization that she didn't want to find new work in the same field.

"Holy horses. You haven't lost any time, and actually you've moved on this a lot faster than I expected."

Charlotte nodded. "I think I've been making decisions almost subconsciously, if that is possible. On the other hand, I admit I like being in control—"

"Most single moms do," interrupted Diane. "Go ahead."

"—and now, without Ellis to support and protect, I can scale nearly everything way back, making it easier to stay in control, and stay independent."

"Money and a room of your own," Diane concurred.

"Exactly. But Helene also said something that stuck in my head, that the people who survive are the ones who are willing to travel light."

Diane nodded, rolling the words over in her head. "It's certainly true financially."

"I'm thinking it works with everything, money, stuff, maybe even relationships."

At this point the waitress arrived with Diane's ribeye sandwich and Charlotte's grilled shrimp salad. After several meals of whatever was left in her refrigerator, the crisp texture of the salad, the smokiness of the shrimp, the sweet tang of balsamic vinegar, and the unaccustomed midday gin buzz combined to lift Charlotte's mood. She and Diane looked at each other and giggled.

"I feel like I'm playing hookey," said Diane, trying to talk and chew at the same time. "This is fun."

Charlotte nodded. "And in a week or so I'll be living just down the block."

"It was meant to be, I mean it has the feeling of it was meant to be, not that I believe in that kind of stuff, but sometimes things really do have a way of working out well in the long run." Diane's tendency to run on was enhanced by the martini, but it didn't stop her from ordering another when the waitress came to see if they needed anything.

Charlotte said no to the second drink. "I gotta pick up the Jeep in a little while and get things done at home. I'll need every bit of time I can get to go through my stuff before Stanton gets there on Friday." She forked a jumbo shrimp and took a bite. "But there's no doubt this lunch is making me feel better."

"You have always had that independent streak, and it's admirable. But just because you *can* be a lone wolf and do everything on your own doesn't mean you *should*."

"How do you mean?"

"Don't be afraid to reach out to your friends, Charlotte. Reach out to me, to Helene, Jimmy Frobisher, even new friends like Simon and Lola. Even if it's just for a cuppa coffee or a beer. Line us up to help you when you're ready to move, too."

Charlotte just smiled, and thanked Diane. And ordered a cup of coffee.

She plunged into housework once she was back home after picking up the Jeep, which ended up costing half again as much as originally quoted. She redirected her annoyance by taking out the trash and sweeping the first autumn leaves off the deck. It calmed her down enough to make a large mug of herb tea, switch on the kitchen TV, and sit down with her To Do list. It was Tuesday; Stanton would be arriving Friday to begin setting up for the sale the following weekend. This left her today, Wednesday, and Thursday to finish going through closets, drawers—and the endless stuff in her basement. She was half-tempted to just let them find what they find, and pick out what she wanted to keep a day or two before the sale. Martin did say, after all, that they usually set aside things like photographs and letters and obviously personal things.

Sunday was the day she set aside to clean and paint the apartment, with the intention of moving in on Monday. So that meant she would be living and sleeping here for less than a week. She wrote the different items down on the list, then made a clean list with everything in the order it needed to be done. Seeing everything organized and in writing made her feel a little better, a little less scattered. One week was not really a lot of time to pick through a lifetime of possessions and select only enough to fit in a studio apartment, though. Or was it?

Charlotte's attention was drawn to a local news bulletin showing the front of Warren Brothers Pawn and Payday, with an overlaid caption that said, "Local Pawn Broker Found Dead." She turned up the volume with the remote. Did something happen to Bosley? She remembered the phone call he received that clearly upset him when he came to her house. The reporter Judy Sargent was once again on the scene, but this time her demeanor was serious.

"Early this morning, police discovered the body of local pawn broker Wesley Warren, who has not been seen since last Thursday afternoon. He was found in his car, which was submerged in a large pond alongside the road leading toward his residence north of Elm Grove. Police are withholding further comment pending an autopsy and toxicolo—."

The picture suddenly went black. Charlotte worked the remote, but nothing came up except the words, "No Signal."

No cable? Confused, she thought about it for a moment and remembered that she had scheduled its cancellation, but her understanding was that the service was paid through the end of the month. If it was canceled, that meant her cable Internet connection might be canceled, too. She opened her laptop and tried to get online. Dead. She wanted to know what happened to Bosley Warren's brother, and wondered if the things she had pawned would still be accessible if the business should close. The atmosphere in the shop was tense and strange the day she was there, which would be no wonder if Wesley was missing and Bosley was out looking for him.

Cursing, she called the cable company on her cell phone and went through Press One for This, Press Two for That, layer after layer of menus until, after several tries, she got someone to check her account, who claimed that billing applied on the fifteenth of every month, and since no further payment was made, her service was canceled as per her request. It could be reinstated at an additional fee of—

Charlotte hung up. She was going to be out of here in a week, anyway; it simply wasn't worth the hassle to straighten it out. Maybe she screwed up, maybe they did. Whatever. She thought about calling Helene or Diane, but decided she was peopled out and could find out whatever she needed to know soon enough the next day. In her irritable mood, it was better to stay put and sort through boxes. At least the electric was still on.

Charlotte looked around her large basement, at the stacks of boxes, shelves of old toys, tools, sacks of decorating items, an assortment of furniture that was in need of repair or refinishing, and a ping-pong table that she and Ellis had never seemed to use. Instead, its surface provided more storage space, covered as it was with an assortment of items acquired from assignments at the magazines: knockoff Noguchi-style lamps (the real ones were in the living room), small tables of unusual design, rustic and cottage-style items that never looked right in her sleek house, little-girl decorative items that Ellis grew out of as fast as they came in, large and small baskets in every conceivable material and color, and stacks of rug samples. Boxes of baby clothes and Ellis' dolls, plus a few boxes from Charlotte's own childhood were stacked against one wall. She hadn't looked in them in years. The washer and dryer area was surrounded by baskets and bags of clothes that Ellis had either grown out of or didn't want to take with to Paris, plus laundry Charlotte hadn't gotten around to dealing with. There was nothing for it but to tackle it, go through every box and, well, *just deal with it,* even if it took all night. After all, this place, this stuff, would be gone once and for all in a matter of days.

Charlotte woke in the dark, thinking the furnace was on full blast. But it was just another hot flash; she sat up and threw the covers off, took a sip of water from the glass on the nightstand. The digital clock said 4:17. And so it begins, she thought, the onset of old. *Dammit,* she swore to herself, *I'm not ready for this!*

It had been a year and a half since her last date. She noticed less, for lack of a better term, *feedback* from men. She was becoming invisible, there was no split-second light of interest in their eyes anymore. Neutral and pleasant was what she got, if anything at all, or, at best, the half-joking flirtation of gay friends and much older men. Inside, she was still young, vibrant, and sensuous. But outside, invisible—even when she took pains to look attractive.

As she lay back down, she thought about past relationships and Brian in particular, the six months they had, from meeting, to dating, to passion. She knew he was the one from the first kiss, even from just holding his hand, the charge of just being in one another's presence. There was just something about the way he looked and moved, the sound of his voice, the way that he made her feel that he *saw* her—and connected with what he saw—that she had never felt before or since.

And then his National Guard unit was called up to the Middle East. He was forty-four years old. Twenty years before, he had joined under pressure from his employer, along with several other mid-level executives at the company he worked for. All the things they'd planned to do, gradually bringing together their families, the beautiful future she knew they were going to have, all of it ended thirty-eight days after he arrived at the desert base. That was six years ago. She still had a drawer of his clothes that he'd kept there.

For months she'd slept with the one sweater that still had his scent, crying herself to sleep. The scent had faded, finally. She moved on, insofar as she could, to the occasional date. And then no one. Forays into online dating services led to nothing, because she couldn't bring herself to actually meet up with any of the people she met there.

By this time the clock said 5:31, and Charlotte resigned herself to not getting any more sleep. One might as well get up and tackle the projects for the day. After making a coffee, she grabbed a box and put everything in it that was too personal to leave out for the estate sale crew: photo albums, mementos, a few journals, a teddy bear from her grandmother that she'd taken to college. To this she added the box of mementos of her months with Brian, and his beloved sweater. Was this why she'd faded so quickly? It was as if a part of her own life ended with his, and never came back. And she wasn't yet fifty. *Here I am in one big giant empty nest, empty of my child, empty of love, work, meaning, life.*

Charlotte broke down in tears, holding Brian's sweater to her face, and as the sobs started to fade, she realized that the sweater now smelled like a mixture of mustiness and furniture polish. I'm an idiot, she thought. It was time to let it go. They hadn't been married, after all, hadn't yet built anything together, and even the flag on his coffin was handed to his mother. She realized she'd suspended her entire emotional life over him, widowed herself inside. It was time to let the past go, all of it. *Keep the love, but let the stuff go.*

She pulled herself together, took a deep breath, and began tossing away everything that could hold back her heart from opening up to a brand-new life: lingerie she hadn't worn in years, high school and college mementos, programs from concerts, birthday cards. A pressed corsage she could no longer connect to an event. The past had *passed.* She would no longer allow herself to become as musty as Brian's old sweater, as dusty and frozen in time as the objects that filled Olivia's house.

Nine

Wednesday, September 18th

Helene was on her cell phone with Simon, striding like a woman half her age. Indeed, she looked like one in chinos, running shoes, and a man's untucked tailored white shirt with a subtle "PLD" monogram on the point of one collar, which after a moment or two Charlotte realized stood for Paul Lucien Dalmier. Charlotte's lingering concerns for her friend's well-being dissipated as she found herself trying to keep up on the walk to Olivia's house. The muscles in her legs were stiff and aching from the hours of moving and sorting through the boxes in her basement. She was also out of sorts from too many emotions and too little sleep; the three coffees at breakfast didn't really help.

Helene was bringing Simon up to date about the conference with the attorney earlier that morning, which clarified the terms of the will. "I can't believe this, either. Charlotte and I are going there now to size up the job, and if at all possible I'd like your input, too. Olivia clearly had this project on her mind at least a month before she said anything to me, as that's when her will was updated." She paused as she listened to him. "Oh, that would be great! Thank you so much Simon, and see you soon." She clicked off, took a deep breath, and turned to Charlotte. "Simon will come by in a few minutes. He's wrapping up office hours."

By this time they'd gone up the porch. Helene unlocked the door and once again the heavy scent of roses made Charlotte feel sad and a little dizzy.

Helene, however, was undaunted, and carefully made her way to the window surrounded by the bookshelves, raising the roller shade and opening the sash, bringing in sunlight and the crisp fresh air. The improvement was immediate. Charlotte wondered if Olivia would have been a nicer person, a happier person, if she'd only opened the windows. But perhaps she didn't because she was not a nice, happy person in the first place.

Helene saw that she was standing close to the blood streak and took a quick step back. "We need to get rid of this rug. Horrible."

"I'm glad one of us is on good form this morning," murmured Charlotte.

"Oh, I'm loaded for bear," Helene said, in a growly tone that was as uncharacteristic as her attire, and Charlotte smiled to herself, enjoying this new side to her elderly friend. Or perhaps it wasn't a new side at all, but something essential to Helene's nature that wasn't necessary in the years Charlotte had known her. Helene was clearly not going to let Olivia's will defeat her the way that Olivia was defeated by Ronson or other elements of life. She couldn't picture her friend giving up her music to go into a self-imposed exile.

They looked over the rug, and at the books and papers still scattered around it. As Charlotte began collecting and handing them to Helene to place on the coffee table, she realized they were all part of a copy of Allen Ginsburg's *Howl.* "This is a well-worn copy, but not a first edition."

Helene had turned to look over the shelves. "Most of these are not valuable, at least at first glance. Old, yes, but that doesn't mean valuable." She turned back to Charlotte. "Of course if there really was something valuable, I'm sure whoever was here has taken it."

Charlotte found some old newspapers, which she placed over the blood stain. "I don't want us to accidentally step in this for the time being." From there she went to put the fallen table and lamp aright, and then the cup and crossword book.

Helene wandered from room to room, shaking her head at the clutter, and at the way her sister had lived. "One thing we can do right now is get rid of the potpourri and open more windows—if we can even get at the windows."

They opened the back door and the kitchen and dining room windows, and tossed the potpourri in the trash, then Charlotte took the trash to the wheeled bins outside. Helene went out to the porch to sit in the swing, taking deep breaths of fresh air. Charlotte joined her.

"I'm trying to think of how to make short work of this," said Helene. "I do want to do the right thing and find those notebooks. Of course I still want you to do everything we'd talked about with Olivia, if you're still interested, but please don't feel obligated while your own situation is so unsettled."

Charlotte nodded her reassurance, while trying not to show too much relief. "I really do want to do this. It's a wonderful opportunity and I have a feeling something good will come of it." She silently thanked her lucky stars that the job was still there, unsettled situation or not.

"Do you have any ideas about how to proceed?"

Charlotte adopted the manner that worked when making suggestions and proposals at editorial meetings. "I think the most important thing right now is to just find the notebooks. Once I have those, you could have an estate liquidator come in like I'm doing. That way you don't have to worry about all the hands-on work, the sorting and the details, and you can turn the house over to Donovan fairly quickly."

Helene seemed to like the idea. "Oh, the sooner the better, in my opinion. I wasn't impressed by that display of his." Her lips were pressed in a thin line of disapproval. "But I need to have a rough estimate of the personal property value for the estate and for the taxes, like an appraisal. The books might not be worth much, but there are some antiques and collector's items in the cabinets and on the other shelves. Maybe I should call Martin Stanton, but I think we need to see what we're dealing with first."

The weather was sunny, but cool, the first touches of autumn on the breeze. Charlotte was glad she'd worn socks and a sweater. Helene shivered, and they rose to go back into the house. Then a motorcycle quietly pulled into the driveway, surprising Charlotte, as she hadn't heard it coming. It was Simon, who smoothed back his hair after taking off his helmet. She had already recognized him, however, by the jeans and the jacket. It had to be long-legged black jeans, she thought. She looked away before he caught her staring.

Simon joined them in the living room, and noted the open windows. "Smells better already."

Helene pointed down to the newspapers covering the blood stain. "I only hope that we won't smell the blood now. This rug has got to go. But I'm supposed to have everything valuated before getting rid of anything. The attorney said to take pictures." She smiled and looked up at Simon. "Would you like the job?"

Simon chuckled in a way that said he knew her all too well. "Yes,

Helene, I will be happy to do it. But you know that."

"No, no," she protested. "I mean as a real job. The estate will cover your time and expenses. My sister has created a huge inconvenience for me, but I don't want it to be an inconvenience for my friends, as well. You both might as well get something out of it. At least that's my feelings about the matter."

Simon looked like he was going to object, but Charlotte interrupted. "Oh, Simon, take the bloody job and make good work of it. I could use the help, too."

He looked at her with amusement. "Alright, I'll take the *bloody* job," he said, stressing the difference in their accents. The creases in his high-boned cheeks deepened as he smiled, and for a moment Charlotte thought that he looked a bit like an aging but well-preserved rock star. "We'll make good work of it, then." He turned to Helene. "When do we start?"

"Immediately." Helene had to look up at him, but seemed taller as she gave the command. Every so often, thought Charlotte, one could get a glimpse of Helene the concert pianist, and the teacher used to dealing with young prima donnas.

"Right, then," said Simon, moving his hands to point out and encompass different areas of emphasis. "I propose we do it as a video, first just a quick scan and set of notes, and then as Charlotte goes through the search for the notebooks, we'll do a detailed inventory of everything in each room. That's also when I can do still shots of groups of items that might be of particular value, such as each shelf in the cabinets, or the things on the sideboard and dining room table. If there is anything of outstanding value, I can set it up as a single-item shot, with perfect lighting and detail."

Helene nodded her understanding. “That sounds like a good plan, and hopefully not too much fuss. The attorney did say something about videos—evidently that’s the way insurance agents do it nowadays.” She went on to say that she would provide both Simon and Charlotte with checks to cover a week’s worth of work in advance, with another if the project required it. Charlotte expressed her gratitude, and hoped she was hiding her relief, wanting to keep things as professional as possible. She would stretch the money as far as she could, but it would help her make ends meet until after the sale.

“The videos might help me spot the notebooks, too,” said Charlotte. “I have no idea what they look like or where they’ve been stashed.” She shrugged. “Or maybe not. I’ve no idea, really.” She looked around the room, feeling a bit helpless and hopeless. Where *does* one begin in a mess like this? Especially when there is a need to find something specific. “These notebooks could turn out to be ten needles in a hundred haystacks.”

“I can help you with that, too,” said Simon. “I can help you move things, maybe make it go a little faster.” He, too, looked around the room. “Moving things might be unavoidable.”

Helene sat down on the wingback chair. “If it wasn’t for the fact that my sister was once an author of some promise and regard, I’d be tempted to say to hell with this and go directly with an estate liquidator, like Charlotte is doing,” she said. “But as it is, my conscience won’t let me, and I am also just plain curious about what’s in those notebooks. So much of Olivia’s life was a mystery.”

Charlotte once again felt torn about telling Helene what was in the last notebook. Now that the project was definitely back on, she would have to set aside the time to read it carefully, and make a typed copy.

Perhaps it would be best not to say what was in it until she had read the whole thing. "She certainly seemed to be well-connected, from what you've told me."

Helene nodded. "Her world back then was like a *salon* of literary stars."

Simon had been looking over the bookshelves. "Here's a first edition of *On the Road.*" He thumbed through it. "And it's full of marginalia. Looks like Olivia didn't like it much." He replaced it. "Marked up like that, it won't bring a lot, I wouldn't think."

"Was she part of the Beat movement, or the French New Wave?" asked Charlotte.

"I honestly don't know," said Helene, with a shrug. "She was French at heart, or at least wanted to be."

Simon pointed at a row of books on another shelf. "Seamus O'Dair, but mostly paperbacks. With Joyce and Beckett, no first editions."

"I think Olivia knew him, too," said Helene.

"Does anyone actually understand Seamus O'Dair?" asked Simon. "I mean, I found *Least Objects* a hard go."

Charlotte remembered reading it in grad school. "It's a very harsh novel, and it is difficult, but it is brilliant. Some people think O'Dair's take on post-war consumerism is a prophecy that has come true in recent years, especially with more awareness of the influence corporations have on the decision to go to war. People have trouble with *Least Objects* because there are endless levels of compromised values, and it is hard to read without having a real hero to root for. Even feminists were divided on his treatment of the main woman character, Margot—some said it was only fair that she was cast out for lying about being part of the French Resistance, and others thought that she was unfairly punished for being young and hero-worshiping. Everyone in it is seriously flawed in one way or another."

"That's what I remember of it, that darkness, an almost pointless darkness," said Simon.

"It's one of the darkest books I've ever read, too," said Helene. "I read it in the original French and came away with a different experience than I did when I read the English translation. It seemed less mean-spirited. Something might have gotten lost."

"There's a quest story in it, too," continued Charlotte, as she recalled more and more of the novel. "The character Jacques, who's probably the closest to a hero in the book, thinks that Margot has stolen his son, and the search takes him into one situation after another. Of course it all ends badly, but that's part of the point—there cannot be a good ending in a world dominated by banks, corporations, and armies."

"That's probably the simplest summary of that book that I've ever heard," said Simon. "Not that I'm ready to give it another go," he put up his hands to stop her reply, and grinned. "Seriously, though, I might have been too young and impatient for it back then, not up for reading much of anything so serious." He imitated a lofty, self-important person. "All about my *art*, y'know."

"Oh, Simon," tutted Helene, "I'm sure you were never that full of yourself."

"Oh but I was, and probably still am!" he insisted, and left to pick up his video equipment.

Charlotte had remembered to bring the one notebook she did have, and once again wondered at the words inside the front cover: *Put the pieces together and bloom.* She showed it to Helene.

"I thought at first that it's the title of this volume, this notebook, but so far I'm not making the connection," said Charlotte. "I admit that the handwriting is difficult to read in the first half, so I might be missing a lot."

Helene nodded thoughtfully. "It feels familiar, but I'm not sure why. Maybe it will come to me." She handed the notebook back to Charlotte.

"Perhaps it's episodic, like a lot of modern fiction, in pieces that are put together to make a whole novel. Or maybe it's because it's literally in pieces, in different notebooks, and it means what Olivia wanted, to put all the notebooks together?"

"That's one way of looking at it. But knowing my sister, it probably isn't that simple."

Charlotte was about to ask Helene why, but Simon returned just then, with lights, tripods, and a camera. She was impressed by how quickly he set everything up to begin the overview video of the contents of each room, along with a commentary. As he worked, Charlotte made written notes, and occasionally asked Helene to identify antique items, such as a pants press and a collection of darning eggs, as well as providing date ranges for certain styles of hats, dresses, and lampshades. It was time-consuming and often awkward, because of the sheer number of things in every room, and because there was so little room to move around in.

The contents of the bedrooms took most of the morning. When she and Simon went back to the living room, they found Helene at the writing desk, absorbed in a ledger book, which she showed to them as they approached.

"Historians say that the most fascinating information about any period of time comes from the small things like household accounts, and

I'm beginning to see why." She pointed to a line that said "coffee," at the end of which there was a price.

Simon looked as if he was suppressing a laugh. "Yes, well, now we know they had coffee as long ago as, what, 1972?" He peered more closely to see the date in the first column. "Interesting."

Helene knew she was being teased. "Oh, stop it. What's interesting is that she's put down an amount that was more like the 1982 price, after the price of coffee skyrocketed. I was just looking through this to remember what one bought and how much things cost back then, and everything seems right except for the coffee, and maybe the milk and eggs."

Simon burst out laughing. "Oh that's an old trick, that one. Clever girl, your sister."

"Why, how do you mean?" Helene looked genuinely puzzled.

"She was skimming. Probably her husband had her on a tight allowance, and it looks like she also had to account for every penny she spent. The only way to get him to fork over more money was to show how much necessities cost, and then she pocketed what she didn't actually have to spend. What about cigarettes? Are those in there?"

Helene checked the list. "Yes. The price seems about right."

"And beer?"

"That seems about right, too."

"Yep," nodded Simon. "She put down the right prices on the stuff he was likely to know the prices of, too, like beer and cigarettes. Some women would skim for their own drink and smokes, or to save up for something special or to slip to a relative who needed it."

Helene sighed. "My poor sister. Her life was so different than mine, so much harder."

These observations made Charlotte recall a friend at school whose family thought buying books was a foolish luxury. The girl collected cans and bottles to turn in for deposit and scrap metal money, and then bought a copy of *Alice in Wonderland*, which she kept hidden under the floorboards in her bedroom closet. From there, Charlotte realized that if Olivia kept detailed grocery purchases, she might have kept purchase details for everything else.

"Helene, is that just groceries, or the other things, too, like the collectibles?"

Helene checked. "Oh, it appears to be everything. I see here there's baseball cards—a rather lot of baseball cards, actually, nylons, a Roseville vase, and even gasoline. I have no idea if the Roseville vase is the right price, or the baseball cards, but the gasoline seems to be about right, ten gallons for $3.50. Of course, Ronson would have known that." She pointed to the bottom row of the bookshelf next to the desk. "There's dozens of these ledgers."

"I find it interesting," said Simon, "that there are things like baseball cards listed, and extras like the vase, which meant Ronson probably knew about them, and was okay with them. He might have been strict and controlling, but he wasn't a tightwad. I mean," he gestured around to the curio cabinets, "clearly he didn't have a problem with her spending money on this stuff. Would the baseball cards be something their son bought?"

Helene shook her head. "The cards were Ronson's, I'm remembering now. He was a baseball fan, but Donnie never cared for sports. Ronson was also a Notre Dame football fan, as was Paul. I remember being glad that there was something he and Ronson could talk about when we would see them during the holidays. I think Olivia was collecting the Hummels and pottery and such when she went to sales and antique shops with him."

Charlotte was sitting in the wingback chair by this time, idly scanning the bookshelves. With the lamp and table upright, she realized this was probably where Olivia sat most of the time to read. From the chair, she could see that a great many of the books had stickers on the spine that showed they were purchased at library sales or second-hand shops.

"Books," said Charlotte. "Are there book purchases in the ledger?"

Helene was silent as she thumbed through page after page. She looked up, with a conspiratorial smile. "Not a one!"

Charlotte sat in thought, continuing to scan the bookshelves as if they could tell her what she needed to know. Simon sat in the recliner and looked over at her. "Penny for them?" he asked.

"Olivia clearly loved to read—and write. But she hid her writing and now it looks like she hid her reading, as well." Charlotte pointed to several books with red heart-shaped stickers on the spine. "I bet a lot of these books were purchased after her husband died. The ones with the red hearts are from Ramona's Resale, which has only been open three or four years."

"That would fit with what I knew of Ronson," added Helene. "He was the sort that would have felt threatened by Olivia's intellectual leanings, or wouldn't want to be outshone by a wife."

Charlotte felt it was now safe to reveal something of the notebook she'd read. "Olivia was actually quite bitter toward him, judging by what little I've read of her writing. Something very warped about their relationship, I'm afraid."

"And it shows in Donovan." Helene sighed. "I wonder what it all means, though, and if it has anything to do with what happened here?"

"I would say it does," Simon asserted. "There are many cultures that believe the way we live contributes to the way we die, that nothing is entirely an accident, even if we can't immediately discern it. Personally I don't think it's karma, just cause and effect. An obvious example would be lifestyle choices affecting our life and health, but more often it's less obvious, like when the choice of work affects the route we take to the job, which in turn puts us in the path of a drunk driver."

"Oh you could take that back to childhood, when seeing something on a class trip triggers an interest that leads to choosing that line of work," said Helene. "Or still further, when one's parents chose a line of work that sent them to the town with the school that had the class trip that inspired the child's profession. We could play the chain reaction game all night."

"True," said Simon. "But this is more direct. Olivia was a collector, and some of the things she collected were valuable. This could have brought her to the attention of someone who wanted those valuable things for himself."

Helene looked worried. "Or she was a difficult woman who ended up alone in her old age, and that made her seem an easy mark."

"Or maybe both," said Charlotte, the inklings of ideas beginning to form. The process was interrupted, however, by the sound of a car with a muffler just about to go out pulling up in front. She stretched up to peer out the front window. "Guess who's here?"

Ten

Wednesday, September 18th (a long afternoon)

They watched Donovan slowly emerge from a rusty Dodge Viper and make his way up the walk. He seemed more tired than angry, and didn't seem surprised that the front door to his mother's house was open. Charlotte and Helene, however, were taut with caution as he entered with a querying "Hello?" Simon moved to stand behind Helene's chair.

"Hello, Donovan," said Helene, and she introduced Simon, who leaned forward to shake hands. Charlotte thought it looked like he was asserting his greater height and physique as a protective gesture, and suppressed a smile when she then realized that was probably Helene's intention.

"Aunt Helene, hello," said Donovan, with quick nods at her and then at Charlotte, "and Charlotte. I owe you both an apology for acting like an ass the other day. Things just kinda caught up with me."

He looked so contrite and defeated that they relaxed a little.

Helene nodded. "Apology accepted, Donovan. It must all come as a shock. It certainly did to me. First there is your mother's terrible misfortune, and now this unexpected arrangement with the estate. I had no idea she had set things up this way."

"I believe it, I really do. You know things have been difficult with Mom for years and years." Donovan shrugged. "Can't take it back now, or change anything."

"Do you know anything more about what happened, have the police said anything?" asked Charlotte.

"Not a word. It's like there's nothing happening on it at all."

"I'm so full of regrets, Donny," said Helene. "I wish that your mother felt she could have told me about what was really going on when you were growing up and that I could have helped you and her both."

"It was long ago, Aunt Helene. But everything that happened to me after I graduated from high school and went to work at the mill was my responsibility, the luck of the draw, whatever. Things weren't too bad until the mills started having trouble back in the nineties. A lot of us got laid off and didn't get back in, and the unions started losing ground. Had a fair-sized pension built up, but it evaporated, like everyone else's, so retiring after twenty-five years wasn't an option anymore. There was a bunch of us in the same boat, and we became contractors, worked on road crews, freelance mechanics, that kind of thing. But now things are even worse, and I'm in my fifties, and, to be frank, I admit I could use some financial security right now."

"You couldn't ask your mother for help?"

He shook his head. "No, that wasn't going to happen, because I never paid her back for the first time she gave me a big loan after I lost my retirement savings and my truck was repo'd. And she was really unforgiving about that. I needed a car to get to jobs, and found a deal, but it had to be cash. She helped me out, but I never got on top of things again, just one deal after another fell through, and there always seemed to be more urgent things to take care of than paying back my mom's loan. I know it makes me look bad, but it never looked like *she* was hurting for anything. If you want proof, I'm still driving that car." He tilted his head toward the Viper, which was just visible through the drapery sheers.

"What about now, though? What are you doing for work now?" Helene was gentle, but persistent. Charlotte realized she had scarcely breathed while Donovan was telling his story. It seemed like the truth to her, and he seemed genuinely contrite.

"Well, my age and the economy aren't a good mix. I just pick up work as a general laborer or mechanic. I got arthritis real bad, plus some breathing problems. Don't have a work history of anything like tending bar or sales, and I'm not that good with people, anyway. Got a friend down in Costa Rica, and thought I'd get together some cash and go there. The dollar goes a lot further, and I can get out of these winters here. I admit I've hit the wall. I was going to see if I could sell some of this stuff over at Warren Brothers or on eBay, raise a little cash. A lot of these things are antiques now. But it looks like Mom had other ideas."

Helene looked as if she had come to a decision about something. "I'd like to help you out, Donnie. I don't need the money and feel it should all be yours, anyway. That being said, I do feel obligated to honor your mother's wishes about finding her notebooks and having them published. You already know Charlotte's role in this, and I've also brought in my friend Simon, who is a photographer, to help with documenting the contents of the house for valuation as per the terms of the will. Once the notebooks are found and the expenses are at least estimated, I believe it will be possible to turn it all over to you. Or, at the very least, it will be ready for a sale and you will receive everything left after expenses."

Donovan looked a little more hopeful. "Did you have a time frame in mind for it, any idea?"

"Well, we're just getting started here today, but I think we could be out of here in a week or so."

Charlotte felt herself gulp. She hoped Helene wasn't making promises that couldn't be kept.

"That would be great, Aunt Helene. I can't begin to thank you enough for that and I'm really sorry I blew up. Is there anything I can do to help you out?"

Helene looked around the room as if assessing an answer. "Anything you could think of to help us figure out your mother's peculiar filing system for these notebooks would be very useful." She pointed at the notebook Charlotte held and explained that there were many more, evidently hidden throughout the house.

"I haven't been here much since I was a kid, and most of this is stuff Mom and Dad accumulated after that time, or even after Dad died. I put those shelves up for her maybe three or four years ago, 'cause she was buying so many books. And since I didn't even know she was writing, I have no idea where she'd keep those notebooks. You probably would have a better handle on that than I do."

"I was wondering," said Simon, pointing to the patch of newspapers over the bloodstain on the rug, "if you could give me a hand in getting this rug out of here, maybe take it to the back yard and see if it can be cleaned."

Donovan paled slightly as whatever hopefulness he had seemed to wither away. "Oh god, yeah, of course."

It took a while, but they maneuvered the rug out from under the furniture and managed to get it out of the house without mishap, which Simon declared, without thinking, a bloody miracle. Helene winced.

Donovan's cell phone rang, and he looked relieved to have an excuse to go back outside and take the call.

Charlotte, Helene, and Simon moved to the front window and watched him as he tensed during the call, leaning forward with his head down in concentration.

"I get the feeling," said Helene, "that the call is important and is not going well."

Charlotte nodded. "You know how a person automatically speaks loudly if they want the other person to speak loudly, as in a poor connection, even though that is not always how it actually works with cell phones? He looks like he's straining to hear, but he's not talking loudly."

"That's what it is." Helene sighed and looked up at Simon. "What do you think of all this?"

"He's definitely hard up. I don't think he'd hurt anybody, but I don't think I'd let him have the run of this place, either."

Then they heard Donovan raise his voice, and rub the back of his head with his free hand. As he turned, they could see his distress, and he was pleading, "It'll just take time, it's out of my hands for a little while, but I'm good for it!" The reply, whatever it was, clearly exasperated him, and Charlotte thought for a moment that he was going to throw the phone out into the street the way he threw Helene's phone at the urn with his mother's ashes. As Donovan came back toward the house, Simon and Helene quickly left the room, and Charlotte moved to the bookshelves, pretending she had not been trying to eavesdrop.

Donovan entered and grabbed his jacket and car keys. "Look, Charlotte, I'm sorry, but I gotta go deal with some stuff, and I don't know how long it'll take, might be a day, might be a couple of days."

"Everything okay?" asked Charlotte, taking note of his paleness.

"No big deal, just a pain in the neck, some guys I talked to about a job. But tell Aunt Helene I'll be back as soon as I can." With that he strode out the door, half-ran to his car, and sped off.

Charlotte was nonplussed. "I'm good for it!" sounded as if Donovan owed money, which would fit with his own admission that he was in need of "financial security," and with his anger at not being able to dispose of his mother's household effects immediately. Just how much trouble was he in, though, and with whom? She looked down at the desk, where there was a small framed picture of Donovan as a little boy in a Dracula costume. He looked about eight years old, smiling shyly instead of snarling and showing off his fangs like she'd known other boys around that age would do when they wanted to be in character. There was white makeup on his face, which emphasized the widow's peak of his hairline. It also emphasized the tired, sad look of his eyes, a look he had to this day, more haunted than haunting.

They gathered in the living room, Simon in the recliner, Helene on the sofa, and Charlotte back in the wingback chair, from where she could study the bookshelves again.

"I really don't know what to think about Donovan," said Helene. "Clearly he was counting on a full inheritance, being an only child and all. I would have been happy to have stayed out of this whole situation, but Olivia really wanted this. I think she suspected that Donovan would just go for the money and not care about the writing part of it."

"Interesting about the rift that started because he didn't pay his mother back for the loan to buy a car," said Simon. "I wonder if that transaction appears in the ledgers?"

"So what if it does?" asked Charlotte.

"It's about where Olivia got that kind of money. I'm thinking that could give us an idea of what was really valuable in this house, but of course that's just a guess."

Helene raised her hand. "I'll volunteer to track that down."

"There are two mysteries to solve here," said Charlotte. "One, of course, is what happened the other day that led to Olivia's assault—what, if anything, is missing, and why. You're right, Simon, that knowing what was worth a lot of money might give us a clue. The other mystery is where are her notebooks? All we've got to go on is the contents of the one notebook we have and the contents of this house, and perhaps the ledgers, but it looks like she stopped keeping them for the past few years. The one thing that connects the two mysteries is the fact that an altercation occurred in this room, in front of these books, and a book was knocked down on the floor. There are, however, several empty spots in the bookcase, not just one."

"Well-spotted, Charlotte," said Simon. He rose to take a closer look at the gaps where books were missing. "They are very dusty, except for two of them, which suggests they were taken out longer ago than the other day. This one," he pointed to a spot in the middle shelf, "is in the middle of books by the Beat poets and a couple of Kerouac novels, so it's likely that's where the copy of *Howl* belongs." He then pointed to a gap two shelves up. "But this one is in the middle of, let's see, Proust."

Charlotte bounced up off the chair and went to see for herself. Simon was right. There was a clean, dust-free gap between the three-volume set of *In Search of Lost Time* and another set in French. She brought over the notebook Olivia had given her and slid it in: a perfect fit.

"Well!" said Helene. "Are there any other notebooks there?"

"I don't think so, Helene. I'm not sure this will help me locate the rest of them."

"Are all the notebooks the same? You know, kind and size and such?" asked Simon.

"I have no idea," shrugged Charlotte. "I've been scanning the shelves to see if there are any more like this, but so far I haven't spotted any. I'll probably have to go over all the books one by one to make sure I'm not overlooking anything. Olivia said, though that they are all over the house"

Simon pulled the notebook back out and looked it over, then looked over the shelves.

"Simon," said Helene, very quietly. "Could I take another look at that, please?"

He handed her the notebook, and she opened the cover to read the words on the inside cover. "*Put the pieces together and bloom.* It's probably nothing, but humor me. What comes in pieces, or is made up of what we call pieces?"

"Puzzles?" suggested Simon.

Charlotte nodded, as that was what she thought of first. "Quilts, maybe?" She thought of the titles of some of Ellis' music books. "Collections of short songs?"

"Five Easy Pieces?" said Simon, "that sort of thing?"

"Very good," Helene said, as if to her students. "Now what about bloom?"

"Flowers, always flowers, I would think," said Simon.

"Flowers, but also blossoming, like coming into one's own," added Charlotte.

"There's also bloom in the sense of efflorescence, in watercolors and special effects." Simon splayed his fingers to imitate the occurrence. "A lot of technical and chemical processes describe various forms of bloom, and then of course there are biological processes like algal bloom on ponds."

Helene just looked at him patiently. "I think, Simon, that Olivia was highly unlikely to be thinking of scientific processes. My bet would be flowers." She closed the book and rose from the chair. "And let's start with puzzle pieces. I'm sure there are puzzles in the place somewhere."

"The kitchen!" Charlotte exclaimed. "There are stacks of them under the table."

They went into the kitchen, and Charlotte crouched down for a closer look at the boxes of picture puzzles.

"Now," said Helene, with a confident tone, "find one with flowers."

There were several, but one in particular was all flowers, a field of bright yellow daffodils. Charlotte pulled it out of the stack and opened it. Inside, there was another notebook laying atop the puzzle pieces. The pages were full from front to back with Olivia's handwriting."

"I am amazed!" said Simon. "Well done, Helene!"

"How did you know?" asked Charlotte, grinning from ear to ear.

Helene looked thoroughly pleased with herself. "Scavenger hunts. Each clue found led to the next. My mother used to make them up for us, based on what we were reading or learning in school. She would level the playing field a little bit by coming up with unusual or nonsense associations for things or words, because I was so much younger than Olivia and the Lamont children. Olivia has left clues, and I think she left them for herself, so she would remember where she hid the books."

Charlotte quickly scanned the tops of the pages and saw, like the first notebook, this new one also spanned many years. "It took her a long time to fill a notebook, so it would be no surprise that she was afraid she would forget where the others were."

Simon now looked confused. "What I don't understand is why she hid them in the first place."

"Oh, I do," said Charlotte. "Even if everything in these notebooks is intended as fiction, it would be very easy to think that she was writing about her own life. There are passages in the other book about a dying husband that sound like first-hand accounts—and maybe they are. She wouldn't have wanted either her husband or her son to read them."

Helene nodded in agreement. "Ronson would not have been supportive of her writing, even if it wasn't about him."

Simon snorted in disgust. "Maybe *because* writing itself wasn't about him."

As they moved back into the living room, Charlotte checked to see if there was anything on the inside cover of the new notebook. "*Where he metamorphosed*," she read aloud.

"So that's the next clue?" asked Helene. "Daffodils were on the picture puzzle box, and they are a variety of narcissus, which of course leads to mythological Narcissus."

"Makes me think of the painting by Dali, *The Metamorphosis of Narcissus,"* added Simon.

"Oh, I think I remember that one! An egg and a sort of a rock-like figure reflected in water?"

"That leaves us with more than one possibility, then," said Helene. "Was Olivia referring to the Dali painting, or to any watery surface that caused Narcissus to see himself and die because he couldn't tear himself away?"

"Well," said Charlotte, "it'll be something reflective, because that's where the change happened. I don't think there's anything with standing water in this house, but there are mirrors and other shiny things."

They looked around the house and checked the mirrors. Simon found the parts of an aquarium in what was once Donovan's room, but there was nothing in or around it that held a notebook. But after a few minutes, Charlotte heard Helene shout, "I've got it!"

Helene was in Olivia's bedroom, holding a mirror; the frame was decorated with sea shells. She held it up to show them the back, where a notebook was attached to the frame with duct tape. Simon used his pocket knife to cut the tape and Charlotte lifted the book out as carefully as she could. The clue inside the cover was, *What Alice found there.*

Helene pointed to the mirror. "Through the looking-glass?"

Charlotte smiled. "Think chess pieces—or a chess board."

They hurried to the living room to take a closer look at the round side table, with its inlaid chess board. There was a drawer with pulls on the front, but it was stuck.

"Some of those old knockoff tables had fake drawer fronts just for looks," said Helene. "Maybe it's taped underneath?"

Simon turned the table upside down, but there was nothing. "It feels a little top-heavy. I think there's something in here." Once again he got out his pocket knife, this time to try to pry off the drawer front.

"Pocket-knives and duct tape," muttered Helene. "Aren't we all clever?"

Simon glanced at her with one eyebrow raised. "We are." He stopped when the drawer front didn't budge. "It's glued in tight. Let me have a go at the top."

The chess board turned out to be a self-contained board set flush into the table top, and came loose with just a couple of tries, revealing the drawer beneath. And in there (almost too good to be true, thought

Charlotte), lay the fourth notebook.

She retrieved it, and turned to the others. "I think this just might be doable."

On the way back to Lake Parkerton, Charlotte decided to make a quick stop at The Coffee Grove. Now on its third location, at the corner of Ramble and Harvey Streets, its current incarnation was in a former old-fashioned corner hardware store across from the courthouse square. Jimmy had moved from a much narrower building in the next block down, which in turn came after his first location, a tiny walkup shop in a cluster of galleria-type spaces, which Charlotte fondly remembered enjoying on afternoons out with baby Ellis. With each move, Jimmy added more offerings, going from coffee, tea, and pastries, to those plus light lunch fare of soups and sandwiches, to the current full-on deli with imported and traditionally-made cheeses, salamis, olive oils, and other fine foods. He also sold fresh breads and simple staples for downtown residents who didn't want to drive to the big supermarkets on the edge of town.

Rumors abounded of Jimmy's mysterious past and how he kept his business growing, outlasting seven other downtown coffee shops in the course of fifteen years. Some said he was a front for a meth lab, some said he was a closet Internet billionaire. He claimed, in a newspaper article a few years ago, that he just had a good nose for what Elm Grove wanted and needed.

Like most coffee shops, it had a decent Wi-Fi connection and now that her Internet service at home was shut off, it was the only way to check emails and send one to Ellis. It was a quiet evening, with students working at several tables, and a couple of lonely-looking middle-aged people like herself. She waved to Jimmy as she set her bag down to secure a small table, then went to the counter to give her order for a cup of tea to a young barista named Kelsey, who bore a striking resemblance to Ellis' roommate Sophie in clothing and hairdo. She wondered if Ellis would end up looking like that before the year was out, but couldn't imagine her daughter's fluffy, curly hair quite that sleek.

The email inbox was sparse compared to a few weeks ago, when her account at the magazines was still active. The highlight at the moment was, as always, the new one from Ellis. She confirmed selling the piano, and reported having a crush-from-afar on one of the younger teachers. Then there was the missive from Jack, also basically giving the okay to sell Ellis' baby grand, but worded in such a way as to imply Charlotte was a worm for not being able to keep it. She shrugged it off, and wrote a quick email to Stanton to list the piano.

Sitting alone in a coffee shop just before sunset made her feel more alone than ever. Best get that email to Ellis written and get out of here, she thought, and opened a "compose" window, in which she quickly wrote an update, including the news about Olivia, the transcription and editing project, and the apartment. Charlotte paused a moment just before she finished writing, thinking that in a week's time she would be living here in Elm Grove again.

"Hello, Charlotte." Jimmy broke her reverie, and sat down in the chair across from her with his own cup of tea.

"Hi, Jimmy." She smiled at his smile, and the world seemed a little less of a deserted island.

"Surprised to see you here this time of day. Back in school or something?"

"Oh, no. My Internet's been shut off at home. I don't know if it's their fault or mine, but I'll be moving back here next week, anyway, and...."

It was a pleasant conversation, as Jimmy had a way of conversing about things that mattered, and even personal things, with a kind and understanding touch. Charlotte found herself telling him about the recent events in her own life, and her enthusiasm for regaining freedom by simplifying her life as much as possible.

Jimmy smiled. "Got a couple of minutes? I want to show you something." He waved to the barista. "Kelsey, keep an eye on Charlotte's stuff, we'll be right back." Kelsey nodded, and Charlotte followed Jimmy into his office, then through a door to stairs that led up to a loft-style apartment.

The apartment seemed to take up the entire second floor of the building. So this was where Jimmy lived, thought Charlotte. The Harvey Street side had windows similar to her future studio apartment, only they were larger and more numerous, and continued around across the west-facing Ramble Street side, which let in the last of the reddish light of the setting sun. Wall panels suspended from the ceiling beams separated the various sections into rooms. The furnishings were simple and few, and, Charlotte could see, expensive.

"Wow. It's beautiful. And peaceful."

"Thank you. My first apartment was small, a studio like the one you're moving to, and my coffee shop was small, as well—I know you'll remember it—and both places were furnished with second-hand things and castoffs that I'd fixed up. Then the next place was a little bigger and a little nicer, and so on, until now I have this. But it's still simple, still peaceful, and still within my means."

"I'm glad you showed me this. Gives me more confidence to see how it worked for someone else."

They went back downstairs to the shop. Jimmy went to help Kelsey with sandwich orders, and Charlotte added a couple lines about his apartment to the email to Ellis, and sent it. Then she checked the online version of the local paper to see if there was anything about Bosley Warren's brother. It said more or less the same thing that was on the television report, and there was no update or any indication that the police knew what happened, other than Wesley Warren drove his car into the pond. The embedded video showed the car being pulled out of the water. There was a side story about Warren Brothers' Pawn and Payday, how Bosley and Wesley started out as a hobby shop, and then expanded to include a pawn shop and related services. There was, of course, reference to Bosley Warren's jackpot rare book sale. Wesley was survived by his brother and a former wife, but no children.

As Charlotte was packing up to leave, Jimmy came back over with a paper bag that he held out to her.

"For you. A submarine sandwich. You can run it under the broiler at home, really brings out the flavors, I think." He handed her a card, as well. "And here's the guest password for my own Internet account. Even if we're closed, you can park outside and log on. Might come in handy until you get settled in."

"Oh, gee, thanks Jimmy!" Charlotte was overcome by his generosity. "I really appreciate this."

Jimmy opened his arms and Charlotte found herself embraced in a big hug. "Hang in there, girl. Everything'll turn out just fine."

Eleven

Thursday, September 19th

Charlotte pulled up to Olivia's house and took a deep breath before getting out and walking up to the front door. The last time she came here alone she had discovered Olivia on the floor, knocked unconscious. But it was time to take the situation in hand and set aside her trepidations, to focus on the task in front of her, which was to find the rest of the notebooks. The heebie-jeebies fought hard with her common sense, however; thus, when she was about to unlock the door and found it already unlocked, they were front and ready to make her seriously consider running away and screaming at the top of her lungs.

But Charlotte remained rational and calm, at least on the surface, and pushed the door open with the back of her knuckles, so as not to smudge any new fingerprints.

Her emotions flipped from frightened to intrigued in a matter of seconds, mostly due to the fragrance of Italian cooking and the sound of someone washing dishes in the kitchen while listening to classical music on a radio. Was it Donovan? She turned to look up and down the street, but didn't see his car. Helene? No, Helene had her own kitchen just down the block, that wouldn't make any sense. Simon? Same thing, just down the block. She rapped sharply on the door to get the cook's attention.

"Hello? Who's here?" she called out. She wasn't aware that anyone else was supposed to be there this morning (Helene had a club meeting, Simon was teaching at the university), so she was cautious, but what could be less nefarious than lasagna (and the distinctive scent of baked cheese and pasta sauce suggested something like lasagna)?

She could make out a moving shadow through the doorway to the kitchen on the other side of the dining room, and then suddenly a young man in a full-length apron over tee shirt and jeans appeared, wiping his hands on a dish towel. He held up his right hand in greeting and his smile shone bright even at that distance.

"Hello!" he called out. "You must be Charlotte!" He strode forward to meet her, and the closer he came the more strikingly handsome he looked, handsome in a boyish way with twinkling blue eyes and close-cropped light brown hair. By the time he was close enough to proffer his hand and say, "I'm Mitchell, a friend of Donovan's," Charlotte realized he was older than he first appeared, probably in his late thirties. He was fit and muscular, yet lithe. He was her height, almost exactly, and she found herself almost stammering as she looked directly into his eyes. Eyes, in fact, that made her feel that they liked what they saw, and she even began to blush.

"Oh! I wasn't expecting anyone to be here, but pleased to meet you," she said, shaking his hand.

"Van ran to the store for some wine, he'll be back in a minute. Want to have lunch with us? It's just lasagna, but there's plenty."

The change in the ambiance that came with the scent and activity of cooking was startling, thought Charlotte. "Well, it certainly smells like a *very good* lasagna. I don't want to intrude, however, and should probably just get on with my work."

"At least have a glass of wine when he gets here," said Mitchell. "'Van feels terrible about everything that's happened. I thought that a bit of cooking in here would get rid of that creepiness, you know?" He grinned at her as if she was part of his conspiracy.

Charlotte couldn't help but smile back. The mood in the place had certainly improved, and it would make the work less stressful. "I like it, and I think you're right. I was so nervous about coming here again."

"Wait 'til the wine gets here, it'll be even better!" A timer dinged, and he turned to go back to the kitchen. "Gotta take it out of the oven now."

Well! Thought Charlotte. This is unexpected. Nonetheless, she looked carefully around the room—after all, she only had Mitchell's word for it that he was a friend of Donovan's, and Donovan himself had great motivation for removing his mother's valuables and cashing them in. The only thing that appeared to be "missing" was the rug, and for that she was glad. The window in the middle of the bookshelves was open again, even though the day was on the cool side. The stultifying fragrance of the potpourri was almost gone, replaced by fresh air and pasta. No headaches this time.

"Coffee, Charlotte?" Mitchell called out.

"Only if you have some made," she called back, and walked toward the kitchen.

"How do you take it?"

"Black, thanks."

As she entered the kitchen she could see that the back door was open, and the porch door leading to the yard was also open, letting in more light and air. The rug, she noted, was still draped over a couple of sawhorses, and from that distance she couldn't see any evidence of the bloodstain.

Mitchell handed her a mug of coffee (that smelled better than anything she'd had for a while outside of The Coffee Grove), and looked out at the rug, as well.

"I got most of it out, but you can still tell there is a stain on the back. At least it's a red rug."

"What did you use?" she asked.

"A salt paste, mostly, then a bit of dish soap and water, and finally hydrogen peroxide in a couple small places where it was the worst. I was worried it would take the dye out, but it didn't. Now it just needs to dry real good."

"You are quite domestic!" said Charlotte. "You're a gourmet cook, and you know how to get bloodstains out of oriental rugs!"

Mitchell shrugged and chuckled. "It's nothing, really. I just like nice things, good food, and delightful women." The boyish smile returned. He was one of those men, thought Charlotte, who seemed to laugh at his own flirtatiousness, to keep things from feeling anything other than fun and in the moment. Couldn't hurt to enjoy it while it lasted.

They talked about the house and its collections, in particular the Eiffel Tower figurines on the kitchen shelves, and then heard the front door open and close and footsteps coming toward the kitchen. Mitchell looked through the doorway and spoke. "There you are, Van! Charlotte's here." He stepped back as Donovan came in with a grocery bag.

Charlotte smiled and said hello. "Your friend here makes good coffee."

Donovan smiled weakly, and handed Mitchell the bag, then stood with his hands in his jeans pockets. The mood, thought Charlotte, had suddenly become awkward. Mitchell seemed to sense it, too, and patted Donovan on the back.

"Van has understandably had a hard time dealing with all of this." Mitchell looked over to Charlotte, his eyes sad and sympathetic. "It's so hard to know what to think, what to do, to make sense of it, and not know enough about what really happened here." He rummaged in the bag and pulled out a bottle of wine. "Ah, a Chianti! Perfect. Let's have a glass right now."

Donovan seemed to collect himself. "Um, I'm not sure where the wine glasses are. Dad drank beer and Mom drank bourbon."

"No worries," said Mitchell, fishing in his jeans pocket and pulling out a Swiss Army knife with a corkscrew. "We'll just use those jelly jar glasses on the windowsill. They look clean enough." He opened the wine with practiced ease. "I've invited Charlotte to join us for lunch."

Charlotte raised her hands to protest. "Oh, thank you but I couldn't possibly impose and should really get on with the work. The coffee was wonderful."

Donovan turned, suddenly, from the windowsill where he had gathered the glasses. "Please, Charlotte, please join us. I know it's a little weird," he stammered, "but I would be grateful if you did. We can sit out on the front porch. What can it hurt?" His expression was almost pleading, and Charlotte couldn't continue to say no.

"Okay, then. Thanks."

During this exchange, Charlotte wondered about the nature of Mitchell's relationship to Donovan. Mitchell seemed to know his way around Olivia's kitchen better than Donovan did, but she sensed that Donovan wasn't any more familiar with Mitchell than he was with the kitchen. She had known people like that, though, usually males who would stand around awkwardly while the womenfolk would move quickly and efficiently to put together a big holiday dinner or lay out a potluck buffet. But she also had a strong sense that Donovan really wanted her to stay—as an ally, almost.

They grabbed plates and forks and Mitchell served big squares of lasagna, which they took out to the front porch along with the bottle of wine and the glasses. Donovan sat on the swing, Charlotte on the top step, and Mitchell lowered himself into a cross-legged position on a sunny spot on the grass. Then Donovan mumbled that the swing was too wobbly for eating, and moved to the bottom step.

Mitchell poured the wine and generated most of the conversation, friendly social chit-chat about the weather, the neighborhood, the school, the town, and life in general, nothing which referred back to crime or Olivia's death. Charlotte felt he was trying a little too hard to be sensitive, but then nothing was likely to make anyone completely forget what happened here.

"I haven't eaten outdoors like this in ages," said Charlotte, finishing her last bite. "It was delicious, and thank you."

Donovan nodded. "I think the last time I did was eating an ice cream bar when I was like, ten or something. There used to be an ice cream truck that made the rounds."

Charlotte nodded. "There still is. My daughter used to complain that it would go by too fast to catch up with."

"That's awful!" said Mitchell. "What's the point of an ice cream truck going too fast for the little kids?"

"The stuff they sell is expensive, too, especially for what you get," said Charlotte.

"Everything is, these days," murmured Donovan.

Charlotte looked up at him, and noted that he seemed lost in thought again. She tried to think of a topic of conversation that he seemed enthusiastic about.

"So, Costa Rica, huh?" she asked him.

He didn't look up but his face flushed in embarrassment. Charlotte reddened, too, feeling that she managed to step in it somehow. Mitchell, however, was ready with a reply.

"Oh, yeah, our boy wants to live amid the bananas and the señoritas, sipping Dos Equis under a shady palm." He swallowed his last bite of lasagna. "Problem is, he's gotta get some money together. It's cheap, but it's not free."

Donovan just nodded sadly, reminding Charlotte of the donkey Eyeore in Ellis' Winnie-the-Pooh videos. Then he suddenly got up. "Time to get to work and get that money together, then," he said, and went back in the house.

Charlotte looked over at Mitchell, who shrugged and rose. "Touchy subject, I guess. Let me take your plate."

Back in front of the bookshelves, Charlotte took the four notebooks out of her bag, plus a notepad of her own, to see if she could work out more of Olivia's clues without Helene's help. She could hear Donovan and Mitchell cleaning up the kitchen, and then looked up as she heard Donovan approaching. He held two more cups of coffee, one of which he handed her.

"Gotta keep a clear head, right?"

"Oh yeah. Wine and pasta for lunch are a good way for me to feel sleepy. Thanks."

He nodded at the notebooks, which she had left on the desk. "Found more of them?"

"Three more. There's a clue in each one that leads to the previous one. Helene said it reminded her of the scavenger hunt clues your grandmother made for them when they were girls."

"Could I see them?"

Charlotte didn't see the harm, so showed him the clues and explained how they worked out so far.

"Good god, that's complicated. Or at least it is to me."

"What's complicated?" Mitchell came into the room, untying his apron.

"Mom's method for hiding her notebooks. I'm only just beginning to learn what sort of person she really was. Never would have guessed." He looked up at Charlotte. "To me she was just Mom, you know, a housewife. But I'm beginning to understand why she thought college was so important, and why she was bitter that I didn't go."

"I haven't really started on the transcriptions yet, but her writing is dark and forceful in what little I've read. I know Helene promised to have us out of here in a week, but a lot depends on how quickly I can work out her clues. My education is more modest than your mother's—certainly I'm not as smart as she was—but I can look up a lot of things online, and hopefully that will make up the deficit."

Mitchell stepped forward and took a quick look at the notebooks, then spoke to Donovan, his voice quiet but firm. "This better not interfere with the date."

Donovan didn't reply, but stared at the floor. Charlotte sensed that the tension in the room had shot up. "What date?"

"Mitchell here," said Donovan, "works for Warren Brothers Estate and Auction. We talked to Aunt Helene earlier today, and she's contracted them to come in on Friday of next week to start taking everything out of here and over to their auction building. Once they start doing that, any scavenger hunt Mom laid out will probably get messed up."

Charlotte's mood fell from reasonably cheerful to dismayed. So Helene made a week's time official. How was she going to handle both the search for the notebooks, which could get complicated, and her own preparations for a sale and moving? She looked around at the room, then directly at Mitchell, "please don't move anything in the meantime, then. Olivia suggested that not all of the notebooks are on bookshelves. They could be anywhere, and as you can see, any shape, size, and anything from spiral bound to cloth bound."

"No problem, Charlotte. Don't underestimate your own intelligence—I'm sure you'll find them all in no time," Mitchell smiled while speaking in an overly soothing tone. "How many notebooks were there, again?"

Charlotte's impressions of Mitchell flipped from positive to negative when she heard the fakey compliment, but she kept her temper. "Olivia said there were nine or ten, she couldn't remember exactly. But they are all in order. Even if one gets found accidentally, I would need to know exactly where it was, because its location might be part of the clue for the next one. This can quickly get more complicated than it already is."

Mitchell seemed to realize she was no longer on his side, and he used the same quiet, firm tone with her as he did with Donovan. "Understood. But I know that date is a firm commitment, and Van really needs to do this."

Charlotte felt her blood pressure spike. The contents of the house were *Helene's!* But she was not privy to the conversation between

Mitchell, Donovan, and Helene, and she was, after all, just an employee for the estate. She would have her own conversation with Helene as soon as she could.

"Okay, then," she said, turning away from them in as much dismissal as she could muster. "Time to get on with it."

Mitchell and Donovan left shortly afterward, and Charlotte breathed a sigh of relief that they were gone, but remained thoroughly annoyed.

If it wasn't for the fact that Helene had students for most of the day, Charlotte would have walked straight to her condo and ask what was going on. It had been a long time since she was in the position of not being able to control her own work schedule. Her work with the magazines was always laid out months in advance, and there was plenty of support staff to provide research and proofreading on the rare occasions when a feature was scrapped at the last moment and needed replacing. Here she was tackling a project whose dimensions were unknown beyond the fact that there were nine or ten notebooks, and those notebooks were deliberately hidden in a house where it would be difficult even to find things that weren't hidden, there was so much clutter. And on top of it all, she had a time-sensitive personal crisis that demanded her focus and attention. It just wasn't fair!

She looked at her watch. Helene had asked Charlotte to come by for tea when she was done teaching for the day, but that was three hours from now. Charlotte closed her eyes, took a deep breath, and envisioned the stress and tension leaving her body as she exhaled. No matter what Helene's reasons were for locking in a deadline, the fact remained that the notebooks had to be found as quickly as possible. Without the distraction of Donovan and Mitchell, Charlotte could now focus on Olivia's clue in the fourth notebook: *In my new red robe at the Café de la Régence.*

As Helene explained, each clue or location was itself part of the next clue. The daffodils of the picture puzzle signified Narcissus, the mirror signified *Through the Looking Glass* (and not *Alice in Wonderland).* The chess board, therefore, signified something about the next clue, but Charlotte was drawing a blank. She cursed her lack of Internet access. It would have made things so much easier. There was the nearby public library, of course, or The Coffee Grove, which was a few blocks further.

Olivia, however, did not need the Internet to weave her clues, and Charlotte wondered how future generations were going to manage if they couldn't retain what they read on their own, or couldn't be bothered to read and study in the first place because the great search engines were the ultimate cross-list of information of every kind. They did the thinking and remembering for you, or it certainly seemed like it.

Café de la Régence suggested something French, something with food and drink—it was starting to come back to her now, the bits and pieces of her reading and education. The Café was the most famous coffeehouse in Paris for well over a hundred years. Writers, philosophers, artists, politicians, and scientists gathered at coffeehouses to discuss ideas and issues—and play billiards, cards, and chess.

Charlotte had a general recollection of famous writers and philosophers of the time, but it was a wide time span. The "new red robe" tugged at her, but she couldn't remember what it referred to, or who. But here she was, in Olivia's house, and maybe it was time to simply look for, well, a new red robe, and not sweat the details?

It took well over two hours of digging through closets and drawers in the bedroom, before she found a bright red flannel robe, the tags still attached, in a box of clothes in Olivia's closet. The box was at the bottom of a stack of other boxes and bags of clothing, and looked as if it hadn't been moved in decades. Charlotte went into a sneezing fit from the dust and the old woolen things she had moved aside. When it settled down, she lifted the robe and saw that it was folded around another notebook, a thick one this time. She carefully extracted it, returned the robe and other things to the box, the box to the closet, and the other bags and boxes on top of it.

Charlotte had a great sense of satisfaction from having found another notebook on her own, without help from Helene, Simon, or the Internet. Of course, it took quite a bit longer, and quite a bit of physical work, as well, but she found it, didn't she? Now it was time to see what the clue was for the sixth notebook: *Elle et lui.*

Ohforgodsake, she thought. Sweating the details might be unavoidable.

Charlotte could hear someone performing the Chopin Nocturne in F# minor as she went up the steps, her arms full of the six notebooks that had been found thus far. She checked her watch, and knew she wasn't early. Perhaps it was Helene herself playing? But, no, Helene was standing behind the performer, a woman in her thirties who was wearing a well-cut gray suit that said *lawyer*. Helene glanced up and acknowledged Charlotte with a slight nod, and Charlotte quietly continued to the kitchen. The music was sweet and sad, and Charlotte recalled the days of taking Ellis to her lessons, when they would sit in awe while listening to the more advanced students.

Then the pianist came to the dramatic *Molto più lento*, and her performance fell apart. Charlotte heard Helene giving suggestions and wrapping things up, then saying goodbye. She came into the kitchen and sighed.

"That was Janet Thompkins, who works in my lawyer's firm. She brought over some papers and then asked for some pointers. The firm has a public relations thing going on to show how their attorneys and staff are not just suits, but people with other accomplishments and interests. I think she would have made a fairly good performer at one time, but she went into law school and has never really practiced much since. Too bad. Or maybe not," Helene shrugged. "Maybe she's better off as a lawyer."

"It's nice that she can still play at all, then."

Helene nodded in assent. "I know, I know, I am being a snob. So, how are things going today? It looks like you've made progress," she nodded at the stack of notebooks on the table, and began to fill the electric kettle with water.

"Yes, one more, but probably more from luck than understanding the clue." She showed the clues in the fifth and sixth book to Helene, who laughed when she saw them.

"Olivia is referencing the philosopher Denis Diderot, and perhaps you haven't—"

"Oh, I remember it now!" wailed Charlotte. *"Rameau's Nephew,* right?"

"Yes! Olivia and I were steeped in French philosophers as schoolgirls, and Diderot was a favorite of us both. The Café was one of his hangouts. The robe was the subject of one of his essays, how buying one new thing made all one's other things look shabby, so you end up buying more new things to go with it and then go into debt."

"Sounds like modern life. But what about *Elle et lui?"*

"Well, we know that *Rameau's Nephew* is written as a dialogue between the narrator and another man, which in French is *moi et lui,* of course. But 'she and he,' I'm not so certain. The way these clues work, however, I would guess that it refers to another dialogue, this time between a man and a woman."

"That could be a lot of things, yet nothing in particular comes to mind for me, either. I'll see what I can find online, but I don't know when that will be. I have to stay at home tomorrow for Stanton's first day, be there to answer questions and such, and I don't have an Internet connection anymore."

Charlotte's earlier annoyance at her friend had softened. She thought of ways to word her questions about Helene's contract with Warren Brothers, buying time by getting out the tea cups, saucers, and lemon slices. Helene got the porcelain tea pot out of the cupboard and looked over her assortment of teas.

"Russian Caravan?" she said, looking over her shoulder at Charlotte with a smile that didn't quite hide the worry in her eyes.

Charlotte knew then that Helene was perfectly aware of the problems she'd created. Her stash of Russian Caravan tea was imported at great expense and seldom brought out. She didn't wait for Charlotte to reply but carefully made the pot of tea and set out, as well, a plate of small squares of pound cake and a dish of sour cherry preserves. Then she joined Charlotte at the table.

"I assume that you know by now what I've gone and done without talking with you first, and I'm so sorry."

By this point Charlotte was more curious than annoyed; Helene's fundamental nature was neither impulsive nor thoughtless. "Apology accepted, Helene, no worries. I'm sure there's a good reason for setting things up like this."

Helene shrugged as if doubtful. "I really don't know, Charlotte."

"Tell me what happened this morning, and then I'll fill you in about this afternoon."

"Donovan called last night and said he'd thought more on what I said about a sale after finding the notebooks, and wanted to come by this morning with a friend who could help us. I agreed, thinking that any help we can get to move things along would be good for everyone concerned. So he came by with this fellow, Mitchell, who was very charming and persuasive and the next thing I know I'm signing a contract. I did hesitate, but, Charlotte, there was something in Donovan's eyes, almost a pleading look, if you know what I mean?"

"You know Mitchell works for Warren Brothers, right?"

Helene nodded. "Oh, yes, that was quite evident, right on the contract form. It's for an estate auction, but they're having it at their auction barn, not at the house, because the house is so small, there's not enough parking, and there's so much stuff, so many collectibles, that they think there will be a lot of people. In the moment it seemed so much easier than bothering Stanton with it, and Mitchell had some valid points. But it was Donnie that really got to me. He's desperate, Charlotte. I just couldn't wait and I don't think I want to know what he's caught up in."

Charlotte wondered if Donovan's desperation was real—or if he was just a really good actor, a practiced con man, able to snooker Helene as well as herself. She relayed her experiences of arriving at the house and meeting Mitchell, his charm, familiarity with Olivia's kitchen, Donovan's ill at ease manner, and Mitchell suddenly turning hardline. "I had to bite my tongue when he said 'Van really needs to do this,' because the contents of the house are yours, according to the will."

"They're certainly my responsibility, but apart from anything I can do to find the notebooks and get them published, I have no desire to be involved in Olivia's spiteful ruling from the grave." Helene's expression was dark and thin-lipped as she took another sip of tea.

"Do you think Donovan is playing you?"

Helene looked up sharply. "I don't care. You know, Charlotte, I've never had children of my own, but I've worked with them most of my life, some of them from toddlers until adulthood, and have observed so many different kinds of parent-child relationships. The parents, almost without exception, set the tone, set the stage for the future. Donnie's path in life started as a reaction to Olivia as much as to Ronson. It's not my place to sit in judgment of him, whether or not he's truly in a bad way. If he's desperate, getting the money to him quickly will help. If he's not, getting the money to him quickly will get him out of my hair."

"Makes perfect sense," said Charlotte. She really couldn't blame Helene under the circumstances.

Twelve

Also Thursday, September 19th

Charlotte rubbed the back of her neck as she surveyed the contents of her basement yet again, and tried to decide what had to be tackled next. Fatigue was setting in. When she was tired, it was hard to stop her mind from replaying the various scenes that led up to this sudden change in life, from the day Ellis learned that she was accepted to the Conservatoire, to the announcement that the magazines were closing. She knew that anger, at this point, was useless. The circumstances weren't personal. Ellis did not go to Paris to abandon her. The magazines did not fold to reject her. Jack did not stop the child support to spite her (as much as it would have suited her to think this). The economy did not tank to nearly bankrupt her. It just was, like the weather. Nothing personal. So many others, like Donovan, were in worse shape.

But was he in worse shape entirely due to circumstances? Or was he a victim of some very poor choices? Charlotte knew that, at one time, the local steel mill workers earned good money with good benefits. They could buy nice homes, decent cars, take vacations, get nearly any kind of medical treatment they needed, and send their kids to college. If they started right out of high school, like Donovan, they could look forward to retirement and retirement benefits at an age young enough to start new careers if they wanted. She knew of a chiropractor who'd started training on his forty-seventh birthday, a week after he'd retired from the mill. Several of the real-estate agents and business owners in the area were once mill workers that had retired in middle age. Then things bottomed out, devastating scores of middle-aged workers and their families, and their loss of buying power impacted the entire region, long before the current recession.

Different people take different steps, though. Maybe Donovan, who was never married or had a family (as far as anyone knew), had less to worry about, or was willing to take more chances. Or perhaps he was more inclined to find an "easy" way to make money, even illegal ones? Charlotte thought of the world around the Warren Brothers pawn shop; even in a small town like Elm Grove there was usually an undercurrent of criminal activity, of drug dealing, prostitution, black markets, larceny, illegal gambling, and money-lending. Just because she hadn't seen much of it before pawning her jewelry didn't mean it didn't exist. Even out in the countryside there were plenty of meth labs amid the cornfields. There had been more than one story in the local paper about former mill workers getting nabbed for anything from shoplifting to gun running or worse.

Once again she told herself, *Snap out of it!* She didn't have the luxury of time at the moment. The best thing to do was to think about Olivia's mystery while in Elm Grove, and her own situation while in Lake Parkerton, or something like that. The stacks and collections of things that were self-evident, like toys and Christmas decorations, she could leave for Stanton to sort out. The things inside storage boxes were another matter, particularly the ones full of old papers, schoolwork, and files. It took her an hour to find them all and move them up to her office to sort and shred.

Mental fatigue, however, was making concentration on the task difficult, as she found herself explaining over the phone to Diane, who called for a friendly update.

But Diane disagreed. "Nope. I mean, sure you're really tired, and you ought to be, given all the stuff you have going on right now, and I'm sure it would drive anyone to drink, or at least wanting to crawl into bed and pull the covers over your head." She paused to get a breath, and Charlotte jumped back in.

"Well, then what is it? And what are you drinking? Buzz juice? I could really use some of your energy right now."

"Just espresso. There's a gorgeous new barista at The Coffee Grove. Too young, yeah, but I don't care. Makes the best shots, so gifted, I swear."

"Oh stop robbing the cradle already! We're talking about me. Why am I spacing out like this when there's so much I need to do here?"

"Because *you're in the middle of a murder mystery*, you idiot! I mean, face it, it's a lot more interesting than packing up your crap for a move, but you also care about Helene, and by extension you care about Olivia, or at least you have concern for your fellow human beings, and in the case of Olivia, there's the whole mystery of the notebooks and the way she lived and why. You have a huge void in your life right now, no kid in the house and no regular job to answer to, just this downsizing stuff and you know how nature abhors a vacuum."

"You have a point, there, about the vacuum. But we don't know that it's a murder, necessarily. It might just have been an argument gone wrong and an accident."

"Somebody left an old lady there to die. Smells like murder to me."

"Maybe. I guess I can't help trying to figure out what happened, what it all means and why. It *is* intriguing, hard to stop thinking about."

"Don't underestimate yourself, Charlotte. I can see the way your brain works, what makes you really good at observing and analyzing trends, would make it natural for you to try to sort out what happened to Olivia. Hold on," she paused, and Charlotte could hear background voices. "Sorry about that. Client's here, I gotta go. Hang in there."

The pep talk made Charlotte feel better, and she tackled the papers with renewed vigor, scanning things which could be saved in digital form, shredding anything too personal or which could lead to identity theft, and throwing the remainder into paper bags for recycling. She found it helped to imagine she was in an embassy about to be stormed by a military coup and she had to evacuate with only a briefcase of the most important things. In a sense, she really did have to leave, and in a hurry, and it sped up the decision-making process. Box by box, she whittled everything down with the goal of ending up with just one expandable file and a thumb drive. Whatever she couldn't do today, she could finish while the crew from Stanton Estate was setting up in the week ahead.

After an hour, her phone rang again, showing Helene on the caller I.D. She welcomed the break and went out to the kitchen as she took the call, taking the opportunity to make a fresh half pot of coffee. It wasn't good news.

"Oh, Charlotte, it's terrible," said Helene. "The police have been questioning me all over again about Olivia."

"Why? Do they know anything more than they did?"

Helene sighed. "I don't know. I don't think so. They just left a few minutes ago. They asked me another million questions about Olivia, her son, her husband's work and his side of the family. They wanted to know everything about her lifestyle, her money, her will, just everything, and I had so little information for them. I might live nearby now, but we hadn't been close in years and they look at me like I'm lying to them. Does everyone really think family members ought to know every last thing about one another, particularly if they are two old widowed sisters?"

"Are they aware of how, well, eccentric she was, that it wasn't easy to have that sort of relationship with her?"

"They seem to understand it when I tell them, but they keep coming back with questions that suggest they haven't taken it on board. I'm not used to having my statements of fact challenged like that. Very disconcerting."

"Do you think you're going to need a lawyer?"

"Oh heavens I hope not! I mean, what could I possibly be guilty of? I'm another old woman. What would I gain from such a thing? I'm comfortable."

Charlotte thought the whole thing odd, and the idea of the police making Helene feel nervous and under scrutiny was unsettling.

Just then, from the window in the breakfast nook, Charlotte could see a black sedan quietly pull into the driveway. The spotlights attached to the side mirrors meant it was an unmarked police car.

"Helene, someone is here, and I will have to call you back, okay?"

"Please do. Thank you, Charlotte." She disconnected.

Charlotte opened the front door immediately, forcing assertiveness for Helene's sake. A heavy-set man in a dark suit and tie got out of the car and hoisted up his trousers as he walked toward her, revealing his gun and holster. He nodded and smiled as he held up his identification.

"Ms. Anthony? I'm Detective Gordon Barnes with the State Police

Criminal Investigations Division, about the incident at Mrs. Targman's in Elm Grove."

Charlotte nodded in understanding and held the door open. If he could be gracious, so could she. "Please come in. I've got coffee on." She spotted a movement on the other side of the privet hedge. Ernie was snooping again. She lowered her voice. "My neighbor isn't shy about eavesdropping."

They entered the kitchen, and Charlotte silently thanked her lucky stars that it wasn't a mess. There were the things she had boxed up, of course, but the rest of it looked clean and welcoming, or at least calm and orderly, unlike her nerves at the moment. What was going on? "Pardon the boxes and such. I'm putting the house on the market and getting ready to have an estate sale."

"I saw the sign. Where are you moving to?" Barnes nodded thanks as she handed him a cup of coffee.

"Cream? Sugar?"

"Both, thanks."

"I've taken a studio apartment in Elm Grove, right above The Good Stuff."

"Downsizing." He stirred and sipped his coffee.

"That's what they call it," she laughed, somewhat nervously. She had a feeling he'd been looking into her.

"My wife's sister did that last year when she got laid off and stayed laid off. It's not easy."

"It's been eye-opening, but in some ways almost exciting. It's really making me think about why I have the things I do, why I thought I wanted them, and just how little of it is really worth it."

He smiled and nodded. "You seem to be handling it well."

"I'm tired, I'm probably trying to do too much too quickly, but, yeah," she smiled and nodded back, and realized her hand was trembling ever so slightly as she held her cup. "I'm all right with it. Drinking far too much coffee, but I'm alright with it."

Barnes nodded briefly and cleared his throat. The niceties were done. "Well, to get down to business, the incident at Mrs. Targman's is now officially a murder investigation."

Charlotte was struck cold on hearing the word "murder" from a policeman, in a way that was much more visceral than hearing it from Diane.

Barnes continued. "Do you know Wesley Warren?"

She paused. Where was this going? "I know who he is, one of the Warren Brothers, but I never knew him, no. He drove his car into a pond, right?"

Barnes nodded. "We've matched the blood on the rug and bat at Mrs. Targman's house with Mr. Warren's."

"Oh my god!" Charlotte's jaw dropped, and her mind raced with trying to make sense of this new fact. "Do you think Olivia, Mrs. Targman, killed him? How did he get in the car, then? Or was it the accident that killed him?"

"The cause of death was drowning. Toxicology came back clean. But the autopsy showed there was a severe injury in the *back* of his head, enough to render him unconscious. There was nothing at the scene to indicate it occurred during the accident, and in fact the injury seems to have occurred a fair bit of time before he drowned."

"So the head injury probably happened at Olivia's, and he drove away, lost consciousness, drove into the pond, and then drowned?"

Barnes nodded briefly. "Something along those lines is possible. It is presumed that Mr. Warren was visiting Mrs. Targman, perhaps in regards to appraising some items she may have wanted to sell, and there was an argument that led to an altercation. This presumably led someone, perhaps Mrs. Targman, to injure Mr. Warren with a baseball bat. In turn, he presumably pushed her down, causing her fall and head injury. Then, as you suggest, he left, and as his injury bled, or perhaps bled internally, he lost consciousness and drove into the pond. But this is all speculation at the moment."

"Do you really think she could have hit him that hard, or even had a chance to? She was in her nineties!"

"It does seem unlikely, yes, but we can't rule it out—it might even have simply been an unlucky blow. We also can't rule out the presence of a third party."

He paused, watching Charlotte take in the significance.

Before she could answer, Barnes began asking a "routine" series of standard information-gathering questions, along with questions about how she was connected to Olivia and Helene. Charlotte knew, from the experience of answering questions on the day she found Olivia, to keep her answers on point and brief, and she resisted the temptation to elaborate or go off on tangents. She was dying to ask questions, but bit her tongue every time one nearly blurted out. She wanted the detective to take her seriously, but she didn't know if it was because she was trying to figure out what happened herself, or if her ego was fragile because of her circumstances. She also couldn't help thinking that Donovan was now much more likely to be a suspect, or somehow involved.

Then he said the magic words: "Do you have any questions, Mrs. Anthony?"

"Oh, I have a thousand questions!" she laughed.

He smiled. “Naturally. Anyone would under the circumstances.”

“Is there any *firm* knowledge about what actually happened at Olivia’s?”

“It’s all speculation at this point. It is assumed that Mrs. Targman knew Mr. Warren, or that there is a connection between them, because there was no sign of a break-in.” He paused and fiddled with the coffee spoon.

“But what about Mrs. Targman? Do they know if she was also hit or if she fell?”

“That is still under examination; the position of her body was different than it would have been if she’d just fainted or passed out. Not impossible, mind you, just not likely.”

“Is Helene considered a suspect?”

Barnes looked at her with the most neutral expression she had ever seen on anyone. “At this time we have not ruled out anyone.”

Charlotte felt her jaw start to drop again, but she managed to talk instead. “So I’m a suspect, too? What about Donovan? I mean, he would have been expected to benefit from his mother’s death, and he was very upset to find out that the property is tied up.”

Barnes nodded as he looked at her for a few long seconds, as if sizing her up. “I know about his blowing up at his aunt. He’s got an alibi, but you’re right that he bears a closer look. We do know that he has a minor record, and some dodgy associates, but nothing serious, no violent crime history. But we’re seeing a sharp increase in crimes of desperation, as would be expected in this kind of economy, and Donovan Targman appears pretty desperate.”

“So I’m considered a suspect because I’m forced to downsize?”

Barnes remained neutral. “We are looking into the possible

motivations of everyone involved."

Charlotte barely repressed a short laugh of disbelief at this turn of things. *Snap out of it, you're not the only one hurting here!* She looked up at Barnes. "The one I'm worried about is Helene. She's just lost her sister, she's being forced to deal with Olivia's overwhelming estate and requests, and her nephew has a temper."

"Have there been any further outbursts?"

Charlotte shook her head. The idea that she and Helene were among the suspects triggered something in her brain, though, gave it a shot of adrenaline that refused to let her become a victim of circumstance. "No, but something odd did happen this morning." She recounted Mitchell's appearance on the scene, and Donovan's unease, which drew a look of intense interest from the detective, and he made some notes as she talked. "So now someone from Warren Brothers is once again in that house. Do you think they know that Wesley Warren was there, or could this be a coincidence?"

"You raise a very good question. I don't like coincidences, especially in a small town. Mitchell Bennett is known to us, but not as an employee of the Warren Brothers. In fact, he's bad news, and I urge you to exercise caution in his presence or while working in Mrs. Targman's house."

"Oh good grief. What on earth do they want with Olivia, or anything in that house?"

"Another good question. Mitchell Bennett is connected to one Toley Banks, who has his fingers in a number of underground pots. Banks is the half-brother of Bosley and Wesley Warren. We know Banks bailed them out of their failing hobby shop several years ago and set them up as a pawn shop, which could be pretty convenient for his activities, but we just haven't caught him yet."

He got up from the table, took out a business card, and handed it to her. "Thank you for the coffee. Here's my info, and don't hesitate to contact me if Mr. Targman continues with aggressive behavior, or if Mitchell Bennett or anyone else is hovering on the scene or giving you the sense that people are acting under pressure or threats. Of course, call me if you think of anything more, or if anything new comes to light."

"Of course."

As he left, he turned and asked, "By the way, what is your impression of Simon Norwich?"

Simon, too? Charlotte recalled his taking pictures of the crime scene, his need to be able to counter what he called "bad cops." Was that based on experience, and actually having committed a crime at some time in the past? She had no way of knowing. She chose to be honest. "Abrupt. Talented. Honest. Helene thinks the world of him, and he of her."

Barnes just nodded and smiled, then went on his way.

Charlotte took a deep breath. Such unsettling times, and had been for a while. She grabbed her phone and began to call back Helene, as she'd promised to do. A hammering noise from the street caught her attention and she walked out on the driveway to see what it was. Another pickup truck full of signs sat in front of the Vanetti's house two doors down, and a man was driving a stake into the front lawn. Then he attached a realtor's sign to it, along with an additional "FORECLOSURE" sign at the top. *Another one bites the dust.*

Thirteen

Friday, September 20th

Stanton Estate Liquidators arrived bright and early. Charlotte worked in her office to make herself available to the crew on this first day, as per Martin Stanton's request, but she resolved to also stay out of their way and let them earn their thirty percent. There was enough for her to do that no one else could do, she thought, such as continuing the monotonous process of going through the remaining boxes of papers. Why did she save everything? Really, why? She wasn't sure, other than a sense of "just in case."

The box she was working on at the moment included everything connected to her divorce from Jack, from the endless missives from her lawyer, between her lawyer and Jack's lawyer, and every hostile note and letter from Jack regarding the division of property and child custody arrangements. Did he have a similar box to go through before his marriage to Mrs. Jack, or before selling the house and moving to Paris? Did he destroy anything, or was it moldering in a storage unit somewhere until he returned to the States? She hadn't looked at any of this in years, and with the detachment that comes from time, she found much of it downright embarrassing. None of it was ever going to be relevant in the future, and she wouldn't want Ellis to read any of it someday.

But as glad as she was to have the chance to destroy it for Ellis' sake, she felt a little sad as page after page (and photo after damning photo) went through the shredder, because reliving those days also made her remember being ten years younger, a young mother with so much of Ellis' childhood still ahead. The past, however, could not be relived—or redone.

Martin Stanton interrupted her reverie with a knock on the door frame.

"How are you doing, Charlotte?"

She smiled and gestured at the stacks of bags and boxes. "Bored, but just fine. Trying to bring myself into the twenty-first century and scan all these old files and papers."

He nodded. "My wife and daughter have taken that on at the office. I'm getting used to it." He lifted his arm to show that he was using the tablet computer today instead of the clipboard. "They won't let me backtrack."

He explained which rooms were being worked on and in what order, and reassured her that she was free to add or remove items at any time during the process leading up to the sale, but ideally to not change her mind about major items, as those were part of the publicity he was using to draw buyers.

"Any chance you'll change your mind about the big Hannah Verhagen?" he asked.

Charlotte was about to insist that there wasn't, but she was curious. "If I did let it go, how much do you think it would bring?"

He named a figure that made her gasp.

It was, on her new budget, enough to live on for a year, even after the thirty percent. Or to buy a second-hand car if she needed to. With more than enough left over to pay for a round-trip flight to Paris. It was more than the equity she had in the house, more valuable than anything else she owned. But it was *hers*, Hannah painted it for *her*, for this house, for her emancipation—.

But these were different times. "How soon would you need to know?"

"Ideally, this afternoon. Another email blast goes out tomorrow morning, plus some last-minute snail mail and posters. It would be a huge draw." He looked at her with more sympathy than urgency. "I can understand not wanting to let go of something so wonderful, especially if she is a friend."

"I'll let you know one way or another later today, then." *I know I should be grateful that I've got the option*, she thought to herself, but the conflict between keeping something precious and getting much-needed money was in itself stressful, and she felt her stomach burning and the muscles in her shoulders tightening.

Before he left, Martin introduced her to Josh, the young man he was leaving in charge. Josh had his left arm in a sling and had managed to nestle a tablet in it, so he could tap and type on it with his right hand. "Josh, here," said Martin, with a wink, "tried to get a doctor's excuse for the day off, but modern technology found a way to keep him on the job."

After another hour and half of sorting and shredding, Charlotte took a break to stretch her legs and make some lunch. The choices were narrowing. There was a loaf of whole-grain bread she had taken out of the freezer that morning to thaw, and she managed to pry off a couple of slices and toast them. She saw a single-serving can of deviled ham in the cabinet.

It was Ellis' favorite until some girls teased her for eating "cat food." Charlotte opened it, spread it on the bread, and added Ellis' other favorite, yellow mustard.

The act of making the familiar combo brought back memories of other shared things, and brought a lump to Charlotte's throat. All this recent busyness was a distraction from the pain of missing Ellis. It was just as well. She took the sandwich and a refill of coffee back to her office, dodging the setup crew coming and going from the basement.

Normally, she would watch the news or browse the Internet while having lunch, but neither option was available. Olivia's notebook was at the top of a stack of things that Charlotte set aside to take with when she moved, and she decided to risk the dark tone and give it another go.

You call for him, and he will not come, you call for me and only part of me arrives. I go through the motions, wash your body as if I were washing the floor: wet, swab, polish dry, just another one of your soldier boys.... The pain seizes you and you blame me. They tell me that you don't mean it, this is the dementia, but it is not, it is the same thing you have always said have always done....Now they can care for you and I walk away, they will wipe my spittle from your face, thinking it is yours....

In the mirror I can see the black marks of your hand, finger stripes where you seize me and name me your pain. I no longer look like myself, I cannot move, I cannot write, I can barely bathe or eat or dress and yet there is nothing new about this except it is now made flesh....

But what was truth, and what fiction? Olivia's description of events was in a manner shared by other *nouveau roman* writers, completely subjective, repetitive, and bleak. It was not a kind of literature that Charlotte favored or even knew that much about. She thumbed through sections of the other notebooks, and each seemed to feel a little different in tone and perspective than the other. Large chunks were in French, as well, which Charlotte could translate literally, but knew that she wasn't fluent enough to translate the sensibility. Perhaps she could get Helene's help with those sections. But first she had to find the remaining four notebooks, and that meant figuring out what Olivia meant by *Elle et lui.*

Of course, without an Internet connection, any research wasn't going to happen from her office. Still feeling restless, she wandered around the house to see what was happening, half-expecting to feel somewhat violated, or at least embarrassed, by having all these strangers go through her things. Instead, it felt surreal to see something from the past going by in the hall, in someone's arms, and to see banquet tables being set up in the living room with an assortment of her possessions on display like a collection of insects. It occurred to her that this was what would be happening if she had died, and thus it was a bit like being at one's own funeral.

She stood at the middle of the second floor balcony walkway, which overlooked the living room. From here she had her favorite view of Hannah's painting, hanging above the fireplace mantel in all its multicolor glory. She had two hours left before giving Martin Stanton her decision. Never in her wildest dreams did she expect her former classmate's work to appreciate in value so much so quickly, nor that she would ever seriously consider letting it go. Hannah hadn't been in touch for a couple of years now; phone calls and emails went unanswered, and her website only said that she was "on a working tour of the world," painting where she landed, without a particular itinerary. Purchase queries were to be sent to her dealers in Chicago and Los Angeles. There was no way to let Hannah know about selling the painting until she resurfaced, whenever that would be.

Charlotte had imagined the painting in the high-ceilinged studio apartment, where it could shimmer in the light from the bank of tall windows. Martin suggested taking digital photos of things she wanted to remember but wasn't planning to keep, but she could not imagine a photo doing justice to her magnificent painting. Selling it could well mean the difference between seeing her daughter within a few weeks or not for a year. The difference between driving a safe vehicle, or none at all. The difference between being able to rebuild her writing career, or to look for a job she wasn't guaranteed to find. She wished she had more time to decide, but knew in fairness that if it was going to draw buyers and go for a higher price, she had to let Martin Stanton know this afternoon.

Josh, who had been going from room to room making notes, heard her laugh and smiled shyly as he approached her. "Everything okay?" he asked.

"Just fine, Josh. I'm okay with everything and I'm ready to move on."

He looked relieved, and scratched at his arm in the sling. "It can hit people pretty hard sometimes. Especially old people who have lived in the same house for fifty years."

Charlotte was uncertain if Josh included her among "old people," but gave him the benefit of the doubt. "I can well imagine. I guess I laughed because I actually feel *lucky* that I'm not going to be one of them, and that's worth more than all the material things in the world."

"That's awesome, Mrs. Anthony." His tablet slipped out of his sling. Charlotte caught it before it fell and helped him get it settled in his sling again.

"What happened to the arm?" she asked.

"It's a sprained wrist, actually. Playing basketball and fell. So I got put in charge of the charts today," he shrugged in resignation, and held up the stylus for the tablet with his right hand. "I'm left-handed, wouldn't you know it. But it's a lot easier than a pen."

Charlotte looked at the checklist on the tablet and understood what he meant. The check marks were clear; the notes were typed in with an on-screen touch keypad.

"So Martin wasn't kidding when he said you were trying to get the day off, hmm?" she teased him.

He laughed. "Glad I can still work, to be honest. The other guy can't even put his shirt on without help."

"What happened to him?"

"Rotator cuff. We collided. I landed on my wrist and he landed on his arm and shoulder. He's a tennis coach, and it's really going to mess him up, at least for a while. Might even need surgery."

"Well, I hope you both heal quickly," she said, and he thanked her and continued down the stairs.

Charlotte was impressed by how something like a tablet could make it possible for an injured person to work, and in her usual way her mind wandered from there to other kinds of technology that helped people perform tasks. She remembered when she went from using a typewriter to a word processor, and then to a personal computer, and had difficulty imagining how she would have done her job over the past ten years using just a typewriter, although that was the way it had been done for most of the previous century. But certain things still required extra help. The tennis player wouldn't be able to use a racquet with an untreated rotator cuff injury. She imagined other kinds of activities that would be difficult, like painting on a large canvas, or, her eye caught by the sunlight reflecting off the tools of some roofers several houses away, carpentry. Just about any kind of sport, tennis, baseball—

Baseball. You couldn't pitch a baseball with an injured shoulder—or swing a bat. Olivia's arm was injured enough to prevent her from writing for months, and even recently still prevented her from lifting—quite likely a rotator cuff injury or something similar, caused by being roughly grabbed by Ronson. It still bothered her as recently as two days before the incident at her house, when Charlotte met her and she said she needed help finding the notebooks because she couldn't lift much. At the moment, everyone assumed Olivia had hit Wesley Warren over the head with the bat. If she had an untreated injury, there was no way she could have swung that bat at all, let alone hard enough to draw blood, unless perhaps she had used her other hand.

Charlotte hurried back down to her office and checked the notebooks, and saw that the older ones had much better handwriting. Yes, Olivia was right-handed. She closed her eyes and tried to recall the scene of the crime. Was the baseball bat in Olivia's right hand or left? Olivia was mostly on her back on the floor, the bookshelves to her right. The bat, Charlotte was certain, lay between Olivia's leg and the bookshelves, meaning it was in her right hand, the one she definitely couldn't have used. That meant that someone had put it there.

Someone else had been there, the mysterious "third party" Detective Barnes suggested, someone who could have hit Wesley Warren with the bat, loaded him into the car, and pushed the car into the pond. The same person who also likely knocked down Olivia and left her for dead, who might have even intended to kill her.

Charlotte suddenly realized that if there was a third party, she and Helene were also likely in danger, unless the killer had succeeded in finding whatever it was he came for. Given Donovan's general distress and

Mitchell's hold over him, Charlotte's intuition told her that whatever "it" was, it remained elusive. Olivia's last words to Helene, "It's *my* book," only added to the sense that the threat remained. And there were the books on the floor. And Bosley Warren found a first edition of *Least Objects*, by an author connected to Olivia's days in Paris, one she quite probably knew.

Books. Everything seemed to be connected to books—notebooks, rare books, secret books, ledger books, writing books, writers. The detective said that he didn't like coincidences, especially in a small town, and Charlotte had to agree with him, at least up to a point. As a detective, he would ferret out the facts, gather the evidence, and assess whatever information would suggest motive in order to lead to apprehending a criminal. Coincidences in a narrow context, such as a small town, would lead to a smaller and likelier range of suspects.

Charlotte, however, saw things in terms of trends. If two or three designers suddenly use wicker, paisley, or turquoise green, a trend is set. Young fashionistas rediscover go-go boots from the 1960's in thrift shops, and another trend is set. Color predictions are developed and refined over decades; an economic recession meant certain colors would be more favored than others. Skirt lengths, too, although that was becoming less predictable as fashion styles became less rigid.

It was not enough, however, for a writer to spot trends—the trends had to *mean* something, to signify something about an individual or a group or society. A trend rarely consisted of a single item. If, for instance, tall riding boots were a trend, there would be an accompanying trend of jodhpurs or tucked-in pants, tweed jackets and hats, and other elements of an idealized "horsey-set" lifestyle. When a radically different trend occurred, it could create a domino effect, causing entire homes to be refurnished from lamps to rugs, entire wardrobes to be revamped. The significance of a single object to its owner could cause the acquisition of more, related objects which shared that meaning, the representation of a certain lifestyle to which the owner aspires.

Collectors were a special breed of consumer, however. Sometimes a collection reflected taste, whim, or aspiration, and had nothing to do with trends in the larger world. But quite often a collection only revealed an interest in the process of acquisition, and as a result many collectors had more than one collection. Such hunter-collectors are inspired by elements outside of themselves: articles on a famous person's collection, decorating trends, items bringing high prices at auctions, and items purportedly in limited quantity.

Olivia had countless collections. Her husband, from all accounts, only had one—baseball cards. His pursuit was much more likely heartfelt, while hers were simply something to do while going on the hunt with him. But the one collection she was passionate about, the one she tried to hide from him, and didn't fully indulge in until after his death, was her books.

Books, again. Whatever the motive, whatever the actual crime, Charlotte sensed that it had to do with books.

"Mrs. Anthony?" came a voice from the doorway, and Charlotte looked up. It was a young female Stanton crew member, who looked even younger than Ellis. She approached and placed on the desk an old lidded cardboard box, one that Charlotte had long forgotten about. "This one looks like it has photos and mementos, and I thought you'd might like to look through it first."

Charlotte thanked her and opened it when she left. It contained various things from high school and her first year or two in college, yearbooks, concert posters, a pom-pom from pep squad, programs from classical concerts in Chicago, ticket stubs to rock concerts, a few issues of the campus literary magazine in which she'd published her first poems and short stories, a book of poetry signed by the author during a campus visit —and a deck of Tarot cards. Oh, those cards! She'd gotten pretty good at reading them, and for a semester or two the girls in the dorm would come down to her room and ask her to tell them if their boyfriends were cheating or if they'd get a scholarship. She held the deck to her nose. It still smelled faintly of incense, the smell of her personal silly season.

It was a traditionally designed deck of cards, and she shuffled them, laid them out in the only arrangement she could remember, a Celtic Cross spread to help the questioner determine a course of action. The center card was the present situation, and on top of it, laid crosswise, was the challenge. Around these cards she laid the distant past, immediate past, immediate future, best outcome, and to the side were four more cards, which she vaguely recalled had something to do with factors affecting the decision, both within and without, one's hopes and fear, and the final outcome. She couldn't remember the exact meaning of the various cards, but they were a mix of coins and swords, which, she thought, was probably an accurate description of her recent life. The only one that she was sure about was the first one, the one that described the fundamental present: The Fool. The happy-go-lucky fellow was ambling along, oblivious to being on the verge of stepping off a cliff.

Ouch, she thought. That was the way she'd handled the whole summer, oblivious to danger, and coasting on faith. Charlotte put the cards back in the box. She didn't need them to tell herself what to do next, and called Martin Stanton to tell him she was selling Hannah's painting.

Fourteen

Saturday, September 21st

There were several boxes that had been moved from the basement into the garage, where the estate service had set up large folding tables. Charlotte thought she might as well take a look through them before heading to Elm Grove. It turned out to be stuff she probably would have thrown out, such as parts to appliances she no longer had, accessories she never used for the refrigerator and clothes dryer, left over craft supplies from Ellis' elementary school days, scraps from Christmas and Halloween projects, plastic Easter eggs, and the like. Nothing, really, worth keeping, but still it was better to check than to accidentally sell something that she or Ellis would have wanted to keep.

"So it's like that, huh?" came the big loud voice, startling Charlotte so much that she gasped and dropped a plastic bag of clothespins, which scattered across the concrete floor.

It was Bosley Warren, who seemed to take up half the width of the garage door opening.

"What do you want? You scared me half to death."

"What the hell are you doing, Charlotte Anthony, giving twenty percent of your haul away to that slick Stanton outfit? And why didn't you think it was worth mentioning to me? We had an agreement!" His salesman drawl was diminished by his fury.

"We didn't have an agreement. I said I wanted to think about it."

He came closer and got louder. "And I said I was going to hold the date for you and I gave you the contract."

"I never signed a contract with you and we never made an agreement."

He jabbed a finger at her, nearly touching her chest, and she backed away as he shouted, "Uppity bitches like you just think you can do what you like without common courtesy, you can break agreements and take your husbands for every dime they got, oh that's all right, huh?"

"What are you talking about? I did cancel! In person! The next day! Maybe the redhead just didn't remember to tell you! Get away from me!" She backed around the end of a table and tried to make her way to the driveway, but the big man was fast and light on his feet.

"I oughta sue your skinny ass for breach of contract!" He flipped over one of the tables in a rage, and several boxes of trivia crashed and clattered across the concrete.

"HEY!" It was Ernie, emerging from around the hedge between their driveways. He was holding a long pole with a sharp serrated pruning saw attached to the end, and he was pointing it at Bosley Warren. "What the hell are you doing? Get outta here, you sumbitch!"

Bosley turned to Charlotte and growled at her. "I'm gonna burn your ass for this, one way or another." He stormed out past Ernie, jumped into his Escalade, which was parked on the street, and peeled off.

Ernie dropped the pruning saw on the driveway and toddled over. "You okay, Charlotte? Want me to call the police?"

Charlotte was trembling from the ordeal, but shook her head. "Thanks, Ernie, but no. I'm so grateful you came by when you did, he was pretty scary."

"I still think you should tell the police, he might come back or follow you or something." He helped her put the table upright and started to help her pick up the stuff scattered on the floor.

"I'm going to call someone, don't worry."

And a few minutes later, alone, she did call Detective Barnes, who arrived quietly and quickly.

Charlotte felt relief the minute he pulled up the drive, and the story just spilled out of her in a burst of nerves.

Barnes was unflappable. "Even if you did break the contract, he was out of line to threaten you like that."

She showed him the contract form Warren had given her. "I don't know where he got the idea that we had an actual agreement. In fact, he got a phone call just before he handed it to me and left in a hurry. And I did tell the woman at the counter, I think Ilona was her name, that I wouldn't need the date saved." She continued by telling him about her visit to the pawn shop.

"Ilona," he nodded. "That's the redhead. Used to be his girlfriend or something. I'm thinking about his hostility, wondering if he knows about your connection to Olivia, and by extension the reason for his brother's presence in her house."

"The thought had occurred to me, too, which is why I called you instead of the sheriff's department."

"Does he know you're moving to Elm Grove?"

"No. I certainly haven't told him. I don't think anyone that knows would have told him, either."

"Don't take it for granted, though. People talk, things get said in conversations that aren't intended to harm. People always know more than they say, although it might not sound like it sometimes." He shook his head as if remembering many examples of this. "If possible, be extra vigilant. I'll make sure Warren is put on notice about this, and will also inform the Sheriff's department and the Elm Grove police. It could just be he is acting out because of grief, and it has nothing to do with you. His brother was also his business partner, and as I understand it, the smarter one of the two, so maybe he's finding out he's in over his head. Could be any number of things."

"Oh, great. The minute I have to downsize, I get mixed up in things I never thought about or even knew about. I pawned my jewelry and silverware at his shop and I want to get it back when I get the money from my sale. Oh, I am so dumb, dumb, dumb," Charlotte groaned and rested her forehead on her palm.

Barnes patted her on the back. "You didn't do anything wrong, Charlotte. Lots of people are going to cross paths that never normally would in this economy. If it isn't this, it would be break-ins, muggings, or something or other."

"I can't wait for this sale to be over with and just hole up in my little apartment."

"When are you moving?"

"I'm cleaning and painting it tomorrow, so I wouldn't be able to move in until Monday at the earliest." She went on to explain her arrangement with Larry, which wasn't necessary for Barnes to know, but she couldn't stop herself from babbling. Fortunately, he didn't seem to mind, and when she looked up at him his expression was a little less neutral and a little more sympathetic than it was the last time she saw him.

She finally started to calm down. "Want some coffee? If you have some time, I, um, I've done some thinking about the murder."

"Have you, now?" he said, his eyebrows lifted in interest. "Coffee sounds good. *You* might want to be careful with the caffeine, though." He pointed at her hand, which was trembling again.

"Good point. Coffee for you, herb tea for me." She poured Barnes a coffee and prepared the tea while explaining her thoughts about the baseball bat being planted in Olivia's hand, and showed him the passage in the notebook that recounted the cause of her injury.

"I remembered what you said, that there could possibly be a third party," continued Charlotte, "and I'm thinking you're right. It's the only way to explain that bat, and Wesley Warren's injury. Olivia couldn't have done it."

Barnes studied the notebook for a few moments more, closed it, and jabbed it with his finger. "This is good. But I will have to take it for evidence."

"Oh, dear. I really need it for the transcription project, and I haven't even read it all the way through yet."

"Let's get a copy made, one you can work from, and I'll make sure this one stays safe. When the case is closed, you can have the original back."

"It's not actually mine, you know, it's Helene's. Part of the terms of Olivia's will, Helene got all the contents. I'm just an employee."

Barnes nodded. "Of course. I'll talk it over with her, then." He paused, and stared out the window of the breakfast nook, as if determining how everything fit together. "Keep these thoughts to yourself for the time being. As I said before, everyone is a possible suspect until we can eliminate them, no matter how unlikely, even yourself and Mrs.

Dalmier. More importantly, the two of you might be in danger, as you've already come to realize. We are dealing with a violent person, even if the deaths of Mrs. Targman and Mr. Warren were unintended. We are definitely dealing with a desperate person, and we don't know if they have found what they're looking for."

"Is Simon a suspect, too?" she asked. "I mean, he's an employee like me, and Helene trusts him so much, he's almost as much a part of this as I am."

"Simon Norwich has been eliminated as a suspect. He was in a plane on his way back from Japan."

The news pleased her more than she'd expected. It must have shown on her face, because Barnes smiled with amusement, and Charlotte blushed like a teenager.

"I'd still be careful about sharing any of this with him or with Mrs. Dalmier, because they might inadvertently let something slip to someone who really does have something to do with all this."

"Well, I don't think any of us are going to say a word to Bosley Warren, Mitchell, or even Donovan at this point. Those are the most likely ones in my reckoning, even if I'm not sure why."

"Do you have any feelings about the motive, one way or another?"

The question surprised Charlotte. "Well, I suppose I do. I'm *sensing* it has to do with books, since that seems to be the one common element among all the players, including myself. Books and writers. And I'm convinced that it's what Olivia held in greatest value, more than anything else in her house."

"Another rare book, like the one Bosley Warren found?" Barnes' smart phone had been vibrating, and he began to get up from the table after checking it, making preparations to leave.

"Seems to be," said Charlotte, "but I find it difficult to believe that that kind of lightning would strike twice in the same small town."

"Then we might have to look a little deeper into the provenance of that book. But remember," he held up a finger in warning, "keep your own counsel, be discreet, and don't work at Mrs. Targman's house alone."

Later that morning, Charlotte sat alone at a window table at The Coffee Grove, reading the latest email from Ellis, writing one back to her, and searching for any updates on Hannah Verhagen's whereabouts (but she found none). The shop was busy, and most of the tables and armchairs were full with friends meeting up and couples having brunch, plus the usual students, business people, and local attorneys. She knew she really ought to be back at Lake Parkerton and finish sorting through her things, but she couldn't face being alone there after the confrontation with Bosley Warren and Detective Barnes' confirmation that she might be in some danger from whoever killed Olivia and Wesley Warren.

She called Helene, inviting her to come down, and told her to bring Simon, as well. The Englishman was growing on her, and his being the one person cleared of suspicion gave him a stability that was much to be desired in her currently unsettled circumstances. She thought, too, of Diane, who had been another source of support and encouragement, and called her as well.

"Hell, yeah!" Diane cheered over the phone. "Any excuse to get out of the office on a Saturday morning! I'm on my way!"

And in fact Diane actually arrived first, tossing her tote bag and jacket on the chair opposite Charlotte's, and waving and calling out to Jimmy to make her "the usual."

"So!" Diane said breathlessly, "Do. Tell. How is everything going?

Did Stanton's start yet? How's Helene?"

"Everything's fine. So glad you could make it. Helene is on her way over, too."

"Ooh, good! I'd love to see her, it's been ages. When are you moving? We could be doing this every day!"

Charlotte laughed. She really needed to be around friendly energy like Diane's. She described the Stanton crew and her own efforts to go through everything and make decisions. They both spotted Simon's motorcycle pulling into a parking space across the street. He wasn't wearing his helmet, but the woman riding with her arms around him was.

"Who's the chick?" said Diane, and they watched as the rider dismounted slowly and carefully, then removed the helmet. Helene!

Diane burst out laughing. "I swear she is the coolest!"

Simon and Helene soon joined them. He was clearly enjoying himself, and Helene looked both exhilarated and like a cat who swallowed a canary. They placed their orders and Jimmy came over to pull two small tables together to make one larger one. He joined them when he brought a tray of coffees and pastries, and Charlotte took it all in, the pleasure of a gathering of good-natured friends over good coffee. It dawned on her that she hadn't really done anything like this with a group since the economy took a nosedive and her Lake Parkerton neighbors turned in on themselves.

"Lola!" cried Diane, waving as the real estate agent entered the shop. Today Lola was wearing a turquoise suit of the same cut as her pink one, with black spike heels and a lacy black camisole. Charlotte couldn't be sure if the lipstick and nail polish were the same color as before, but they were certainly as shiny.

Lola gave Diane an air kiss and a quick hug, and the same to Jimmy, who went to get her a chair and a coffee. She then came around and gave Charlotte a hug, as well, and flashed her billboard smile when introduced to Helene and Simon. Charlotte caught herself watching Simon's reaction to Lola, and was disappointed when he flashed her a big smile right back. Oh well. Men.

Lola herself brought the conversation around to Wesley Warren, reporting on local chatter. Of the two brothers, Bosley was considered the more likely to have a car crash, given his liking for drink and his impulsive nature. Wesley was the quiet and cautious one. Charlotte knew not to contribute anything to the conversation, in light of Barnes' warning, but decided it wouldn't hurt to ask questions. She directed one at both Diane and Lola, who were sitting next to each other, and with a glance included Jimmy, as well.

"Do any of you know somebody named Mitchell, I think his last name is Bennett?"

Diane shook her head, Jimmy just looked down at his coffee, and Lola went quiet and pale.

"Oh, yeah," she said with a sigh. "I would just as soon not know him."

Jimmy looked over his shoulder, checking out the rest of the people in the shop, before asking Charlotte, "How in the world do you know him?"

"I just met him once. He's a friend of a friend. Gave me a bad feeling, and I guess it is warranted."

Lola nodded, then leaned forward, talking quietly, and the others leaned forward to hear her.

"Several years ago, I was married to a drunk, and needed money to get divorced and support my little girl and get some kind of career training. Had it all planned out, but life doesn't tend to work according to plans. To make a long story short, I ended up owing money to Toley Banks."

Simon and Helene looked confused, and Jimmy muttered, "Local loan shark." They then understood. Charlotte kept her expression neutral, and nodded as if the information was new to her, as well.

Lola continued. "Mitchell is, essentially, Banks' collector. Looks so sweet, y'know? And so charming. That's what gets you."

Helene, Simon, and Charlotte glanced at one another in mutual understanding: if Donovan was associating with Mitchell, he was mixed up with Toley Banks.

"Anyway," continued Lola, "it took a while, but I finally got squared up with them. In theory, anyway. Part of getting squared up with people like that is they always seem to want another favor, as part of their so-called 'interest.'"

"Is that why you pushed Warren Brothers' estate services?" asked Charlotte.

Lola had the grace to cringe. "Yeah. They're into Banks, too, even though they're relation. I heard you're going with Stanton's, though."

Charlotte nodded. "It's a better fit. Sorry about that."

Lola shrugged. "It's okay, Charlotte. You're better off."

Jimmy had finished his coffee and was pensively tapping the empty cup on the table. "There have always been slimeballs who take advantage of people when they're vulnerable, and not many other options for vulnerable people to go when they need help. But right now there's a lot of people needing help, and it's just going to make loan sharks richer."

Diane had her own opinion about the "legal loan sharks," banks and mortgage companies that convinced people they could afford more house than they really could, and the conversation gradually rippled out to the difficult economy, and the things many people had to do to cope without good-paying jobs. Helene and Jimmy had stories of charities, both local and international, Simon had tales from England and other countries, and from there the topics spread to more mundane and personal concerns.

Helene was going to have her hair done, as she was attending a fundraising gala in Chicago on Sunday, staying overnight with a friend; Diane was going to a weekend rally for MG owners; Lola was excited about having one showing after another, and two houses with sales pending, but she had to stay on top of the buyers' various demands that the sellers were balking at; Simon had a field trip for his students in the afternoon, and had "another godforsaken faculty party" on Sunday evening; Jimmy had an out of town visitor coming in, a cousin he hadn't seen in years.

Charlotte had thought about Diane's encouragement the other day, to reach out to friends for help, especially when she was ready to move, but as she listened, she realized that each one's life was so full, whether as teachers, artists, businesspeople, family members, and members of the community. They weren't spring chickens, either. She couldn't bring herself to ask more of them than this fellowship. Her original instinct to whittle down her possessions to only what she could personally manage, what she could move on her own steam, in her own vehicle, was the right one.

Fifteen

Sunday, September 22nd

The entry door was tall and narrow, deeply carved, painted shiny black, and squeezed between The Good Stuff and Cindy's Nail Salon. The hardware was real brass and original to the late 19th-century building, including the number 222. Charlotte's hands shook a little as she fumbled with the still-unfamiliar lock and deadbolt; the door squeaked softly as it opened into the tiny foyer. She reached for the pull chain to turn on the light.

The foyer was little more than a hallway which ran from the front door to the back of the stairwell, where there was another paneled door, half in shadows. Larry said it connected to the store office but was kept locked. Charlotte noted that there would be enough space under the stairs for storing Ellis' boxes, and maybe even a bike.

The fresh air streaming in from the front door cleared out some of the stale air in the foyer, and in her head, as well. It was just after six o'clock in the morning, in addition to being a Sunday, and she was able to park immediately outside of the apartment door. She wanted to be able to clean the place and rip out the old carpet without getting in anyone's way

—or without anyone getting in her way, either. The dumpsters were at the back of the building, clear around the corner and halfway down the block through an alley. Charlotte planned to load up bags of trash into the Jeep, then drive the Jeep around to the dumpsters, rather than dragging them bag by bag on foot.

As she reached the top of the stairs (and once again the light coming in from the wall of windows gave her spirits a lift), she saw that Larry was as good as his word, and had provided a step ladder, paint, spackle, brushes, rollers, an extension pole, dropcloths, and various cleaning supplies. She brought a few cleaners and scrubbers of her own, plus rubber gloves, her own broom and dustpan, and a small bag of tools. Charlotte hadn't always had a cleaning lady and a handyman service, and as she looked from the supplies to the mess surrounding them, she realized that those lucky days were likely over for good. There was a cheap full-length mirror attached to the outside of the bathroom door, and as she approached it, she saw herself as she was now: bandana tied like a kerchief around the top of her head, a washed-out oversized chambray shirt with the sleeves rolled up to the elbows, and beat-up jeans and sneakers. *The spitting image of a woman paying the piper*, she thought. She pulled on the rubber gloves and went to work, first scrubbing the bathroom from the ceiling down to the floor, making it feel clean enough to use. She did the same with the efficiency kitchen and the little refrigerator, and then put in the peanut butter sandwich and bottle of orange juice that she'd brought from home. So far, so good.

The walls were a mess, of course, as she knew from seeing them the first time, but she patiently removed all the posters, tape, and thumbtacks, and patched dents and holes with spackle. Next came the carpet, which she ripped into strips with a retractable knife and rolled up into manageable bundles. It was dusty, sneezing work, and she hoped there wasn't cocaine or something mixed in with the dirt and fibers. Just in case, she moved the bandana from her hair to around her nose and mouth, and opened the windows. It was chilly, but at least it was fresh. Larry was right about how heavy the sofa was, but she managed to push it out of the way; there were probably metal slides on the bottom of the bun feet. The big library table was, thankfully, on casters.

Rip, roll, bag, dump, sweep, pull, patch, sand, wash, scrub, paint. It took hours, and she was thankful that the whole place was just a little over four hundred square feet: one long hard day would be enough to fix it up.

Charlotte finally took a break just before noon, and sat on the sofa with her juice and sandwich. The sofa was extremely comfortable, but she supposed that anything softer than a bed of nails would feel comfortable at the moment. Her aching arms were covered with tiny white dots after rolling paint on the ceiling and the first coat on the walls. No doubt her face looked the same, but she wasn't going to check. The white paint was a bright, slightly warm white, which she liked but she didn't think there was going to be enough of it to do the entire apartment. Larry had also provided a half-filled five-gallon bucket of an interesting soft warm color midway between beige and grey. It would have to do.

The second coat of paint was next, and then she could clean up the floor, which was spattered here and there with several generations of paint, a century of varnish, and decades of stains and dents. *Gives it character,* she thought. She had a room-size rug to cover it up, a knockoff of a kilim that wouldn't bring much money at the sale. It would be worth more to her here. The big table and the tufted, studded, roll-arm sofa were more gentleman's club than she would have preferred, but they were solid pieces, and she appreciated the quality. If needed, she could even sleep on the sofa until she could afford a bed.

She could hear activity in the shop below, as it was nearly time for it to open. Elm Grove was a town where more shops and restaurants were open on Sunday afternoons than on Mondays. She could smell the different cuisines from either side of the block: pizza, Chinese, grilled steak, barbecue, tacos. It made her mouth water, but none of it was affordable at the moment. She couldn't help but note the irony of having money to eat out when living at Lake Parkerton, but it was so far from everything that it wasn't convenient. Here it was convenient, but she had no money, at least for a while.

Would it ever feel like home? Charlotte wondered. After all, what constitutes home? Is it one's stuff, or who's there? The house in Lake Parkerton hardly felt like home anymore without Ellis. Yet it couldn't be about who else lives there, because people who live alone still have a sense of someplace being home; it was more than just a place to hang one's hat and sleep. But living in, say, a hotel room, where everything was already set up and in place, nothing personal, that wouldn't be home, would it? Some people seemed to live that way, but Charlotte couldn't imagine it. A home is made to some extent by what we choose to put in it, the way we make our mark on it, the way we compose it.

The west wall was where she had planned to hang Hannah's big still life, the one thing that would help make the new place feel like home. There lay the conundrum: the beloved painting currently hung in a house that had been home, but no longer felt like home, but she had planned to hang it in this place that was not yet home in order to make it feel more like home. But now that option was out.

Time would make it home, she supposed. Time, and the actual living in the space. Spaces could tell you what they wanted, she always believed, much like Hannah used to say that the canvas always told her what it wanted. So what did this space have to say? She opened her mind to it, only to get the sense that she was being watched.

She turned quickly to look over her shoulder at the stairwell, but there was nothing there, except perhaps a hint of movement that could just as well have been the shadow of a bird flying past the windows. Fatigue was surely having its way with her, making her see things that weren't there, and dust and cleanser fumes probably didn't help. *Snap out of it!* She took a deep breath and got up off the sofa, stretching her back and legs. The sooner the apartment was cleaned up, the sooner she could move in, and know for certain which things she absolutely needed from home, what would fit and what wouldn't. And she would feel safer here where Bosley Warren wasn't likely to find her, either.

This line of thinking gave her enough renewed energy to finish painting the walls, and it went quickly, as second coats often do. As the clean soft grey covered the last streaky bits of the first coat over the black and purple walls, Charlotte couldn't help but feel as if she was erasing the old in her life, as well. Back and forth, up and down, purer and purer, until at last the job was finished, and the dropcloths could be gathered up and the brushes washed.

By this time the sun was far enough in the west to play up the streaks and grime in the tall north windows. Charlotte knew she should stop working and clean them another day, but she *couldn't*—simply couldn't let it be. She scraped and cleaned the glass panes from top to bottom, one after the other, like an assembly line, like a machine, then cleaned the Venetian blinds slat by patient slat. This place *had* to be ready for tomorrow! She desperately wanted this for herself, a clean, bright space ready to move into, ready for creating her new life, whatever it would be.

This was the set for the next act in her life, she was not going to give up, she was going to pull herself up and carry on, onward, upward, and never give up, unsinkable—

And then, just before it got dark, it was done: clean and fresh from ceiling to floor, inside the closet and cabinets, every surface from the toilet and tub to the kitchen sink and stove. The big table was scrubbed and polished, the sofa gleamed from cleaning and an application of leather creme. Tomorrow night she would be sleeping here, eating here, perhaps even writing here. She cleaned her face and arms as best she could with dish soap and paper towels, then locked up the place and walked down to The Coffee Grove to use the Internet before driving home.

Jimmy wasn't there; she remembered that he said something about a cousin from out of town. The shop was quiet with only a few students, and even the music on the speakers was low. It would be closing soon, so Charlotte settled in with a cup of tea and wrote to Ellis and checked for messages. Nothing much. Social media: someone she followed had recently gone more in the direction of positive thinking and daily affirmations. Today's bit was about needing to believe in spite of all evidence to the contrary.

The barista was making closing-up noises, and Charlotte packed up her computer and left, feeling conspicuous in her grubby, paint-stained clothes, even next to the students. The sky was dark now, the waxing moon in and out of clouds, the air chilly and a bit damp. She had just enough energy left to drive back to Lake Parkerton and zap the last convenience dinner in the freezer. As she unlocked the Jeep, she looked up at the windows of the apartment, and once again had the sense of being watched, of a suggestion of movement. Great. The place was haunted, just what she needed. She shook her head at her own silliness.

The Jeep cranked, but wouldn't start up. She tried again. No go. Again. Still no go.

Several hundred dollars on a repair job not even a week ago, and it was in worse shape than ever?

She tried one more time, to no avail, and pounded and pounded the steering wheel, cursing the Jeep, the repair shop, the economy, her luck, everything, and broke down in tears. It was too much.

She shivered. Her stomach growled. It was going to be too cold to sleep in the Jeep, too cold to sleep in the apartment. Helene was still in Chicago, and Diane was out of town. Lola was working day and night, and even if she wasn't, Charlotte was bothered by the fact that Lola had foisted Bosley Warren on her. Simon had a faculty gathering, Jimmy a house guest.

Then she thought of Olivia's house. She had the key. Nobody was there, and she could at least sleep on the sofa. Barnes warned her about working there alone, but nobody would know she was even there, right?

Charlotte wiped the tears off her face, then crossed the street and started walking to Olivia's. She would check to make sure Donovan—or Mitchell—wasn't around, then get inside and find a blanket. If she could just get some sleep, maybe somebody could give her a ride back to Lake Parkerton tomorrow, or at least figure out what to do about the damned Jeep. She walked with her head down and her arms crossed, trying to stay warm, but feeling defeated, as well. Tomorrow was supposed to be moving day, and if the Jeep was out of commission again, she didn't know how it could come about, or even when it could come about at all, at least until after the sale, which wouldn't be until the following week.

She was so lost in her own gloom that she actually walked right into Simon and scared herself half to death.

"Hey, Charlotte, it's me," he said, and reached out to hold her flailing arms. "What happened?"

Her nerves were shot, but she managed to collect herself and tell him what happened with the Jeep, and her intent to stay at Olivia's house for the night.

She looked up at him. "But what are you doing here? I thought you had a faculty thing or something."

He pointed to the camera slung from his shoulder. "Night shots. Stayed at the party as long as I could stand it, then decided to do something better with my time. There's always something interesting in the light and shadows." He pulled the camera up and aimed it at her. "Like you, for inst—"

"No!" she hissed, putting her hands up to hide her face, and she started stomping off. What an ass, she thought.

"Hey, I'm sorry, I was just teasing. I wouldn't actually take a picture of a girl when she's down." He caught up and kept walking with her.

"I just wanna get inside and get some sleep. I've been working since six this morning, and I'm so pissed off about my truck not running again, and I really can't spare the money to fix it, and without it I can't move, and I've just had it, you know?"

"Charlotte, I had no idea. Many apologies."

He truly looked contrite, and she nodded in acceptance. By this time they were approaching Olivia's house, and Simon suddenly stopped her. He spoke quietly. "Somebody's in there."

She, too, could see a soft light in one of the windows, and the shadows cast by movement. Donovan's car was parked out front, and another one was in the driveway.

"He's not supposed to be there," she whispered.

"Let's get closer, behind the hedge," said Simon, and they moved quietly in the shadows to a hidden vantage point.

He worked the lens of his camera. "Wish I had my longest lens, but this is better than nothing."

"Can you see anything?" Charlotte shivered. It was damp close to the ground like this.

"It's Donovan, and I think two other guys, one big and the other shorter, maybe that Mitchell fellow."

"The big guy—could it be Bosley Warren?"

"Possibly." He noticed her shivering. "I wish I'd bothered with a jacket, too, you're getting chilled." He put his arm around her shoulder, and they sat there for a while, watching the house.

Charlotte took in his warmth, the texture of his sweater, the scent of the soap or shampoo he used, the scent of the damp earth, the clear air with leaves just beginning to turn, the dark sky lit by a waxing moon, the crickets and other night insects, the occasional car going by, and gradually, very gradually, relaxed. The movements behind the curtained windows at Olivia's house were just a blur.

"Charlotte?" whispered Simon, giving her a little shake, but not removing his arm from around her shoulders.

"Hm?" She smiled up at him.

"You poor girl. You're so tired you're falling asleep. C'mon." He helped her up, slung her bag over his shoulder, and they began walking toward the condos at the end of the block. "You're not going to be able to stay at Olivia's with all that going on. I've got a sofa."

Charlotte's legs and feet were aching, but she carried on, or rather she was half-carried along by Simon. She started to protest, feeling self-conscious and grubby, but he was having none of it.

"If I didn't offer you a place to crash, just imagine what Helene would do to me." He unlocked the door.

Even tired as she was, the idea made her chuckle. "I suppose you've got a point." She followed him up the stairs.

Charlotte wasn't sure what to expect in Simon's condo. Would it be a man cave, all TV and sound systems, with beer cans and smelly socks laying amid pizza boxes? Or would it be an artist's abode, with cameras, prints, lights, shelves of lenses and cases?

It was neither. It was nice, actually, she thought, if a bit conservative, then remembered it was a furnished unit provided by the university for visiting faculty, with standard furniture groupings, neutral colors and fabrics, carpeting, drapes, etc. The only difference was the artwork, which was not the usual safe framed prints selected by committee, but an assortment of paintings, photos, carvings, and digital prints, some of which were familiar.

Simon noticed her studying a Tibetan mask. "Yes, it's Helene's. She let me borrow a few things she wasn't using. I put the university's visual muzak in a closet." He gestured across the living room. "Welcome to my abode."

"It's nice. But I'm afraid to sit down. Look at me." She pulled at her grubby shirttail.

"How about a nice hot shower? I've got a track suit you can borrow, it'll be a little big, but still—." He disappeared into the bedroom.

"I'd be so grateful." She really was, and felt tears welling up. Fatigue was giving her the emotions of a teenager. She tried to tell herself to snap out of it, of course, but instead she accepted the stack of towels, track suit, and a pair of thick socks that he held out to her and pressed them to her face. "I'm glad you found me. I don't know what I would have done if I'd gone to Olivia's and then found out I couldn't even go in there."

"I'm glad you weren't already there by yourself when they showed up. Go. Shower." He nudged her in the direction of the bathroom. "Shampoo and all that is in there."

The whole thing felt a little surreal, stripping out of her clothes in an unfamiliar bathroom, being rescued by Simon, being back in Elm Grove after a decade of living in Lake Parkerton, doing more physical work in the past week than she had since she was in her 30's. The hot water helped to ground her. Simon's shampoo, with its hint of cedar, helped to clear some of the smell of paint that tended to linger in one's sinuses.

By the time she scrubbed clean and came back out, Simon had made sandwiches for them both and was heating up a cup of tomato soup in the microwave for her.

She sat on a stool at the breakfast bar, and waited for him to finish prepping, but he gestured encouragement.

"Go ahead and eat. You must be starving. Soup's almost hot. Hope you like tomato."

"I do," she nodded, and took a big bite out of the sandwich. Stacks of salami, ham, and cheese on a hoagie roll, chewy and heavenly. She didn't worry about looking like a pig. The man was seeing her at her worst, and any likelihood of appearing attractive was long since gone. "So good," she mumbled with her teeth closed, in the middle of chewing.

Simon grinned. He didn't grin very often, thought Charlotte, but when he did she could see something of what he must have looked like as a kid.

He put the mug of soup and a spoon in front of her. "Pepper?" he asked, holding a grinder over the mug.

She nodded. "Lots." Took another big bite of sandwich. As the minutes ticked by, she started to feel more human. They ate companionably. He dripped mustard on his sleeve, she helped him daub it off. He asked about the problem with the Jeep, and she described it the best she could. She wondered about Donovan at Olivia's house, and who else was there with him, but was too tired to pursue it.

By the time she'd finished the sandwich and soup, she was getting sleepy again. She felt her hair. A mess, but it was dry.

"If you have a blanket, I think I'd like to crash on the sofa now."

When she woke up, however, she was in Simon's bed, and the clock said it was mid-morning.

Sixteen

Monday, September 23rd

Charlotte groaned as she tried to remember the events of the evening before. She was still in the track suit; the only clothing removed was the socks, which were at the side of the bed, and she bent down to put them back on. She didn't think anything erotic occurred, but it was good to confirm it. A look in the mirror above the dresser confirmed it further: she looked like a train wreck, hair sticking out in every direction, dark circles under her eyes. Every muscle and joint was throbbing in pain from the work and getting chilled. Then she sneezed, and realized her throat was scratchy, as well. She longed to get at her own bathroom cabinet, with its collection of remedies and palliatives. Another sign of being middle-aged.

She padded out to the kitchen and saw that Simon had left her a note and coffee in the coffeemaker. She poured a cup and sat at the counter to read the note:

Good Morning! Had an early class and appointments. Helene is back and expecting you for breakfast. Told her what happened. Hope you're feeling better. S. PS—I've got an idea about the Jeep, and took the keys. Hope you don't mind.

Now she remembered. He had insisted she take the bed because he was leaving early, and she was too tired to protest. He had slept on the sofa, and she saw the blanket folded up on the seat cushion. What a nice guy he turned out to be. She kept thinking about his arm around her while they were watching Olivia's house, and the day she met him, when he caught her as she started to feel faint. A hot shower and a sandwich. Clean clothes to sleep in. His long legs and black jeans, the shaggy hair, the eyes that looked right into her, and yet—

—the attraction, as far as she could tell, was strictly one way. The current episode wasn't going to help things, either.

Charlotte sighed, turned off the coffee pot, and after the usual bathroom activities, plus a dab of Simon's toothpaste on her finger to clean her teeth, and twisting the bandana to make a tieback for her hair, she gathered up her things and made her way around to the next condo over. The sun was shining, and it was going to be a perfect day to move, except she wasn't going to be able to move. Damn. She hoped Simon would be able to figure out what the problem was with the Jeep.

Helene let her in, and looked like she was trying not to laugh in spite of making sympathetic noises and remarks.

"You poor dear! You've had a rough time of it, haven't you?"

Charlotte resisted the temptation to protest too much, lest Helene think something more went on than actually did. "Simon's note said you were expecting me. Thanks so much." She could smell something baking, and realized she was hungry again as she followed Helene to the kitchen.

"Oh, I only wish I was here last night! Just got back an hour ago, threw a little something in the oven."

There was more coffee, and Charlotte curled up on the cushioned chair, allowing herself to be pampered. Helene removed ramekins of baked Eggs Florentine from the oven, and put in thick slices of French bread to toast. Charlotte gradually became aware that Helene kept looking at her with what appeared to be an increasing level of concern.

"Something wrong?" she asked.

"I'm worried about you, Charlotte. You're working too hard, trying to do too much." The toast was ready, and she brought it over and poured more coffee.

Charlotte nodded. It was true enough. "I know, Helene, but it's like I *have* to. It's so important to me to have a nest, my own nest. I feel so lost without one, and with all these changes, it's more important to me than ever. Plus, I want to know what I need to take, what I can leave behind to sell, and be at peace with all those little decisions. This is the time that I have to do it."

Helene nodded ruefully. "I can just kick myself for agreeing to contract Warren Brothers so soon, when you have all this going on and trying to find those notebooks at the same time. I feel responsible for getting you into this bind. Please let me help, Charlotte, with everything. Anything I can do, just say the word."

"Hey, Helene, you're doing it already," Charlotte said with a smile and holding up a forkful of eggs. "This is delicious."

They ate and talked about Donovan breaking the terms of the will by moving things around at his mother's house.

"Simon is afraid they may have messed things up for you, making it harder than ever to find those notebooks."

"I want to go there now, but I can't go out like this."

"Most of my things will be the wrong size, but I can loan you a clean overshirt if you can stand wearing your jeans again."

"That'll work! Let's see what's been going on over there, and then I'll have to decide what to do about the Jeep." She explained how she had planned to move that day, but the Jeep broke down again.

"Simon told me. He said he had an idea about that, though. Didn't elaborate, and I'm not sure I would have understood, anyway. But I am glad, in a way, that you can't move today. You need to take a day off. No work, just try to rest."

After Charlotte changed into Helene's shirt and her own jeans, they drove instead of walked to Olivia's house, since Helene thought she would give her a ride to Lake Parkerton. Things had clearly been moved, but mostly put back. Charlotte had the sense that Donovan and the others had been looking for something, but had not necessarily taken anything. She would have to view the video Simon made to be certain. Just the fact that they had been looking, however, made her nervous—it meant that whoever came here and killed Olivia and Wesley Warren had not yet found what he was looking for.

"I'm fed up," said Helene. "Donovan is not supposed to be here until after the auction. Nobody is supposed to be here except you, Simon, and myself until Warren Brothers comes to start getting things for the sale, which isn't until this weekend. I'm calling him and giving him a piece of my mind, especially after caving on having the sale so quickly." She found his number on her phone and dialed.

The call did not go as expected, however. After chatting a moment, Helene got Charlotte's attention. "Donovan is over on Harvey Street. He and Simon are working on your Jeep."

Donovan and Simon both? "This I've gotta see," said Charlotte.

Helen thought for a moment. "It makes sense, actually. Donnie said he'd been working as a mechanic, and he'd have to know a thing or two about cars to keep that Dodge going so long, wouldn't you think?"

Charlotte shrugged. "Could be. Let's find out."

They found a place to park near the Jeep, but only Simon was working on it when they walked up. The hood was propped open and a screwdriver, a socket wrench, and an adjustable wrench were lying around, along with some other tools.

"Where's Donovan?" asked Helene.

Simon stood upright and wiped his hands on a towel. "Good morning, ladies. Donovan has gone to get a replacement part." He turned to look at Charlotte. "With any luck, our diagnosis is correct and your Jeep will be up and running good as new."

"Really? What's wrong with it?" she asked.

"A bad crankshaft position sensor. Not a hard job, but awkward."

"You're up to something," said Helene.

Simon smiled. "Wanted an excuse to talk to him alone about his shenanigans last night. The fact that he really did seem to have an idea what was wrong with Charlotte's Jeep is a bonus. The only problem, though, was trying to change the subject, because once he gets going on the subject of cars, there's no getting him off of it." He turned to Charlotte again. "Sleep well?"

She felt her cheeks start to redden, but she smiled and nodded. "Yeah. Thanks again for everything." She gestured toward the engine. "This too." Then she spotted paper under the windshield wiper. A parking ticket. She said nothing, but groaned inwardly. Was there no end to this?

"Have you learned anything yet?" Helene asked Simon. "Charlotte and I were just at Olivia's house. We can't tell if anything is missing, but she thinks things have been moved as if they were looking for something."

"That was the impression I got from what I could see last night," he said. "People moving around, but carefully." He looked at Charlotte. "I'll finish editing the valuation video that we have so far, and use it to see if anything is missing. Then we can get the rest done maybe Wednesday or Thursday."

"I don't understand why Donnie keeps going back there when he knows he's supposed to leave it alone," said Helene, who then explained to Simon about agreeing to contract Warren Brothers for the estate auction because she felt Donovan was at his breaking point.

Simon looked surprised, but took it all in. "I'm thinking you're right, he's desperate. We can be pretty certain he's into that loan shark for money, given what Lola and Jimmy said about Mitchell."

Helene nodded, and Charlotte added her concerns. "I'm almost positive that Olivia and Wesley Warren were assaulted for something that's in that house. If Donovan and Mitchell are still looking, then whatever it is hasn't been found. The only reason I can think of for them not to wait until this weekend to look for it is because they're worried we'll find it first."

"Oh, dear," said Helene. "What on earth could it be?"

"I think that whatever it is, it's a book or something to do with books. Didn't Olivia say something to you before she died?"

Helene nodded slowly. "Yes. She said, '*C'est mon livre.*' 'It's my book.' But I wasn't sure she knew what she was saying."

"I'm beginning to think that she did," said Charlotte. "And I'm almost positive she didn't hit Wesley Warren with the bat. Olivia was right-handed, wasn't she?"

"Yes she was. I am left-handed, and Olivia was right-handed."

Charlotte turned to Simon. “Do you happen to have the pictures you took that day we found Olivia?” When Simon nodded and began to retrieve his smart phone, she continued, “I want to double-check which hand the bat was in.”

Simon found the picture, then showed it to her. The bat was, indeed, in Olivia’s right hand. “This seems to go against your argument.”

Charlotte expected his objection. “It actually supports it, because Olivia has had difficulty with that arm since right before her husband died. In one of the notebooks there is an account of his grabbing her in a fit, and there is a noticeable deterioration in her handwriting, which only got slightly better toward the end. She did say that difficulty in lifting things was one of the reasons she needed help in gathering the notebooks.”

“Of course!” exclaimed Helene. “I remember asking her about pouring coffee or something with her left hand, but she just said it was arthritis in her right hand. She didn’t want to admit what really happened.”

“So you see, she couldn’t have swung that bat with her right arm, at least not with any force, and I wouldn’t be surprised if she couldn’t even pick it up. If she did pick it up and use it, it would have had to be with her left hand, but I doubt if she would have had the strength and coordination for that.”

Simon put the phone back in his pocket. “So that means someone else used the bat on Wesley Warren—and planted it in Olivia’s hand afterward.”

“Exactly,” said Charlotte. “There was almost certainly a third person on the scene, someone who got Wesley Warren into his car and made sure it ran off into the pond.” She went on to explain what Barnes said about

Wesley Warren's head injury, and that he was still alive when the car went under the water.

After a moment or two of silence, Helene asked, with a pained expression, "Donnie?"

Simon shook his head. "I can't see him leaving his mother for dead, to be honest."

"But he's clearly tangled up in this," said Helene. She sounded tired. "I don't think I want to talk to him in person at the moment. I need to think about this for a while." She asked Charlotte, "Would you mind if we left?"

"How about I stay here, and see if the guys are able to get the Jeep fixed, or if it needs towing. Then if I still need a ride, I will come back to your place."

"I'm pretty sure we'll have it sorted out within the hour," said Simon.

Helene was reassured, and Charlotte walked with her to the car. She retrieved her tote bag and gave Helene a hug. "We'll get to the bottom of this, Helene. If nothing else, we should have all the notebooks in a few days."

Helene held on to Charlotte's arms. "Just be careful. And promise me to take the day off—no packing, no painting, no moving, just give yourself one day off."

"I promise."

As Charlotte returned to Simon and the Jeep, Larry strode out of The Good Stuff, his hands on his hips.

"So uh," he said to Simon, gesturing at the Jeep, "this gonna take long, or what? Parking's for customers, and this truck's been here since yesterday."

Charlotte spoke quickly. “Sorry, Larry, it wouldn’t start, but I think it’ll be fixed in just a little while.”

Larry’s face cleared on seeing her. “Oh, it’s *you!* I was wondering if it was your truck or not. Problems, eh?”

Charlotte explained about working on the apartment the day before, the recent repair, and introduced Simon. The men shook hands.

“You painted yesterday, then? You didn’t make a peep, had no idea!” Larry seemed pleased with this fact.

“I’m glad! There were a couple of times when I dragged the ladder and it made some noise, but I got done with the carpet and the trash and stuff before the store opened. Want to see it?”

“Sure do.”

Charlotte turned and asked Simon if he wanted to see the apartment, as well.

Simon just leaned against the Jeep and smiled. “Donovan will be back any time now. Maybe I’ll take a look after we’re done with this.”

As Charlotte followed Larry up the stairs to the apartment, yesterday’s exertion came back to haunt her with aching leg muscles. The place still smelled like fresh paint, with overtones of various cleaners and artificial lemon.

“Holy mother of margarine!” Larry exclaimed, turning to beam at her as she reached the top of the stairs. “This is *great*!”

It did look rather nice, she thought, especially with the bright sunny sky shining through clean windows, the walls freshly repaired and painted, and the wood floor gleaming with the warm patina of age. Larry looked over the kitchen, bathroom, and closet, nodding his approval, but Charlotte remained at her vantage point near the stairs, trying to visualize which of her furnishings would work. The entire apartment was only slightly larger than her living room at Lake Parkerton, and most of her furniture was designed for a larger space.

"So when you moving in?"

She shrugged. "Tomorrow. I was planning to move in today, but then the Jeep broke down—and I have to admit I'm awfully tired."

"I'm not surprised you're tired, I'm tired just imagining what you did yesterday. But it sure looks nice. I'll make sure the thermostat is on for this zone later today, and I'll get the paint stuff and the ladder outta here for ya."

Charlotte thanked him and went back outside. Donovan had returned, and he and Simon were installing the new part. Then Charlotte spied a meter cop coming down the sidewalk, stopping to write a ticket three cars down from the Jeep. Oh great. The ticket was going to be exponentially larger with every two hours it sat in that space.

"Hey guys," she said to Simon's back and Donovan's legs, "how's it going?"

Donovan grunted something about rust and Simon made a "so-so" gesture with his free hand. The meter cop came closer, then stopped to talk to someone. Charlotte's palms started to sweat. She was grateful that Simon had taken the initiative to get the Jeep going again, but she wondered how much the part was, and how pricey the ticket was going to be by the time they got done—if they got it done at all. If they didn't, she'd also have a towing expense. She felt as if the money from Helene's check for Olivia's project was evaporating before her eyes.

Donovan called out for something, and Simon handed him a different tool. The meter cop finished her conversation, and was checking the next car. Donovan then scuttled out from under the Jeep, dusted himself off, and gave Charlotte a hello wave that was not unlike a cop's hand signal to stop. She waved back the same way, hiding her conflicting feelings about him. Would she get a chance to tell him that she was onto him and he had better stay away from his mother's house the rest of the week?

Simon got all the tools off the truck frame, and Donovan got in the driver's seat. The Jeep started just as the meter cop walked up, and Charlotte almost hit her when she jumped up and down in excitement.

"Oh, oh, I'm so sorry, I didn't see you behind me," Charlotte apologized. "They just got it fixed. Oh please don't give me another ticket, I—"

"No problem, ma'am," said the cop, setting her cap back on straight. "So you're saying it's been here because it broke down?"

Charlotte nodded. "I was here yesterday to get my apartment ready so I could move in today," she pointed up at the windows above The Good Stuff, "but by the time I got done and was ready to leave, it wouldn't start, and I'd just spent hundreds of dollars getting it fixed last week, and I—," she stopped when the cop held up her hand.

"Let me check something," she said, and stepped away to talk into her radio.

Charlotte looked over at Simon, who was placing socket wrench bits back into a case, and wiping fingerprints off the hood. Donovan was nowhere to be seen. "Where'd he go?" she asked him quietly.

He nodded toward a small parking lot down the street, and she saw Donovan getting into his car and driving off. "Cop came up. Doesn't want to be seen, I suspect."

Wow, thought Charlotte. Everything pointed to Donovan being involved in something criminal. She felt uneasy that she was now obligated to him for his help.

The cop came up and handed Charlotte a ticket slip, but said, "This isn't a ticket. Take it in to the station and tell them what happened. I think they'll waive the whole thing. I told them you were clearly having it repaired and you weren't just shopping too long or something. Should be okay. You're moving up there, eh?" She pointed up at the windows.

"Yeah, tomorrow, if things just go right for once."

The cop laughed and nodded at the ticket, "Well, I hope that helps. When you go into the station, apply for a resident sticker so you can park on the side streets overnight. Have a good day, and welcome to the neighborhood." She waved at Charlotte and Simon and continued her rounds.

Charlotte was so relieved—the Jeep was running again, the tickets were waived, Larry liked the job she did on the apartment—that she had to hug somebody, and Simon was it. She didn't even care if he hugged her back, her happiness was complete.

He did, however, laugh a little and hug her back, if a little more reservedly. "You should be okay now. It's a pretty straightforward fix once it's diagnosed."

She realized they were talking nose to nose—his arms were still around her, and hers around him. She suddenly felt shy. "How, uh, how much do I owe you, and of course Donovan?"

"Not a dime. Part was cheap. The knowhow was priceless." He looked at her with deadpan seriousness, then winked and let her go.

"Simon, I don't know how to thank you. You know, last night, and now this. I hope you were able to learn something about Donovan."

"Not a thing, other than that a cop, any cop, makes him nervous as hell. He's a tough read. But you," he said, putting a hand on her shoulder, "need to get home and try to relax the rest of the day. Don't try to move in today. Promise me that."

She felt as if his eyes were looking right into her brain, and nodded. "Helene made me promise already."

"Good. Got my number in case you get stranded again?" He got his phone out again.

"No, actually. Good idea. Does it have to keep running like this for a while, or can I stop at The Coffee Grove for a few minutes? I don't have any Internet service at home anymore, and I want to see if Ellis emailed me."

She handed him her old "dumb phone," and he looked at it for a moment before adding his number to her contacts. "I'd like your number, too, okay? Didn't you have a different phone last week?"

"Oh yeah, I did, but I downsized that, too." She entered her number in his contacts. "I admit I really miss it sometimes."

"You can stop and start the Jeep as much as you want now, but if there's a problem, get hold of me right away." He looked at the time on his phone and reacted with surprise. "Running late, and I've got to shower and get to class, but see you soon?"

She nodded and watched as he walked down the sidewalk towards Pierce Street.

Charlotte moved the Jeep into a different parking space, even though it wasn't much closer to The Coffee Grove, but she didn't care. It was running. Things would be back on track tomorrow.

It was still early enough in the day to catch Ellis, who was luckily online, and mother and daughter had a good chat, catching up on news. Martin Stanton hadn't left any messages, so Charlotte assumed things were progressing smoothly. She wanted to go back to Olivia's house and take another look around, to see if there was any clue as to what Donovan and his associates were looking for. She knew, however, that she needed to get home and check on things in person, to start making decisions about what pieces of furniture were going to go in the apartment, and not left for sale. Her phone rang. Helene.

"Hi, Helene. They got it fixed!"

"I heard. I'm so glad, Charlotte. You are going to go home and rest now, right?"

"Yes I am. Again, thanks so much for breakfast. I feel guilty that I won't be able to work at Olivia's tomorrow, but I've got to get out of my house as soon as possible."

"Well, don't feel guilty! It's my fault for jamming you up, I'm the one that should feel guilty. I wanted you to know that I did reach Donovan, and I read him the riot act. He has promised me that he will keep his associates out of there, and avoid the place until after the auction." She paused. "I don't know that I believe him, though."

"I hope you aren't too upset, Helene."

"I'll be just fine, and it won't be long before it's out of our hands altogether. Now go home, dear girl."

"I will probably see you tomorrow."

"Are you sure you're going to move tomorrow?"

"Absolutely. Going to get an early start loading things up, and hope to be back in town by noon or just after. Thanks for the wonderful breakfast, Helene. It's kept me going today."

"Any time, Charlotte."

Back home in Lake Parkerton, Martin Stanton's crew had everything under control, at least as far as they were concerned. Charlotte, however, found it bewildering, partially because she was tired, but mostly because they'd made so much progress in the day and a half since she was last at home. There were tables set up in nearly every room. Even in the upstairs hall there were shoe and garment racks, where a Stanton employee had been organizing her wardrobe by tops, bottoms, coats, and accessories. The rod in her closet had been fixed. The suitcases she'd filled with the clothes she knew she was going to keep were luckily still in there. She had since added some boxes with a few other things she'd pulled out at the last minute—extra clothes, mementos, spare sets of linens and towels, things both sentimental and stylish, as if she had been impulse-shopping in her own house.

She realized now, however, that there wasn't going to be room in the apartment for everything. If she could let the painting go, she could let these extra things go, too. Time to be realistic, to be strong. She gave the boxes of extra things back to the crew, and began to make the final list of what she was going to take with, as small and efficient a list as possible.

Seventeen

Tuesday, September 24th

It was six in the morning again, barely daylight, and Charlotte walked out on the deck overlooking the lake for the last time, red coffee mug in hand. This was it, she thought. Moving day. Everything changes. She was both excited and sad.

Stanton's crew wouldn't be there until eight, giving her a couple of hours of peace and quiet. She planned to make no more than three trips back and forth between Lake Parkerton and Elm Grove today, and then only one trip more on Friday, the day before the sale, to sign off on everything. Whatever needed moving had to be done today, because she needed to finish trying to find Olivia's notebooks before Saturday. There was just enough gas in the Jeep for five trips. She had it all planned out, everything under control.

A flock of Canada geese took off from the water, their stately flight moving up and arcing around to the south. A pair of deer moved carefully down a hill, then jumped over the fence into a neighbor's back yard for a breakfast of shrubbery. Squirrels ran back and forth to stockpile their winter hoard. A ground hog stopped at the edge of the street and looked both ways before scuttling across and disappearing under a storage shed. She was unlikely to see this from her apartment on busy Harvey Street.

Time to get going. Clothes and toiletries were already packed, so Charlotte loaded them first. She decided on using an air bed for the time being, as it was portable, and loaded that up with the boxes of things Ellis wanted to save. Next she packed towels and sheets, then kitchen things, which was easy because she had already sorted through them the night she cleaned the kitchen. That night felt like a month ago.

She poured another cup of coffee and began to pack up whatever was left to do in her office, and felt proud that all the essential paperwork and files had been scanned and saved digitally. The office chair would probably have brought a nice price at the sale, but Charlotte's aching back and legs reminded her that a good chair was worth its weight in gold. It would come with, too, and she wheeled it down the hall, out the front door, and lugged it down the steps. When she reached the driveway, a battered green pickup truck pulled into the driveway behind the Jeep.

Her first instinctive thought was of Bosley Warren; the early morning sun glared off the windshield, preventing her from seeing the driver. Both truck doors opened, and she tensed, trying to remember where she set her cell phone.

"HELLOOOO!" Charlotte almost went limp with relief at hearing Diane's big cheerful voice. The passenger waving at her was Simon, who was carrying a bag from The Coffee Grove.

"What on earth are you two doing here?" asked Charlotte.

"Helping you move," said Diane, giving her a hug. "We brought carbs, too!" She grabbed the bag from Simon and held it out to Charlotte.

"Good morning," said Simon, friendly, smiling, but not giving her a hug.

"How did you know? And don't the two of you have to work?"

"I'm free this morning, as luck would have it," said Simon.

"I just moved appointments around. Helene alerted the troops. Why didn't you tell us the other day? You *know* we would have been glad to help and there's no way you should be doing everything by yourself when you don't have to—"

"Oh, but I couldn't, you all are so busy and I'm only taking what I can handle by myself, and Simon, you just helped me yesterday, and—"

"Charlotte," said Simon, "It's okay. Really. Many hands make light work."

Diane nodded fast in agreement.

Charlotte was almost speechless, but managed a few words. "I don't know how to thank you."

Diane grinned. "Well, then, put on more coffee! Put us to work!"

There was no better way to turn the bittersweetness of leaving her house into a celebration of the future than to have friends help with the moving and what remained of the packing. In some ways, it took a little longer, partially because of stopping to converse, but also because the nature of the project shifted now that there were two trucks and three sets of hands. Diane and Simon repeatedly cautioned her against taking too little, especially since she wouldn't have to worry about restricting herself to only what she could carry on her own.

"Oh, I understand what you're trying to do," argued Diane, when Charlotte explained her intent to live as frugally, independently, and minimally as possible, "and it's admirable, and it's part of why I think you're going to rebound from this setback fairly quickly. But there's a lot of things you'll only end up having to buy again, and while that might be okay for things that will wear out, like a toaster oven or something, it's not so much for the really good things like, well, *chairs.*"

"I suppose," said Charlotte, knowing that her friend was probably right. "But it's a really small apartment."

By that time Martin Stanton had arrived with his crew, and Charlotte made introductions, but it turned out that Diane and Martin already knew one another.

"Charlotte's moving into her apartment today, and we'll help her get out of your hair in no time," Diane said to him.

"That reminds me," said Martin to Charlotte, "the crew is to give you a hand loading up whatever you want to take. If you like you can also use our van."

"Oh, Martin," said Charlotte, "that's very kind of you, but I'm sure I wo—"

"That's great!" Diane interrupted. "So we can take anything we want?"

Martin laughed and shook his head as he placed a calm hand on Diane's shoulder. "The advert has already gone out, so I discourage taking anything that's listed on it." He showed Charlotte a copy of the brochure that went out to advertise her sale. There, on the front, was Hannah's painting, its bright colors glowing on the shiny paper.

"It's beautiful, Martin."

Diane and Simon leaned over to look, and Diane gasped. "Ohmygod, Charlotte, you're selling *the painting*?"

Charlotte nodded. "It might bring enough to live on for a year, or replace the Jeep, and I'll be able to fly to Paris to see Ellis, too. I love it so much, but I can't justify keeping it."

They went to look at the painting itself. Diane put her arm around Charlotte in sympathy. "That's a brave thing to do. I only hope it's worth the heartbreak of giving it up."

Charlotte summed it up. "If I can deal with an empty nest, I can deal with selling the painting."

"Well that's that, then. All the more reason to take a few things for creature comfort, especially now that you have us to help you lug it around."

Simon's expression was neutral, but he was clearly taking in the painting, the surroundings, and the view over the lake. "This is a beautiful house. Impressive. What about the rest of the artwork? Not taking anything with?"

She shook her head. "Nope. Some day I'll start a new collection."

Charlotte and her friends conferred and debated which pieces of furniture not listed on the advertisement would fit the apartment without crowding it. She described the sofa and library table already in the apartment, and how much space they took up. In the end she decided on a set of folding chairs that could be used for dining and extra seating but kept in the closet or under the stairs when not needed, the big kilim rug (which Charlotte had told Martin she was taking, so it was never listed), wicker storage cubes that could double as a coffee table, a shelving unit with more cubes that could serve as a dresser, a couple of floor lamps, a table and reading lamp, and a pair of folding screens to divide the sleeping area from the living area. Charlotte wanted to take the overstuffed armchair and ottoman set that were in the guest room, thinking it would look good with the sofa, but it was listed. She'd use the office chair as extra seating instead. Simon went to tie the rug to the top of the Jeep.

"So," said Diane. "Which bed are you taking?"

"I've packed an air mattress already. It'll do for now, or I can sleep on the sofa."

Diane thought about it for a few seconds, then began shaking her head. "No. No no no no no. Won't do, Charlotte. You need a bed. If you don't take one of the ones here now, you'll only end up with doctor bills and shelling out big bucks for a new mattress. And what if you get a boyfriend? Gonna use the floor? I don't think so!"

"I think my dating days have passed, Diane."

"Nobody's dating days pass if they don't want them to. If I can get a date, you can. Let's go." Diane grabbed Charlotte by the arm and marched her up the stairs.

Charlotte's own bed was part of a suite listed on the advertisement, so it was out. Ellis' bed was a twin-size trundle, but extremely heavy. Then they went to the guest room, which had a double mattress atop a platform with storage drawers and a bookcase-type headboard. It also wasn't listed specifically, as apart from Charlotte's suite, the advertisement only said "other bedroom furnishings."

"This would be perfect!" said Diane, testing it out. "No wasted space, either!"

"We could get the crew to help us load it up, but wouldn't it be awfully heavy and awkward to get up the apartment stairs?"

"Let's find out," said Diane. She went to the door and yelled, "Siiiiiimon! C'mere!"

Charlotte hoped she wasn't blushing, remembering her night in Simon's bed. He came in, taking in Diane's chatter and giving Charlotte an amused glance.

"These are usually assembled components, smaller units attached together." He moved the mattress to check the frame and structure.

"Shouldn't be a problem with one other person to help me carry them, and there's no big box spring to worry about getting around corners." He moved the mattress back in place, then laid down on it with his hands behind his head. "Comfy, too. I must say I rather like it."

Diane jabbed her in the ribs. "See? He likes it."

"Fine. Fine," snarled Charlotte, trying to hide her reaction to seeing Simon stretched out on the bed. "I'll find some tools." She descended the stairs quickly, but was smiling to herself by the time she reached the bottom.

The Stanton crew helped them take down and load up the bed. Josh was supervising again, and he reaffirmed the offer to help Charlotte move out anything she was taking.

"How about a TV?" asked Simon, pointing to the one on the kitchen wall. "This one would make a nice monitor, too."

"Go ahead and take it," said Josh. "That particular one is not listed. Most electronics depreciate so quickly, that you wouldn't get much for it."

Diane helped Simon dismantle it and the wall bracket that held it.

Charlotte appreciated what they were trying to do, but thought it was pointless. "It might be a long time before I get cable again, you know."

"You can get a lot of movies and shows on the Internet now, either free or cheap," said Simon, lifting the television off of the bracket.

"Oh, I know that, but it might be a while before I get an Internet connection again, too."

Diane turned to look at her, and actually didn't say anything for a moment. Then she smiled. "I've been thinking about your decision to sell the painting. It changes your budget situation a little bit. There's no reason you can't at least have a decent Internet connection at your new place."

It was as if a light bulb went on in Charlotte's head. "You know, I hadn't even thought of that! I'm going to call the cable company right now and see what I can do."

As she waited to talk to a live representative, Charlotte realized that her sudden happiness at being able to get online again was an indication that she was a lot less enthusiastic about downsizing than she tried to convince herself to be. But just having this one thing back, being able to get online for work, for entertainment, for staying connected to Ellis, meant she could keep an important way of doing things intact, no matter the surroundings, no matter how much she cut back on everything else.

This time she talked with a representative who connected her to a supervisor. He looked over her account and seemed willing to help her get it straightened out and write up an order for a new connection at the apartment. The down side was that it would take a week. He softened the blow (and apologized for the early shut-off without actually admitting culpability) by giving her the six-month introductory rate usually given to new customers, making the cable TV almost free.

"Well?" asked Diane, when Charlotte got off the phone. Simon, who was about to carry the television out to the Jeep, paused to learn what happened, as well.

"All set. It won't kick in for a week, but I get free TV for six months. Thanks so much for pointing it out to me, Diane. This really cheers me up more than I can say, and it's going to make life so much easier."

"Oh, sweetie, that's what friends are for!" cheered Diane, giving Charlotte a big hug. Then she rummaged in her pocket for her phone. "I gotta make a phone call, though. 'Scuse me." She walked out to the deck.

Simon smiled and picked up the television again. "You'll feel at home in no time flat."

"I think you're right," Charlotte agreed. "I really think you're right."

They were finished by eleven.

"I thought this would take longer, to be honest," said Simon. "You're really not taking much at all, and most of it is pretty easy to move."

"Yeah," said Diane, looking over the tables of stuff that were already set up for the sale. "Imagine if she wasn't having a sale and we had to pack and move all *this* crap!"

"Exactly my point in selling it!" exclaimed Charlotte in defense. "I'm embarrassed you guys are seeing all of it, to be honest."

"After Olivia's house, this is nothing," said Simon.

"Ah, but I gotta say something," said Diane. "If you think this is bad, just come by my parents' place out at the farm. It's got fifty years of their stuff, *plus* most of the stuff from my grandparent's house. Easily ten times what you have here, and most of it's useless. I really shouldn't be poking fun at you, Charlotte."

"No, no, I'm not upset. But I think I'm ready to leave now. I'll be back on Friday to sign off for the sale, so if there's anything else I need from here, I'll get it then."

"Yay! Let's go!"

Once they arrived back in Elm Grove, Jimmy joined them with two young staffers, evidently by prior arrangement with Simon and Helene.

Charlotte's legs were grateful, and she stayed up in the apartment to direct where she wanted everything to go. Diane went to check on things at the office.

One advantage of a small place, thought Charlotte, was not only could it not hold a lot of furniture, there were only so many ways the furniture could be arranged: table over here, bed over there, rug and sofa in the middle. Simon picked up a large pizza from the joint across the street. Diane came back with a bottle of bubbly she'd been saving in her office, which she now poured out into plastic cups.

"Here's to Charlotte's new life!" she cheered, and they all clicked glasses.

They chatted a while about the merits of the apartment, then Simon and Jimmy decided to tackle setting up the TV

Charlotte didn't think it was worth bothering with—she had neither cable nor Internet service, yet.

Simon just smiled. "Trust me."

Charlotte just shrugged, and she and Diane unpacked kitchen things and linens, then started reassembling the bed frame.

"This is such a great place, Charlotte," said Diane. "It's small, but those big windows and the high ceiling make such a difference."

Simon had finished attaching the television to the wall bracket and was taking photos with a small digital camera. "The light is pleasant, but it presents certain challenges for a photographer."

"Oh, Simon, stop being a professor for five minutes!" Diane teased. He started a rapid set of photos of her; she responded with silly faces.

"Ready?" said Jimmy, into his own cell phone. He looked around the room. "Where's the remote?" Simon tossed it to him, and he aimed it at the TV.

The next thing Charlotte knew, it was on. She wandered over, unbelieving. "How did you do that?"

Jimmy spoke into the phone again. "Working great. Yeah." He disconnected and smiled at Charlotte. "You've got cable." He pointed to a small box on the floor. "And wireless Internet."

"*I do?*" She looked from Jimmy to Simon, who looked very pleased with himself.

"Your friend Diane," said Simon, pointing at the culprit, "called Mr. Connections here," he then pointed to Jimmy, "who made it happen today instead of next week."

"I'm going to miss seeing you at the coffee shop when you do your work, but—" said Jimmy, shrugging in mock resignation.

"But I only ordered it a couple of hours ago. How did you do that?"

She didn't find out because there was the sound of someone knocking on the front door, opening the door, then calling out, "Hello?"

"Hey, Helene," Jimmy answered, and went down to help her up the stairs, carrying the gift basket she brought.

Everyone was glad to see Helene, who looked equally glad to have made it up the long flight of stairs to see Charlotte's new home. She loved the view from the bank of windows, and particularly admired the sofa and library table.

Charlotte of course thanked Helene profusely for the basket of gourmet goodies, which included, she noted, a precious box of Russian Caravan tea. They caught one another's eye and smiled in understanding.

Charlotte got Jimmy aside and thanked him, as well, but he just shrugged and said "he had a good friend" at the cable company. Once again she was reminded how it just took the right person talking to another right person for things to happen. And they weren't always bad things.

Yet also once again, Charlotte experienced a momentary twinge of panic at things being out of her direct control. *Snap out of it,* she told herself. *You've won the lottery!* These happy, friendly people meant well, every one of them, and did what they could to help her reverse her string of bad luck. After years of working alone and independently, having control over choices that affected herself and her daughter, and money to throw at problems she couldn't directly fix herself, Charlotte found it strange to be on the receiving end of others' largesse.

It wouldn't do to let them see her mixed emotions. She got out her laptop, and Jimmy helped her connect to the wireless network. The technical activity was neutral and calming. But it was more than neutral to be online again, as a wave of completeness washed over her when she saw the word "Connected" on the computer screen.

Maybe that was her real home now, she thought. All those years of telecommuting and developing professional relationships online had shifted her sense of community to short bits of text and information from regular, virtual sources. On top of it, it was the only way of having Ellis around anymore. Interactions with real people in real spaces around her was still not quite as real, as if she couldn't believe that this kind of real-life good fortune could happen to her. Yet there it was, right in front of her: her new family.

Ellis had sent her a link to a video clip with the name, "A New Moon," and she pressed the forward arrow to play it.

"Hi Mom! Hi Helene! Happy moving day, Mom! I wrote a piece to commemorate the occasion as part of an assignment. It's a little bit classical, a little bit electronic, new and old, just something I was having fun with."

The performance was in a digital media studio class. Charlotte could see the other students sitting in an arc behind Ellis, who was at an electronic keyboard surrounded by what looked a small version of a space ship control panel in a science fiction movie. The piece began with the opening bars of Debussy's *Claire de Lune,* then the opening bars of Beethoven's *Moonlight Sonata* came up under it, picking up speed, both themes reshaped and shimmered by the electronic sound effects into something altogether different and fascinating, then released into a slow, poignant glissando. It was short, about four minutes; her classmates were enthusiastic.

"Oh, my," whispered Helene, who had come to stand behind her. "It's a new world, isn't it?"

It was, indeed.

Later, long after everyone left and she had finished unpacking and making up the bed, Charlotte stood at the windows overlooking Harvey Street, sipping tea from the big red mug. The traffic grew lighter as dusk grew. It was certainly a different view than the one from her deck and living room at the house, but it had its own charm. Sunset was sunset, after all; the mood was in the changing light of day, and not necessarily the view. The street lights had come on. They were ornamental replicas of ones that had graced the street a century ago, nicer and warmer than the cold, utilitarian ones that lit the street when she lived in Elm Grove before. The town was making an effort to thrive, and she felt much farther away from economic troubles in this modest apartment than she did amid the luxury of Lake Parkerton.

Charlotte had the sense, again, of being watched. She scanned the windows of the buildings across the way, but saw nothing, nor saw any indication of anyone watching from the street, the sidewalks, or the parking lot. She turned away, and nearly dropped the mug.

There was a large, black and white tuxedo cat sitting on the newel of the staircase rail, just staring at her.

Charlotte's first thoughts ran along the lines of *how did you get in here?* The next thoughts were, *Friend or Foe?* This was The Good Stuff's shop cat. The chances, were, then, that it was a people-friendly cat. Of course, that did not necessarily mean it was Charlotte-friendly, as she sometimes evoked violent responses from cats whose owners swore "we've never seen him do *that* before!" then glared at her as if she was abusing the poor feline when they weren't watching. Thus, she approached slowly and cautiously.

The cat adjusted its position from sitting upright on its bottom to down on its belly, tucking its front paws in, looking thoroughly contented. Charlotte could hear it purr, and as she got closer, she could have sworn it was smiling, but also swore she would never tell anyone this.

"Hello, cat. What brings you here?"

The cat just kept purring, and blinked at her in a sleepy way.

She reached out to let it catch her scent, but it skipped that cagey preamble and rubbed its head and ear against her knuckles.

Friendly. So far.

When Charlotte got very close, the cat sat upright again, then raised itself up by the hind legs, placed one of its front paws on her chest, and stretched up to look at her nose to nose. She remained still, and after a moment the cat went back down on all four paws, looking at her with its head tilted to one side, as if wondering why she wasn't being affectionate. So she started petting it, and then it wanted cuddling, and then, with what felt like twenty pounds of cat in her arms, she realized that its white markings were beautifully symmetrical. She also confirmed it was a he.

The cat decided it had enough of the cuddling and twisted out of her arms, leapt onto the desk, then down to the floor, around the newel post, and down the stairs. She followed, pulling the chain of the stairwell light on, only to see the cat disappear into the shadows around the door at the end of the foyer. There was a soft slapping sound, then nothing.

Charlotte moved cautiously into the shadows, closer to the door, and tried the knob. Locked. Good. Then her eyes adjusted to the dark, and she saw a small flapped pet door at the bottom. Maybe not so good. She considered calling Larry or going around to his apartment, but decided it wasn't an emergency. It was a rather nice cat, after all, and maybe it wouldn't be so bad to have the occasional visit.

Instead, she went back upstairs and switched on the TV to catch the local news, still amazed at having the luxury to do so, and the luxury of her own Internet connection again. She listened to the news and weather reports (rain was moving in overnight) while writing Ellis an email to thank her for the music video. Then she heard the name "Seamus O'Dair," and looked up to see a picture of Donovan on the screen. Only it wasn't Donovan, she quickly realized, but O'Dair, and wondered at the uncanny resemblance. Could it be—?

The program was a university-sponsored talk show called Courtney at Corton, that covered the arts and current events. Tonight's installment was an overview of Seamus O'Dair's life and work, in light of his book recently being in the news. The expert being interviewed was a professor at Corton University, one that Charlotte assumed came in after she and Jack divorced, as she had no recollection of meeting him. Most of what was discussed was commonly known, but Charlotte listened patiently on the off chance that something would be relevant to Olivia's notebooks. Or to

Donovan. The picture of O'Dair was not the usual old man of letters on book jackets, but a candid one of when he was younger, wearing glasses and holding a cigarette between his long, bony fingers. The program host commented on this, and the professor explained that it was a photo taken around the time O'Dair wrote *Least Objects,* in 1959, when he was forty-eight years old and coming into his writing prime.

Donovan was in his early fifties. When was he born? And just how well did Olivia know O'Dair?

The professor went on to describe O'Dair's involvement in the French Resistance during World War II, and how he and fellow artists and writers in the Resistance gathered in Paris and worked to restore a theater which they themselves had sabotaged and set on fire while it was being used by the Nazis. O'Dair was Irish by birth, but lived in France, and wrote nearly all of his early and middle-period books in French; the author said on more than one occasion that English was too full of words and phrases that were beside the point. He never translated his French work into English, nor the English into French, claiming "it was not philosophically possible."

Courtney (who was a youngish professor of communications, and knew the camera was making the most of her mixed ancestry) asked if the story in *Least Objects* only confirmed that the French hated Americans. The professor chuckled, and said the hatred was a myth—for the most part. He explained that the French distinguished between a people and their government, and have looked askance at American power and foreign policy for a long time, especially after World War II. O'Dair wrote *Least Objects* when the Resistance hero de Gaulle came back into power. During this time, the Resistance was glorified, romanticized, and those who were not enthusiastic were looked at as if they were Nazi collaborators. The Americans may have helped to liberate France, but they took their time and made little secret of their reluctance to work with General de Gaulle during the war. The professor found it interesting that O'Dair used the phrase "military-industrial complex" almost two years before Eisenhower used it in his farewell speech, but there was never any attribution given by the White House.

The time allotted for the interview was running out, and the hostess concluded the segment with more commonly-known facts about O'Dair, including his other works and his Nobel Prize for Literature.

Charlotte got up from the chair and stretched. Her legs and back were still aching from all the lifting and moving, but on the whole, she thought, looking around at her brand-new apartment, it was worth it. She was normally a shower person, but for tonight she ran a bath in the big claw-foot tub, and enjoyed being able to stretch out and recline in it as she soaked. It wasn't the Jacuzzi she had at Lake Parkerton, but it was still good, and certainly quieter. She made a mental note to bring a couple of pillar candles from the house, and perhaps a low table for setting a glass of wine next to the tub.

It was early, but she didn't care, and got into her favorite plaid pajama bottoms and an extra soft tee shirt. She rummaged around the kitchen and put together a snack from the gift basket. There was a bottle of calvados and a chunk of camembert, plus some savory crackers to work with. Perfect. She brought it over to her bedside table, along with her laptop and Olivia's notebooks, and turned on the reading lamp. The bed was behind the row of screens she had set up to use as a room divider, creating a snug and cozy place, and helped to diffuse any light from the street below that managed to get past the window blinds. She was glad now that Diane had talked her into bringing a proper bed and extra pillows as she climbed onto the soft duvet and sighed with pleasure. What was it that Simon once said? *The older I get, the more I appreciate home comforts.*

The brandy went down nicely, warming her joints and relaxing her muscles. The various scenes of the day played through her head, coming back again and again to Simon stretched out on the very spot she was lying on herself. There might be little use in hoping for anything to happen, she thought, but if she enjoyed thinking about him, she would. No one would have to know.

She opened a notebook, planning to scan through each one to get a sense of what they covered, and to see if there was anything to illuminate any of the mysteries of this case: why Olivia stopped writing; why she wrote again, but in secret; why Donovan was the spitting image of Seamus O'Dair; what was it Donovan and Mitchell were looking for; why Olivia and Wesley Warren were killed. But after just a few minutes, she was blissfully sound asleep.

Eighteen

Wednesday, September 25th

It was the concrete truck roaring by that startled her awake, but there was also white noise that tempted her back to sleep. For the first few seconds, she didn't know where she was, and then, seeing her favorite duvet cover, the familiar folding screens, and her robe hanging from a hook on the closet door, reality fleshed out. It was the apartment in Elm Grove, on the busiest street in town. Her new home. The white noise was rain.

Charlotte yawned and checked her cell phone on the side table. Six a.m. She'd been in bed for at least nine hours. Olivia's notebooks were still spread on the other side of the bed, along with a patch of dark soft stuff that looked like cat hair. Right. The cat must have come up to sleep on the bed at some point during the night. She smiled.

The usual morning routine felt a little awkward. She was used to having ample counter and cabinet space in the bathroom, but there was almost no place to set anything down here. It made her aware of every movement: hold toothbrush, remove cap from toothpaste tube and set it on small area next to the cold tap, put toothpaste on toothbrush, hold toothbrush in mouth while replacing cap on toothbrush tube and putting tube back in small medicine cabinet, then brush teeth. She did pack her electric toothbrush, but would have to find a place to set the charger. *Mental note: bring some kind of bathroom storage or shelf thingy from home. Correction: from house in Lake Parkerton.*

Making coffee was a little easier. While it brewed, she opened the window blinds and surveyed the rainy townscape. At this hour, there was light commuter traffic broken by the occasional truck or semi, but almost no pedestrians. She moved the screens away from the bed and climbed back in, this time with coffee in the big red mug and her laptop. From this vantage point, she could see the entire apartment, save for the door to the bathroom.

She recalled Diane's loose quote of Virginia Woolf over lunch at Cole's Pub, "money and a room of your own." Here's the room, Charlotte thought. In a few days, with any luck, there will be some money. She opened her laptop to write a journal entry.

My new home feels like a cross between a waiting room and a room at the Lotus Spa. It is small, well-lit, airy, and there are very few things in it, but they are good things. It is serene, but it isn't home. At least not yet. I feel self-conscious in it. I miss having books on the shelves, art on the walls, and yet I suppose the blank walls are soothing in their own way. My closet looks like I'm on a two-week vacation somewhere, but if I'm honest those are the things I usually end up wearing, anyway. I feel like I'm meeting myself as I really am for the first time, yet that can't be write. Oops, right.

She wrote for another twenty minutes, stopping when the rain stopped and the sunlight broke through the clouds. She dressed for a bike ride, and found just enough money in the bottom of her purse for a bagel and egg sandwich at The Coffee Grove.

Elm Grove was the same as ten years before, yet it wasn't. Enough time had passed that Charlotte felt herself on a weird cusp between the familiar and the new as she rode her bike around the neighborhood. A familiar figure in a trench coat and fedora was walking with a distinctive lope along the sidewalk on Cortland Street. Was it her old neighbor, Frank? She nearly stopped to say hello, then suddenly remembered that Frank had passed away several years ago. Perhaps it was his son. Or perhaps her mind was playing tricks on her, making similar things seem like things she once really knew. A familiar-looking rusty Volvo station wagon passed by on Sheffield Street, and she expected to see one of her former colleagues driving it, but once again it was a trick of memory. Here among the old houses, the stage had changed very little as the actors came and went.

She shared this observation with Jimmy, who came over with a coffee while she ate her breakfast.

"Will this town always seem full of ghosts?"

He seemed to consider the question, but she had the feeling he was filing it away for later reference, as well—she had come to understand that there was more to Jimmy than met the eye.

"I'm certain it won't if you open yourself up to it," he said. "Replace the bad old memories with new good ones."

She looked at him askance. "Sounds like positive thinking, that I'll draw new and good things to me if I just have the right attitude."

Jimmy burst out laughing. "Oh, c'mon, Charlotte. I'm the last person to believe in magnetic nonsense—that kind of lack of reality played a big role in our economic troubles. No, the good things are there, but you have to be open to the possibility, be open and lie in wait for things to reveal themselves."

"Sounds like wildlife photography," said Simon, who had walked up with his own breakfast. "Or espionage?"

"Good morning!" said Charlotte. "It's neither, actually."

"Charlotte here," said Jimmy, "is experiencing a sort of Brigadoon in reverse. She's reappeared in town after a long time and her brain is playing catch-up."

Simon nodded in understanding as he sat down next to Charlotte at her invitation. "I've had that happen a couple of times when I've gone back to my old neighborhood. But he's right. If it is logical that something is there, or that you have it on good authority, then it is reasonable to be open to the possibility and, well, wait for the shot."

"I guess it'll just take time. But I'm glad I'm back. I'm seeing a lot of possibilities for how my life here could take shape."

Jimmy went back to the counter to help out, and Simon ate his breakfast in a hurry.

"Sorry to run, but I don't want to be late for the faculty meeting this morning. Want to get a proposal in for next semester, and then I need to face the hordes begging for mid-term extensions. Going to Olivia's today?"

"Yeah, in a little while. I'm actually waiting for Ramona's Resale to open up, to see if I can find out anything about Olivia's book collection."

"Good idea. I'll be by as soon as I can get away, and maybe we can get the valuation video finished up."

"See you soon, Simon."

He looked down at her as he slipped into his leather jacket, with an expression she couldn't interpret, and then just turned and left.

There had been a dusty, musty, junk shop in the big old three-story building across from the Post Office for at least thirty years. It closed for a while when the owner became too old and ill to operate it, then, according to a newspaper article Charlotte read some years back, Benny Ramona bought it, cleaned it up a bit, brought in some new stock, and named it Ramona's Resale. He used a red heart as the shop's logo, not only for the "I (Heart) Ramona's Resale" bumper stickers and tote bags, but on the spines of paperback books, because he ran a paperback book exchange from the shop, as well. Those stickers were on many of Olivia's books.

The door at the front of the building was locked, with a sign saying "Entrance in Alley" and an arrow pointing one in the right direction. Charlotte went that way, and walked about a quarter of a block down the brick-paved alley until she reached a heart-shaped sign hanging over the pavement from a bracket. There was a bike rack, which she took advantage of, and with the realization that there were many, many more bike racks around town these days than ten years ago.

The shop door was a cheerful, red-painted new one styled like a full-length French door, and she went in with a more positive attitude than she would have in its previous incarnation. She knew that Ellis and her friends went there to find cheap and unusual clothes and jewelry, but up to this moment she had never had cause to go there herself.

What she saw amazed her. It was as if the owner had taken ten houses like Olivia's and spread out the contents, from furniture to clothing to knickknacks. The checkout counter was next to the door, manned by a stout, muscular young woman whose bleached-blond hair was swept back off her face in a lion's-mane halo. Her name tag, appropriately enough, said "Aslan." Charlotte murmured hello, and Aslan nodded back.

There were several rooms on the main floor, mostly full of furniture and large items like a popcorn wagon and two pinball machines, and a back room with nothing but large appliances. A sign by the staircase said "Books, Clothes, More Furniture," with another arrow, this one pointing up. Charlotte went that way, too.

The rooms with clothing were distinguished by funky (where several flashy college girls were sorting through the racks and having a laugh), and not-so-funky (where a handful of quiet older men and women did not appear to be shopping for fun). There were two rooms of books, one with mostly hardbacks and the other with all paperbacks. A large handmade sign explained the book exchange regulations in the paperbacks room. The hardback room, however, had no signs other than "Priced as Marked," and included a couple of old-fashioned horsehair-stuffed armchairs for one's reading comfort. A curly-headed man in his thirties, wearing tan corduroy trousers and an argyle sweater vest over a pinstriped shirt, was sitting in one of them and reading an old historical atlas. He looked up through thick-lensed glasses as she came in.

"Hello. I'm Benny Ramona. Let me know if there's anything I can help you with."

"There might be," said Charlotte, and she explained her relationship to Olivia and why she was there.

"Oh, yes. I saw the obituary, and of course the article about what happened to poor Olivia," he said. "I rather liked the old girl—she was one of my first and best customers, and then she suddenly stopped coming a couple of years ago. Probably the stairs were getting to be too much. She bought hundreds of books, including a lot from the old stock that was already here when I bought the place. Two or three times she bought so many that I delivered them to her house, they were too much for her to carry with that wonky arm of hers."

"Do you know if she purchased any first editions?"

"She might have. She purchased quite a few books in French. There was a whole slew of books here in French and German, a lot of discards from the university library and possibly from retired professors' stockpiles. I don't read either language, and my profit margins don't really allow for appraisals. If it's new stock, I've put a sticker on it, like so, and specify the title on the sales slip." He pointed to one such book on the shelf next to him. "If it's from the stock that was already here when I bought the place, I sell it at the price already marked inside the cover, and just write 'old stock' on the sales slip."

"Do you know if she bought any Seamus O'Dair books?"

Benny smiled in understanding. "Like a first edition of *Least Objects?* Oh, if I knew that she did, I'd be kicking myself right now. But I honestly don't recall having come across any copies of any of his books, at least not in the new stock."

Charlotte thanked him for his help, and complimented him on the store.

"Thank you, Ms. Anthony. Please feel free to come back if you have any more questions, or anything you think I could help you with." He rose and proffered her his hand, and they shook. Then he continued, "May I ask you a personal question?"

Charlotte was surprised, but nodded her assent.

"You look familiar, as is your name. Would you happen to be related to Ellis Anthony?"

"Yes. That's my daughter."

He looked thoroughly pleased. "I knew it! Tell her I said hello, and that Aslan and I both miss her."

Things had definitely been disturbed in Olivia's house since they were there two days earlier. Helene shook her head sadly. "I don't know what to do, Charlotte. Drat Donovan, anyway." She turned to close the front door, and turned the deadbolt.

"I do," said Charlotte, determined to keep cheerful and professional. "We'll pick up where we left off with the notebook clues, and when Simon gets here, we'll have him take pictures of how things are today and compare them to earlier ones. The most important thing is to try to find the notebooks, and then get out of here for good."

"I suppose," Helene sighed, and pursed her lips. Charlotte knew that her friend was not used to having her wishes ignored.

They once again looked at the clue in the most recent notebook: *Elle et lui.* Charlotte told Helene that she had entered the words in an Internet search and came up with it as a title to the 19th-century author George Sand's account of her affair with the poet Alfred de Musset. "It's French and literary," she explained, "so maybe there is something to it. It looked like the strongest candidate of all the search results that turned up."

Helene looked genuinely perplexed. "George Sand? Are there any books by her on the shelves?"

They looked along the shelf with 19th-century French writers, and found one book by Alfred de Musset, but no George Sand.

"She was also known for her affair with Chopin," said Helene. Maybe there are records or tapes of his music somewhere?"

Charlotte wandered through the rooms, but saw no signs of music or anything that played music, other than the radio in the kitchen. A search in and around it proved fruitless, as well.

"There aren't a lot of homes where there is nothing on hand for playing music, especially if there was once a teenager living there," said Charlotte.

Helene looked perplexed again. "You're right, now that you mention it. Olivia was crazy about jazz at one time, as I think I've said before. I don't know if Donnie was a music buff any more than he was a sports buff, though. But I would have thought Olivia would at least have a few jazz albums around, if not classical."

Charlotte thought for a moment. In her experience, if someone was of a demographic that was highly likely to have a certain product, then there was usually a good reason if they didn't have that product. "Maybe she did, but she either sold them, gave them away, threw them out—or Donovan got them."

"Oh, my!" Helene exclaimed. "I hadn't thought of that. Maybe we should think about what else ought to be here that isn't here."

"My thoughts, exactly. There's so much stuff in this house, so many different kinds of things, that it might be easier. You were looking through an old ledger book the other day. How recent do they run?"

Helene went over to the small bookcase and looked it over. "The last one in here appears to be several years ago—the year Ronson passed away, in fact, but let me see...." She thumbed through the pages of the last ledger, then slammed the book shut. "It goes up to about six months before he died. Simon is right. Ronson was the one who forced her to keep detailed expense ledgers, and when he got too sick to check up on her, she stopped."

"I think that is when he hurt her arm, and she wouldn't have been able to write in the ledgers even if she wanted to. Even recently, writing so small would have been difficult for her, if not impossible."

"How awful. I feel like I've failed her by not knowing what was really going on, but I didn't even know to ask the right questions. She was too proud to tell me on her own." Helene looked around the room sadly.

"What other things do you think should be here that aren't?"

"Well, let me see." Helene sat down on the desk chair and looked around the room. "I know that she loved jazz, and of course to read and write. Ronson was every inch an Army man. He liked sports, in particular baseball. He collected baseball cards. He was a meat-and-potatoes—"

"Baseball cards!" Charlotte interrupted. "I don't think I've seen any baseball cards in the house, at least not yet."

"There's something, then," agreed Helene. "I will go through the ledgers, I can do that sitting down. That might tell us where the missing things have gone if Olivia entered their sales."

"Good idea. Work backward, from the most recent book. I'll check the basement and the garage."

Charlotte went to the basement door in the kitchen, but discovered that the key was no longer hanging on the nail on the trim around the door, nor was it in the lock. She tried the doorknob again, and it was indeed locked. Perhaps Donovan had been down there and pocketed the key.

She then decided to take a look around the garage, and went through the back porch. The oriental rug had been brought in from the back yard and was rolled up and laying across the stacks of plastic containers. She continued into the back yard and then to the side door of the garage, which was unlocked. She felt for the switch and turned on the light.

It was a typical one-car garage for the neighborhood, barely large enough to contain the twenty-year-old beige Ford Taurus that looked as if it hadn't been driven for the past ten, it was so covered in dust. There was a small workbench along part of the back wall, and tools hanging on the pegboard above it. Everything was typical—lawn mower, garden tools, hedge clippers, partial bags of grass seed, fertilizer, and concrete, a ladder, a rolled up garden hose, and here and there signs that Ronson went on fishing trips, including a small outboard motor lying under the bench and a fish net hanging on a nail by its frame. None of it appeared to have been disturbed in years. There were no boxes that looked as if they could have held baseball cards.

Charlotte returned to the house and thought she heard Helene talking to someone. In the straight shot from the kitchen through the dining room she could see Helene standing near the desk in the living room, one hand on the back of the chair, and looking up and nodding with polite interest at someone Charlotte couldn't see but whose voice she now recognized: Bosley Warren's.

A sharp wave of alarm ran through Charlotte's stomach and throat, culminating in tension, and she rubbed the back of her neck as she tried to think of how to handle this, of what to do. Helene did not look worried or threatened, that was good. There was no other voice than Bosley's, which indicated he was either alone, or with Donovan. Should she quietly sneak back outside? She didn't want to leave Helene alone with that ape, but she was afraid that if Bosley Warren saw her, he would erupt violently. And why was he here, anyway? She pulled out her phone and called Detective Barnes, whispering her message to his voice mail.

Helene must have seen or heard her, because she turned, smiled, and beckoned her to join them.

Here goes, thought Charlotte, and she walked toward the living room, ready for a fight.

"Charlotte," said Helene, "I presume you know Mr. Warren?"

As Charlotte came into Bosley's view, his eyes widened and betrayed his own alarm, and his knuckles went white as he gripped his clipboard tighter.

"You! What the hell are you doing here?" he snarled.

Helene answered first, with a teacher's calm authority. "My sister hired Charlotte to find her notebooks and transcribe them, and I've kept her on. She has found over half of them, but if your people keep coming here and moving things, it will become incredibly difficult to find the remaining notebooks, and thus fulfill my obligations as the estate administrator."

Bosley didn't say anything for a few moments, and looked as if he was trying to decide on the right approach under the circumstances, glancing at Helene, then Charlotte, and back again. Helene remained calm, and kept her gaze on him steady. It seemed to be having an effect, taming Bosley's inner beast to the point that he let out a deep breath, and set the clipboard down on the coffee table, rattling a set of keys attached to the clip.

"This is real uncomfortable," he said. "I was just informed this morning that we have a contract to do the Targman estate auction, but I'm not the one who booked it, and I'm usually the one that handles all the auction bookings. I came here to look over what all we were going to have to move to the auction barn, and found you, Mrs. Dalmier, which I'm cool with because it's your signature on the contract. I also just learned yesterday that my brother was here last week, and was evidently assaulted in this very house, right before he drowned in that pond. Nobody tells me what's really going on. I'm standing here feeling like a fool, and kinda insulted because everybody treats me like I'm an idiot. And not only do they not tell me what's going on, they don't tell me what's *not* going on." He turned to Charlotte. "I asked Ilona if you canceled that sale date I gave you, and it turns out you did. She just didn't bother to tell me. My brother went missing. I was worried, and trying to handle his side of the business as well as my own. I know I shouldn't've hauled off on you like that. I was there when they pulled his car out of the water. Everything's spinning outta control."

Charlotte was taking all of this in, and didn't get a sense that it was an act. Bosley really was at a loss. She decided to attempt a question.

"When was the last time you were here?"

He shook his head as if the question didn't compute. "This is the first time I've ever been in this house."

Helene and Charlotte looked at one another. Simon had said he was pretty sure that someone big like Bosley and someone shorter, like Mitchell, were in the house with Donovan the night Charlotte's Jeep broke down. Could the big man have been Toley Banks' driver, Doc?

Charlotte looked again at the keys on the clipboard. One of them was an old-fashioned skeleton key, the kind that would fit the lock on the basement door. "So how did you come by those keys?"

Bosley looked at them, then at her. "They were there at the shop, along with this order, signed by Mrs. Dalmier here."

"I didn't have the keys," said Helene. "I just signed a contract with Mitchell Bennett, who said he was authorized to do so for Warren Brothers."

Some of the mystery was clearing for Bosley, and he nodded slowly. "Yeah, Mitchell. He works for my older half-brother, who has a big stake in the shop. If Toley told him to do it, there's nothing I can do to say otherwise. But it really messes with the schedule. Wes was the one who kept all this stuff straight between us and Toley."

"Do you know Donovan?" asked Helene

He shook his head again. "That name isn't familiar. Doesn't mean I don't know him, but I don't know the name."

But Charlotte remembered something about the name. "What about Van?"

This time Bosley's face cleared with recognition. "Oh, yeah, I know a Van, yeah, he's the skinny guy who—uh, yeah, Van T-something." He paused as it sunk in, and he picked up the clipboard to read the auction order form again. "Ohhhhh man." He muttered some invectives and looked at Helene as if he had received more bad news. "He's the guy whose model train parts I bought at a swap meet. The O'Dair book was in the box."

Helene's hand went up to cover her mouth.

Charlotte was astounded. "The book was *Olivia's?"* She looked at Helene. Was that what Olivia's last words referred to, that the rare edition of *Least Objects* was hers?

Bosley looked confused again. "Who's Olivia?"

"Mrs. Targman. She was Van's mother," explained Charlotte. Bosley looked suitably astounded, as well.

"Well, I'll be. Maybe that's got something to do with why my brother was here. Maybe they were trying to get the book back or the money for it, and things didn't go too well."

"No, they didn't, Mr. Warren," said Helene, who looked at him in grim sorrow. "My sister received the injuries that killed her, too."

As this sunk in, Bosley pulled himself together. "I got a feeling I shouldn't be talking about this. I just want you to know, though, that the authentication process was all above board. I told the auction people how I acquired the book and showed them my copy of the sales slip. Van had a box of model train accessories that I bought without looking through it much, because it had a bunch of those crossing signals on top that I wanted, so I made him an offer for the whole box, and he agreed. He seemed happy about it. When I looked through the box back at home, I found the book at the bottom, wrapped in brown paper, and painted to look like a school or a factory or something, real little kid stuff. Anybody else might've thrown it out. But in my line of work, you look inside anything that can open and unwrap everything that's covered, because you'll never know what you'll find. It looked like a first edition, and I asked Wes to check out, 'cuz he's the one who knows books."

"Did Donovan realize what happened?" asked Helene.

"I don't think so," said Bosley. "At least, he never tried to get back in touch with me."

Charlotte tried to picture how events unfolded. "Did Wesley approach Mrs. Targman, or did she contact him? Or did he say what it was for?"

Bosley shrugged. "I don't have any idea who called who. If Wes went out on a valuation, it woulda been for books. We got another guy who appraises everything else for us. 'Cept trains. I do trains."

Charlotte recalled her trip to the pawn shop. Toley Banks appraised the silverware, but it was the man called Doc who appraised the jewelry. She was about to ask if it was Doc when there was a sharp rapping at the door, and she went to see who it was.

It was Barnes—and Simon.

There was considerable tension at first, as Barnes had been

prepared for trouble. But in the course of questioning him, Barnes relaxed slightly as he realized that Bosley was cooperating, and no longer a threat to Charlotte. Simon was less relaxed, but said nothing. He pulled together the pictures and videos he made to show the detective how things had been moved out of place—and how some things were even missing, particularly from the dining room and the curio cabinets. Since there was no sign of a break-in, and the door was locked when Charlotte and Helene arrived, someone had to have had a key, which implicated Donovan.

Barnes was satisfied with the results of his questioning, and Bosley agreed to leave the basement key on the premises for Charlotte's use. After they left, Helene sank down on the sofa with relief.

"Oh, my word," she sighed. "I was so startled when that huge man just let himself in the door like he owned the place!"

"I couldn't tell you were frightened at all," said Charlotte.

"Good on you for keeping your cool," added Simon.

"Thank you very much. It seems we now have more information than we did before."

The three friends considered the implications of the book having originally been Olivia's. Helene thought it likely that Olivia would have tried to get it back—if she knew it was gone in the first place. But Olivia gave no indication in the weeks before her death that she was missing that book. Helene said her sister's focus was on the notebooks of her own writing, and on eventually publishing them. If her copy of *Least Objects* was something Donovan used as a child to make a prop for his train set, she apparently didn't value it enough to keep it out of his hands. Or perhaps she didn't know he took it, and considered it lost or permanently misplaced. If the book was at the center of whatever altercation caused the deaths of Olivia and Wesley Warren, there were still a lot of unknowns, including who was the third party.

Nonetheless, it appeared more than ever that Donovan was that third party. He was much more likely to realize he'd given away the find of a lifetime, if he had followed any of the articles and reports on how Bosley had acquired the book. If he was angry enough to throw a fit at Helene's house, there was no reason he couldn't get angry enough to do damage at his mother's. Barnes had made it clear that, between Donovan's outburst and the proof that things were going missing with no evidence of a break-in, there was sufficient cause to get a warrant for Donovan's arrest.

"What it doesn't explain, though," said Charlotte, who was slouched down on the wingback chair, "is what they're still looking for. They're taking random objects out of the dining room and curio cabinets. There's no pattern there. But they're moving a lot of stuff around without taking them, as if they're looking for something in particular."

"Maybe it's a smokescreen, or something to throw us off the track," added Simon.

"Well, if Donovan is arrested," said Helene, "I will go to the jail and ask him myself. Besides, I think I know where Olivia got the money for his car—she and Ronson sold some baseball cards for several thousand dollars in 1998."

Nineteen

Also Wednesday, September 18th

Simon wanted to get on with making the rest of valuation video, and Charlotte wanted to see the basement before continuing working on the clues in the notebooks.

The key to the basement door had a long shank and scalloped bow, which Charlotte grasped as she turned it in the old brass lock. The dark stairwell sent up a whiff of stale basement air mixed with moth balls, but it didn't smell of anything that suggested excessive damp, mildew, or decaying mice. Charlotte could not abide the smell of a dead mouse stuck somewhere out of reach in a house. She tread down the stairs carefully, hanging onto the wood rail, into a classic old basement of the kind she hadn't seen since early childhood. At the bottom, she pulled on a string that turned on a bare overhead bulb.

A forced-air furnace on the opposite wall was new enough to gleam here and there in the light. There were stacks of cardboard and wooden boxes on pallets, a pair of workbenches with tools hanging on pegboards, a laundry area with a washtub and an avocado green washer and dryer set from the late 60's, and a table made out of sawhorses topped with a sheet of plywood supporting stacks of more boxes and large items like a 50-cup coffeemaker. There were also dry-cleaning type bags filled with curtains and bedspreads, and a few boxes of toys from the 60's, building block sets, and boxed games that were popular at the time, many of which Charlotte once played herself. Two medium-sized containers held several vintage model railroad cars in original orange Lionel boxes. Neither container was full, and Charlotte supposed that Donovan had been raiding it a few cars or props at a time.

A darker area closer to the center of the house held the remains of an old boiler, which was near a raised area in the floor that ran all the way to the outside wall. There were cobwebs here and there, but nothing too awful.

Simon had to stoop occasionally to avoid hitting his head on various pipes and beams. "Well," he said, looking around slowly, "it's not as bad as I feared it would be. Probably only because it was hard for Olivia to get up and down these stairs."

Charlotte nodded. "I don't think anyone's been down here for a long, long time, either, maybe not since her husband got sick."

"I'll bring down the camera and stuff. Might as well get it over with." Simon went back up the stairs.

The basement really did look as if it were frozen in time. Some of the boxes on the pallets looked out of alignment, but it was impossible to say how, when, or why. Charlotte thought of her own basement, and how easily things got out of place when one searched for something that had been stored in a stack of boxes. Olivia's boxes were labeled, for the most part. Some were even the colorful printed-cardboard storage boxes that were popular back in the 70's and 80's, which were labeled with writing on masking tape on the ends: Blue Bedroom Set, Pink Bedroom Set, Ron's

Uniforms, Coats, Tablecloths and Towels, Donnie's Clothes, etc. Charlotte lifted the lid on one of the ones on top of the stacks, labeled Tablecloths and Towels, and saw nothing special, just various cloth and vinyl tablecloths and placemats with various kitchen towels and hotpads that coordinated with them, the vast majority in the green, yellow, and orange colors popular in the 60's and 70's. These were the things that Olivia and her family had used themselves, not things that she had collected just to collect them, as many of the things were upstairs. She didn't value these things in quite the same way, did not worry if they became damaged from damp. But for some reason she didn't let go of them when she no longer liked them enough to use—much like myself, thought Charlotte. These were just the things Olivia was tired of or wanted out of the way, and to Charlotte they looked highly unlikely to contain the valuable notebooks. Out of sight, out of mind.

Simon came back with the equipment and once again she was impressed by how quickly and efficiently he set it up. The smell of mothballs in the boxes with clothes and blankets was beginning to give her a buzzy headache, and the dark basement in general made her feel claustrophobic. She sighed, stretched her back and neck, and went back upstairs, where she helped Helene to successfully decipher the clue in the notebook (it turned out to refer to the film *Hiroshima, Mon Amour,* and the notebook was taped to the back of a framed poster of the film); by the time Simon finished with the videos of the basement and kitchen contents, they'd found three more volumes.

Charlotte read the latest clue: "*Painting the Music of Time.*"

Helene took it up. "This one sort of makes sense. The last one referenced *Books Do Furnish a Room*, which is part of Anthony Powell's *A Dance to the Music of Time.*"

"So maybe we go look on the bookshelf?"

Simon interrupted. "Poussin. There's a painting of that name by him in the Wallace Collection in London. Got any Poussin?" He smiled ever so slightly.

They went looking around the house again, but found no prints of the painting, not even among the stacks of jigsaw puzzles or among the art books on the bottom shelf in the living room.

"Well!" sighed Charlotte. "We know there isn't any music in the place, nor any Poussin paintings depicted in the things we can see up here. What about the basement, Simon? Did you spot anything worth looking at?

"The only things I wonder about are a couple of boxes that aren't labeled, that probably bear looking into."

Charlotte followed Simon down to the basement and helped him to uncover the boxes, which were stacked near the containers with Donovan's model train set. Both boxes turned out to be full of books.

One of the books was a worn-looking copy of *The Paintings of Nicholas Poussin.*

"Huh," said Simon. "The old spy Blunt wrote that."

The binding was broken, and pages appeared to be missing. As Charlotte went through it, she saw that it had been forced to hold one of Olivia's notebooks.

"There's a couple of Seamus O'Dair books, too," said Simon, as he checked the various titles. "Reprints, no first editions. But what have we here?"

The small dark book he pulled out looked as if it had seen rough treatment, but was still intact. The gold leaf title was almost worn away: *Faux Silence.*

Inside, the title was repeated, with the subtitle, *Poèmes de la Résistance.*

The author: Olivia Bernadin.

It was published in 1948 by the Sibylline Press, Paris.

"I wouldn't be surprised if this was the only copy," said Charlotte, feeling as if she was holding the very essence of Olivia's existence.

"It's nice to see it for real. Shame it was left down here."

"We should take these up to Helene. I bet she'll be surprised."

"Check the clue in the notebook first. We might get lucky."

Inside the cover of the eighth book, Olivia had written: *Wheel of Fortune!*

"The game show?" she wondered aloud.

"Or the board game. A stack of them over here." Simon moved to the end of the table and started looking.

Charlotte recalled that Olivia didn't remember if there were nine or ten notebooks. "You know," she said, "if there's no clue inside this next notebook, that means we've got them all, that there were nine, and not ten."

"Keep 'em crossed, then," he said. "Found it." He pulled it out of the stack of other board games.

The ninth notebook lay inside.

And it's clue: *Snakes and Ladders.*

"That one ought to be here—"

Charlotte was puzzled. "I don't know that it's right. I know there's "Chutes and Ladders," but not snakes."

Simon insisted. "You Americans have to rename everything. Everywhere else on the planet it's called "Snakes and Ladders," and it's an old, old game. Here we are." He found the game (and the cover said

"Chutes and Ladders"), and pulled it out as well.

There was no notebook inside the box, however.

They both sighed.

"That would have made it too easy, of course," Simon grumbled.

"Of course."

Helene was thrilled at their finds, and couldn't stop looking through the little book of poems. "I can't believe I'm actually holding this book. There were so few copies printed, you know. My parents had a copy, but I don't know what happened to it. This might have been theirs. In fact, I think that box of books you found might have been my mother's. Olivia got most of their things when they died, because Paul and I moved and traveled so much. I often wondered what happened to them."

This gave Charlotte an idea. "Could the copy of *Least Objects* that Donovan sold have been your parents'?"

"Yes!" said Helene, nodding in agreement. "It's very likely. My mother, especially, would have kept up with literature, and her preferences were high-brow. A Nobel-winning author would have been right up her alley, and in New York you could get any book the minute it came out."

"I'm going to bring those boxes up here," said Simon. "You can have a look, then."

"Oh, Simon," said Helene, "that would be wonderful, but maybe we should wait and not move anything until we find that last notebook. Just in case?"

"Right. I forgot about that." He opened up the ninth notebook and showed her the clue. "Does *Snakes and Ladders* suggest anything to you other than the game?"

Helene shook her head. "Nothing other than pythons and stepladders."

"Plumbing snakes?" Charlotte speculated. "Ladders in pantyhose?"

"How about sleeping on it?" Simon was looking at his watch. "I've got to get back to campus. I hope you don't take this the wrong way, but I'm uneasy about the two of you being here alone when the likes of Toley Banks and Mitchell are involved."

"Oh, I agree, Simon." Helene rose from her chair, still holding the book of poems. "I need to put my feet up a while. You two are doing all the hard work, but it's making me tired, anyway."

Charlotte wanted to plow through with finding the last notebook, but knew better than to argue with Simon and Helene. She would use the time to think and read.

"I'd like to take the most recent ledger books with me, along with these notebooks. If there's anything I need to double-check online, I can, and then maybe I can sort out what we know from what we are just guessing at." She turned to Simon. "I could use a copy of your pictures and videos, too."

"Absolutely," he said. "I'll get it to you later on today, if that's okay."

"Perfect."

Charlotte walked more slowly than usual back to her apartment, as her canvas messenger bag was heavy with notebooks and ledgers. As the blocks were covered, she still experienced the past overlaid with the present. To the right, for instance, there was the library, now doubled in size from the decade before, but she still *felt* the way the old front steps were spaced, and the way it felt to hold Ellis' hand as they went into the lobby, then around the pillars to the children's section. Further down the block, across the street, an architectural firm had renovated an old feed and seed store to serve as their offices. As she looked at it, she could still vividly remember the smell of fertilizer, the cool dampness of the bulk containers of seeds and bulbs, and the shiny troughs of the hanging scales.

The smell of pizza, however, brought her firmly into the present, as it usually did. She was now across the street from The Good Stuff and her apartment, waiting for the "Walk" sign at the busy intersection. The pizza joint next to her beckoned, but she resisted, despite her watering mouth and growling stomach. There were still some good things to eat from Helene's basket. The "Walk" sign came on, and as she crossed the street, she could see the tuxedo cat in the shop window, watching her. She went into the shop, looking for Larry, but didn't see him.

The woman behind the counter looked up, then eyed her bulging messenger bag, as if Charlotte was a potential shoplifter. "Can I help you with anything?"

"Um, yeah. What's the cat's name?"

"Shamus. Why? You want him?"

A rather unfriendly woman, thought Charlotte. Good thing there weren't a lot of customers at the moment. "Well, he's the shop cat, isn't he?" Was it Shamus or Seamus, she wondered.

"By default. One of Larry's customers gave us the cat, and that was okay for a while, but our younger daughter is allergic. Larry won't give him up, so we compromise by keeping the cat down here."

"Oh, you're Larry's wife! I'm Charlotte Anthony, I've taken the studio apartment."

"Yeah, he was telling me about you." The woman was looking Charlotte up and down, as if she were a rival. "Wendy." She didn't proffer a hand, but at least set down the catalogue she was reading. "Thanks for taking care of the cleanup, 'though I'm surprised he gave you that much of a break on the rent."

Her manner insinuated that Charlotte had done something more than clean up the apartment to get the rent break. "It was pretty bad. A lot of work, but I'm grateful to get a place I can afford."

A customer came in, and Charlotte took the opportunity to get away. "Well, um, nice meeting you. Gotta go." Wendy just gave a nod and went back to looking at the catalogue.

Charlotte looked by the window for Shamus/Seamus on the way out, but he wasn't there.

He was, instead, sitting on the newel post in her apartment, waiting for her to come up the stairs. She was pleased. Clearly, she and this cat had an understanding: *Wendy doesn't like either one of us. We don't like Wendy, either.*

"Hello, Shamus." She reached out to give him a pat, but he reached out with his own paw, and they played a silly pretend-swatting game for a few moments before she went over to the table and unloaded the bag of notebooks.

"So, are you a Shamus, or a Seamus?" She watched him leap from the newel to the table, and then try to see what was in the bag. He stuck a paw down in a gap along the side, and pulled out a pen, which he then batted around the table top.

"You're a snoop. Shamus it is."

Charlotte fixed a light lunch of cheese, crackers, and apple slices while waiting for a fresh half-pot of coffee to brew. She'd been drinking far too much coffee, and it was probably time to wean herself off the caffeine. There would be a small grocery run on Friday, on the way back from signing off with Stanton Estates, since the supermarket was out on the highway. She made a list of what to get from both the store and the house, and then wondered what, if anything, would be left after the sale? Martin had said that she could keep anything that hadn't been sold, or let them donate it to charity.

The dark red leather of the old sofa gleamed in the soft sunlight, and brought out the faded reds of the kilim. Shamus was sitting on the back of the sofa, looking out the window, watching birds coming and going from the young tree planted in the sidewalk below. Charlotte wondered how big the tree would get, and if she would ever be eye-to-eye with a crow, or at least a cardinal or blue jay.

The big library table stretched across the west wall, from the window on the right to the stairwell on the left. It was a handsome table, if a little too big for the space, same as the sofa. But within minutes, she was grateful for every square inch of it, spreading out the notebooks in chronological order. There was still room for her laptop and her lunch. Her scanner/printer was propped on a file box under the table, ready to go. The table had four deep drawers, as well, of which only one had a few office-type supplies and batteries and charging cables. The rest of the drawers were still empty.

Now, where do I begin? Each notebook had dated entries, so she labeled them with the year each one began. The autobiographical passages, combined with ledger entries from the same time period, might give some idea of what was going on in Olivia's life. She began with the earliest notebook she had, which started in 1969, even though it really wasn't the beginning, typing the passages in English on the computer, and making notes of passages in French, including a loose translation if it didn't take too long.

But as she progressed through the notebook, she found herself abandoning the typing and just reading, curled up on the sofa with Shamus dozing on the back of the sofa, next to her head.

In our house we spoke both English and French. My mother, Sophie Vinerman, was a Jew from Edinburgh, Scotland, where her father was a scholar. When she was seventeen, she traveled with her parents to find various relatives left in Europe after the Great War. In Paris, they lodged with Mme. Bernadin, a widow with a bookish daughter named Anastasia and a son named Marcellus. Marcellus was an apprentice chef. My mother and Sasha became fast friends, as mother was quite well-read, and she enthusiastically supported Sasha's dream of owning a bookshop. When my mother and father first met, they were quite shy around one another. Sasha thought my mother would make the perfect wife for her brother, and was shameless in her matchmaking. My grandparents, though, were so absorbed in looking for their relations that they didn't even notice the blossoming romance growing beneath their noses. When they returned to Edinburgh, Sophie and Marcellus wrote to one another faithfully for two years, while Marcellus advanced and began to earn something of a living. That was when he traveled to Edinburgh and spoke to my grandfather, asking for my mother's hand in marriage. Grandfather reluctantly agreed, because Marcellus was not Jewish, but a Huguenot. He only agreed because my mother threatened to run away with Marcellus.

I came along a year after they married. We lived with my Grandmother Bernadin in Paris, and my mother helped her with the lodgers and the cooking and cleaning. Sasha lived there, too, and we read books and went to plays and lectures and art exhibitions. Sasha knew so many people, and she would often bring me along, being quite okay with people thinking that I was her child. Later I realized it was because she had no liking for the male sex, and most men would not want to be bothered with a woman who already had a child. No, Aunt Sasha preferred the company of women, as I came to realize when I was older. She introduced me to her friend Henriette one day at a café, and said that they were going to open a bookshop together. I was thrilled. Grand-mère Bernadin was less thrilled, but my mother, as always, was very supportive and persuaded my father and grandmother that this would be a very good thing for Aunt Sasha and she would be very successful and very happy.

I adored the bookshop, which they named Sibylline. It was probably not the best sort of environment for a young female child—this was the time of the Lost Generation, after all, and everyone came to Paris to drink and loosen their morals. I read things that I probably should not have read at such a tender age, and let myself be touched in ways that I should never have allowed, but that was how things were in Paris in those days.

My mother and my grandmother remained sheltered from much of this, because I knew, instinctively, not to tell. Nor did my father, who was also exposed to licentiousness, because he had worked his way up to sous-chef at a small but well-known restaurant.

When I was ten, two things happened which changed everything. My grandmother died and my father came to the notice of Mr. Lamont, a very wealthy American who lived in Monte Carlo. Mr. Lamont wanted my father to become his personal chef. This was attractive to my father in many ways. First, the pay was phenomenal—and steady. Second, Mr. Lamont entertained frequently, and his guests were wealthy and sophisticated; some were even royalty. Third, it was a live-in arrangement, and a wife and two little girls were more than welcome. Fourth, as I later discovered, my father had great concerns about my exposure to Aunt

Sasha's world, and saw this as a way to protect me.

I, however, did not like it one bit! Monte Carlo was not Paris. The people were so different. I loved my aunt's scruffy friends who wrote great things and made great art, the whole world of books and paint and café crème. I did not like the marble floors and the salty sea air of the mansion at Monte Carlo. I did not like the feeling of being of the servant class after running loose as an equal, if a child, among the men and women of talent. But my father thrived in the appreciation and the security, and if my father thrived, so too did my mother.

My sister Helene, however, was as if born to the manor. She had no self-consciousness and her outgoing nature and blonde looks made her adorable to Mr. Lamont's children, whereas I always felt they looked down on me.

But a chef was not like a maid, particularly not one of my father's quality. He was regarded as a talented asset to be treated with respect, in much the same way as the Lamont children's music teacher. Monsieur Czerny followed his nose to the kitchens, where he would discover all sorts of delicacies and pastries being made, and Monsieur never met one he didn't immediately proclaim as perfection and devour it on the spot, along with several more if he could get his hands on them. Both my parents thought him great fun, and my mother, in particular, saw an opportunity to provide me with the piano lessons like she herself had had as a child. With Mr. Lamont's permission, I took lessons with M. Czerny in the music room, but only when it wasn't being used by the children or guests. I was a tolerable student, and felt somewhat accomplished—until my sister Helene turned three and began to show an interest in the piano herself.

How can I explain the deflating realization that my baby sister, ten years younger than myself, could easily play—and by memory—what I struggled to learn? This cheerful little blond prodigy won everyone's heart and attention. We were taught to play Solfiegetto as a duet, my left hand on the melody, her little hands the bass line. By the time she was five, she played the treble, and I the bass, and she played it with more musicality than I ever managed, even while I lurched high above her and her feet couldn't even reach the pedals. They dressed us in identical white lace frocks with pink ribbons, which suited her and made me cringe. But she became so good so quickly, that soon I got away with staying in my room to read while she performed.

My mother promised me that I could visit Aunt Sasha for my fifteenth birthday. Little Hell was to be left behind with our father and the Lamont's old nanny. I had my mother all to myself for the journey to Paris and back, and we talked about books and I told her that I wanted to be a writer. It was 1936. Things were much the same at Aunt Sasha's, there were still all the familiar faces, the writers, the artists. Picasso was there, and Hemingway, Gertrude Stein had just come back from a tour of America, there were strikes in the factories, and arguments about the Olympics going to Berlin instead of Barcelona. There was talk of a strange political situation in Germany, of the Depression in America and in Europe, as well. I felt as if I was let out of a box, seeing and hearing all the things I'd been missing in the sheltered dream world of Monte Carlo.

I begged my mother to let me stay, and Aunt Sasha begged her, as well, but my mother knew my father would not approve. After a blessed three weeks in my most favorite place on earth, we returned to the coast. When I was sixteen, my parents and Mr. Lamont began to introduce me to various young men, mostly local tutors, but after knowing the brilliant young men (and old) of Paris, those poor insipid boys held no charm—

and I made no secret of it.

Thus, by the time I was seventeen, I was able to persuade my father to let me travel on my own to Paris, and I would stay for a month or two at a time and help Aunt Sasha and Henri at the bookstore. This went on for almost three years. The talk became more political than artistic among the bookstores and cafés. One day I met a young writer from Dublin named Seamus O'Dair. He was so tall and slim, with jutting cheekbones and his auburn hair was so thick it almost stood on end. He had such long slender fingers, like a pianist. He had come to Paris to help organize the strikes, and after the settlements he stayed in flats down the street from Sibylline. I thought he was so passionate and brave, and Aunt Sasha said he was brilliant and had a great future. I do not think he noticed me, though, other than a polite "thank you," when I rang up his book purchase, and once when he forgot his cap and I ran for blocks to give it back to him.

Then France declared war on Germany. My parents were frantic, and Mr. Lamont sent my father in his car to retrieve me, and to bring Aunt Sasha and Aunt Henri, too. But my aunt was adamant: she would not leave Paris, nor would Henri. They felt such responsibility to the writers and artists there, and to Paris itself. It was the last time I would ever see Aunt Sasha; she was later executed by the Nazis for being part of the Resistance.

It was the Resistance, in the end, that would destroy me, as well, because I had not stayed. I was old enough, but I had not stayed, I had allowed my father to scoop me up and take me back to a world of privilege, to escape the war and reality itself in the entourage of the American, Mr. Lamont. Yet I was French. It was my country, I loved my country, and I loved Paris.

Twenty

Still Wednesday, September 25th

Charlotte read for hours, without realizing it was for hours, going faster as she became accustomed to Olivia's handwriting, and as things made more and more sense. She felt compelled to keep going, all for the desire to know: *what happened next*?

The oldest notebook in her possession began in 1969. Olivia's mood was dark and extreme; she was suffering anew from a deep sense of betrayal and guilt that she thought she had gotten past. As far as Charlotte could tell, it was a mix of attack, apology, resentment, and guilt. Passages seemed to be written as if to Ronson, with references to "your son," and "I told him he could have his father's book—why ever not?"

I know who it is you write about so cruelly, who you put through all the horrors of banishment, but I have taken, I really did take, the things you wanted most, just like you stole mine. You will never have them! I will kill him before you can have him, just like you killed me. How I wish I had not seen this, how I wish I had never met you....

Her eyes did not reflect the pictures that she saw in her mind, but they still told stories that broke my heart. Why couldn't I tell those stories for her? I never meant any harm....

Something had happened prior to 1969 that triggered Olivia's need to write again, after at least ten years of silence. She gave Helene a quick call to firm up some dates in Olivia's life as best as possible, then made notes of her own.

Olivia spent the war years as a college student in Manhattan. She returned to Paris as soon as she could, around 1947, and wrote and published a book of poetry by 1948. She came back to New York after Aunt Henri died and the bookstore was sold, which was around 1952. She frequented jazz clubs and kept writing and publishing, before suddenly returning to Paris in '56. She sent a postcard to Helene to say she was in love with another writer, and writing plays. Then nobody hears from her until she suddenly reappears back home with Ronson and baby Donovan, in early 1959.

Something shattered Olivia between 1956 and 1959, something which caused her to stop writing and, essentially, disappear from the literary scene. Back then, having a baby out of wedlock stopped a lot of women in their tracks. Donovan was the spitting image of Seamus O'Dair, and she now had proof that Olivia had known him.

Charlotte looked up some entries on O'Dair. He was, indeed, living and working in Paris in a twenty-five year stretch from 1936 to 1961. He was also commended for his role in the French Resistance. As the professor said on Courtney at Corton, O'Dair and a group of other writers who had been in the Resistance got together and restored an old theater which they themselves had sabotaged while it was being used by the Nazis. There, they staged the unorthodox and experimental plays O'Dair came to be known for, and launched the careers of several New Wave actors, screenwriters, and directors.

In a side note, the theater once again burned down, during the 1968 student riots, but was not rebuilt. It was also the year O'Dair was the co-recipient of the Nobel Prize for Literature, along with Yasunari Kawabata.

It was a good fit. Would O'Dair have rejected Olivia if she was pregnant with his child? Or would she have told him? Either way, what would have happened if Olivia found herself pregnant, but, for whatever reason, could not involve Seamus O'Dair? A marriage of convenience was not far-fetched, if done early enough. Strict, controlling Ronson did not seem a likely candidate for marrying a woman for her convenience. Given Olivia's secrecy about her writing, Charlotte thought it was a good bet that she let Ronson think that Donovan was his child. The things revealed in the notebooks, then, had to remain secret, hidden from both Donovan and Ronson.

Charlotte felt confident that she now had Olivia's motivation for hiding the notebooks the way she did, in and among things that both Ronson and Donovan knew about—but didn't concern themselves with. And if O'Dair was Donovan's father, then the passages Charlotte first thought were written as if to Ronson were actually addressed to O'Dair—and made more sense. "I told him he could have his father's book" could well have meant she gave Donovan the copy of *Least Objects* she had inherited from her mother. A nine- or ten-year old boy of the time would have played with model trains and turn a book into a homemade prop, especially back in those days.

As she continued reading, Charlotte picked up the rhythm of Olivia's shifts between her life at the time of writing and the story of her life leading up to why things were as they were at the time of writing, past and present, present and past, back and forth. The furious anger ran through the first two notebooks Charlotte had, the ones that began in

1969 and 1970, respectively. There were more passages that only made sense if O'Dair was Donovan's father, such as how she explained to Ronson that her grandparents were from Scotland, and that's why Donovan's hair was red. One passage said she kept Donovan in a buzz cut so he wouldn't look so much like his father. Ronson was a military man, and very likely in a permanent buzz cut, so it only made sense if Donovan's stiff auburn hair was inherited from O'Dair.

There were an increasing number of passages about the tediousness of the trips Ronson would make to track down baseball cards. He did, however, encourage her to start a collection of something of her own. Olivia had nothing but contempt for "collected junk," and out of spite went to extremes with it, forming not one, but dozens of collections. Yet Ronson never complained. He complained about everything else, she wrote, but never about the one thing any sane man would have raised objections to. She suspected that he saw their collections as their children, and had more interest in them than in Donovan, which made her very uneasy.

Then there was a gap, with the next book beginning in 1976. That was the year Donovan graduated from high school, and Olivia wrote about her disappointment that he rejected college, even as she felt spiteful glee that he didn't go into the military as Ronson wanted, all which corresponded with what Donovan himself said about his life at home. He liked to read and write as a child, until Ronson shamed him for not liking sports, after which he avoided both. Many sections sounded similar to things Olivia had written in the previous notebooks, like a retelling of scenes or incidents, but each time altered in some way, with a few words changed, or a shift in their emphasis. With the end of the Vietnam War, Ronson was home more often—and they went on more forays to shops and auctions for their collections. Olivia's attitudes to the collections seemed to shift when some things suddenly skyrocketed in value. She was both fascinated and repelled by what she called "the American desire to turn mediocrity into a legacy."

A knock on the door brought Charlotte back into the present, and she realized it was almost dark. Who could it be? She couldn't remember if there was a peep hole in the door or not, but at least there was a chain across it, so she decided to answer it, and was relieved to see it was Simon.

He held up a thumb drive. "Got a copy of everything for you."

She remembered he was bringing her the pictures and videos of Olivia's house. "Thanks! I'm about to make some tea—would you like to join me?"

"Yes, actually, a cuppa sounds good."

As he came in, there was a whiff from the pizza joint across the street.

"That's the one bad thing about living here," she said, pointing to it before closing the door. "I don't know how long I'm going to be able to resist eating pizza all the time."

"Why resist?" He smiled and followed her up the stairs.

"Unhealthy and expensive." Charlotte was terribly aware of Simon's closeness behind her, and wondered what would happen if she suddenly stopped on the stairs. Would he put his arms around her again, and then maybe leave them there a bit? *Oh, snap out of it!* Her mind was getting as bad as a chick flick, and she was far too old for such nonsense.

But even without the staged cuddle, Charlotte was glad Simon was staying for tea, and that she had a bit of milk on hand for the way he took it. He leaned against the end of the cabinets to listen as she brought him up to date about the content of the notebooks, her near-certainty that

Seamus O'Dair was Donovan's real father, and Olivia's reason for hiding the notebooks the way she did.

Simon was impressed. "Bloody hell! To think of Donovan as the offspring of someone like O'Dair! I know from you and Helene that he has a temper, but he comes across as gormless."

"I think that's an act," countered Charlotte. "I always get the feeling that he's holding a lot in, like what he really knows about what happened to his mother and Wesley Warren. I imagine he feels he needs to play his cards carefully, and right now he can't make a move without Mitchell and Toley Banks knowing about it."

"That might be, but then that makes him a very good actor." Simon took his mug of tea over to the table to look over the notebooks, and received another surprise when Shamus jumped up and walked across to meet him. "I didn't know you had a cat."

"I didn't either, until about twenty-four hours ago. That's Shamus."

Simon stroked the cat's back and was rewarded with Shamus flopping down on the table and rolling on his back to have his tummy rubbed. "Seamus, as in O'Dair?"

"I don't know for sure, but I prefer to think of him as Shamus, as in private investigator." She sat down on the sofa and enjoyed watching Simon and the cat get on like a house afire.

"You're a bit of a shamus, yourself, on this project. Ow!" He pulled his hand back from the cat, who was getting carried away, like cats often do. Simon joined her at the other end of the sofa. "What's your next step?"

"I'm going to keep reading, to get whatever facts I can out of the notebooks, and then go over the ledgers to see if anything stands out.

We're all pretty sure that the copy of *Least Objects* that Donovan accidentally sold was his grandmother's. She died in '67, when he was nine. Now, I think it is a fair assumption that Olivia did not read it until she received those boxes of her mother's books."

"She could have gotten if from the library, I would think," said Simon.

"Sure, she could have, but think of it from her point of view, and given the kind of man Ronson was. If she went and checked out that book from the library, that would indicate a particular interest in that book or author, not something she would want to draw attention to. Ronson was the sort that would have asked her about it, and she'd be forced to lie. But if it was just one of a whole bunch of books that was given to her by her mother, then it would have looked like she was just sampling something from it. More random, and less likely to require an answer as to why she chose it."

"So you're saying she didn't read it when it first came out, but like nine or ten years later?"

Charlotte nodded. "Probably around the time he won the Nobel."

They sat musing this in silence.

She continued to speculate. "So many of Olivia's actions seem sudden. She suddenly goes to Paris, suddenly comes back, suddenly goes back again, suddenly reappears with a baby and the last kind of man you'd expect her to marry, and suddenly disappears from the literary scene."

"Would have been hard work, being her." Simon shook his head sadly.

"She went into everything with great passion, a sort of all or nothing person, not the sort who would stay friends with an ex, for instance."

"Not even if they had a child together."

"Not even," she agreed. "So who's the father? An incredibly well-regarded writer, a hero of the Resistance, and someone she's had a crush on since she was a teenager—she first met him 'way back in 1936. But for whatever reason—they had a bad argument before she realized she was pregnant, she caught him with another woman, he was secretly married, or he was just using her or treating her like a convenient groupie—she is upset enough to careen away from him and into the arms of Major Ronson Targman."

"But she was a writer, herself." Simon sipped more of his tea. "The falling-out might have been professional."

Charlotte told him that Olivia's last known project was co-writing a New Wave screenplay. "There's a lot of evidence that it was one that O'Dair went on to finish on his own."

"Maybe he criticized her work, and that would have cut her as badly, if not worse, than catching him with someone else."

Charlotte nodded enthusiastically. "Exactly! And in typically melodramatic fashion, she would have burned everything she ever wrote, flung herself into despair, and renounce the literary life forever and ever."

"Sounds like bad fiction," he laughed.

"That means that it might have really happened that way, since they say that the truth is stranger."

He looked at her as if in challenge. "Well, then, Detective Anthony, how do you explain the notebooks? What made her start writing again?"

Her eyes locked on his. "The pattern will tend to repeat itself. There is one more notebook in that house, the very first one, and we don't know when she started writing it. I'm guessing it will be 1968. She's finally read O'Dair's most important novel, and has to face the fact that she cut off her nose to spite her face when she gave up her writing career like she did. Then he goes and gets the Nobel. It puts her in one of her reactionary tizzies. Only this time, she can't write openly. But she writes."

"Possibly," he said, as he considered the idea. "But here's one for you. What's all this got to do with Olivia's death?"

Charlotte sighed. Simon was right. The great reveal about why Olivia did and didn't write, and Donovan's true parentage, seemed to have nothing to do with the mystery of what happened to her in the end.

"The pawn shop is a common denominator in all of this," said Simon. "You're right, I think, that the entire mystery is connected to a book or books, and your idea of a personal connection between Olivia and Seamus O'Dair is also compelling. Ronson is dead, and now Olivia, so the great secret about Donovan's parentage is no longer valuable. Yet we know that people connected to Warren Brothers are still intensely interested in something that's in Olivia's house. I say a visit to the pawn shop is in order, to just see what we can see, maybe spot something there that we know was in her house not too long ago."

"I was there about a week and half ago," said Charlotte, and she explained about pawning her jewelry and silverware. "It has trains and books, and you can tell that Bosley and Wesley combined their hobby shop stock with the pawn shop's."

Simon rose as if he was preparing to leave. "How about we go there tomorrow—I'm free in the morning—on the pretext of getting your things back?"

"I'd love to, but I won't have enough money to redeem them until after the sale."

"Ah. Well, don't write it off yet. Take a look at the video, and some of the ledgers. We'll talk tomorrow. Thank you for the tea, it was spot on."

Charlotte saw him out the door, and locked up, the scent of pizza again wafting into the foyer. Her stomach growled, and she wondered if she should have ordered one, just once, and invited Simon to stay. Too late now. Besides, she really needed to get back onto the job.

Simon was right about looking through the ledgers. Charlotte began, as planned, with the most recent one, which covered the time before Ronson's death before abruptly stopping, which she speculated was when Ronson had hurt Olivia's arm. There were many entries of items sold, particularly of baseball cards—none as valuable as the ones sold for Donovan's car loan, but there were other entries, such as several thousand dollars for "sterling silver." Charlotte looked up silver prices for that date online, and saw that it coincided with an unusual spike. Clearly, the Targmans had kept an eye on fluctuating values, which implied they collected what they did as an investment. This was evidently quite common in the seventies.

This would tie in with Charlotte's own impressions of Olivia. She was not someone who did "cute," or "precious," despite the number of her collections which could be described as such. Not long ago there was a fad for small stuffed animals, which were bought and sold for strangely inflated prices for a number of years before petering out as the market became saturated. She checked the ledgers for that time period. There they were: three lots of the stuffed toys sold for thousands of dollars, and two individual ones that sold for several hundred dollars each. The Targmans had unloaded their stuffed toy collection before the market for them crashed.

Other items did not seem to do as well, and in fact some, such as Hummel figurines, were entered as sold for far less in the last two ledgers than they did in the earlier ones. Because the ledgers stopped before

Ronson's death, there was no way to tell for certain if Olivia had continued to sell off valuable collectibles in the past several years, or which ones were still valuable. Perhaps Detective Barnes could find out if Wesley Warren left any record of why he was going to visit Olivia that fateful night. Maybe whatever it was he was looking for—and didn't get—was what everyone else was looking for? Yet nothing suggested itself. Charlotte made notes of what she found, in the event that she and Simon would find something of Olivia's for sale at the pawn shop.

Shamus suddenly reappeared, and Charlotte realized she hadn't even noticed when he'd left. The big cat leaped up onto the table, rubbed his chin on the corner of her laptop monitor, then sprawled out on his side and began to give himself a wash. The night was chilly and windy, with a bit of a draft coming through the north-facing windows. She grabbed the throw off the sofa and wrapped it around her shoulders, and cobbled together something to eat while she sat and considered the entire Olivia problem.

Was there any connection between Olivia's hidden notebooks and whatever it was Donovan, Mitchell, the Warren Brothers, and Toley Banks were looking for? She was stumped. Then the thumb drive Simon brought over caught her eye, and she decided to take a look at it. If she could identify anything that was missing, they would know what to look for at the pawn shop, assuming Donovan took things to convert to quick cash, or someone else just plain stole them and the shop was fencing them.

She had already seen the early pictures, the ones that showed Olivia prostrate on her living room floor. Then came pictures Simon took of each room on the same day, followed by the still shots taken on the day he made the first valuation video, and then the video itself. Some things were immediately evident—missing vases and serving pieces from the dining room, and a bit of thinning out on a couple of shelves in the curio cabinets.

She made more notes and closed the video file, thinking that was everything, when she spied another file on the drive: "charmove." Curious, she opened it.

There were dozens of still shots, all taken on the day she moved. Shots of the house at Lake Parkerton, clowning around with Diane, Hannah's painting hanging above the fireplace, Ellis' piano, other works of art, her neighbors Ernie and Lorraine, Martin and Josh, and several of herself talking with Diane, standing alone on the deck with her red coffee mug, and getting into the Jeep for the drive to Elm Grove. There were actually quite a few shots of her that captured the mixed mood of that morning, looking forward and backward at the same time.

There were several pictures of the drive to Elm Grove, including Bosley Warren's billboard. At the apartment, there were funny pictures of her furniture being unloaded and brought up, quick snapshots. More refined ones came later, no doubt after Simon himself was done helping with the move. One shot caught her pensive mood, when she felt anxious about things getting out of her control, the mood she tried so hard to hide from others. Her favorite was a shot of herself and Helene watching the video Ellis had sent. Helene's expression revealed her love for Ellis, something Charlotte hadn't seen before.

But Simon had noticed.

Twenty-One

Thursday, September 26th

"Oh, for goodness' sake, Charlotte!" said Helene, with a motherly sigh of exasperation. "If you needed a loan, you should have asked me, not pawn your lovely things!"

This time Charlotte was in the brown leather armchair in Helene's sitting room, somewhat slouched down, hair hanging limply on either side of her face, and looking not unlike Tenniel's famous illustration of a sulking Alice in Wonderland at the Mad Tea-Party. She started to explain herself, but Simon, who was leaning against the archway to the kitchen with his arms folded across his chest and looking like he was trying not to laugh, jumped in first.

"I can see why she didn't, Helene. One doesn't want to be a bother, especially if there are options, and especially when there's actual cash money involved. Wouldn't do to have it go sideways."

"I just hope it hasn't gone sideways at that shop," Helene retorted. "Charlotte, dear heart, I don't mean to sound like a scold, I'm just worried for your sake, and the Warren Brothers are such bad news, as we all know now. Please let me loan you the money so you can get your jewelry and silver back."

"It'll be a good cover story when we go and have a look around," added Simon.

"Okay, I'll do it," said Charlotte, nodding in resignation. It would be good to get the things back, even if she ended up turning them over to Martin Stanton to sell. "I spent a lot of time looking at the ledgers and the videos, and I have some idea of what objects are missing from Olivia's house." She looked up at Simon. "I'm glad you're going with me, though."

"I was wondering," added Helene, "if you should tell Detective Barnes what you're about to do."

"I'll call him and tell him on the way there. I need to give him an update, anyway." Charlotte took a deep breath. "I need to give you an update, as well, some things I figured out last night."

Simon began to go into the kitchen. "I'll put some coffee on, if that's okay?"

"Thank you, Simon," said Helene, who then turned to Charlotte. "What have you learned?"

Charlotte told her about the likelihood of a relationship between Olivia and Seamus O'Dair, and of Donovan being O'Dair's son, supported by corresponding dates and the anecdotal references to O'Dair in Olivia's notebooks.

"This is the great secret of the notebooks, why they were hidden in the first place. I strongly suspect that Olivia did not read *Least Objects* until nearly ten years after its publication, when she received the boxes of books from your parents. It triggered something in her, causing her to write again. But of course," she concluded, "the story she had to tell had to remain a secret."

Helene sat in silence as she absorbed this information. Finally she spoke. "Donnie does look just like O'Dair, doesn't he?"

Simon came in with coffees. "I'm wondering if anyone else has noticed this. But there's a lot of people who think all redheads look alike."

"True. Anyway," continued Charlotte, "I kept reading the notebooks. Olivia's style is to replay certain key scenes, changing just a few words or details in each version in order to say something new about it. Some of the passages felt familiar, or some of the story did, especially about things that happened in France. Then it dawned on me, in one of those middle-of-the-night bursts of insight, why that was. They're passages from *Least Objects,* except told from Margot's—the main female character's—point of view. And her point of view is very, very different than O'Dair's."

"Oh, my word," whispered Helene.

"How do you mean, exactly?" Simon asked. "Is it a word-for-word sendup, or what?"

Charlotte shook her head. "No, the familiarity is in the story told. The words are Olivia's own. There's a copy of *Least Objects* online at Project Gutenberg, so I was able to compare, and not just rely on memory." She took a sip of coffee before proceeding. "Now, Olivia has also written many passages in French, which I can translate just enough to know that they, too, follow the pattern of retelling with small changes in words or details. What strikes me most, though, is that the story feels real, like autobiography. In O'Dair's version, Margot was caught in a lie about being part of the French Resistance, and was not only castigated, but outcast. A lot of horrible things happened to her as a consequence. Olivia writes about the story of her marriage and life here in Elm Grove as if it were the same sort of cold horror, as if she was Margot."

"It sounds dreadful," said Helene. "Perhaps we shouldn't pursue this project, if my sister was delusional?"

Charlotte shook her head quickly. "No, no, no. Don't get me wrong. *We* might know that she thinks she's writing about her own actual life, but as a novel, it stands on its own. There's craftsmanship there. It was deliberate, not delusional—she knew what was fact, she understood that she was being relentlessly subjective—but she knew it could hurt. She didn't actually want to hurt anyone, even though this was the story she had inside her to tell."

"Now I'm feeling sorry for her again," said Helene. "So it is worth doing, then, this project? Is it worth transcribing and publishing?"

"No doubt in my mind," Charlotte asserted. "In fact, now I want to find that last notebook more than ever, both to confirm the reason she resumed her writing, and to add the critical first passages and chapters."

"That means keeping Donovan and Mitchell out of that house at all costs," said Simon. "We can't take the chance that they'll do something to mess up finding that notebook."

"Oh, absolutely," said Helene. "I'm actually hoping that the detective catches up with Donovan. Maybe he'll put a detail on the house?"

Simon smiled at Helene's uncharacteristic phrasing. "Wouldn't hurt. Then I'd feel better about you two working there when I'm in class."

"Helene," said Charlotte. "I need a favor. In the notebook that Olivia gave to me, which is the final volume, the entire middle part is in French. I believe it is the same sort of thing she's written all along, except there's a difference in tone, as if she realizes something she didn't know before. I'd like you to translate those pages for me, if you think you can bear it."

"Of course, Charlotte." She finished her coffee and set the cup down with determination. "I guess I never really knew my sister, and this is one way I might be able to understand her better."

There's more to it than that, Charlotte thought to herself. *I think it says that Olivia had another copy of Least Objects.*

Simon offered to drive to the pawn shop, and at first Charlotte refused, thinking she wasn't up for riding all the way out there on the back of a motorbike, but he gestured at a black Land Rover parked on the street behind her Jeep. "That's yours?" she asked, not hiding her surprise.

He grinned. "The winters are long and cold here."

Once they were on the road, Charlotte called Detective Barnes and left a message to say where they were going, why, and requesting a meeting for an update and some new theories. She barely ended the call when the phone rang with Barnes calling her back. She filled him in with many of the things she had shared with Simon and Helene.

"I think Olivia might have left some indication her final notebook of what Mitchell and Donovan are looking for, but I'm having Helene translate those passages in order to be accurate. The handwriting is also pretty bad in that one, so it might take some time."

"Anything solid you can come up with is more than welcome, Charlotte," said Barnes. "We've got a lead on Donovan Targman's whereabouts, and should be able to bring him in later today. The only thing I worry about is they have keys and can just let themselves in, like Bosley Warren did. I'll let you know the moment we have Mr. Targman in custody, and then I want you and Mrs. Dalmier to be on the alert for the other players in this drama."

While Charlotte was talking with Barnes, she occasionally glanced at Simon, taking in the way he drove. He was clearly used to driving on the right-hand side, perhaps because he'd spent so much time in different countries, or perhaps he was just an ambidextrous driver. She didn't think she could easily drive in the left-hand lane in England, herself, or at least not without a lot of practice.

"By the way," she said to Simon, when she rang off with Barnes, "I saw the photos of my moving day. Thank you for those. They were great."

He smiled. "You're more than welcome, Charlotte. Do you miss your house yet?"

She shook her head. "Not really. It's still a little bit like I'm on a vacation. But that could change in an instant. Tomorrow is the last time I will see my stuff, you know, before the sale. And the house is on the market, so that could go at any time, soon. Maybe that's when I will finally feel dispossessed."

Simon nodded as he listened. "I've done a bit of traveling light, myself. Obviously. Sometimes I have to remind myself that not everyone does, or even can. People do get attached to places, stuff, their homes, and they just pine for them." He turned toward her for a moment, with that undefinable expression of his again. "I don't think you're one of them, though."

"Is that good or bad?" she asked.

He didn't answer immediately, his attention focused on maneuvering through a badly-designed interchange that would take them onto the highway leading to the pawn shop. Charlotte wondered at herself, for being attracted to a man who left her confused as to where she stood with him. If a friend was experiencing the same kind of attraction, Charlotte wouldn't hesitate to advise stepping back and taking a closer look at her own motivations: was the attraction because the inscrutability was hard to crack, to tame? And if she succeeded, would the appeal dissipate, and the respect for the man be lost?

"Good," he said, startling her back into the present. "Very good, I should think."

Oh! Charlotte thought. Then, just to be contrary, she said, "I'm a nester, you know. I'm not happy unless I have a place I can call my own."

"But it doesn't have to be the same exact place, does it? I'd bet you could turn a tent into your nest if you were so inclined." He glanced at her sideways, with a hint of a smile, then pulled into the dusty, pot-holed parking lot in front of Warren Brothers Pawn and Payday.

Charlotte's palms were cold and clammy as they entered the shop. Now that she knew who Toley Banks was, and aware of what he could do, the prospect of facing him again made her stomach hurt, even with Simon there to back her up. She remembered Banks' driver, Doc, and wondered if Simon could handle him in a match. *Snap out of it!* This wasn't a crime show on television. If Toley Banks decided to pull a gun on them, there was nothing either she or Simon could do about it. No, she had a legitimate reason to be there, ticket in hand, the cash borrowed from Helene in her purse. Just stay cool.

Simon didn't look the least bit worried as he walked around, taking in the variety of things for sale, with particular attention to a display of motorcycle helmets. Charlotte had given him a list of items she thought were missing from Olivia's house, but they agreed that he shouldn't be too obvious about looking for them in the shop.

Ilona was gabbing on the phone *(did she ever stop?)* as Charlotte approached the counter, but when the clerk caught sight of Simon, she hung up quickly, ignored Charlotte, and strutted over to the counter nearest the helmets. Her cleavage was on fine form for his viewing pleasure, and Charlotte's annoyance increased as Simon smiled at Ilona the same way he did at Lola. She sighed, and continued to the counter, where she rang the metal bell for service.

She had put so much thought and energy into expecting to deal with Toley Banks, that when Mitchell came out from the back room and greeted her like an old friend, she didn't know what to say.

"Charlotte!" he crooned, "what a surprise! You're looking beautiful, as always." He grasped Charlotte's hand with both his own, and gave it a little squeeze. "What brings you all the way out here today?"

"Oh, um," she stammered, then handed him the pawn ticket. "I've come to get my jewelry and silver back, if that's okay." *Oh, stop being a wimp,* she told herself. *Of course it's okay!*

"Not a problem, not a problem. Just give me a moment, and I'll track them down. You're redeeming everything, then, the full amount?"

She nodded the affirmative, and he went into the back room. Or rooms. Charlotte had no idea how extensive the "back room" was, then imagined it had to be substantial if it held all the things that couldn't be sold. She decided to browse through some shelves herself, in particular the collectibles, since Simon continued to flirt with Ilona.

She spotted a trio of Olivia's Capodimonte flower baskets almost immediately, and two small McCoy vases, as well. One of the vases, she knew, was purchased for sixty dollars in the 1970's, but here the sticker said only $45, which Charlotte found odd. The basket trio was marked at forty dollars. She didn't know if this was a fair price or not, but suspected that it was lower than it ought to be. Nonetheless, a mental calculation of the estimated number of small collectibles in Olivia's house, times, say, an averaged-out price of twenty dollars apiece (some were worth far more, others were nearly worthless), would be around thirty thousand dollars. They would likely bring more at an auction, where collectors would bid against one another. If Donovan was selling off things now, he was throwing money away.

Seeing Mitchell again, his insistent charm and too-knowing eyes, convinced her that Donovan was not selling things off willingly. She moved over to the bookshelves, where there were two framed newspaper articles hanging on the wall nearby: one was of Bosley Warren's luck with *Least Objects*, and the other was Wesley Warren's obituary.

"Isn't it just the saddest thing?" Ilona had finally stopped trying to seduce Simon, and came up next to Charlotte.

"I imagine it's been a shock. What will happen to the business?"

"Oh, I don't know, I suppose it'll go on, 'cause you couldn't buy the kind of attention Bos' book got. It's a shame, though, 'cause Wes was the one who knew what the book was worth, *and* he thought he knew where to find another one, too."

Ilona now had Charlotte's full attention. "He knew where to find another one? You're kidding!"

Ilona shook her magenta hair off her shoulder with an air of authority. "I'm not." Her eyes followed Simon around the shop. Charlotte scrambled to think of another question before Ilona's short attention span evaporated, but Mitchell came back out to the counter just then, with her jewelry and silver. She walked to the counter, and Ilona walked over to Simon. Of course. I might as well have come here on my own, she thought.

"Here you are, Charlotte." He opened the bag with the jewelry and checked off the itemized list as he chatted. "How is your search for the notebooks coming along?"

Charlotte hesitated to answer. What should she tell him? The truth, that there was only one more to go? Perhaps that would reassure him that she was almost finished with the search, and he would be more patient about waiting until the place was turned over for the auction.

"Very well, actually. We've found nearly all of them, in spite of quite a few things having been moved around against Helene's explicit wishes."

Mitchell feigned surprise, not quite pulling it off. "I wouldn't know anything about that. I've no interest in the notebooks apart from wishing you the best of luck in finding them."

"Oh, I know you don't care about the notebooks," began Charlotte, and then suddenly stopping as she felt an arm move across her back, settling with a hand at her waist.

"What about the notebooks?" asked Simon. He left his arm around her, and she felt her brain go blank for a couple of seconds.

But only for a couple of seconds. Her thoughts raced from one misgiving to another: was he patronizing her by acting like her "protector," was he doing this out of genuine concern, or was it purely subterfuge, because he knew something that she didn't? There was only one thing she could do that would both cover the legitimate possibilities and her own sense of dignity: act as if the attention was both welcome and expected.

She tilted her head a little to look up at him adoringly. "Darling, this is Donovan's friend, Mitchell. He was asking how our search for Olivia's notebooks was coming along, because I know he's in a bit of a rush to get in there, himself."

She felt Simon's hand press hard against her waist in warning. "Oh, yeah," he put out his other hand and shook Mitchell's. "Simon Norwich. So you're the fellow who makes lasagna." The inflection in his tone opened up a wide range of interpretations.

Mitchell, for once, looked as if he didn't know what to say—which meant he wasn't in control of the situation. "That's right. Well, then," he looked down at the jewelry to hide his irritated expression, and finished checking things off.

As Mitchell moved to the silverware, Simon, whose hand hadn't left Charlotte's waist, began talking to her about the jewelry that was in another display case, in particular a "pearl choker" that he thought would look lovely on her. She looked at him in alarm, but he pressed his hand hard again, so she played along. Ilona came back around the counter, her heels clacking loudly, and her face in a thorough pout. Charlotte put her own arm around Simon's waist and pulled him a little closer.

"You spoil me," she cooed.

"Anything for my favorite wench," he murmured.

Wench? She bit back a retort, and made the most of the moment of cuddling, resting her head against his shoulder as Mitchell finished up the paper work.

He looked up at her. "That's it, then. If you have the amount due?"

Charlotte and Simon let go of one another as she retrieved the money and gave it to Ilona, who ran it through the cash register.

Mitchell looked tense, as if forcing himself to be professional and cordial. "Nice seeing you again, Charlotte, and meeting you, Simon." Then he turned and went into the back room.

Charlotte wished she could ask Ilona more questions, but the moment had passed, and the clerk's obvious irritation made it highly unlikely she would be forthcoming with answers.

Simon continued their charade by taking Charlotte's elbow and leading her over to the jewelry counter, pointing out a pearl choker that probably really would look good on her. But she was certain the "couple" act was coming to a close, and fought back the temptation to get snarky.

It didn't help matters that as soon as they got back in the Land Rover, he burst out laughing.

"Well done, Charlotte! That'll keep the smarmy git off balance."

"You really think that bit of theater will stop him from moving stuff around Olivia's house? That he'll think my big bad boyfriend will make his life difficult if he gives me any problems?"

He sobered up. "That I don't know, to be honest. It might even make things worse. But one thing I know about his kind, if they haven't got all the angles worked out, it makes them nervous. And when they're nervous, they make mistakes. Mistakes that might give away what the game really is."

Charlotte had to give him credit for the attempt. "And here I thought I was actually going to get a pearl choker," she joked.

He started the engine, then gave her a pat on the knee. "Anything your little heart desires, love."

She clobbered his arm.

Simon had to get back to campus, so he dropped Charlotte off at Helene's, where she gave as light-hearted an account of their adventure as she could.

Helene saw right through it. "Hmm. You sleep in the man's bed, serve as his damsel in distress, and blush nearly every time you hear his name. You have it bad, Charlotte."

"Well, it isn't reciprocated, so please don't tease or say anything to him, okay?" Charlotte's stomach growled, partly because it was lunch time, and partly from being so nervous at first at the pawn shop.

"I'm sure I won't have to," said Helene. "He's not stupid."

"That makes it even worse. I know he likes women that look like

Lola or that tramp at the pawn shop, lights up like a Christmas tree around them. And that isn't, and will never be me, I'm afraid."

"And thank goodness for it! He likes you a lot more than you think, my dear. He certainly respects you. I know that seems like cold comfort right now, and it wouldn't surprise me if you are feeling a bit lonely at times. But he might not want to start something he wouldn't be in a position to continue in a few months' time."

Charlotte looked up at Helene, and realized she could be right. Simon wasn't a citizen, and probably only in the country as long as he could have a work visa. If the university didn't give him another year's contract, he would likely have to leave.

Her cell phone rang; it was Detective Barnes.

"We got Donovan Targman," he said.

The first thing Helene did was call her lawyer, who in turn called another lawyer better suited to represent someone charged with burglary or criminal trespass—or even murder. Then Charlotte drove her to the city jail, where Donovan was being held.

"I will do what I can to get him out on bail, but I want to talk to him first. The detective said that could be arranged. I want to know, once and for all, if he is being coerced by Mitchell and that loan shark, and just what it is they think they're looking for." Helene looked and sounded determined—just short of imperious, Charlotte thought.

"That's the the sixty-four thousand dollar question, isn't it?" Charlotte came to a stoplight, and as she waited, she had a worrisome thought. "Do you think he'll be charged for Olivia, you know—"

Helene's lips pressed into a thin line. "Detective Barnes said he's being questioned about it. This is awful."

They drove in silence the rest of the way, and said little until Barnes met them in the waiting area and expedited their access. Barnes and Charlotte went into the observation room, and Helene went to talk to Donovan in the interview room.

Donovan was already there, seated at the table. He hung his head when he saw her, and spoke quietly. “I’m so sorry, Aunt Helene.”

“Oh, Donnie. Please tell me what this is all about.” Helene sat down at the table across from him, her back to the two-way mirror.

Charlotte was surprised by how similar the set up was to things she’d seen on television crime dramas, and it calmed some of her initial nervousness. Her heart not only went out to Helene, but to Donovan—as he looked up at his aunt, he looked twenty years older than he was, as if he was wearing every hardship, heartbreak, disappointment, humiliation, and loss of hope that he’d experienced in his life all at once. He seemed exhausted and afraid, a man at the end of his rope.

“Whatever you do,” he whispered, “do not break the contract with Warren Brothers.”

“What are you looking for?” Helene pleaded. “What is in that house that is worth all of this?”

“Mom told Wesley Warren that she had a first edition of *Least Objects,* but that it was more valuable than the one they sold.”

“That’s why he was there that night?”

Donovan nodded. “They own me, I’m trying to pay them off, but I can’t, not without Mom’s stuff. Too much interest.”

“What happened that night, Donnie? Can’t you tell me?”

He shook his head. “Just don’t break that contract. Don’t go there alone. Be careful, you and Charlotte both.” His eyes were glazed with fear. Then he wouldn’t answer any more of her questions.

The guard indicated that Helene's time was up, and she sighed. "I've retained a lawyer for you, and we'll take care of bail."

He shook his head. "You shouldn't do that."

Helene rose to leave. "Well, I can't leave things like this. Be careful, Donnie. And stay in touch." She turned and the guard let her out.

They stopped at The Coffee Grove for a late lunch, and Helene used her cell phone to cancel her afternoon student.

"I can't face teaching right now, my head is just too full of this tragic mess." She took a bite of chicken pecan salad. "Besides, I've started translating those passages in the notebook that you mentioned, and I'd like to finish it. It's a lot of pages, but it's absorbing."

Charlotte nodded. "I wouldn't bother you with it, but something tells me it's important to know what it says right now, and I don't want to get it wrong or miss any nuance. Too much is at stake."

"I wonder why Donovan wouldn't tell me what happened that night."

Charlotte had the salad, as well, and had to force herself not to eat too quickly, she was so hungry. "I think he probably didn't want to upset you even more. He really is scared, I think. They must have something awful on him."

Helene looked thoughtful. "Do you think he realizes that he gave away Olivia's copy of *Least Objects?* He's confirmed that Olivia had contacted Warren Brothers about the book, and Bosley Warren now knows that the book he sold was originally Olivia's. Either the left hand isn't talking to the right hand at Warren Brothers, or there's reason for them to think that there is yet another first edition of that book." She wiped her lips with her napkin. "But that is highly unlikely, isn't it?"

"Extremely," Charlotte agreed. "Yet it would explain their determination to find it—and to find it before we do."

"But we aren't looking for it," Helene pointed out.

Charlotte gave her a sly smile. "Maybe we should be."

She had no sooner reached the top of the stairs in her apartment when Shamus came dashing up the steps, bolting by her in a blur toward the bathroom. *What on earth?* She went to look to see what he was doing, and found him hunched down in the tub, behind the shower curtain. He shied away as she bent down to pick him up, and growled. Then came loud, insistent banging on her door.

The events of the day, plus Donovan's naked fear, made her wary. She peeked out the window to the sidewalk below, and could just make out Larry's wife Wendy. She reluctantly made her way down to the foyer as the banging continued, and answered the door.

"I want to get that damned cat. I know he's in there." Wendy started to come in, but Charlotte held her ground.

"Yeah, he's here, and he's scared to death! What's going on?"

"I'm taking him to the shelter. My daughter is allergic, I told you. I'm also tired of his cat hair all over the shop. He's been sleeping on a stack of silk scarves and they're ruined!" She held out her arm and showed Charlotte a fairly deep cat scratch. "On top of that, he's mean. I'm fed up."

"Wait a minute, wait a minute. Why don't I keep him here for a while? He's good company for me."

Wendy thought for all of five seconds. "I'll be back with his food and box. And I'm going to block off that pet door." She strode back to the store entrance.

"What was *that* all about?"

It was Diane, who had come down the sidewalk from the other direction.

"I've just become a cat owner. I think. C'mon in!"

As Diane came in, there was the sound of something heavy scraping on the floor coming from the other side of the door at the end of the foyer, then a sharper, snapping sound: Wendy was sliding in some kind of panel in the pet door. Then more scraping sounds. Charlotte felt herself being watched, which by now she took as some sort of telepathic communication from Shamus (and swore to herself she would never, *never* let on to anyone that this was the case, along with the fact that the cat smiled). She caught him peeking around the newel post.

Diane looked at her with a *What?* expression. Charlotte held up a finger. "Just give it a minute."

Forty-five seconds later, there was banging on the front door again: Wendy had arrived with the litter box and food bowls.

"Larry's got the vet info, you'll have to get it from him later," she said, setting the cat things down on the floor. "Thanks." Then she abruptly left.

"Wow!" Diane exclaimed. "What a—"

Charlotte handed her the food bowls. "Wanna meet Shamus?" she asked, picking up the litter box and going up the stairs.

"Hey, sure! I love cats! In fact, I adore cats! Is this the black cat that's always hanging around the store? He is so cool!"

By this time Shamus had figured out that Wendy wasn't coming up after him, and he was sitting on top of the table next to the computer. Charlotte set his box down near the bathroom door and smiled happily as Diane cooed and fussed over him. A pet certainly helped the place feel like home, she thought. She filled his bowls with water and the kibble Wendy provided, and set them in the kitchen area. As she worked, Shamus jumped down from the table and trotted over, tail high in the air, and sat politely until she finished.

"That is a great cat!" said Diane. "How could anyone *not* like that cat? And he's so friendly!"

Charlotte explained Wendy's grievances.

Diane wasn't having it. "Animals know when they're not wanted, you know?"

"I think you're, right," Charlotte agreed. "But Larry really likes him, and I don't know if he'll want this to be a permanent arrangement."

"He ought to get rid of his wife and keep the cat!" Diane flopped down on the sofa and surveyed the apartment. "The more I see this place, the more I like it. How about you? Do you like it here?"

"It's definitely growing on me. I've been so busy dealing with the Olivia project, and tomorrow I have to go back to Lake Parkerton and sign off on the set up for the sale. But I'm glad that I'm here, that I'm not trying to work and sleep in the middle of all the upheaval. Want some tea? Or how about calvados?" she added, spotting Diane's slight hesitation at the suggestion of tea.

"Calvados, for sure! How's the project coming along, and how's Helene holding up?" Diane kicked off her brown suede demi boots and tucked her legs up on the sofa. She was wearing a long, fuzzy brown cowl-neck tunic sweater over brown cable-knit tights, and her dark hair was set off by a wide, light brown knit headband. She looked like a big cuddly teddy bear with glasses.

Charlotte shared as much as she could, leaving out anything Barnes would have wanted her to keep to herself, which actually was most of the bits about Donovan, the Warren brothers, and Toley Banks' operation.

"Finding that last notebook is giving us fits, though," she said. "I want it more than ever, now that I have some idea of what Olivia was writing about."

Diane, for once, was quiet, lost in thought and looking into her glass. "Does any of this have anything to do with Olivia and Wes Warren? You know, why they died?"

"Simon is wondering the same thing. My intuition tells me there may be a connection, but not necessarily a direct one. I don't think that whoever is involved with their deaths is looking for the same thing I'm looking for."

"Maybe it's a red herring!" Diane's expression was completely serious. "Maybe they *want* you to think they're after one thing, when they're after something else altogether."

Charlotte shook her head. "I really doubt that. If there's any red herrings at all, it's the natural distractions of everyday life—the stresses, the confusion, limitations of imagination and stamina, things like that can leave one operating blind. Or I make my own red herrings by thinking there's significance in certain objects in Olivia's house, when there might not be any at all."

"Oh, what's the fun in that?" Diane teased, but halfheartedly.

Shamus had finished eating, and was sitting on the floor in front of them, washing his paws and face.

"Shamus," said Diane, who then asked, "is that Seamus, like O'Dair, or Shamus, like a private eye?"

Charlotte was again struck by the sort of group-think that occurred among her friends: Simon had asked the same thing.

"Who knows?"

Twenty-Two

Friday, September 27th

Charlotte was surrounded by boxes and boxes of picture puzzles, and the pieces were mixed up between boxes. She was in a large room lit only by the glare of the sun coming through a single large window. Each box of puzzles was emptied and set up with the picture visible next to the pile of pieces that was in it. She went from pile to pile, with hundreds of pieces in each, turning every piece face up, and grouping them by color or some distinguishing feature. It took hours and she was sweating with fear that she would not finish in time, time was running out—and then a great wind started up, blowing away pieces from the piles, and she tried to grab them, but the wind got stronger—

She woke up. It was dark, save for the glow from streetlights that managed to find cracks in the closed blinds. Other elements of the dream were still with her, the aloneness, the sense of not really knowing what to do, but feeling responsible for doing it. She still wasn't used to living here, the noises of the old building, the cars going by on the street, the vibration of a train going by somewhere, all the night sounds which would wake her, put her on alert because she hadn't yet accepted them as normal.

Charlotte didn't recall feeling quite this skittish when she and Ellis first moved to Lake Parkerton, but she was a decade younger then and still possessed a bit of youthful invincibility. These days, not so much. Her joints and muscles still ached from the move, and she still felt emotionally drained from all the changes. It also didn't help that she was in the first circle around not one, but two murders, that she was worried about Helene, and had an unreciprocated attraction to Simon. And she still had to sell her stuff and her house. And to find that last notebook.

The time on the cell phone said 4:27. The last time she'd had problems with insomnia, Dr. Lauro said not to fight it but to embrace it —lay back and let the mind wander where it will, and even if sleep didn't return, the relaxation would still help her body recover and her mind process all the changes. So Charlotte adjusted the duvet, fluffed the pillows, and lay back down, looking at the ceiling, and gradually realized her mind's eye was still seeing her house at Lake Parkerton, every room, every item, as if it was still the way it was, and she was still there.

She saw her bedroom closet, felt the fabric of the clothes, the texture of sweaters, shoes, scarves. Memories of when she acquired each piece, where she wore them, why she bought them or why she stopped wearing them. Fleeting moments of guilt, of wishing she now had the money she had spent on them, and the time back, as well, that she had spent on shopping trips. Charlotte's mind moved through the house, to Ellis' room, remembering the teenage mess of clothes and schoolwork, of friends visiting. There was the first winter there, when Ellis had a bad case of flu and Charlotte stayed up all night in a rocking chair next to her bed, worried about pneumonia, relieved when her little girl pulled through. The hours and hours of listening to Ellis practice, of sitting quietly in an armchair in the corner while she had lessons with Helene, and the walks around the lake to Helene's house and back.

Ellis was the common thread through most of her memories, of shopping trips and day trips, of camping with the families of her friends, of worrying while watching her learn to sail, even on the placid waters of the lake. Was that only two summers ago? And was it only earlier this year that she played so well at the state competition? Charlotte had hung a series of photos along the wall above the dresser, and did not need to have the light on to know which one was which: pictures of Ellis, from her toddler days playing in the sand at Lake Michigan until her last state competition, in the midst of performing the lyrical solo *cadenza* from the Haydn Piano Concerto in D Major. It was not the most difficult of the works performed at the competition, but it was the perfect showcase for Ellis' light touch, technical precision, and youthful exuberance. The expression on her face in that moment was almost as if she was singing the melodic line. Charlotte would never forget that night, when she knew in her bones that her daughter was going to enter a level, a world, which would take her far, far away. And it did, ever so quickly.

A sudden crack of lightning and loud thunder startled Shamus, who jumped off the bed and ran, she assumed, to hide in the bathtub. It was now 6:11, and the wind and rain pelted against the windows. Sleep wasn't going to happen.

She put some coffee on to brew, opened the blinds, sat on the sofa, and from there she considered the apartment in the weird light of the stormy sky. She noted that the kilim rug looked so much nicer here than it did at the house. Here, it seemed larger, more significant. The slightly worn areas were as beautiful as the rest. It was *the* rug. Over in her closet, there was *the* pair of black jeans, *the* pair of blue jeans, *the* black skirt, *the* white shirt, and *the* gray sweater, whereas in her former closet they were each one of several, and the several amid many more. In the kitchen area, there were one set of white dishes, one set of glasses, one set of flatware, small sets, just enough, having left behind the bone china set for twelve, and various sets for holidays, picnics, and such. Same with everything else.

It had only been a few days, but with each day of seeing only the things she loved most or most needed, other options never seemed to enter into consideration. An almost sacred relationship was emerging with the few things that she kept. In turn she found herself noticing excess wherever she went. *How did this all start? Why did I buy so many things over the years, and why did it seem like such a good idea at the time?*

The shop downstairs was exactly the sort of place she used to go to, delighting in the shapes, the colors, the newness, and buying things to feel a part of them. The irony of living in reduced circumstances in the apartment above it was not lost on her. But this recent act of choosing to live with a few essential things made her feel more like she belonged to herself, that she was more clearly Charlotte, a Charlotte with a distinct point of view.

She moved from the sofa to the kilim, and did some stretching exercises, leaning forward slowly to touch the toes on each outstretched leg, then laid flat on her back, palms down on the rug, absorbing the bumps of the weave, the tiny fibers that escaped the twist of the threads, a spot that was worn thinner than the rest. From the floor the ceiling seemed like the sky, even the tall windows seemed to stretch up forever, the whole space simultaneously calming and stimulating, an atelier of *being alive,* of *intent.*

There was the word of the hour: intent. Charlotte got up and poured coffee into the big red mug, then took it over to lean against the back of the sofa and watch the rain. When she first met Olivia, the elderly woman's intent seemed clear: to find all the notebooks, then turn them into something publishable. The past two weeks, however, revealed that there were actually layers of intent—not only to keep the notebooks hidden until such time as was suitable to reveal them, but also what was intended by the notebooks in the first place. Olivia may have been rash, but she was not stupid. Any chance at a brilliant writing career was not going to happen, that ship had sailed decades before. But she had a story she intended to tell, the other side of *Least Objects.*

Likewise, she would not have contacted Warren Brothers without intent. She had long since acquired valuables that she would periodically sell off when she needed extra cash, like the loan for Donovan, and a trip to Yellowstone Park and the Grand Canyon. Later, during Ronson's illness, this method paid for extra things for his care. It was a long-established pattern. If she sold something, it meant she had a specific intent for the money—and the most obvious reason immediately before her death was to pay for Charlotte's help and any other expenses related to publishing her work.

Olivia was as certain that she had a first edition of *Least Objects* as she was that she had "nine or ten" notebooks stashed away in various locations in the house. The question now, in Charlotte's mind, was whether that first edition was the same one Donovan had given away—or if there was, incredibly, a second one. Since the parties looking for the second book were aware of the provenance of the first book, it increased the likelihood that there was, indeed, a second book. That book, however, was not on the shelves, in the boxes of books in the basement, propping up the bed, mixed in with cookbooks, or in any other place in Olivia's house where books were found or likely to be.

This meant that Olivia either: a) did not have a second book, b) hid the book somewhere, in the manner of her notebooks, or c) the book was not *Least Objects*, or did not look like *Least Objects.* Charlotte thought about how the other copy of the book did not look like a book, wrapped as it was in brown paper and painted to look like a building. Maybe there was another "building" made out of a wrapped book? But wouldn't Donovan have already thought of that and looked in what was left of his model train accessories? What else could a book be made to look like, without damaging it?

It could be made to look like some other book, just by changing the book jacket. Charlotte sighed. That would mean removing every similar-sized jacketed book in Olivia's shelves and boxes, and uncovering it, or opening it to the title page—at least half the books in her collection would require checking, unless the missing tome turned up. Then she remembered the notebook hidden inside the large, broken copy of the Poussin book. Hidden that way, *Least Objects* would fit in an unabridged dictionary, for instance, or in Olivia's copy of the Riverside Shakespeare, increasing the number of books to look through.

Shamus jumped up onto the back of the sofa, and rubbed his head against her arm.

"Hey there, kitty cat," she said, giving him the long strokes from head to tail that he seemed to love. "I could use the help of a real shamus right about now. Are you any good at finding books?"

He sat and looked up at her with a sleepy, contented cat-smile, but didn't commit one way or the other.

Simon joined her at Olivia's house, to help out for an hour or so before heading to class.

"It's a reasonable theory," he said, when she explained what she was trying to do. “But it might end up taking more time than we have.”

Charlotte nodded, then grasped the shelf to balance herself. She had retrieved the step stool from the kitchen, and was standing on it to reach the top shelves. “That’s what I’m afraid of. But I’m also hoping that if I spend more time here, I might figure out where the last notebook is, too. Sort of by osmosis.”

“What was that clue again?”

“*Snakes and Ladders.*”

“Right. The one you thought ought to be Chutes?” He began to tease her. “Is that what you called it, Chutes and Ladders?”

“Yes, that’s what ‘we Americans’ call the game,” she retorted with mock patience.

“Nonetheless, the clue is Snakes.” He stood back and began to scan all the shelves. “Have you seen a book about snakes, or reptiles, or serpents, or—”

“Adam and Eve?” she interrupted. “Here’s a book on the history of religions.” She looked it over, but it wasn’t hiding either the notebook or *Least Objects.* “I don’t think the notebook is going to be on these shelves. The older notebooks were written before Olivia had these shelves put up. We found the last one in the basement.”

“Could be an allegory.” Simon went back to searching through right-sized books. “You know, good versus evil.”

“Could be absolutely anything. The only thing consistent about Olivia is that everything she did, she did intentionally.”

It had been three days since Charlotte was last in her Lake Parkerton house, and she went through the rooms feeling exposed, spread-eagle, like a specimen for dissection, on seeing every item she owned laid out to be sold.

She felt as if she was walking in slow motion, out of time, almost disassociated. She was there to make sure there was nothing more she wanted to hold back from the sale, but the initial impact of seeing everything—literally *everything*—in the house laid out on tables, counters, and floors, seemed to shut down her thought processes.

"Just take your time, Charlotte." Martin Stanton came up next to her. "It hits a lot of folks like that."

She barely nodded, and continued in a blur. After a few minutes, a sort of rhythm set in, and the meaning of the things she was looking at finally made its way through her brain. Every so often something would trigger a memory, a flashback, and she would be stopped in her tracks.

It wasn't the most valuable or obvious things that would do it. There was, for instance, a bit of lace left over from trimming a pillow for Ellis' first "big girl" bed, which took Charlotte back to the early summer day in the back yard of their house near the university, sitting on a glider on the little brick patio she and Jack had laid themselves, and Ellis romping on the fresh-mown grass with Lady, their Golden Retriever. Charlotte was hand-sewing the lace around a pretty pink pillow and noting the contrast between what Ellis wanted for her room and the grubby, grass-stained tyke running with the dog and playing in the sandbox. An ordinary day a dozen years in the past, yet like yesterday upon touching a bit of leftover lace.

If someone were to ask how she *felt* about divesting herself of nearly all her possessions, she still would not know how to answer. At times it felt like self-amputation, or how she imagined it would feel. At other times it felt as straightforward as throwing out the trash or making a donation to charity. Mostly she felt in a daze, because it was all happening so quickly.

Martin was learning against the rail of the deck, with his back to the lake, and sipping from a travel mug of coffee. Charlotte poured a cup for herself from the crew's coffeemaker in the kitchen and joined him. He made light chit chat, recounting some lighter incidents of past estate sales, nothing too silly, just gentle talking that Charlotte found soothing and interesting enough to take her mind off of her moment of sadness. She was grateful that it was this kind and unpretentious man she was talking to, and not the aggressive and phony Bosley Warren.

"What happens during the sale itself? I mean, what kind of people will come, are they dealers or homeowners or what?"

"In general, it's about fifty-fifty. Even individual buyers might turn around and sell what they've acquired to a dealer or another individual. You don't have a lot of antiques, so you're probably less likely to have dealers, but I could be wrong. If there's a current demand trend for, say, contemporary kilim rugs, or mid-century furniture, your collection might draw dealers with interior design businesses. Since you're selling the Hannah Verhagen painting, I know for a fact that there are going to be both dealers and collectors, along with decorators and higher-end homeowners. Quite possibly a few of your neighbors."

"When dealers buy things, does the stuff end up in their shops?"

"In their shops, yes," Martin nodded, "but sometimes they have a specific client in mind and they'll just hold it back until they connect with the client, or the client commissions them to purchase specific items."

Charlotte wished she could have been there over the weekend to observe the process, but there was no doubt a good reason for owners to stay out of the way during the sale.

"So," said Martin. "How are you doing at the new place?"

"Quite well, actually. Better than I expected. I love not having to take care of a large space with a lot of stuff in it, and I love being able to walk to just about every place I need to go." She took another sip of coffee. "I've got a cat, too, by default." She told him about Shamus.

"I take it you've seen Helene, then? How is she doing? I heard about her sister. What a horrible thing for her."

They talked about Helene and Olivia, and Charlotte told Martin about the notebook project. "We came across Olivia's first collection of poems, which was published in France."

Martin was impressed. "Some of those small-press first editions are real collector's items, particularly if the author is well-known. Helene's sister isn't that well known, but maybe some other things they published were by writers who later became big names. Now *those* would be worth hundreds, maybe even thousands."

Charlotte was intrigued. She tried to recollect if there were any other books published by Sibylline Press in the box in the basement, and seemed to recall seeing several with the imprint's gowned woman holding an open book on which rested a crystal ball. "There might be other books in there, I'd have to look."

"If you want, I can connect you to Aldo Madiveros, our rare book guy in Hyde Park—"

"Yes!" Charlotte exclaimed. She suddenly had an idea, and a rare book expert would be most likely to help. "I'd like to talk to him as soon as possible, it's in connection to some things related to the project."

Martin seemed pleasantly surprised. "I can do that right now." He got his smart phone out and made the call. Charlotte wondered if Martin had the same sort of calling-in-favors network that Diane and Lola had. After a few moments of small talk and explaining about Charlotte, he handed the phone over to her. "All yours."

Aldo Madiveros had the voice of half a million cigarettes, but he was talkative, and, after Charlotte apologized for bothering him, he assured her that he loved talking shop more than anything.

She began by explaining the nature of her call, referred to Bosley Warren and the auction sale of *Least Objects,* and then Madiveros interrupted her with enthusiasm.

"I know all about that book! I verified it for the auction house!"

"Well, then, you really are the person I want to talk to, Mr. Madiveros." She went on to explain about discovering that the book had belonged to Olivia, and then who Olivia was.

To her surprise, Madiveros said that "Olivia Bernadin" rang a bell. "She was one of the *nouveau roman* crowd, if I recollect. Let me see now," he paused, and Charlotte could hear the tapping of a keyboard, then the rustle of papers. "Got it, a list of her published works, a spot of bio, not much. Presumed dead for decades."

"Um, I'm afraid she was alive and well until a couple of weeks ago."

"No!" he exclaimed. "You are kidding me, Ms. Anthony! Well, how about that. I'd love to know more, to fill in my files here."

"I'll be happy to do so, Mr. Madiveros. I'm working on a manuscript she left behind, and I might find out more in the course of the project."

"This is so exciting!" he exclaimed again. "It's like having another piece of the puzzle around Seamus O'Dair's years in Paris, and all his associates."

"Actually," said Charlotte, now ready to launch her main question, "I'm calling to ask you about O'Dair's book, *Least Objects.* What would make a copy of it even more valuable than the one that sold a few weeks ago?"

"Ahh," Madiveros pondered for a moment. "Well, several things, the most obvious would be if it were O'Dair's own copy, or one with his autograph in it, although I don't think he ever autographed *any* of his books, made quite a point of it, actually." Madiveros coughed, and Charlotte could hear him taking a drink of some kind. "Then there would be the first French edition, of course, but there were so few of those printed that only a handful are known of, most of them in and around Paris."

"So it was printed in France before it was printed here?" she asked.

"Oh yes. O'Dair wrote the original version in French, you know, and it's barely more than a novella. *Une Mort non Perçus.* Published by, let's see now," he paused, and Charlotte again heard the tapping of keys and the rustle of papers. "Sibylline Press. In fact, it was the final publication by that press, just a short run of one hundred. That was the book that made his international reputation. The American publisher had him write a new version in English, and that's the one most of us know. He either wrote in English, or wrote in French, never translated from one or the other."

"When did Sibylline Press shut down, or when was it sold?"

"Let's see now," and once again he paused as he looked it up. "Established by Anastasia Bernadin and Henriette Munier in 1930, then sold in 1952 to Beauregard Lamont. Insignificant publication history after it was sold until *Une Mort non Perçus*, and shut down for good in 1959."

The name Beauregard Lamont rang a bell. Wasn't that the wealthy American for whom Olivia's and Helene's father worked? Perhaps Olivia appealed to him to buy the bookstore, so that Henriette could continue running it, and she, Olivia, could continue editing their publications?

"Makes sense, you know," said Madiveros. "Lamont held a majority share in one of the biggest publishing houses at the time, Beauregard Books, and let's see now—yes, the same one that published *Least Objects* in English. Small world, isn't it, Ms. Anthony?"

"Smaller than you know, Mr. Madiveros."

There was no time to act on this new information, however, as she had to deal with what she came to do, to go over the entire house and confirm, room by room, that the items in it were to be sold. She also had her own list of things to retrieve, if at all possible, to take back to the apartment. She had also brought along the sterling silver flatware she had redeemed at the pawn shop, along with most of the jewelry, and showed them to Martin, explaining why they were not available earlier.

"I'm glad you brought these, Charlotte. On the average, you'll get three times as much money selling them here as you would get from a pawnbroker. Josh," he called to his assistant. "Call Lindy and have her bring a jewelry display case from the office. Add the flatware to the other silver and crystal."

Charlotte moved on and found various things she could use: a small rattan wall cabinet for the bathroom, a plant stand that she could use as a table by the bathtub, several candles and holders, a rubber-backed runner for the foyer, a pair of tapestry-covered throw pillows that would look great with the Chesterfield sofa, and a basket that looked the right size for Shamus, along with an old squishy red pillow that would work for a cushion.

As she thought about how she was using the space, taking meals and snacks on the sofa or on the bed, she took an old painted tray. Then she seriously considered a kitchen cart with a butcher block top. It had shelves, hooks, a drawer, a towel bar, and a small wine rack. "Hey Josh," she called out when she spotted him walking by, "is this cart listed?"

He looked his tablet, scrolling to the right page. "Afraid so, Mrs. Anthony."

Bummer. Maybe it wouldn't sell.

The upstairs hallway was full of garment racks the crew had brought in to make her clothes easier to get at. The amount would have filled her favorite boutique twice over. Would they bring anything? There were quite a few high-quality labels among them, good things of wool, leather, and silk, and several evening gowns, including a couple that hadn't even been worn, but which she'd bought impulsively. There was one rack, in fact, of items with their tags still on, and she shook her head at her own stupidity. Thousands of dollars' worth of unworn, brand-new clothes, many of which she'd forgotten buying. Funny how things looked more desirable when they weren't crammed together in a closet.

She selected a few items from the rack of still-new things, a simple charcoal gray knit skirt with a matching cardigan jacket that she could wear as a suit or mix and match with other pieces, a black wool and cashmere wrap, and a white linen sleeveless tunic with pintuck pleats, and a mid-calf halter-neck summer dress in an abstract floral of purple, rust, black, and beige, bought on her last spree with Ellis. Hanging around Helene was having a noticeable effect. She took the clothes into the bathroom to try on, promising herself to keep them only if they fit perfectly. They did. She also found a pair of waterproof shoes that were like new, and actually quite comfortable. Walking in the rain that morning had made her wish she'd had them on hand. Now she did. She would be walking nearly everywhere, now, rain or shine.

As she made her way through the rooms, and back down the stairs, other things appealed to her, but she had what she really needed, plus a few new (literally) clothes, and, after all, she still needed the money she could get from them. Then she sat down on the sectional, to look at Hannah's painting for the last time. Who would buy it? Where would it go from here? Would she ever know?

Passages from Olivia's notebooks came to mind:

I brought you back to life, my mentor, my muse, my mother, my goddess, I took on your pain and the fear of the gunshot that you felt within the suffocating cloth sack over your blonde locks cut to look like a boy's. You embodied everything good and true, the true queen of the hour, and you were doing what I should have done, what I wanted to do, but I was trapped. Now I am free, and I've chosen to resurrect you, to embody you, to let you live once again, a hero cut down far too soon in life.

In another world, another country, another time they would have seen me for what I am, they would have seen what I did for what it was, the ultimate sacrifice I could make for you, Anastasia, to lose myself and become you. I wore your clothes, I lived your stories, I wrote your words, I kept your work alive—and they called me a liar, the crabbed souls who would deny my honoring you, and even them, spitting on my ripped open soul.

Her cell phone rang. Helene was calling, and she sounded excited.

"Charlotte, I've finally finished those passages in the notebook. You were right that they shifted in tone, and much of it was about looking at things a second time, and of looking at oneself a second time, to consider what others might see. She hopes that what she has written will recapture a part of the story that has been lost. A way to triumph over time and death."

"I've got news, too, Helene—I think I know a little more about what caused Olivia to stop writing, and then to resume writing. I'm also pretty sure there really is a second copy of *Least Objects*. I'll tell you all about it when I get back."

Two more rooms to cover with the Stanton crew, a thousand or more items to check off, to let go, to consign to the ages, or at least to other owners. The mass of her possessions were laid out like a blanket of objects, screening the floor and the rooms, a smokescreen of objects that told about her life but didn't actually tell anything other than a small part of the truth of her life—

A smokescreen of possessions, she thought. Our possessions can tell a lot about us, but they can also hide a lot about us, and misguide those who would know us better. In her own case, what it hid was the real reason for coming to Lake Parkerton, to connect Ellis with Helene. What it revealed was the extent to which she was willing to fit in, was willing to make it happen financially and socially—the right sort of writing job, the right sort of activities, the right sort of possessions, clothes, furnishings, etc. The art collection was probably what revealed her most truthfully. The rest was baggage.

It was similar with Olivia's possessions. None of them revealed her true passion, only their role as a sort of coping mechanism. And a coping mechanism is not the truth itself, but only a sign that the truth is unworkable. In both my house and Olivia's house, thought Charlotte, the objects are spread like the ruins of ancient history. One might hold a magnifying glass over them, try to decipher their meanings, to look for some sort of Rosetta Stone that would help one translate their meaning, but only to learn that it is all one very large red herring. The stuff had absolutely nothing to do with the story within the story, and the sheer mass of it provided endless hours of traveling down the wrong road. Charlotte now realized, however, that in Olivia's case, it was done with conscious intent.

The last space to check off was the garage, which was almost wholly filled with things she would not need as an Elm Grove apartment dweller, or as a middle-aged person who could no longer finance skiing trips in Colorado or snorkeling in the Caribbean. She looked through the piles on the tables, anyway, and came across something familiar, a square assemblage of odd bits of wood, metal and brackets and hinges. She remembered. Ellis made it when she was four or five years old, imitating herself and Jack as they worked on a remodeling project. It had been on the wall above the window in the garage, and covered up by pool toys and skis until it was forgotten. It was clearly by a child's hand yet it was a charming, whimsical composition—a triumph over time. Charlotte untangled it from the pile, and took it home.

Twenty-Three

Saturday, September 28th

When Charlotte arrived at Helene's condo, she found Detective Barnes enjoying tea and cake in the sitting room; Helene invited her to get another cup.

"The detective was wondering if we have seen Donovan since his release, but I said I haven't, and I assumed you haven't either," Helene explained.

"No, I haven't. Things have been quiet, as far as I know."

Barnes nodded. "Not surprised. Mr. Targman is probably afraid for his life right now, and laying low."

"It's that bad? Life-threatening?"

"Could be. When I told him that Wesley Warren was still alive when his car went into the pond, I don't think I've ever seen a guy look so surprised—and scared at the same time. Now, the simplest thing would be to think he's panicking because he's guilty. But Wesley Warren was a big guy, and if he was a big dead weight guy, Targman would have had to have help loading him up in the car. That, to me, puts a fourth person on the scene—and somebody with a cooler head than he possesses."

"Mitchell," said Charlotte, both from instinct and from logic.

"Mitchell." Barnes took a big gulp of tea and set the cup down on the table. "Or someone similar in the Toley Banks organization."

"I don't think they'll hurt Donovan, though," said Charlotte, "not if they want anything at all in that house. Right now everything belongs to Helene, but they'll be able to sift through all the stuff when it's moved to the auction barn."

"So can Mrs. Dalmier," Barnes countered, then looked at Helene. "They don't want it to get to that point, because once you've identified whatever it is they're looking for, it's on the record. The time for them to get their hands on it is now, or while it's in transit."

Helene looked confused. "But they're the ones who pushed for the early auction date. They want what Donovan owes them, and they want it *now*, right?"

Charlotte began to see things from Mitchell's perspective. "We are obviously looking for something, which increases the likelihood of our finding what I'm fairly certain is another first edition of *Least Objects*. The sooner our search is stopped, the less likely we will find the book before they do. They've got the manpower to sift through everything between the house and the auction barn without our knowing about it."

"Detective Barnes," asked Helene, "what would happen if I break that contract, because I want to have more time? Why was Donovan so insistent that I don't break the contract?"

"He's afraid they'll take even more drastic measures, Mrs. Dalmier. I believe your nephew was concerned for your safety, and by extension Charlotte's."

"I knew it!" Helene asserted, her fist firmly hitting the arm of the sofa. "If he's concerned for our welfare, he couldn't have hurt his mother, either."

"There is that," agreed Barnes. "He has had some minor run-ins with the law, but nothing violent, and certainly not against women. His outburst that the two of you witnessed is, in fact, uncharacteristic, and I believe indicates a high level of stress and frustration. We know that he owes Toley Banks money, and he would not be the first to act out from the pressure—or be forced to do things he doesn't want to do. I'm inclined to advise the same thing, if it is at all possible."

Charlotte recalled Lola's frustration at still being forced to do favors for Banks, even after she paid back the money she owed. There were some things, however, that did not add up for Charlotte. "I've spoken to a rare book expert about *Least Objects,* and the auction houses do like to confirm provenance. If that book is what they're looking for, and they steal it before Helene can confirm that it is part of Olivia's estate, wouldn't they have a hard time selling it?"

"Nah," said Barnes. "Look at the other one, the one Bosley Warren found—how likely a story was that? Yet it was accepted, and sold with great publicity. All they have to do is concoct a similar tale. What matters most is that the book itself is authentic—and that nobody else can prove it was theirs."

"Possession is nine-tenths of the law," said Helene.

"Not literally, but in the absence of clear and compelling documentation or testimony, the person in possession of property is assumed to be the rightful owner."

Charlotte saw a now-familiar look of determination on Helene's face. She was feeling it, herself. "I think," she said to the detective, "we ought to have one last go at Olivia's house before they come for her stuff." Helene nodded in agreement.

Barnes sighed and nodded in resignation. "Got me on speed-dial?"

After the detective left, Charlotte and Helene put together everything they knew about the notebooks and the assumed second copy of *Least Objects.*

"I have to admit, Charlotte, that after all the grief those loan shark people have caused, I almost want that book as much or more than I want the last notebook. How sure are you that that is what they are looking for?"

"Just short of positive. My reasoning is that Olivia herself contacted Wesley Warren about such a book, after there was so much publicity about the one Bosley sold. This is what Donovan himself said, that she told Wesley that she had a copy 'even more valuable than the one they sold.' Now, even if she didn't know that Donovan had already let go of the copy we know about, it's reasonable to assume she's not talking about the same book. The one she has in mind has something to *distinguish* it from the one that was sold, something to make it *more* valuable." Charlotte made certain Helene was following her line of reasoning, then continued.

"That is why I talked to the rare book dealer, to ask him what version of *Least Objects* would be more valuable than the one sold, assuming Olivia knew what she was talking about. And—given all the years she'd been buying and selling off collectibles—she probably knew what she was talking about more than those people who lined up with their books outside of the pawn shop after Bosley Warren made the news."

"That would be reasonable to assume, yes," Helene agreed.

"So Aldo Madiveros—that was the name of the man I talked to, he authenticated the copy that Bosley sold—Madiveros said a more valuable copy would have to be signed by Seamus O'Dair, or be O'Dair's own copy. The only other possibility was that it was a first edition of the original version in French, but that was highly unlikely, as there were so few." Charlotte went on to explain to Helene the role of Sibylline Press in publishing *Least Objects,* and the fact that Mr. Lamont, the founder of Beauregard Books, had by that time purchased the little press from the estate of her Aunt Sasha's partner, Henriette.

"What a coincidence! Or is it?"

"I don't think it was," said Charlotte. "Your aunt was dead, and Henriette was not in the best of health, struggling to keep the book store and the publications going. She might have appealed to your parents, who in turn might have taken the request to Mr. Lamont. We may never know for certain."

Helene looked thoughtful, as if trying to recall the events of so many years ago. "Let's write out the dates, so I can see. We have the year Donovan was born, the year Mr. Lamont purchased Sibylline, and the year *Least Objects* was published. It was published well after Donovan was born."

"The English-language edition was published after he was born. The French one right before he was born. Beauregard Books had O'Dair write it again in English, because he never translated any of his books, any more than he autographed them."

"Moins d'Objets?" asked Helene. "That doesn't sound right for the French title. Do you know what it was? I can't remember."

"Madiveros said it was *Une Mort non Perçus."*

Helene smiled with satisfaction. *"An Uncollected Death.* Just like Olivia wrote."

This time, Charlotte merely scanned the books at Olivia's house, instead of looking inside one after another. After having spent so many hours looking at those shelves, she recalled seeing a cluster of books in French that she hadn't paid much attention to, since they were not what she had been looking for. Within five minutes, she found it, the gold-leaf title and Sibylline logo nearly worn off: *Une Mort non Perçus.* No one would have noticed it if it wasn't especially looked for.

Charlotte's hands had developed a recurring tremor over the past few weeks from too much stress, caffeine and fatigue. But this time, her hands trembled at the realization that she was holding an extremely rare book of great value. This very book played such a large role in Olivia's life, from her choice to abandon her career, to the way she met her death. A distinctive light pencil marking inside the cover showed the price, and Charlotte knew then that Olivia had purchased the book within the last few years from the original stock at Ramona's Resale.

She handed it to Helene, whose expression relayed the mix of excitement and sadness, relief and fear, that Charlotte felt herself.

"She never read this edition until, perhaps, the past two or three years," said Charlotte. "At one time, this book might have belonged to a long-ago French professor at Corton."

Helene thumbed through it carefully, as if to see if Olivia had left any margin notes or other objects inside. "I read a reprint of this that came out when O'Dair won the Nobel, and found it to be quite different than the English version. It was less harsh, more poignant. Perhaps that explains the change in her tone in her final notebook—she'd read what he had written much closer to the time of their parting ways." She paused and closed the book. "That's not to say the story line is any different, but the attitude, the difference in perspective—."

"The passage of time can do that, too," said Charlotte. "Maybe there's something in the first notebook that would explain it all."

"This is it," said Helene. "If we don't find that notebook now, it might be lost for good." Helene offered the book to Charlotte. "I'm putting this in your keeping for the time being. I just know that first notebook will have my sister's version of what happened."

Charlotte took a deep breath and put the book in her jacket pocket. "Well, then, let's give it one more go. *Snakes and Ladders.* I'll do the basement, since that is where the last one was found, and it is reasonable to think Olivia would have left the one before it there, too. I don't know that you'd be too keen on those steps, though."

"I'd rather avoid them, Charlotte. I'm going to have a look around the garage, there's at least one ladder out there, and maybe there's a plumbing snake. I found Olivia's car keys, so I'll check the Taurus, and in the trunk, too."

"I'll try the game box again. I still can't shake off thinking it's Chutes and Ladders."

"Your guess is as good as mine at the moment," Helene murmured as she went toward the back door.

Luck, thought Charlotte, maybe our luck will hold out. She looked around the house, as if for one last time, to see if there was anything remotely to do with snakes, ladders, or, as Simon had suggested, good and evil. An odd-looking vase atop one of the dining room curio cabinets reminded her of vines wrapped around a tree trunk, and a closer look revealed it was interwoven snakes. *Could this be it?* She lifted it down carefully and looked inside: empty, save for dust and a dead moth. Likewise, with a cookie jar in the shape of a fire department ladder truck: nothing inside. She set her tote bag under the table by the puzzles, as there was no room on the chairs or on the table itself, and unlocked the basement door.

Very little had changed since she was there with Simon: there was the same slightly musty basement odor mixed with moth balls, and a hint of damp after all the rain. The boxes of books where they'd found Olivia's volume of poetry were still where they left them. Charlotte went through them again, this time knowing what to look for, and saw that several of the books had the Sibylline logo. If nothing else, she would bring them upstairs for Helene, in case she would want to keep her mother's books. After today, Olivia's thread of clues would no longer function—everything would be in disarray, and everything they didn't take now would go to the auction barn.

First, she once again confirmed that there was nothing at all like a notebook in the Chutes and Ladders box, nor was there any other edition of the game. What if, she thought, Olivia put the notebook in the Chutes and Ladders box, thinking that Donovan was unlikely to ever play the game again, but he found the notebook and used it like he used his grandmother's copy of *Least Objects?* And Olivia simply never knew about it? If that was the case, it could be in any game box or anything Donovan could have played with or utilized.

She started to go through every box of games and toys and models, when she heard footsteps upstairs. At first, she thought it was Olivia, coming back in from the garage, and nearly called out to her, then she heard many heavy steps, loud men's voices, and the sounds of things being thrashed and knocked over.

The sounds came closer, moving from the front of the house toward the kitchen. Charlotte quickly turned the lights off and moved behind the furnace, suppressing the desire to gasp at the touch of cobwebs against her face and hair. *Where was Helene?*

"I told you, I don't know where it is, I don't *knowww*," wailed Donovan.

Charlotte could hear them punching him, and Donovan grunting and gagging. Then the cold, flat voice of Toley Banks cut through: "Take his phone and keys. Throw him down the stairs and lock it up."

She could just make out a large man, perhaps Bosley Warren—or, perhaps, it was Doc—grabbing Donovan off his feet, and literally throwing him down the stairs. The door slammed shut, plunging the basement into complete darkness, and Charlotte could hear the key turning in the lock. Then the sound of many heavy footsteps going back to the front part of the house.

What is going on? What do I do? Have they killed him? She felt around in her pockets for her cell phone, to call for help, to use the light from the screen to find the light cord, anything—and then realized with dismay she'd left it in her purse upstairs.

She heard Donovan groan in pain. He was alive, at least.

"Donovan?" she whispered. "It's Charlotte."

"Wha—" He sounded confused. "Charlotte? Why are you here?"

"I'm going to try to turn the light on." She felt her way toward the stairs, almost completely blind, following the edge of the workbench. It was just enough to orient her; she flailed her arms around, hoping she was close enough to find the string pull for the light bulb. No go.

She moved forward a little more, and her foot bumped into Donovan, who gasped.

"It should be right over my head," he moaned quietly. "I can't get up. My leg's messed up."

She flailed again and this time found the cord, and pulled on the light.

Donovan winced in shock at the sudden brightness of the bare bulb. Charlotte, on the other hand, was shocked at the sight of *him:* blood coming out of his nose and from his lips, his face and eyes swollen from a beating, his hands scraped and bleeding. His glasses were twisted and broken at the bridge. He was leaning on his side, holding his leg.

"Oh my lord! What did they do to you?" She looked around for something to press against his nose, raiding some of the boxes of old linens and towels. She found old throw pillows and quilted bedspreads to give him something to lie on, and he situated himself with difficulty. Towels dampened with water from the laundry tub cleaned him up as much as he could stand her touching him.

"I think my leg's broke, or I've got a very bad sprain." Donovan's face was pale from the pain.

"Why have they done this to you? What is going on? Do they have Helene?"

"I didn't see Helene. I don't think they know you're here, either. They're coming in tonight, going to clear the place out."

"But they're not supposed to do that until tomorrow!"

"He's not—" Donovan winced with pain, and put his hand over his stomach. Charlotte was afraid he might have internal injuries. "He's not going to take chances."

"Who? What chances?" She felt it was cruel to badger him with questions in his condition, but she wanted to know what was going on so she could help him.

"Toley Banks. He thinks you've been asking about the book, thinks you might be getting too close."

Charlotte instinctively felt for the book in her pocket, and was relieved that it was still there.

"But why beat you up for it?" she asked.

"They wanted me to find out if you or Aunt Helene found it or knew. I refused. Wanted to buy you time—to find Mom's notebooks."

Donovan winced and groaned as another wave of pain struck his abdomen. "Call for help?" he asked.

Charlotte shook her head sadly, and in sympathy when Donovan swore. "My phone's in my bag, in the kitchen." She looked around the basement again for an outside exit, but could see none. "There's no way out of here, is there?"

To her surprise, Donovan didn't say no. "Maybe. Dad used to lock me down here when I was little. For punishment. I used to get out through the old coal chute. Comes out by the driveway."

"What coal chute? Where is it?"

"Over there, up at top. Dad blocked it off, but I still got out. When he realized he couldn't stop me, he just knocked me around."

Charlotte walked to the area Donovan pointed her, trying to understand what she was looking at among the remains of old ductwork and metal parts that looked like nothing she was familiar with.

"Look for the green board," he whispered. "Trust me. One way or another, it's your way out."

She spotted the faded green board that covered a large rectangular duct, but it was too high up to reach. She grabbed the step ladder resting on the wall opposite the furnace, and opened it up, trying to be as quiet as possible. An old coal chute, she thought, put here when the house was built.

A chute. A ladder. Could it be?

She pulled on the board, but it was stuck, so she pulled harder and harder, determined to get at it, to get at this one last hope of finding Olivia's first and last notebook, of getting herself and Donovan out of there in one piece—

It popped off with a squeak that Charlotte was sure anyone still upstairs would hear. She peered inside the chute, full of cobwebs and lord only knew what else, but saw nothing. There wasn't enough light. She held her breath and reached inside until her fingers touched cardboard and paper: a notebook. Maybe two notebooks. The chute was too small for her to crawl through, at any rate.

She started to pull a notebook forward, and into the light, but the floorboards began to creak again. Toley and company were coming back. She shoved the notebooks back, and at the last second, added the copy of *Least Objects* that was in her pocket. She popped the green board back into place, and quietly folded the ladder and put it back where it had been.

Donovan pointed at the light. She pulled the switch off and sat down next to him in the dark.

If ever there was a time to find out what happened to Olivia that night, it was now, but Charlotte struggled to find the right words. She didn't think Donovan would have hurt his mother, but she didn't *know*, and she was sitting right next to him in the dark, with even more dangerous men upstairs. Talk about being between a rock and a hard place, she thought.

When in doubt, ask outright. "What happened that night?" she asked.

Donovan sighed. "That was probably the worst night of my whole life. Mom had called Warren Brothers to ask for an appraisal, and evidently Wesley offered to come over after work, instead of having her go to the shop."

Charlotte could hear him trying to shift his position, to take pressure off his leg. Her eyes had finally adjusted to the dark, and with a bit of waning daylight coming through the glass block near the top of the walls where window wells would have been at one time, she could just make out that Donovan was in a lot of pain. But there was nothing she could do for him. They were stuck until help came. "So, that's why Wesley Warren was here, to do an appraisal?"

"Yeah. I was doing a collection run with Mitchell for Toley Banks. You know I'm having a hard time paying him back. When he says do this, do that, I gotta do it. Somehow Mitchell knew that Wesley was going to be talking to my mother, but he didn't trust him. He wanted me to go see Mom while Wes was there, maybe listen in on the conversation."

"Why didn't he trust Wesley?"

"It's complicated. Toley Banks is the Warrens' half-brother, and they're into him for bailing them out when their hobby shop failed. As far as Toley's concerned, any big-money items they come across should go into his pocket. When Bosley found that rare book, he claimed it was his to do with as he pleased, because he bought the book with his *own* money, not the shop's. Toley suspected Wes was going to try the same stunt, especially since he wasn't talking to my mother on the shop premises."

"I see."

"Anyway," Donovan continued, "Mitch drove us to Mom's house and stayed in the car while I went in. Mom was surprised to see me, but didn't seem to mind I was there. Wes was surprised, too, 'cause I think he knew I was working for Toley. The thing was, though, Mom was trying to play coy with Wes, and Wes was trying to be persuasive with Mom. She'd probably asked him about the book Bosley found, because he was in the middle of telling the story when I got there, how Bos went to a tailgate sale and bought a box of model train props he wanted, and the book was in the bottom of the box, wrapped and painted like a building. That's when I realized it was me that sold it to him." Donovan snorted at his own bad luck. "It was my box of train stuff, and I remembered making that building out of a book when I was a little kid."

Charlotte could just make out Donovan's eyes, shiny with emotion, wide open with the disbelief he still felt. "Can you imagine what it is like to stand there, desperate for money, and suddenly realize you'd just given away a small fortune? Can you imagine how utterly stupid you'd feel at that moment? And angry at the whole world, but most of all yourself?"

"It would be horrible," she agreed, as sympathetically as she could. There was more movement on the floor upstairs, reminding her that their conversation could be interrupted at any moment. "So what happened then?"

"Well, that's when Mom and Wesley both realized what I'd done. To my surprise, she wasn't as upset as I was, just did that rolling of her eyes that meant she thought I was dumber than a box of rocks. But Wesley burst out laughing. He was laughing at me, and he got abusive about it, probably because he suspected I was there to spy on him and he wanted to get back at me for it. Mom, though, didn't know that, and she flipped out. She started railing on him, grabbing at a book he was holding, calling him names, telling him to get out and all. He pushed her away, and she just got madder, and went for her baseball bat. She always kept a baseball bat by the door. I tried to stop her, and she's trying to lift the bat, but she's so old, so—." Donovan choked back a sob.

"Did she hit him?"

Donovan took a deep breath. "No, she just kind of half-swung the bat at his ankles like it was a croquet mallet. But she was cussing a blue streak at him, and he was yelling back, and then she screamed at him that she's got another book, anyway, and he was never going to get his hands on it. I'd gotten the bat away from her, but she's poking him in the chest, and that's when he shoved her even harder, and she stumbled back and fell and hit her head on the coffee table. I ran over to help her, but she was completely gone. Wes came over to check on her, too, and says to me, "Good! The old bitch is dead!" That's when I got him, I was so angry. Just one big swing, and he was down."

"You know you didn't kill him?"

"I didn't find that out until later, when Barnes told me. I was in shock, you know, I can't describe the noise and chaos in my head, I was in shock, and—and in a complete panic. At some point, Mitchell came in, kinda took over, and called Toley. He wanted it to look like Mom hit somebody, even asked me which hand she used. Wanted it to look like whoever hurt her had gotten away. Mitch said then I would inherit Mom's stuff and that way I could pay off Toley. We got Wes loaded up in his car, drove it out to the pond, put him in the driver's seat and then sent it in. I think Mitch really did think Wes was dead, and I think it was Toley who told him to run the car into the pond."

"But what about the blood? And you know your mom hadn't been able to use her right arm in years?"

"I forgot!" he hissed. "And we missed the blood! At night, you couldn't see it on that rug like you can in the daylight. And we were in hurry. It took so long to get Wes out of there, into the car—my god, I can't believe I helped with that, it seemed to take all night." Donovan was wringing his hands and taking short, sharp breaths. "Mitch was going to come back and get rid of our fingerprints and bust a window, make it look

more like a break-in, but by that time it was daylight, then you got there, and the police were all over the place. I found out Mom was still alive on the news. But I had to make like I didn't know and wait until the police or Aunt Helene reached me. By then, it was too late. And then the lawyer said Mom had left everything in the house to Aunt Helene, and there were the stipulations, and—."

The footsteps were in the kitchen, along with several voices. The men were back, and one of them was opening the basement door. Charlotte ran to hide behind the furnace, and watched as Mitchell came down the stairs and pulled on the light switch. Then Toley Banks and the man named Doc came down, as well.

"Charlotte, dear Charlotte," Mitchell looked around for her, calling out in a singsong voice. "We know you're here." He held up her tote bag, then looked down at Donovan. "Nice job on Van, too."

Twenty-Four

Sunday, September 29th

Everything inside Charlotte went cold: fear, panic and anger were suppressed as she faced the reality of her situation and her survival instinct kicked in. She made a conscious decision not to admit to finding the book, unless worst came to worst. The most important thing at the moment, though, was to get herself and Donovan out of there in one piece, to make Toley Banks think that they were no threat to him. She hoped that Donovan would play along.

These thoughts flew through her mind as she walked forward. As she approached Mitchell, she held out her hand for her bag, but he pulled it out of her reach.

"Uh, uh, uh. It's not time for that, yet."

Toley Banks spotted the boxes of books and nodded for Doc to go through them.

Mitchell flashed Charlotte his well-practiced smile. "You know what we're here for, so why don't you just hand it over and save yourself and Van, here, a lot of trouble?"

She fake-smiled back. "That's just it, Mitchell, I know you're here for something, but I don't know what. You know I'm here to look for Olivia's notebooks, but I've never been under the impression that those are of much concern to you. I don't have anything to hand over, even if I wanted to."

Mitchell moved so fast, she didn't have time to react as he threw her bag on the floor and reached around to grab the hair at the back of her head, twisting it until she was forced down on her knees.

The pain of having her hair pulled threw sharp white flashes across everything in the room, and more pain shot through her legs and back as she landed on the concrete floor.

"Don't mess with me," Mitchell hissed, "or your face will look like his." He pointed at Donovan with his other hand. "Bet your boyfriend wouldn't like you so much then, would he?"

Charlotte's eyes were watering from the pain, and her heart was pounding, but she said nothing. Donovan, likewise, said nothing, but she could see the veins in his temples raised from stress.

Toley Banks remained standing in the same spot, watching Mitchell and Charlotte without a trace of emotion, then looked at Doc, who had finished looking through the boxes of books. Doc shook his head.

Banks sighed, then crouched down next to Donovan.

"Mr. Targman. We have a situation."

Donovan didn't move or look at him. Banks was not bothered, and turned to look straight at Charlotte. "I believe you do know what we are here for, Ms. Anthony, and if you co-operate, we will not only release your lovely hair, but remove ourselves from your life, Mrs. Dalmier's life, and even Mr. Targman's life, little as he deserves it. We know you've been in contact with Aldo Madiveros—we were, too. Like Mr. Targman, here, you are in serious financial straits, and we naturally understand that you'd want to find a jackpot of your own to turn things around, keep your lovely house, and perhaps even join your daughter in Paris." He spread his hands to emphasize the world of advantages she'd have if she had the book, the only expression she'd ever seen him display.

"Sounds lovely," she said, her voice strained from the way Mitchell had her head tilted. If she appeared to be willing to talk, maybe Mitchell would let go of her hair.

It worked. Banks nodded to Mitchell, and he released her. She rubbed her scalp and neck, feeling sore and bruised.

Charlotte did not know at this point how long she'd been in the basement, but she hoped Helene was aware of what was going on, and sent for help. The worst thing would be if she walked in on them and endangered herself.

Time to keep Toley talking. She cherry-picked the truth. "I did talk to Mr. Madiveros. Mrs. Targman's notebooks make many references to her Aunt Sasha, and to her days in Paris at Sasha's bookstore. It was part of my research."

Mitchell snorted at this. "Oh, it's pretty clear what the old girl got up to in Paris. A little research on the 'net showed she knew O'Dair, she was living in Paris back then." He gestured toward Donovan with his thumb. "Spitting image of his father! Of course she'd have a first edition of O'Dair's book—she said she had a book worth even more than the one Bos got hold of. Any other old lady, we'd just say yeah, yeah, thank you very much, have a nice day. But her—with his kid, no less—that one was likely to know *exactly* what she had. *He* owes us every penny of what it's worth, so as far as we're concerned, the book is ours. Now tell us where it's at or the next time I grab your hair, you won't be getting it all back."

She played dumb. "Donovan is *Seamus O'Dair's* son?" She looked at Donovan as if she was seeing him for the first time. "Well, there's the hair, for sure. Wow. So is that just a guess, or did he tell you that, or what?"

"The dumb shmuck doesn't even know. Probably never looks in the mirror. O'Dair's face is all over the news." Mitchell looked at Donovan with utter contempt.

To Charlotte, Donovan did not look surprised at this revelation. Did he know? Or was he just a good actor?

Toley Banks stood up again. "So you claim you have not found the book Mrs. Targman mentioned?"

Charlotte shook her head. "If I have, I am unaware of it. What book is it? What's the title?"

Mitchell jumped in. *"Least Objects,* same as the other one. Only we figure it's got O'Dair's autograph in it or something. Maybe even love letters. It'd be worth three times as much as the other one."

So they didn't realize the book they were looking for was the French version. Charlotte would have loved to call them out on what happened that night when Olivia and Wesley Warren received their fatal injuries, but these guys played hard. She was afraid that if they knew that Donovan had told her the extent of their involvement, they'd both end up in the bottom of a pond like Wesley. Staying on the topic of the book was the safest bet to buy time until Helene brought help, or Simon got back from the university. "I have not come across a single copy of *Least Objects.*" Strictly speaking, she thought, that was true. The French version had a different title. "There are a couple of O'Dair books on the shelves in the living room, next to other Irish writers like Joyce and Beckett." She nodded to the boxes of books near Doc. "There are some old books in there, which used to belong to Mrs. Targman's mother. That's about it, I'm afraid."

There were sounds of a door opening and closing upstairs, and then footsteps. "Charlotte!"

It was Helene. Charlotte's heart felt like it was moving up to her throat. Helene called out again, "Charlotte! I think I've found the book! Come and see!"

Helene sounded excited. *What was she up to?*

Mitchell and Toley Banks looked at one another, as if able to weigh their options without speaking a word. Mitchell went up the stairs, and this time Charlotte felt as if it were her stomach, not her heart, in her throat.

She heard Helene's expression of surprise, then a shout, and the sounds of a struggle. Charlotte started for the stairs, but Toley Banks quickly raised an arm to stop her.

"Oh, Charlotte," came Helene's voice, practically crying. "Are you okay? Answer me, please! I've fallen!"

Toley Banks gestured for Doc to go up, and the big man moved quickly and silently, reaching inside his jacket for what Charlotte assumed was a gun. *Oh Helene, be careful, be so careful.*

Charlotte could hear Helene saying, "Who are you? Where's Charlotte?" And then more sounds of struggle. Then silence. Doc did not return, nor Mitchell. All was eerily quiet. She turned to Banks, who by this time was looking up toward the top of the stairs, and said, "I'll bet Mitchell took the book and ran."

Toley Banks looked at her as always, without any expression, except this time the pupils of his eyes were almost red. He suddenly pulled a gun out of his jacket, which he raised as if about to cold-cock her, when Donovan leaned over, grabbed Banks' ankles from behind and pulled hard. Banks fell face down onto the concrete with a scream that left no doubt he'd broken his nose and several teeth. The gun fell out of his hand when he landed, and skidded across the floor.

There were shouts and footsteps now. Was it Mitchell and Doc? Banks was beginning to raise himself up. Charlotte quickly grabbed the gun before he could get it back, then stepped back into the shadows around the furnace. Donovan had fallen back in pain and exhaustion. Men's legs were rushing down the stairs.

The first pair of legs belonged to Detective Gordon Barnes, who immediately restrained Toley Banks. The second set of legs, the ones in the black jeans—

Simon called out, looking around hurriedly and peering into the shadows. "Charlotte?"

She stepped forward, gave the gun to Barnes, and fell into Simon's warm and supporting arms.

The EMTs, who must have already been on the scene, rushed down to help Donovan immediately after uniformed officers took a handcuffed and bloody-nosed Toley Banks up the stairs. Charlotte had her arms around Simon's chest, forcing herself to let go when they had to shuffle out of the way for the stretcher. She noticed a wet spot on the middle of his shirt, and then realized she had been crying. Simon confirmed that Helene was okay, and put his arm around her shoulders as they leaned against the laundry tub. The whole ordeal was not like a crime show in the least, she thought, where the sleuth was able to smugly wrap up the solution and take high fives from the other characters—the effects of shock and adrenaline made everything seem odd and out of sync to her, even dissociated. She watched the EMTs check Donovan over, and work as a team to lift him onto the stretcher with the least amount of discomfort.

Once they got Donovan on the stretcher, though, she came back to reality enough to want to connect with him, to walk over and take his hand.

"Thank you so much, Donovan—you know, for stopping him like that."

He squeezed her hand, and looked up at her with the tiredest eyes she'd ever seen. He was undoubtedly seriously injured, and she felt frightened for his sake. "The least I could do," he whispered. "This was all my fault."

Barnes came up, asked one of the techs if it was okay to ask Donovan some questions, and was told it would be better after they got him to the hospital—he was showing signs of internal bleeding, and time was of the essence.

Everyone stood out of the way as the EMTs carried Donovan up the stairs. Charlotte could hear him gasp as the stretcher jostled. Then they got him into the kitchen, turned, and were gone.

"Charlotte?" Helene appeared at the top of the stairs, and began to carefully make her way down. "Oh, Charlotte!"

Barnes assisted Helene down the rest of the stairs, and she immediately embraced Charlotte.

"Oh, Charlotte, I was so frightened for you! Are you okay?"

"I'm fine. Just shook up. And what about you? What happened up there?"

Barnes folded his arms across his ample abdomen and smiled. "Mrs. Dalmier here deserves an Academy Award for that performance. She was in the garage when she spotted Banks and his crew going in the front door with Donovan, who appeared to be injured. She contacted me immediately, and I lined up the uniforms and the ambulance, making sure everything stayed quiet. We were afraid of a hostage situation, especially with you possibly being trapped in the basement, which, as it turned out, you were. Mrs. Dalmier then remembered that Mr. Norwich was expected at any moment, so she contacted him to make sure he didn't come in here. Instead, he managed to get close enough to the dining room window to hear what was going on inside. That is how we knew Donovan had been thrown into the basement. Then Mitchell Bennett found your purse, so we knew you were down there, too. It also made it probable that you did not have your phone on you."

"We had to come up with a way to lure them out of the basement," said Simon. "Helene is the one who thought of pretending to have found the book they were looking for."

Helene looked quietly proud, and Charlotte smiled. "So that's what was going on! When I heard you calling me, saying you found the book, when I knew you hadn't—." She stopped, then remembered there was more to it. "Then Mitchell went up. I heard a scuffle, and then you calling out that you had fallen. What happened?"

"I was in the front room, so he had to walk out there, and once he got past the door way, Simon and the detective ambushed him!"

Charlotte looked up at Simon, who was nodding. "Did the same thing to Doc," he added.

"Then they told me it would worry Toley Banks more if there was no response," said Helene.

Barnes shook his head at the memory. "Neither one of us would have been able to sound like either Mitchell Bennett or Doc, so our only option was silence. Of course, that increased the chance that Banks would use you for a hostage, but we had something in place for that, too. As it was, it looks like you were able to take matters into your own hands."

Charlotte nodded. "It was all Donovan, believe me." She described the way Donovan pulled Toley Banks off his feet. "We were just trying to buy time until help got here. I was so worried about you, Helene."

"Well, fortunately, it looks like we are all okay. I only hope Donnie's injuries aren't too serious," Helene looked at the bedding still on the floor, and at the small puddle of blood from Toley Banks' nose. Then she suddenly looked at Charlotte. "The book! Do you still have it?"

Charlotte smiled, walked over to the ladder, and began to carry it back to the coal chute. Simon came forward to help her set it up. She pointed at it, and said to the others, "This, obviously, is a ladder." Then she climbed the ladder, and pointed at the duct with the green board. "And this is the remains of a coal chute." She pulled off the green board, took out the book, and handed it down to Simon. "Here's the book, *Une Mort non Perçus, An Uncollected Death,* a first edition of the original French version of *Least Objects."*

Simon's look of amazement was worth the price of admission. "You found it!"

Helene shared her excitement. "We found it right before Donnie and Mitchell and those other men got here. It was right there on the bookshelves in the living room this entire time."

Barnes chuckled. "So this is what they were looking for? This book?"

"Yes, detective," Helene affirmed. "This very rare and costly book." Then she looked up at Charlotte. "So it was Chutes and Ladders, after all? Was the notebook in there?"

"I think so." She started to feel around the inside of the chute. "It was Donovan who told me what this was. When he was thrown down here, they locked the door. Donovan said there was a possible way out, but it's too small." She explained how Donovan was punished as a child by being locked in the basement. "Olivia would have had to use the ladder to hide the notebook in it. I think she wrote *Snakes and Ladders* as the clue because that was what she had always called the game." Her hand finally felt paper and pages, and she pulled out the notebooks. "There's two of them." She brought them down.

The larger one was, indeed, the first notebook Olivia had written, and was dated 1968—and there was no clue on the inside of the front cover. It was, at long last, the first volume of the series.

"You were right, Charlotte," said Helene, looking at the first page. "She started writing again after O'Dair won the Nobel. But what is the other notebook?"

The smaller notebook was a student's composition book, and the handwriting was a young person's, as well. On the first page, the title read, "A Story," and underneath was written, "by Donovan Targman."

"How sweet!" said Helene. "How like a mother to have kept something like that, something she had in common with her child."

Barnes made motions to leave. "Well, everyone, I need to get to the hospital to check on Mr. Targman," he said. "It looks like you have found everything you wanted, and then some. And I don't think you will be bothered by Toley Banks, Mitchell Bennett, or the mysterious Doc anymore. They will have the book thrown at them—as it were—for every felony they committed today alone."

"What a relief!" said Helene. "I want to get out of this basement and go see Donnie, too, if someone will lend me an arm?"

"Allow me, Mrs. Dalmier," said Barnes, who was downright courtly in his assistance.

Twenty-Five

Saturday, September 28th, through Sunday, September 29th

Shamus hopped up on the bed, brought his face close to hers to sniff for a few seconds, then curled up against her tummy. Charlotte was neither awake nor sound asleep, just conscious enough to wrap her arm around the cat and hold him a little closer, as Ellis used to do with her stuffed bunny rabbit. Shamus purred, a soothing noise that did, finally, send her into a deeper sleep for a little while.

It was raining again, and the particular way it sounded here was starting to become familiar. Charlotte had lowered the upper sash of one of the windows, to take advantage of the warm front, and the rain-intensified autumn scents finally overcame the new-paint smell. Dawn was breaking. Shamus had moved out from under her arm, but was still close by. She hadn't bothered to put the folding screens back in place, and could see the whole apartment from where she lay.

Her sense of smell and touch were still in place, maybe even taste, but she still felt numb, exhausted. Shamus opened an eye, then yawned and stretched. She stretched too, but it only emphasized the aches and pains of her exhausted body, especially in her bruised knees and neck. The rain quieted as the daylight grew. Charlotte could see more and more of the apartment, but part of her didn't want to see it, didn't want to embrace being in a new space, or the idea that this was her home now, with its bare walls without art, with its scruffy masculine sofa and not her butter soft sleek one. She wanted the comfort of the old and familiar, of Ellis in her room down the hall, of an entire lake to view from the deck, of a place in the working world, knowing what she was going to do next for the magazines, of scheduling meetings and video conferences, of going shopping, of planning vacations, of Lake Parkerton before the steel mill closed and the economy went bust, all the old familiar things and ways, even the annoying parts.

Shamus hopped down and a few seconds later Charlotte could hear him crunching on the kibble in his bowl. She rubbed the light coating of black cat hair that he left on the duvet, and rolled it into a clump. Wendy hadn't brought over a brush. Maybe Larry had one. *I'm becoming a cat lady—living alone and becoming a cat lady. Maybe I'll have ten cats by the end of the year—*

Oh, snap out of it. Get up, put on a pot of coffee, have a shower and breakfast.

Charlotte leaned back in her office chair and propped her feet on the work table, ankles crossed. This, she thought, was the moment she'd been waiting for, to be able to sit down and read Olivia's first notebook, the one she hoped would explain the whole sad saga. The big red mug was full of coffee, the cat's litterbox was clean and his food and water bowls were topped up. The computer was fired up and online, ready for notes and research. Shamus hopped into the basket she brought for him and placed close by on the table. He settled himself in and watched her.

It all began with my first return to Paris after the war. Aunt Sasha Bernadin was a Resistance martyr, and Aunt Henri was keeping the bookstore and press on as best she could, with the well-earned good will of the literati of Saint-Germain-des-Prés. Henri was so full of sadness, pride, regret, and reflected glory, and she would keep taking my face in her hands, and tell me how much I looked like a dark-haired version of my dear aunt. Indeed, as I walked through the store and their apartment, and walked through the mix of the familiar and the devastated in the neighborhood, I felt myself taking on my aunt's very soul. Or was it her soul taking possession of mine?

As the weeks went by, I felt I had become Sasha and stopped being Olivia. Night after night I would sit by the small fire with Henri, and listen to the stories that Sasha had told her, of the quiet ways in which messages were sent and scenes playacted, of the atrocities she'd witnessed first-hand. At what point did the words no longer matter, at what point was the story told only in Henri's eyes? It was as if Sasha had transmitted what she'd seen into Henri's eyes, and Henri in turn was transmitting them into mine. I could see, I swear I could see, what Sasha had seen, I could feel what she felt, I knew every sensation of every step she'd taken, from delivering a loaf of bread with a message baked inside, to swiping a German uniform for a refugee.

I knew every moment, and I knew what it felt like to face the firing squad, in a line with a dozen others from my team, and to be thrown into a pit before I was even dead. And I knew what it felt like to be glad that at least Henri would know what had happened to me, that I wasn't whisked away in the dark, never to be heard from again, an anonymous naked body on a pile of others in a gas chamber.

The bookstore was part of Sasha's cover—and she never, not once, hid anything in any of the books she carried. Instead, she would be given a complex series of numbers to memorize by those in charge, which she would relay in person to the recipient of the books. The numbers represented the page and word position in a book of each word of the message. She deliberately never looked for the messages, in case she was ever questioned or tortured. Twice she was held and questioned, and twice she was let go—she was able to convince them that she did not know any messages. She likely would never have been caught, but for the traitor on her team, who was executed with them.

Then followed many short stories of different ways in which Sasha served as a courier, and then later as a saboteur, mixed in with the periods of waiting and emotional pain that Henri endured. Olivia's immersion into her aunt's persona was only reinforced by Henri's love and grief. Olivia was aware of what was happening, but welcomed it, seeing it as her way of honoring her aunt, and of fulfilling her own thwarted desire to stay in France and fight, instead of being coddled in New York. The first result of this immersion was the book of poems that Charlotte and Simon found: *Faux Silence.* It brought her encouraging reviews. But the literary scene in Paris was no longer the same one she fondly recalled from before the war. With Henriette's encouragement, Olivia returned to New York to advance her writing career and to be part of the vanguard in Greenwich Village. She took a staff position at *The New Yorker* magazine, and wrote another book of poems, this time in English: *My Enemy, My Mercy,* which garnered solid critical acclaim.

While she loved the Village jazz scene, she soon tired of what she considered the "Beatnik coarseness." She learned of the *nouvelle roman* writers and New Wave filmmakers "back home," but hesitated to leave her job and growing professional profile. When she learned of Henri's failing health, however, she dropped everything to return to Paris and help out.

This was when she became re-acquainted with Seamus O'Dair, whose group of friends and fellow writers—every last one of them involved in the Resistance efforts—often met at *Sibylline.* After the odd and self-indulgent literary world in America, this group, by contrast, were heroes. Olivia wrote that, in retrospect, they were probably no less full of themselves than the Beatniks—or herself—but at the time they could do no wrong in her romantic eyes. Her teenage crush on O'Dair in the 1930's renewed itself with the power and conviction of a woman determined to have what she wanted—and she wanted O'Dair, body and soul.

But he only noticed her when he was made aware that she'd written *Faux Silence,* and the person who brought it to his attention was under the impression that it was autobiographical. She wanted O'Dair's attention so deeply, she did not dissuade him of the notion that she was a Resistance courier based in Marseilles.

We loved, we wrote, we drank, we acted. You called me your muse, I called you my demon.

When Henriette passed away, Olivia continued the book store and the Sibylline Press, although it became more and more difficult as time went on, as Henriette had accumulated bills. An American made an offer for it to Henriette's attorney, who made the arrangements. There was only a small amount of money left after the bills were settled, but it went to Olivia, by way of Henriette's will. Olivia then gave the money to O'Dair's group, to enable them to purchase an old theater that was burned out during the war. In fact, it was O'Dair's Resistance team that had sabotaged it in the first place, when it was occupied by the Nazis. They wanted to restore it, and use it for their theatrical productions, calling it a phoenix that would rise from the literal ashes. The money Olivia brought helped to make it possible, and raised her esteem in their eyes.

All went well until one day a fellow Resistance fighter from Marseilles came to pay his respects to his hero O'Dair and the troupe rebuilding the theater. The passage of time and hardship of the war had changed his appearance, so that Olivia did not recognize him as one of what she referred to as "local tutors" and "poor insipid boys" from her days in Monte Carlo—but he recognized her. In this way it was revealed that far from being a Resistance fighter, she had escaped with her family to America, in the entourage of the millionaire Beauregard Lamont.

At first, Olivia was not concerned, convinced that she would be forgiven for her way of memorializing her Aunt Sasha, and that any of that group of friends would have been grateful to be memorialized in such a manner.

What she didn't expect was the vitriol and contempt she received for her deception. O'Dair himself was the worst. And then she realized, shortly after, she was pregnant. By then, his rejection of her was so complete, he refused to believe her. After a few weeks, she realized he would never forgive her, nor would anyone else. She was a pariah. She was so full of her own connection to Sasha, that she had completely underestimated the depth of their Resistance convictions, and could not see what their objections were.

Her poetry and fiction were her manifestation of Sasha, as well. But O'Dair and everyone in her whole world in Paris now claimed her work was fraudulent, insulting to the Resistance effort. They swore they would expose her for the liar she was and condemn every word she had published, would ever publish. They took every copy of her books and every issue of *Sibylline* in which she had an entry, and burned them in a pile on the street. She could have handled all the contempt, all the rejection, in time, but it was O'Dair's look of utter disgust when she told him she was carrying his child that destroyed her. She wanted, quite sincerely, to die.

Friendless, homeless, and pregnant, she spent her time going from church to church, praying and sleeping during the day, and nightclub to nightclub in the evenings, making superficial friendships along the way and finding solace in music and alcohol. One night a group she fell in with drove to a club in Orleans, where there was an American military base. Tired of dancing, she remained at her table with a drink, brooding over the wreck of her life, of the meaninglessness of her art, her love, her home.

Ronson Targman was at the next table over, also alone. Small talk ensued. He asked her to join him for a meal, and, by this time quite hungry, she accepted. She could tell he fancied her. She liked the fact he was an officer, if a low-level one. He was sensible, solid, and had no trouble telling her new friends she was with him now. His quiet confidence calmed her, made her feel protected, a little less like wanting to die. It suited her just fine.

She could tell that the fact that she was French by birth, fluent in English, and with American connections—yet, somehow, a bit hard up and lost, like a refugee—appealed to him. Her survival instinct grew into self-preservation. Once again, she didn't dissuade the man in her life from what he wanted to believe, and said "yes" the second he proposed. He had no idea who she really was, and that suited her just fine, too, because she had decided she would never write another word as long as she lived.

This bitter vow held fast until shortly after her mother's death:

I had expected the box, but not my reaction to it. There they were, my mother's books, and seeing the titles and the authors was a sudden plunge back home, back to who I'd always thought I was, back to my youth in Paris and listening in on these very writers as they talked and argued and pontificated and flirted and swore, back to the days when I was determined to be there with the best of them when I grew up. And the books were in different languages, English, French, German, Italian, and Hebrew. The Hebrew ones I quickly threw in the trash, because Ronson must never know about my mother's heritage. I didn't think he would care about the rest, just assume that it was common for a European like my mother to read many languages. But there were three of Seamus' books in there, all three in English. Two of them I'd read years ago, but the one, the one I tried to ignore when there would be fleeting mentions of it in the newspaper, in the magazines, on television, was the one that came out after I left France. Ronson was on base. I was bored. When Donovan was in school, I would read.

What I read, I could not believe. I could not believe that my story, my life, my love for my aunt could be so twisted, so abused, so tortured. All my sense of betrayal and rage fomented, burst anew in an eruption that I thought would kill me. Six weeks after I read it, they announced his Nobel Prize. It was my story—my story, told with his hatred.

I write this, in secret, for now. I will write until I cannot write anymore. Some day, perhaps, I can tell my story, and tell Sasha's story, the way it was meant to be told. And as I write, I find the will to go on. I am not Margot, I will not die as Margot. I damn you, Seamus O'Dair. I damn you.

Charlotte was not aware of the passage of time, that she'd read from sunup to long after sundown. The notebook was larger than the others, and written in a very small, strong script, as if Olivia thought she would be able to get everything into a single volume. Page after page, she remained engrossed as Olivia went through a complete and devastating critique of *Least Objects,* sometimes line by line, showing which parts were not true, which parts were things she'd actually said—and written—herself. She and O'Dair had, after all, collaborated on several projects, including a screenplay based on Sasha's life that they were working on at the time of their breakup—the original concept for *An Uncollected Death*. O'Dair's spiteful treatment of the Margot character as a version of Olivia did not happen until he rewrote *An Uncollected Death* in English, when it became *Least Objects.*

Thus, decades later, when Olivia stumbled across the original French novella, which she wrote about in her final notebook, she saw something much closer to the truth, with much more heartbreak than spite, and an element of self-doubt. And she saw that it was published by Sibylline Press, four months before Donovan was born. In the last volume of her notebooks, in the passages that Helene had translated, Olivia speculated that O'Dair had begun to soften his stance toward her—but by that time, she had married Ronson Targman, and no one in Paris knew where to find her. The *prima donna* O'Dair would have taken her disappearance as an act of contempt—which, in a way, it was, particularly if she did, indeed, have his child. She could see how he would express his fury at her by altering the character and story of Margot when he wrote *Least Objects.*

Charlotte's phone rang, startling her back into the present: it was Simon.

"I know this is short notice, but would you like to have dinner with me tonight?"

Charlotte's jaw dropped a little, and she sat up much straighter.

"Yes, I would like that very much. When and where?"

"I caught an opening for eight-thirty at Amaretto. It's a bit posh, but I—"

"I would *love* it, Simon. I haven't been there in years." She looked at the time. It was already a quarter to eight.

He laughed. "I'm glad, then. Shall I call for you and we walk down, or meet at the bar, if you need a little more time to get ready?"

"Let's meet there. I think I can manage to look respectable in half an hour, but an extra few minutes couldn't hurt."

Showered and in her robe, with a towel wrapped around her head, Charlotte stood in front of her only closet and was glad that her choice was practically made for her: one single little black dress, a sleeveless sheath. Finished with black pumps and with the short denim jacket to keep it from looking too stuffy, she would feel attractive and comfortable. But her nails were a mess from everything she had been doing the past two weeks, and an extra ten minutes went for a quick manicure. Fluff the hair, add the lipstick and a bit of mascara, the hoop earrings and the silver bracelet—done.

Walking in pumps on the way to Amaretto felt odd after not wearing them for so long—the last time was at Ellis' performance at the state competition. It seemed like years ago now. The sidewalks were full of people walking to and from the restaurants and bars, and here and there a couple kissed, or a group of young adults laughed at something one of them said. It was a lively little downtown, much more so now than it had been a decade before.

She'd long wondered what a date with Simon would be like, and now she was about to find out. Her palms were slightly damp again from nervousness. *I wish I didn't like him quite so much, and could just be cool about it. Whatever I do, I mustn't gush. Ellis would be more mature than this.*

Amaretto was full, as was usual on a Saturday night, and Charlotte was impressed that Simon got a table at such short notice. She spotted him standing at the crowded bar, his back to her, talking to someone she couldn't see. Even if she didn't know who he was, she would have picked him out in a crowd as "her type." He turned toward the bar just then, and she took in his gray sports jacket over a plain black knit sweater and a fresh pair of black jeans. As Charlotte approached, she could see a woman standing next to him, put her arm around his waist and pull him toward her, and he placed a hand on her shoulder and laughed. It was Lola, in spandex, cleavage, and very shiny red lipstick, a good bit of which was left on Simon's cheek.

Charlotte almost turned around and left, and probably would have, except the bartender noticed her and smiled, and Simon turned to look, as well, with an expression that was, for him, hapless.

"Charlotte!" Lola squealed, and strutted over in red stilettos to give her a hug and air kisses. "You look fabulous!" She then went on a bit in a tipsy monologue about how great it was that Toley Banks was in jail, at long last. Simon, standing behind Lola, made a face that almost sent Charlotte into hysterics.

To Charlotte's relief, however, they were called to their table, and it was in a quiet corner.

When they sat down, she pointed to his cheek. "Lola left her brand on you."

Simon winced at the realization. "She means well, but she's awfully full on." He picked up his napkin to wipe his cheek, and handed it to

Charlotte to finish when he missed a spot. When she handed it back, he looked at it with distaste and set it at the edge of the table. "I think I'll ask for a fresh one."

He picked up the wine menu. Charlotte took in the details of his face, the line of his nose, the way his hands held the menu.

Simon looked up, first at her face, then at the rest of her, taking in the way she looked, and somehow managed to make her feel, without saying a word, that he liked what he saw. "Let's do this properly, what do you say? A good bottle, an appetizer, an over-the-top main course, and maybe even a little dessert if we've room? Something to make the whole world go away for a while?"

He gets it. He read her expression, and chuckled. She grinned, inside as well as out.

Sunday, Charlotte slept in, after ten solid hours of the kind of sleep that had eluded her for weeks. She'd had a lot to drink and eat at the restaurant, but there were no ill effects, and she practically purred at the memory of an utterly enjoyable evening. Simon had walked her back to the apartment, where he gave her a long, warm full-body hug, and then a kiss that landed on her jaw, close to her earlobe, as if he was going to kiss her neck and then stopped to move up to her cheek and didn't quite make it. They laughed and tried again, this time getting it right. Then once again he looked at her with an inscrutable expression, thanked her "for a wonderful evening," and went on his way. No matter where it went from here, they had a connection, of that she was now absolutely certain. It made her feel ten years younger.

As she moved to get out of bed, something shiny on the duvet caught her attention: a stainless steel tea ball. What on earth? Then she noticed Shamus sitting a few feet away from the foot of the bed.

"Did you bring this to me?" she asked him.

The tip of his tail moved, but that was the only answer he had.

The tea ball still had a price tag attached to it, and then Charlotte recalled there was a box of them in the kitchen section of The Good Stuff. How in the world did Shamus get it in here, with the pet door closed off?

"You are one very mysterious cat."

He looked up at her, and once again she could have sworn he was smiling, a happy, pleased with himself, feline smile.

They all met at The Coffee Grove for brunch, sharing the Sunday paper's headline story about Toley Banks' arrest and his ties to Olivia and Wesley Warren. Diane, as usual, was effusive in both her surprise and praise, and Jimmy looked thoroughly entertained. Helene set aside her usual elegant reserve for a moment in the limelight, retelling the story of luring Mitchell and Doc from the basement. Lola staggered in late with a hangover. Simon gave her his chair, then grabbed another chair and squeezed in next to Charlotte.

"So, then?" Diane asked Helene. "Is the whole thing figured out? You've got all the notebooks, you've got a rare book you didn't know about in the beginning, and you've got the people responsible for the crime. But do you know why, or did I miss that?"

Helene gestured toward Charlotte. "There's the one to ask, Diane. Charlotte's been trying to make sense of all this from day one."

Charlotte put up her hands in protest. "Hey, I couldn't have done it without you and Simon, or without everyone's help when I moved and tried to get settled in the middle of everything." She shared an encapsulated version of Olivia's story, then concluded, "I still have a few more things I'm wondering about, but maybe the answers will turn up over time. Or maybe not. Some of it might always remain a mystery."

Jimmy nodded at the last bit. "Human motivation is rarely as clean-cut in real life as it is in a detective story."

As the conversation around the table continued, Charlotte thought of Olivia's promise as a writer, a whole career lost to spite, and how it contributed to Donovan's wasted potential, as well. She recalled Helene's remark about how parents set the stage, set the tone for the future, and hoped that she gave Ellis a chance to blossom by letting her go to Paris so young.

"People sometimes make terrible choices," said Helene, "or are afraid to make any choices at all. The next thing you know, entire lifetimes are wasted."

Simon shifted to get comfortable in the tight space, stretching his arm across the back of Charlotte's chair, and settling in closer to her. She turned to give him a big smile. He grinned back.

"It was never easy to please Olivia," Helene was saying to Charlotte, "but I like to think you would have come close."

Regardless of Helene's praise for her efforts, after a couple of hours more research into the French Resistance, Seamus O'Dair, and the various people known to associate with him in his Paris days, Charlotte debated whether she should continue with the project or not—it would, in essence, amount to a comprehensive research project that might be best left to O'Dair specialists. Then again, there was no reason she couldn't become such an expert, given time and devotion. Olivia's story could certainly change some perceptions about O'Dair, *Least Objects,* and his Nobel Prize.

She read through the composition book with Donovan's story in it. Like Helene, she could see Olivia cherishing something that showed a shared interest between herself and her son. Charlotte expected an immature tone, a naive point of view, or something cartoonish, but to her surprise Donovan's story was about a soldier in the Vietnam War, one that seemed to be based on Ronson Targman, and in a decidedly negative light. The structure was simple: a scene where the soldier describes cruel treatment of captured enemy soldiers, then of locals suspected of being guerilla fighters, and then finally of innocents, interspersed with scenes of the same soldier's harsh, abusive treatment of people and family members back home, including firing at protesting college students "like the ones at Kent State." It was a rough draft, but the descriptive passages were perceptive and direct—too well written, she thought, for a ten-year-old, which was how old Donovan was in 1968. Perhaps it was placed in the coal chute at a later date? She looked up the Kent State shootings: May 4th, 1970. The story was written when Donovan was at least twelve years old. Much more plausible.

Here and there the pages were torn and stained, as was the cover. The notebook had suffered abuse. Had it been thrown away, and Olivia found it and saved it? There was no mention of it in her own notebook from 1970, or the next one from 1976. Charlotte did spot a passage where Olivia mentioned cringing at times at how much Donovan resembled O'Dair, yet at times bursting with a sense of rightness, because he was conceived from love, no matter what happened afterward.

The story of the composition book was added to the list of questions that Charlotte still had for Donovan. She recalled his complete lack of shock at hearing that O'Dair was his father, or any sign of embarrassment or unease. It was something, she was convinced, that he had known about for a long time. If he did, it opened up a lot of questions about his involvement in his mother's death and in the search for the book.

An odd noise from the direction of the stairwell interrupted her thoughts. It sounded like scratching. She went to investigate, moving quietly down the steps in her socks. She could just make out Shamus by the pet door. He turned to look at her, then back at the door, pawing at the flap until his paw went under it, then moving against the wall in such a way that he was scratching *upwards.* Charlotte perched on the steps and watched as he scratched and scratched, until the panel blocking his way began to slide up, and he stuck in his head, then the rest of his body, and Charlotte heard the panel land shut after the last of his tail disappeared.

So that's how he did it, she thought. I've got a cat burglar. Literally.

An hour later, after she heard more scratching noises, he presented her with another tea ball.

Twenty-Six

Monday, September 30th

It was Monday before Charlotte was able to talk to Donovan, who had been rushed from the basement of his mother's house into emergency surgery. For a while she had wondered if there would be a third death connected to O'Dair's book, but the surgeon assured her and Helene that the bleeding was stopped, and that Donovan's prognosis was good, once he started healing and had a good long rest.

A uniformed officer stood watch at the door of the hospital room. Detective Barnes was inside, taking Donovan's statement, but he waved for Charlotte to come in. After the usual greetings and updates, she took the composition book out of her bag and handed it to Donovan.

"I found this in the old coal chute, along with your mother's first notebook."

Donovan said nothing for a few moments, just looked through it, nodding to himself.

"Yeah, I'd forgotten about this. Wrote it when I'd just turned thirteen. Dad saw it in my room and damned near killed me. I think he would have, too, if Mom hadn't gotten home from the grocery store just then."

"You put it in the chute, didn't you?"

He nodded again. "Went out in the middle of the night and fished it out of the trash can before the garbage collectors came. Thought the chute was the one place he wouldn't think to look."

"But you found your mother's notebook in there, didn't you? And you read it."

He just looked at her, and said nothing.

So much became clear to Charlotte. "You've known since then that O'Dair was your real father. You've known all along."

Donovan bit his lower lip and nodded slowly, and looked back down at the composition book. "Yeah, it was a lot to take in, what she wrote, and I didn't understand a lot of it, like the bits in French, and the parts where she went on and on about some book he wrote, but I knew it was her big secret, and I understood why she couldn't tell my dad—Ronson, that is—about any of this. I was glad to find out he wasn't my father, though, as you can imagine. I know she felt betrayed by everyone, and I felt bad for her, but I also felt a kind of unity with her, like it was Mom and me against both dads. But I was too embarrassed to ask her about it, you know? Even later, after he died."

"So you knew she was once a writer?"

"I got that much, yeah, but I also got it was really important not to mention it. You wanted to lay low around Dad, not draw attention to anything he didn't like or approve of. So I stopped writing, too. At least until I left home, and after that, life sort of got in the way. She wanted me to go to college so bad, but I was worried that if I did, and did well, he'd make her life miserable, you know? 'Cause it would prove she was right?" He paused, and rubbed at a stain on the book's cover. "Always worried about her, always felt helpless. I wanted to read and write, but it didn't feel *clean*, you know? Mom was ashamed of her connection to it, and Dad thought it was sissy stuff—or subversive, in the case of this one."

Barnes was taking this all in with great interest. "Were you aware of the existence of the rare books?"

"No, actually," said Donovan. "That first one, that was from when I was a little kid. I just thought I was wrapping up an old book Mom didn't want anymore, didn't even pay attention to the title or the author, it was just a grown-up book with small print and no pictures, you know? Didn't mean anything to me more than being the right size and shape. The French one, I had no idea about. I guess she bought that after Dad died. A few years ago she went on a book-buying spree, and I put up the shelves for her and put the books where she wanted them, and it made her happier than I'd ever seen her. She said they reminded her of a bookstore from her childhood. So I asked her about that, and she told me a lot about her Aunt Sasha and Aunt Henri—and that definitely was not a story she would have wanted Dad to know. I have a feeling she had a lot of stories like that."

"We know that you were in your mother's house several times after her death with Mitchell Bennett, and the person known as Doc, and that some things were removed and put up for sale in Warren Brothers Pawn shop," said Barnes. "Can you tell me more about what was going on, and why?"

"Yeah, no problem, not now," Donovan sighed. "Like I said before, I owed Toley Banks a lot of money, because the interest escalated faster than I could pay back the loan itself. It got to the point where they were threatening violence, so I agreed to do some work for them to help pay it down. When Bosley Warren sold that book, I had no idea he'd gotten it from me. It was in the news, and so was O'Dair, like a renewed-interest thing. Mitchell started making remarks about how much I looked like O'Dair, and I admit I might have given something away by getting irritated at him. Mitchell is like that, uncannily good at finding out people's weak spots. Makes him useful to Toley Banks."

A nurse came in to say that Mr. Targman needed his rest, and would they kindly leave? Donovan held up his hand. "Please, just five more minutes, I gotta finish this. Please?"

She looked at her watch and reluctantly agreed.

Donovan took a deep breath, and continued. "Where was I? Right, um, as luck would have it, my dear mother called the shop about another first edition of that book. The way I think it happened, Toley and Mitchell did some digging in the sales records and figured out Bos got the book from me, the guy who looked like O'Dair, so when my mother said something about yet another first edition, they were inclined to take her seriously. They were less convinced that I didn't know anything about it, though."

Donovan's voice had begun to crack from dryness, and Charlotte handed him the cup of ice water from his tray. He sipped from the straw a couple of times, shifted his position to recline a bit more, then continued.

"It only got worse after that horrible night. What made it complicated was the terms of the will." Donovan squeezed Charlotte's hand. "I'm still mortified about the way I blew up, Charlotte. After I calmed down, when I came to terms with not being able to get shut of Toley Banks as quickly as I wanted, I was determined that Mom's wishes would be carried out. I knew about the one notebook, and thought it was safe where it was at—I didn't want to tell you about it, because then I'd have to start explaining what I knew and how I knew it, and I had to play dumb at all costs. It really was news to me, though, that there were so many more of those notebooks, but I figured if they were anything like that first one, it was important to find them. Your legal right to keep coming around kept Doc and Mitchell from trashing the place altogether. I let them have things here and there to keep Toley pacified—it paid the interest. It was weird, because legally I was stealing from Aunt Helene, but I rationalized that at least it wasn't stealing the things that were most important to her or to my mother."

He took another sip of water. "It was like a balancing act, keeping those guys under control as best I could, and giving you as much time as possible to find those notebooks—and maybe even that other first edition Mom thought she had. I know it was so little time, but obviously I couldn't look for any of it myself because they were watching me like a hawk. Then when I found out Toley was willing to drown his half-brother, I knew it was just a matter of time before he'd do the same to me, or to you—anybody at all that got in the way of his getting his money. That's why I said not to cancel that contract at all costs, so you'd have to leave before things got to that point."

The nurse came in again, and this time she wasn't taking no for an answer.

Donovan was worn out from talking, but he managed a gaunt, dark-eyed smile. "Thanks, Charlotte. Things are going to be okay now. For us both."

Barnes walked with Charlotte as they left the hospital. "We're going to need you and Mrs. Dalmier to come down and give your statements, this morning if possible."

"I'll let her know. What will happen to Donovan, since he was involved in Wesley Warren's death?"

"I've already spoken with his attorney and the D.A.'s office. The charges will be either dropped or greatly reduced in exchange for his detailed testimony of Toley Banks' loan shark and enforcing activities. I'll be happy with that."

Charlotte thought she'd be happy with that, too.

Once again, they were at the police station for a round of questions to answer and statements to make, all proper procedure, which Barnes wanted to make certain was executed perfectly. There was no way, he said, that everything everyone went through was going to be for nothing all because of a technicality, and no one could blame him. Helene and Charlotte also had the satisfaction of knowing their statements would help Donovan, as well.

While waiting for their interviews, they were surprised to see Bosley Warren on his way out. Charlotte tensed up at the very sight of him, even more so when he spotted them and walked over, his huge bulk blocking their view of the rest of the waiting room.

"Miz Dalmier, Charlotte," he nodded to them in greeting. "I wish to offer my deepest apologies on behalf of Warren Brothers Pawn and Payday and Estate Sales. None of the crimes that were committed on your persons and property was planned by us or done with our knowledge. That's all I'm allowed to say, other than that I hope you bear me no ill will, and I'll understand perfectly if you wish to terminate the estate auction contract drawn up by Mitchell Bennett."

"Thank you, Mr. Warren," said Helene, who was sitting up straight and exuded dignity. "I think it is best all around if the contract is voided. If necessary, I can have my attorney send you a letter to confirm it."

Bosley nodded, resigned to the loss of business. "Whatever you think best, ma'am. I stand ready to provide any reassurances you and your attorney require. Again, my sincerest apologies, my condolences on the death of Mrs. Targman, and my deepest hope that Van Targman recovers quickly. Goodbye."

"Well!" said Helene, after Bosley strode away. "That was easy enough, but I'll make sure the lawyer really does check everything. Now I can call Martin Stanton, which will be such a relief after this circus."

"Oh, right! Martin! My sale!" Charlotte cringed at the realization she had completely forgotten about her own estate sale over the weekend, she was so entranced by the contents of the last notebook, caught up in solving the mystery, and on an emotional rollercoaster since Friday's ordeal. "I'm going to have to call him as soon as we get out of here." She pointed to the sign that said "NO CELL PHONES OR OTHER ELECTRONIC DEVICES."

"That's one upside of all this," said Helene. "You were too busy to fret about your sale. A good thing, I would think."

"Oh, sure," Charlotte grumbled. "Like breaking an arm to stop worrying about a hangnail."

"I wonder how it went? If it all sold, or if there was anything left. Maybe you even have a buyer for the house!"

Charlotte shook her head. "Lola hasn't said anything, so I doubt it. I think she was waiting for Stanton to clear out before scheduling viewings. It was pretty full in there, the way they had everything pulled out and in the open."

Then they were called in to give their statements.

Charlotte met Martin Stanton at the Lake Parkerton house, where the crew was doing a thorough cleaning job, after consolidating all the unsold items in the garage. There was, to her great surprise, very little, much of it things she would have been tempted to throw out. She looked around for her big painting, but of course it wasn't there, nor was any of the other art. Some of the older pieces of her wardrobe were left, and the more beat up of her pots and pans and dishes. The kitchen cart she wanted to take was gone, as well.

"Hey, Charlotte," Martin called out from the door to the kitchen. "Not much left, eh?"

"No, there's not! I don't see anything I want to take back, although I should probably look more carefully."

"Come on in, and I'll show you the figures."

It was a little strange to be invited in to one's own house, and yet it wasn't. She realized that she was already settling into the little apartment, and into life in Elm Grove, and it hadn't even been a week.

Martin had the itemized lists and their selling prices spread out. Some things went for high prices, some things were all but given away. She noted the sterling silver flatware did indeed go for nearly three times the amount she'd received for it at the pawn shop. Then she spotted the sales figure for the big painting—Martin's estimate was very close, even slightly low. The trip to Paris to see Ellis was on. But where did it go?

"Who bought the big painting?" she asked.

Martin showed her another list. "Bennington Eastman, the art brokers. They've been buying up Hannah Verhagens left and right."

"Oh." She was disappointed. It would have been nice to know where it went, but brokers tended to be confidential about that information. Yet "Blossoming" was painted for her, and she would never really lose the sense that it was hers.

"Here you are, ready to deposit." Martin handed her the check.

It seemed like such a lotta, lotta money, but she restrained herself from too much giddiness. If the house was sold for less than the mortgage, she'd have to make up the difference with some of this check.

"Wow!" Then she suddenly had a question. "I'm supposed to give you 30% of this, right?"

Martin laughed. "No, no Charlotte, that's your net. We've already taken the thirty percent out, see?" He showed her the total on the sales sheet. Yes, there it was: her check was, indeed, 70% of the total sales.

"You are good," she said.

"We're the best," he said.

Charlotte deposited the check immediately upon returning to Elm Grove, happy to have such a substantial return on her shopping investments and giving up things she liked and loved, but sad, too, knowing that she would never enjoy those things again. There wasn't even anything left worth bringing home. Her house itself was now empty, ready for Lola to stage for prospective buyers. It was done. All that remained was selling the house, and to sell it as quickly as possible.

She pulled into the parking space Larry had set aside for her in the delivery area behind The Good Stuff, locked up the Jeep, and made her way around the building to her front door. As she passed the shop windows, she thought of Shamus, realizing how happy she was to have him around all the time, and wondered if Larry missed him yet, or if things were bad between him and his wife.

The lock on the front door opened quickly, now that she knew the exact way to wiggle the key. Shamus was waiting for her in the foyer, and as she started to bend down to pick him up, she saw what looked like a dead mouse nearby. Oh no. She couldn't abide mice. Then she spotted its cross-stitched eyes. Shamus flopped down and rubbed his head on it, then flipped over on his back. It was a toy mouse filled with catnip. The price tag was still on it. Crazy cat.

She started up the stairs, and the cat ran ahead of her, with his toy mouse in his teeth.

The afternoon sun was doing its thing again, warming up the walls and bouncing light around to form a sort of aura around the bed, the sofa, the rug, the big table, and the big painting—

The Hannah Verhagen still life was on the table, and propped against the wall. It looked magnificent in the high-ceilinged room, and in bold, joyous scale with the windows.

Shamus jumped up on the table, sniffing at the edges of the painting, then batted a note card sitting on the lid of the computer.

Charlotte caught it before it fluttered to the floor.

All it said was:

"With all my love and deepest gratitude,

Helene."

About the Author

Meg grew up an only child on a small Indiana farm, where Nancy Drew became her best friend and she eventually developed a crush on Agent 007. Her reading expanded sufficiently to achieve a Master of Arts degree, but her imagination continues to reside (while knitting and gardening) in various mysterious English, American, and Canadian villages, with occasional forays to more exotic times and locales.

In a different genre, she was an artist and owned a gallery with her English husband, photographer and writer Steve Johnson. Since then she has written a blog, The Minimalist Woman, and its associated lifestyle and cook books, as well as a tiny collection of very short stories.

An Uncollected Death is Meg's first mystery novel. She is currently creating more perils to deflect and clues to unearth for her new friend, Charlotte Anthony.

Contact: megwolfewrites@gmail.com

Web: megwolfe.com

HBL1A

Made in the USA
San Bernardino, CA
01 April 2014